RUN

BY

PAT ADAMS-WRIGHT

WWW.RAVENPRESSLLC.COM

Published by Raven Press LLC

Copyright © 2015 Pat Adams-Wright

Run

First Edition

Library of Congress Control Number:

2015940785

ISBN-13: 978-1-938988-66-0

ISBN-10: 1938988663

DEDICATION

To Denise — I love you today...

CHAPTER ONE

CHARLOTTE REINETTE, OR Charlie as her friends call her, was daydreaming again. The break room at Bamber and Brooks had a soporific effect on her, and apparently, on the other two co-workers in the room with her judging by their vacant expressions. The dark grey walls of the prefabricated building were incapable of reflecting even the smallest glimmer of light back from the dim fluorescent tubes and made the room sleepy and dull. Sitting on a large industrial estate on the outskirts of Walden and having worked there for over ten years, its appeal was beginning to lose its lustre like the shine missing from a new penny.

The view from the window was even less inspiring. It looked out to grey painted railings where the black night watchman's hut nestled against the side of the six-foot railing gate. The night watchman, George Mason, spent his nights in the small, temporary home. He tried to make it appear homely with a horseshoe nailed above the door, but it was never going to work. It was a small plain wooden hut painted black, big enough to take a small table and a chair with an electrical point so George could have a single dangling light from a twisted cord and somewhere to plug in a small heater during the winter months. It was what it was. Dull.

She decided her life definitely lacked colour. She wasn't sure about the night watchman. Charlie liked George. She liked his refusal never to give up on life when the years had not been kind to him. His wife had died from a heart attack during the first week of his retirement. At the time, he should have been celebrating and enjoying his wife's uninterrupted company, but instead, he was in mourning. He could have ended up bitter and twisted, but as he told Charlie later, he'd never been one for wallowing in self-pity.

"Much easier to find a solution to the problem, Charlie," he had said. "Mine was the long nights. This little job solved the predicament. Plus, a little extra cash never did anyone any harm."

Each night, on her way to her car after work, she dropped him off a coffee from the half-decent machine in the break room while he tried to pick out winning horses for the next day from the evening paper. She wondered if he actually won anything on his bets or if he only worked to pay for them.

Enough, thought Charlie, still absorbed in her daydream. You could only stare at a bottle of orange juice for so long trying to figure out what '*made from concentrate*' meant. The packaging of the egg and slow-roasted tomato stack sandwich had also lost its appeal. It still had the same contents and calorific value it had ten minutes ago, except now it was inside her figuring out where on her body it was going to deposit itself. Apparently, the orange juice had deposited itself directly in her bladder. A trip to the bathroom was in order.

The moment she'd risen to her full five-foot-eight-inches, her mobile rang. The spooky sounding music she had set for her ringtone echoed throughout the room. The two other people in the break room lifted their heads. One woman smiled and shook her head slightly as if not quite believing the tune she'd heard, and the other put her head straight back down to resume reading her newspaper.

She was about to have a bathroom break, so she assumed it must be Gavin on the phone. Charlie was so convinced it was Gavin, she didn't even look at the caller display. He was psychically tuned into her bladder—she was certain of it. At home, at work, or at play, it didn't matter to Gavin.

"Hi, Gav! You caught me on the way to the bathroom for a change. What's up?" she asked as she brushed stray crumbs and little black poppy seeds from her black trousers and maroon cowl neck jumper.

"Not much, sweetie. I was hoping, it being First Friday, we might go out cruising and get blasted. What do you think? You up for it?"

Charlie could tell from the tone of his voice it was a desperate plea to help him get laid. Gavin's love life had been a little lean of late, so he felt it his duty to drag her around the gay clubs, all two of them, under the delusion he was trying to get *her* fixed up with a date.

She started her walk toward the bathroom, discarding the packaging from her late lunch in the rubbish bin along the way. It made a satisfying *clang* as it hit the side of the metal bin and a further *bang* as the metal lid swung back into place and connected to the base. Charlie wished her life could be so easy—tossing away the bad bits like unwanted rubbish. "Yes, I think I might be able to manage that," she answered, "although I was going to get my haircut later this afternoon. It's nearly touching my collar." She instinctively brushed her dark brown hair using her fingers as a comb. "Same place and time?" Charlie waited for a different answer than the usual 'keeping his place' response, but she was disappointed

"Of course. Keep my place warm for me!"

Suddenly, Charlie was listening to dead air.

Charlie loved Gavin like the brother she'd never had, but sometimes, he was such a drama queen. Especially on these nights out. Each little encounter with a prospective conquest often led to hours of unending questions about suitability, long-term prospects, dress sense, until suddenly the night was over. Gavin had missed his chance again. Charlie had told him a number of times to get on with it and take a risk. It had never worked. Gavin's life seemed filled with dramatic moments and going home alone.

Secretly, she thought she might be getting a little too old for the First Friday tradition. The first Friday after payday meant the pub and a booze up. Alcohol and picking up one-night stands didn't hold the same fascination at thirty-three as it had at twenty-three. The horrendous hangovers, which lasted into Sunday morning, or the nameless women who temporarily warmed the other side of her bed—if they stayed long enough—were becoming a chore. Personally, she was tired of all the crap and secretly yearned for a special person in her life she could cherish. Such an apt description. She'd heard a similar description in the film *Desert Hearts* a long time ago. Perhaps her evening would be better served and more rewarding if she watched the film again. The thought cheered her.

As she made her way through the outer door of the bathroom, she heard a gentle weeping, stopping her from going any further. She cracked open the inner door as gently as she could and peeked through.

At the sinks, she recognised the back of a small woman staring into the big mirror. She was fidgeting and her fingers pulled and readjusted her polo-neck sweater. As the weeping became a sniffle and a hiccup in the woman's throat, Charlie thought the worst must be over. With the woman looking as though she were regaining some kind of composure, Charlie pushed the door open confidently, giving the impression she had arrived momentarily.

4

The woman turned in surprise. She obviously thought everyone but herself had gone back to their workstations. She looked embarrassed. Her eyes were red at the rims as though she had applied a thin layer of red eyeliner, and Charlie's heart gave an unexpected lurch at the sight.

She resisted the overwhelming urge to run over to the woman and take her in her arms, give her a hug, and tell her everything would be okay. Instead, she asked quietly, "Are you okay?"

The woman looked back with dark-brown eyes, which set off Charlie's inner voice. *Look at those limpet pools.* Charlie began to stroke her hands down the tops of her thighs as though straightening the outer seams of her pants. She had no idea where she'd picked up this habit, but it normally meant she was in trouble. No, not trouble—*emotionally screwed.*

The woman replied with a simple, "Yes." It was only then Charlie noticed the large, dark-purple welt running beneath the woman's left ear hidden partially by her chestnut bob cut.

Charlie reached out and caressed the bruise—in an attempt to heal it as Charlie's mother had always tried to do when she was a child in an effort to make her daughter feel comforted. The skin was warm and soft under her fingers, and then Charlie froze, snatching her hand away. *What was she doing?* The woman locked in on Charlie's gaze, looked at her strangely, then lowered her head and was gone. Charlie was left looking at the door swinging closed and the feeling she needed to get a serious grip on her emotions.

Charlie looked to the stalls, urged forward by her bladder. Sitting down gave her the chance to ponder this mystery woman, and she wondered how she might get to know her better...in the biblical sense. She thought she might finally be back in the game and smiled.

Suddenly, a little colour returned to Charlie's horizon.

CHAPTER TWO

CHARLIE FELT MORE at ease now since her car was safely stowed in her garage. Her Audi was the only love in her life but not dwelling on her current fit of melancholy, she was hoping the situation might change. The sooner, the better. She stroked the car's sleek lines as she walked along side of it, feeling the hardness of the wax cool under her fingertips. She leant forward over the wing. She was rewarded with her reflected image, albeit in muted colours and out of focus, but still glossy, like an expensive, artistically produced photograph. Old habits die hard, and she never failed to enjoy the touch.

The car was only one of two compromises she had made as far as her father was concerned. He had insisted on a decent car, for not only her safety, which still, after all these years, was paramount to him, but it also represented her status as a director of the family company. Maintaining image was part of the game. She only had to attend three to four board meetings a year. Doing so came with the car and a decent salary.

Charlie had qualified from University with a degree in Psychology, and it was her parent's fervent hope she would put it to some use in the family's company of diamond trading.

Charlie hadn't been interested. She admitted to herself a long time ago she had completed the degree for herself. It was her one true act of selfishness, in the hope it would give her some kind of insight into the horrendous experience she had as a young teenager. Her parents would never understand, and she didn't expect them to.

They hadn't been with her in the hellish, isolated garage, tied to an old bed smelling of urine and had felt damp beneath her. Her school cardigan and blouse had stuck to her back like a wet swimming costume when you get out of the pool. The blindfold and the gag still haunted her dreams, day and night. The waking nightmares were the worst, enveloping her consciousness like a second-rate horror film. Charlie shook her head at the thought as her blood pressure began to elevate. The whole time she'd been a prisoner, Jessica's pretty face was etched into her mind. Why hadn't the kidnappers taken her sister instead? Did they see some kind of naivety in her they didn't see in her sister? Perhaps they found her stupid. A stupid, easy target.

Charlie took a deep breath and calmed herself, practising the methods she had studied in college from the degree she refused to utilise in the family business.

So, instead of diamond trading, she chose to work for Bamber and Brooks Limited, a small company based out in the sticks where she was quite happy to input account information from all over the country. From Monday to Friday, nine to five, at desks set out in three rows of six so they were ergonomically spaced and efficient for file sharing, Charlie transferred information into the database.

She was sure they must all look like out-of-sync ensemble rhythms trying to make sense of the beat as arms and heads appeared above the top of the desks in random fashions. Here, she was away from life in the capital and away from her family connections. It suited her to escape from the rat race to wallow in the anonymity of Walden. A medium-sized town with a medium-sized attitude. It kept her obscure and away from any kind of limelight.

She was in the happy position she could choose what she did with her leisure time, whether it was clubbing with Gavin, a weekend in her favourite five-star spa, or a long weekend in a log cabin in the woods. When someone accused her of being a rich bitch, she smiled and said she'd had a kind grandmother who had left her an inheritance. It was all true. Amounts, however, were never discussed. Another plus as far as Charlie was concerned.

The only other compromise her father insisted on was Charlie owning her own home.

"No sharing, so as to limit the risk, darling," he had said to her. Outwardly showing concern, but how much of his concern was true?

So, because he was paying, she acquiesced and chose a modest four-bedroom home on a new estate. The internal garage had been the clincher for Charlie, although large rooms throughout did add to its charm, not to mention the state-of-the-art security system with its beams and pressure pads. *Security, security, security,* her father's mantra echoed in her head each time she entered her six-digit code, waited for the beep and for the red light to change to green.

She wondered if the concern he had shown had been a manifestation of his guilt—guilt for not protecting his youngest daughter when he had the chance or for choosing money over her. The feeling still stung her consciousness and created an almost physical pain. It had been twenty years, but the memory materialised as if it were yesterday.

She had never wanted a home as large as her family's home. She thought their eight bedrooms a waste of space. They had only used three on a regular basis. Her mother liked her own bedroom, which she used as a dressing room rather than for sleeping. Her parents shared a bed in another room, and her sister Jessica, who was a year older, but ten years more worldly as her bedroom attested, had a room also. Technically, another was designated to Charlie. However, she rarely visited to use it.

Where Charlie had posters of girl bands adorning her childhood room from a young age, Jessica preferred modern art prints, no doubt an early precursor to the successful art gallery owner she eventually became. Jessica was truly her mother's daughter. Art was one common interest, but so was the excitement for every hunt and ball on the calendar. Charlie had to be dragged to those events kicking and screaming, preferring instead to read or watch sports on television.

She would never understand the excitement of hunting down and killing a helpless fox, letting a pack of hounds tear it limb from limb. At the mention of each hunt, she used to cringe, knowing it was time for the nightmares to begin. Jessica had called her a worrywart, accusing her of being swayed by other people's opinions in the *real* world. Charlie didn't want to believe her sister and mother were shallow, but she knew it to be the truth.

Charlie was no mercenary, but she wasn't going to look a gift horse in the mouth. The house and the four rings of the Audi symbol shining brightly in the dim garage always added to her feel-good factor. The stars in her universe. It didn't do any harm in the pulling department either. *She was such a guy sometimes*, she thought. A smile crossed her face as the woman from the toilets crossed her mind.

The crying woman continued to play in Charlie's thoughts as she entered her house. The strange feelings continued, even in replay. Each time she thought about those big brown eyes set in the delicate, beautiful face, her heart quickened its pace. Not to sprinting level, just an even jogging pace, and her stomach was aware of some outward stimuli, as yet unclassified. Charlie's hands made their way to the seam of her pants and began to stroke. *She had to be sensible*—especially as they presumably worked at the same place.

On Monday morning, she was going to ask around to see if she could find out more about this mystery woman. She had never seen her before. She definitely would have remembered those eyes if she had—the colour of mahogany with an odd fleck of gold. Charlie knew for sure she wasn't in Inputting because that was her department. Maybe she was in Financial Accounting or Legal though Gavin hadn't mentioned anything, or perhaps she was in HR.

It was unusual for Poppy Ryder, the company gossip and probably the nearest thing she had to a best female friend, not to have come round and let her know about any new recruits in the company. There weren't many these days and probably wouldn't be many more until the financial crisis was over.

Charlie dropped her mobile on the bed. No messages from Gavin so he hadn't changed his plans since lunchtime. She stared at the mirrored doors of her wardrobe and pushed her fingers through her hair, wishing she had turned Gavin down and gone to the hairdressers instead. She was refreshed from her shower and her blue silk robe felt good against her smooth skin. What a temptation it was to just curl up with a book for the evening. She hated this part of going out more than any other and often wished she could just wrinkle her nose like Samantha in *Bewitched* and be instantly dressed. Did she want to impress tonight or not? *Not.*

She opened the door of her wardrobe and grabbed her black jeans, then glanced out of the window. It was absolutely pouring with rain. The slight breeze forced it against the windowpanes with a loud patter as the rain swirled. It was cold outside, too. *Terrific,* she thought. She was going to freeze unless she put on something warm when she left the house. Then, when they got inside the pub and later in the club, she would be shedding clothes like a stripper. Sultry music began to ramble around in her head making her smile.

Taking off the layers didn't bother her but what the hell was she supposed to do with them? Gavin, who she knew would be clad only in designer jeans and a T-shirt simply because he wouldn't dream of being seen dead in anything more, could wander off for a dance or go to the loo uninhibited. She, on the other hand, would be sitting there like a bag lady, clutching her layers of clothes.

Charlie hated bags with a passion. She always said it was why God had invented pockets. Jessica thought her mad and told her so, as she paid a fortune for her Palladino handbag on their last shopping spree together.

Oh, to hell with it! She dressed her medium-sized, muscular frame with black jeans, a dark blue sweater, and black boots, all topped off with her Red Valentino coat. It had been her online bargain-of-the–year. *Time to flaunt it!* No doubt, it would pass Poppy's scrutiny with flying colours. A quick look in the full-length mirror assured Charlie she looked okay. Her bright blue eyes stared back at her reminding her of the grandmother who she had inherited them from. She missed her. The large hole in her heart had opened wide when she watched her grandmother fade away years ago. Charlie wasn't sure she wanted the place in her heart filled.

Shaking off the sadness, she spiked her short dark hair a little more, for once glad for the natural wave. It would only increase the wave if it got damp, but she thought what the hell. *She wasn't looking to get laid…but it had been a while since her hands had had something soft to caress…*

CHAPTER THREE

THE TOWN SQUARE was cold, damp, and miserable. The lamplight was weak and ineffectual, bathing the stone coloured buildings in an eerie, orange glow. The light penetrating rain covered all reflective surfaces with a high polish giving the whole scene a kind of picture-book enchantment. The same rain penetrated to the core, soaking clothing in minutes, purveying the cold directly to the bone. To avoid this, people were scurrying from one doorway to another or sharing umbrellas trying to stand side by side. A good excuse for lovers to get close.

Eight o'clock came and went with no sign of Gavin. Bloody typical! Here she was in the town square, freezing her butt off waiting for him, again. Tell him to meet her in the pub at eight, and then show up at nine—this would give him the chance to be late, and she wouldn't be hanging around like a lemon. It sounded like a thorough plan for the future!

Just then, her mobile rang with the spooky music heralding Gavin, and she blushed as the people passing her turned and stared from under their umbrellas. Mentally, she noted to change the ringtone when she got home.

She juggled with her umbrella until she eventually managed to press the green tab. All she heard was a loud hissing sound and intermittent speech. "…on… way… bus… broken… late." With slight annoyance, she pressed end and accessed her contact list. She selected 'Gavin' and then pressed 'Send Message.'

Gavin, she wrote, I'm going into the Fleece to stop myself from freezing to death. I will be there when you get here. You owe me an orange juice!

She wasn't joking about freezing either. The ice was beginning to form around her boots she was sure. She began slamming the soles of her boots onto the floor just to get her circulation going before she tried to walk. What she did not need was to go flat on her face in the middle of the square. Embarrassment times ten!

***

GAVIN SAT ON the bus looking out the grimy window trying to ignore the slight smell of urine and the dry dustiness clinging to the inside of his nostrils. He watched the amber flash of the bus's hazard lights as it reflected off the rain soaked road. He decided he was going to write to the bus company and complain about the conditions of public transport. The government banged all the time about people giving up their cars and using public transport. Yeah, right!

He closed his eyes. He preferred the inside of Charlie's Audi any time. The smell of the leather made him feel good as it mingled with the other smells—Charlie's perfume, for instance. He loved it! If he had the confidence, he would wear women's perfume. He wasn't sure he possessed a skin to complement men's aftershave—perhaps he had too many female hormones. He giggled to himself at the thought. The people around him didn't even lift their hollow heads.

The light rain clung to the window panes, waiting for a while before joining together to form steady rivulets—pooling together at the bottom, then running off to goodness knows where—somewhere on the outside of the bus—to oblivion. Charlie would be getting so annoyed with him. He wasn't sure if her heart was really into going out tonight, but she was a good friend who needed to find someone. A string to her bow—the steam in the kettle. She needed to get laid. It wasn't like her to go so long without female company. She was beginning to get tetchy.

She would be standing in the square getting soaked. Why the hell did the damned bus have to break down here? The one place in the whole of Walden where the mobile signal was intermittent. He would try again to see if he could get through. He looked at his phone. It was showing one bar, no bars, one bar. The signal settled on one bar. He selected Charlie's number.

The phone began to ring. He was hopeful. It was answered. "Hi Charlie, it's me. Charlie, can you hear me?" Silence was the reply. "Well, I just wanted to let you know I'm on my way, but the bus broke down and I'm going to be late. Wait in…" The call was disconnected. "Bloody hell!" Gavin began to look at the other passengers around him hoping for some moral support. He didn't get any.

Gavin stared at the display on his phone watching for the sign of decent signal strength. Two bars—yes! As he was about to call Charlie, the sound of a doorbell ringing interrupted him. Great, she'd sent him a message. Thank goodness—she was going to go to the pub and wait. At least she would be dry and warm, which was more than he was going to be.

He had been tempted to grab for the one coat he owned on his way out of the door tonight…but no. It wouldn't do to arrive at the club wearing a coat. What would the boys think! Covering up his black Armani T-shirt with its rainbow stripes boldly emblazoned across the front—unthinkable. Worse still, his swaying hips in his black Armani IV's with the ruched legs having their lines interrupted...O–M–G—Never! Wasn't going to happen. Anyway, what was a little water between friends?

***

THE BUZZ OF the message alert echoed around each of the toilet stalls and empty room like an angry wasp looking for revenge.

Buzz. Buzz. Buzz.

Michelle shuddered. She felt like a schizophrenic— mind split in two, trying to juggle each persona within any given circumstance. Struggling. Here in the Fleece—the new Company Secretary—efficiency personified in relaxation mode; drinking wine, talking, laughing, joking— endeavouring to make new friends, acquaintances...even enemies. Socialising. The same things she and Martin had done countless times in the past. Over and over and over. The golf club. The gym. The cinema. Every up-market bar and club in Newcastle...privy to their presence. It's what they did. It's who they were.

Like a dark being pressing heavily on her chest, dread enshrouded her. What would be in the message? Breathe. She would have to read it. He would be angry if she didn't. She needed him to stay calm. Martin and angry in the same sentence, she didn't want to contemplate. Not after this morning. If she had to placate him, then so be it. She would re-apply her makeup first. Would the small delay count as defiance? No, the make-up would be a bad idea. If he upset her again, she would only have her mascara to do over. She wished she had bought the water-resistant kind now.

At home, her other persona was played out. At home, she had become a crying fool. Her tears to Martin had been like water running off a duck's back. He had become immune to her tenderness. Her tears were an irrelevance. An annoyance. A fuel igniting his internal fire of anger like no other spark.

He had peaked this morning. The rain and the paperboy. Such an innocent beginning to their conversation and then…she began running her hands over her body to see if she had imagined the events of the morning.

She had lifted her head from her coffee to speak up on behalf of the paperboy and he caught her unawares by grabbing the back of her hair, swinging her around, and pinning her to the kitchen wall. His huge hands had enveloped her neck, and he began to squeeze.

At first, Michelle looked at him in astonishment, wondering how he could have reacted so violently to such an innocent remark. Then, as he moved his face slowly towards hers, contorted and ugly with anger, fear had crept into her eyes. She was so frightened her bladder had threatened to spill its contents.

He slammed her again—hard, sliding her downward with a vice-like grip on her throat. He grabbed her hair again and began dragging her across the kitchen floor towards the lounge. She remembered banging her leg on the kitchen table as she passed it and thought it should hurt, but she didn't feel a thing. At least she was able to take a semi-normal breath, although the urge to gasp and gag was a strong one, she didn't dare, in case he would begin choking her again. She could tell he had an erection from the tenting in the front of his dressing gown. The sight sickened her.

Once in the lounge he stopped and began looking around the room aimlessly. From table and chairs to couch and then to the coffee table in front of it. She was sure he was looking around to see if he had enough room to do what he was going to do. So cold and calculating. Her brain slowly engaged the situation, suddenly aware of what his plans may include. Another bolt of terror shot through her.

As he continued to drag her behind him, he kicked the coffee table away from the couch. In one movement, he lifted her from the floor, turned her over, and threw the top half of her body onto the couch, lifting her dressing gown above her hips in the process.

His weight was tremendous, his entry into her unforgiving and brutal. He had no thoughts now of being the gentle giant as he forced her head into the cushion, and soon, she was gasping for her breath again. This seemed to spur him on even more as her increasing fear seemed to coincide with his vengeful thrusts. The inside of her thighs screamed with pain as he shifted his position to pin her in place with his knees. Every thrust brought her new pain, but she dare not cry out. She felt the tearing of her insides and knew she was bleeding.

Then, he withdrew and climaxed all over her back. He turned her roughly over on her back and began gorging himself on her breasts. He lifted his head and looked her in the eyes. She wasn't aware of what he saw—pain, terror, disgust? Whatever it was, it stopped him in his tracks.

As he walked away from her, she heard him mutter, "Go clean yourself up, you filthy whore. You'll be late for work."

Now, the results of his blows remained. His bites would remain hidden forever. The other…no one would ever know—she would have to make sure of it. He had been her life—now, who could tell?

Buzz. Buzz. Buzz.

Michelle looked at herself in the mirror. She looked down at the phone and then reached for the make-up bag from her handbag. As she took out her blusher, she heard the voices from the lounge growing louder as the creak of the door announced the arrival of company. The inside door flew open and Poppy Ryder rushed to the nearest cubicle, slamming the door behind her.

17

"I thought you got lost," Poppy called above the sound of toilet paper being pulled from its holder. "I couldn't hold it any longer, as much as I wanted to. Gordon is making such a fool of himself with a woman out there. Honestly, posh as you like and gayer than Christmas, and he's still trying to get her into bed." The flush of the toilet muted the high-pitched squawk of Poppy's laugh.

Michelle was glad for the distraction—dragging her from her home mindset and back to the one of her own. "I hope you're being kind to him," said Michelle applying a little blusher to each cheek and raising a smile at Gordon's plight.

Poppy turned and smiled as she washed her hands. "Not a chance! I'm going to let him dig himself in really deep. Hell, I'll even provide the spade. I need to get a little revenge for myself—but that's another story. So, come on, hurry up and get your make-up done, or you're going to miss all the fun." Poppy headed towards the door and was quickly gone.

Buzz. Buzz. Buzz.

Michelle looked down at the mobile sitting beside her handbag on the sink, knowing she would have to look at it. Her whole body began to tremble as though transported to some dark, dank, cold void. Her hand shook as she reached out. Terrified the message was from Martin. Terrified.

Willpower held the phone. Willpower swiped the message open.

YOU CAN'T STAY IN THERE FOREVER.

He was right. She couldn't.

18

CHAPTER FOUR

THE HEAT AND humidity in the bar hit Charlie like a sauna. Every inch of her exposed skin felt clammy and she immediately felt uncomfortable. As she opened the front of her coat, she glanced around knowing for sure she would see someone from work. After all, it was First Friday, and this was their usual haunt. Over in the far corner, she spied Poppy and a few of her other colleagues, so after a quick wave of acknowledgement, she made her way over to the bar.

It was heaving! People were standing four and five deep, and, as usual, the barmaids were serving the men first. Hells bells! How irritating. Why were women so faceless in bars? Just her luck to be standing behind a man-mountain in the queue. Not only was he ruggedly handsome, which was a guarantee to be served quicker, but he could just reach over the top of everyone's head in front of him, pass his money, and retrieve his drink. Nice advantage. Luckily, three or four people were served at the same time, pushing past Charlie on the way back to their tables, not caring about slopping drinks over her boots and coat. She decided, with an irritated brush of her hand, she should remove the drink slops before they stained— she was going to kill Gavin. No doubt about it.

The man-mountain had reached the bar. "A double Grouse—no ice," Charlie heard him say in a voice barely audible. He looked round and faced her, but looked over her head as if looking for a friend, but nobody was forthcoming. Out of curiosity, Charlie turned and followed his gaze. He seemed to have zeroed in on her group in the corner.

Suddenly, his sparkling blue eyes narrowed and his stare became menacing—his eyelids dropping, lips puckering, contorting his face to make him appear quite ugly. A thought suddenly popped into Charlie's head—*I wouldn't like to meet him in a dark alley.* The thought made her shiver, a bad feeling resonating deep inside. His vibes were awful. His aura clung to him like a bad smell.

At the barmaid's behest, he turned and paid for his drink. Charlie, at last, could begin to think about ordering. She waited patiently for him to move away from the bar, but he didn't. He merely turned his back and leaned nonchalantly against the counter, nursing his glass, arms folded against his chest. Consequently, Charlie had to force her way in beside him, trying her best not to touch. As quickly as possible, she attracted the barmaid's attention and ordered a glass of fresh orange juice, paid with the correct change, and moved away from him. She didn't want to spend another minute breathing the same air as the man who oozed hatred.

Charlie was going to complain about the man as she reached the table where her friends were seated, but her mind skipped the thought when she noticed a newcomer in the group. It was the woman from the restroom. Her stomach lurched as she looked at her, blood flowing conspicuously to her nether regions. Her throat began to dry up by the second, like water on a pavement in Cairo. She had to take a sip of her drink—just to lubricate it enough to talk to the others. Her free hand reached for the seam on her coat and she stroked. For some unknown reason, she could also feel her face deepening in colour. What the hell was going on with her body? Why on earth did this woman have this strange power over her? She didn't even know her. Perhaps sitting was the best option as her legs began to feel weak. Perhaps she was sickening for something.

"Where have you been, you lightweight? You've missed most of the best bits, namely Gordon trying to get a date with some upper-class woman, who I'm sure got on your bus!" Poppy said in the shrill high-pitched voice, which really took some getting used to. Then Charlie was subjected to fifteen seconds of ear-splitting laughter, probably fuelled by drink, as they would have been drinking solidly since a quarter past five. Well, it was First Friday.

"It can't have been so funny, surely?" asked Charlie still struggling to get a voice.

Gordon held up his hand to make a claim in the conversation, his mop of blond curly hair shaking as he giggled. His rotund face was red, even though his tie had been pulled down far enough to open the top two buttons of his shirt. As his giggling subsided, he managed to give his answer. "I'm sorry to say it was, indeed, funny as hell. You will probably have better luck than I did should you be lucky enough to run into her tonight. She'll be the one with the brown slacks and low cut top. Honest to goodness, Charlie—she threw it on and nearly missed. You could see almost all her…" He looked down to his chest and began juggling his hands, palm up. He looked towards the newcomer and blushed, making his face even redder than before.

The mystery woman merely smiled. "I assume you and Gav will be hitting the clubs?" he said to Charlie, obviously trying to hide his embarrassment.

"We will if he ever arrives. I think his bus broke down. It would have been quicker to go pick him up. If he's not here in half an hour, I'm heading home. I'm not really in the mood, to be honest. I only came to keep him company. His love life is a little bit lacking lately," Charlie replied as she fanned her face with her hand.

"I can't see yours has been much better," said Poppy from across the table, pausing briefly to take a large slug of white wine. "It's been a while since you've mentioned going out with some hot, young lady."

"I don't tell you everything, Poppy. You only think I do," replied Charlie with a hearty laugh.

Poppy consoled her ego with another large draught of the wine. "So it would seem. Looks as though you've taken to going shopping without me, too. Nice coat," she said as she shifted her body to get a better look.

Charlie laughed at the feigned hurt look on Poppy's face but took the opportunity to slip off her coat and put it on the back of her chair. "Now would I go shopping without you?" Charlie tilted her head to one side. "This one was an online buy and it was a steal, so I bought it. I've been saving up for a winter coat, and even though the weather says not, the shops say we are in spring."

Charlie could feel eyes on her, and as she turned from Poppy, she had just caught a glimpse of the mystery woman turning away from her to take a quick look at the bar. Charlie noticed a strange look in her eyes—a mixture of sadness, pain, and what looked like a little foreboding. The strange feeling came over Charlie again—the one she had in the ladies room earlier in the day.

She wanted to take the woman in her arms and hold her. Not in a sexual way but to offer protection. Although, why she thought the woman needed protection was beyond her, aside from the welt beneath her left ear. As Charlie followed the woman's gaze, she just knew where it was going to end...on the man-mountain who stood at the bar.

His look was threatening. His eyes bore across the room like two laser beams homing in on their target, but he also projected a quiet intimidation as though he was slowly bubbling, like a pan of water on simmer. It was too much for Charlie.

"Sorry, I don't know your name." Charlie stood and held her lower back as if in discomfort. "Do you think it would be possible to swap seats? These chairs are playing havoc with my lumbago. I could do with a little lumbar support." A couple of heads turned in her direction as though conveying the fact she had lumbago was news to them. She was ready to blame Gavin for having her standing around in the cold and damp, but it wasn't necessary.

The stranger dragged her gaze away from the bar. She blinked—slowly. She looked at Charlie and then took a few seconds to process the request. She answered in a slow velvety voice, "Of course not. I don't mind at all. My name is Michelle, by the way. Michelle Bailey. I'm the new Company Secretary."

"I'm Charlie Reinette. I work in Inputting. Pleased to meet you, and thank you for doing the honours. I can't even rely on them for an introduction." She turned and nodded in the direction of the others around the table. They shrugged their shoulders. Charlie didn't want to acknowledge the earlier events from the ladies room at the office. She didn't think this was the time or the place.

As they shook hands, they changed places, their bodies briefly touching in the move. Charlie jumped as though an electric current had passed through her body. She looked into Michelle's eyes and laughed. "Cheap carpet," she said, as though static electricity was the cause of her discomfort. What the hell was happening to her? Was this woman a witch or something? Was she beguiling her? Yes, that must be the answer, but it didn't worry her. Charlie smiled to herself, and then caught Poppy turning her gaze away from her, smiling knowingly at Gordon.

However, it didn't look as though the man at the bar was overly pleased with the manoeuvre. Charlie could feel his eyes boring into her, but she was determined not to look at him. Obviously, something was very wrong between them. She could tell Michelle knew him because she had held his gaze longer than you would the look of a stranger. *Boyfriend she ditched?* Perhaps the best scenario Charlie could come up with until she noticed the rings on Michelle's third finger, left hand. Wedding band, engagement ring, and eternity ring. Husband then. This situation was not looking good.

The conversation around the table was jocular, fuelled in the main by the wine, spirits, sexual conquests and innuendoes. Gavin hadn't shown his face, and Charlie was nearly at the end of her orange juice. She was about to make the announcement she was leaving when Michelle beat her to it.

"I'm sorry to be a party pooper, but I'll have to run. I promised my husband I wouldn't be out too late. We still haven't unpacked all our boxes from the move yet, so I promised to give him a hand. It was a lovely evening and thanks for inviting me."

Her smile was genuine, as was the sentiment. Charlie felt a sudden sadness. *Bloody hell! Will you get a grip! You're acting like a moonstruck teenager!* "I'm going to make tracks, too. It doesn't look as though Gavin is going to show, so I'm going home to curl up with a book or a good DVD. A visit to the loo before I go out into the cold though. See you all on Monday, and Poppy, are we still going shopping on Sunday?"

"Of course! Is the Pope from some South American country I can never remember? Are you driving or shall I?"

"Do I want to remain alive or not? Mmmm, I think I'll drive. I'll pick you up at ten forty-five." She smiled, knowing Poppy would take the insult to her driving in good spirit.

After she had stood to put on her coat, Charlie watched Michelle leave, the outside door swinging closed behind her. She felt an overwhelming sadness pass through her and she shivered—as though she had been an obstacle in a spectre's path. The woman was definitely a witch Charlie decided but didn't labour on the thought as she was in

24

desperate need of the loo. As she walked towards the restrooms, she saw the big man swill down what was left in his glass, his menacing air surrounding him like a black cloud. She hoped Michelle had her own transport or had gone for a cab across the street. He did not seem in a good mood.

CHAPTER FIVE

CHARLIE WAS GLAD the rain had stopped as it lifted her mood slightly, but the clearing skies heralded a cooling of the air, and even so late in the spring, she feared a sharp frost. Gavin had finally managed to let her know he was going straight to the club—during her trip to the loo, of course, but she had begged off, citing a non-existent headache as the cause.

She headed toward the car park on the street behind the square. Normally, especially late at night, she and Gavin would have gone the circuitous route to avoid the alley at the side of the pub, but at this time of night, there were still plenty of people around should she need any help. Mugging was alive and well—and living in Walden.

As she reached the alley, she heard a man's voice raised in anger. "You fucking bitch! Which one is he? Come on, fucking tell me! Which one of those lame brains has been screwing you?"

Charlie felt a shiver run down her spine. It looked as though she had walked into the middle of a domestic fight—and she knew whose *domestic* it was! As she rounded the corner fully, a tsunami of anger like she had never known in her life rolled through her. Her heart began to pound in her chest, and her fists curled into tight balls. *How dare he speak to Michelle with such hatred? He is nothing but a bully, and it's about time someone told him so. What an absolute bastard!*

Charlie could hear him muttering something in a low, conspiratorial voice, his head bent toward Michelle's face. Suddenly, his hand was raised and came down with such force on Michelle's cheek, Charlie expected her to fall down, or at least scream out in pain. The sound, like the crack of a whip, reverberated off the walls of the alley.

Michelle's only response was a muted whimper. Thank goodness it had only been a slap, but even so, coming from a man of his size...she looked so small in comparison to him. So weak, and helpless. She was cowering like a whipped dog, bowing so low, the front of her coat was trailing in the puddles at her feet. Michelle looked as though she may throw up at any second and seemed to be heaving hard as a precursor. Charlie could see her ribcage expanding and contracting in the heaving motion as though she had run further than her body would allow.

Charlie was enraged. She couldn't remember feeling this angry...ever! Even as she remembered her own plight in her early youth, she couldn't remember feeling like this. Her stride lengthened, but he seemed oblivious to her approach, blinded and deafened by his own rage, as he started another tirade on the defenceless Michelle. "You are nothing but a filthy whore who will open her legs for any Tom, Dick, or fucking Harry. You are an utter disgrace. I don't know what I ever saw in you. You make me want to vomit!"

By the time he raised his hand again, Charlie had reached them. He turned as his peripheral vision was breached, the look of surprise evident on his face like a rabbit caught in headlights. Charlie turned her left foot to a thirty-degree angle to open up her right hip to improve the kicking path of her right leg.

To him, it looked though she were turning away, but no such thought crossed Charlie's mind—just the thought of all the weeks and weeks she had spent practising the Muay Thai leg kicks. The next few moments seemed to happen in slow motion, not a sensation Charlie had ever experienced in her life. She swung out with all her weight coming sideways as she connected squarely with the outside of his right knee.

She felt the impact on her instep and lower shin, and she was thankful she was wearing her leather boots, which at least afforded her some support and protection. She knew she would pay a heavy price later with sore lower shin and foot for at least a week. It had been a couple of years since Charlie had used the kick so wasn't used to it anymore but was so glad all the weeks of training had paid off. The self-defence class was another knee-jerk reaction in a moment of terror to her kidnapping, but all the same, she was saddened it had come to this because she never thought she would use her self-defence to attack anyone.

A twang and a grinding sound pierced the air, and Charlie knew the kick and all her weight had reached its target successfully. *More by luck than judgement,* she thought, but she would take any advantage she could get.

The man screamed with a force so strong he sounded like a bull elephant. It shook Charlie to the core, and she saw Michelle cower and cover her mouth in horror, reminding her of Eduard Munch's 'The Scream'. The only thing Charlie wanted to do now was to run like hell.

But she didn't. Charlie waited for a short time, each moment sliding slowly into the next, just to make sure he was truly disabled, and then she addressed Michelle, cupping her chin and lifting her head to bring her back to a full standing position.

She could see the whites of Michelle's eyes as she looked sideways in a state of terror, never taking her eyes from her assailant as though she expected him to leap to his feet any minute and start dishing out a repeat of what she'd just received. She was truly terrified. She flinched as Charlie took her gently by the shoulders and looked at her—square in the face. She could see her left cheek beginning to swell and the eye beginning to puff in preparation of its closing. She could also see trickles of blood coming from a slight nick in the left eyebrow and a split lower lip. Michelle opened her mouth to speak, but could only mutter, "I...I...I..."

She heard writhing behind her on the ground, and Charlie secretly hoped the man was soaked through to the skin from the large freezing cold puddle he was sitting in. She said in a firm, but calm voice, "You try to get up, and I'll break the other leg, you fucking bully. You're an utter disgrace." And she meant it. He was holding his knee, his huge hands trying to support the right kneecap, head bent forward looking at his crotch. The great bully brought down to the level he deserved to be—in the gutter.

"Michelle, come with me. We're going to get you sorted out," Charlie said in a voice so gentle, she didn't recognise it as her own.

They headed out of the alley towards the car park with Michelle holding Charlie's hand and Charlie's other arm placed protectively around her back holding onto her waist. Michelle moved gingerly with a shuffling gait, which Charlie just put down to shock. She hoped the car didn't prove too low for Michelle to get in.

After driving a couple of miles towards her own home, Charlie had a sudden thought. What if Michelle needed a doctor urgently? Charlie had been so intent on getting her away from him, she hadn't thought to enquire how Michelle was feeling. She pulled her black Audi into a convenient driveway and switched off the engine.

A feeling of complete helplessness swept over Charlie. She had never been in a position where she had taken responsibility for someone else's welfare. She felt as though a great abyss was opening in front of her. She didn't know what to say or what to do. She only knew Michelle needed help. The trick was to find out how to help her. The one way to find out for certain was to ask.

"How you feeling?" seemed the most inane question in the world—but she couldn't think of another. Michelle didn't answer verbally, though. She merely turned her head towards Charlie, as if to say, *Look at this! What do you think?*

Charlie felt sick as she studied Michelle's beautiful face—blood streaked and bruised. What kind of sick, fucking animal could do this to this to a woman? Any woman! Michelle looked so small and fragile. So—helpless. The slap was only done on a whim, no proof to show Michelle had been unfaithful. It was patently obvious from his comments in the alley. Charlie felt distraught. It was the same feeling Charlie had when she saw cruelty to children or the wholesale slaughter of defenceless creatures. She felt —gutted!

Charlie reached across and gave a soft touch to the swelling under the eye. A touch so gentle, it hardly registered at all, but it conveyed everything Charlie was feeling— compassion, caring, helplessness and—dare she admit, a little seed of lust. She inwardly berated herself, telling herself Michelle was a married woman, even though she was married to a brute, if indeed it had been her husband who was slapping her stupid in the alley. It had to be. Michelle didn't seem to be the type to cheat on anyone so Charlie couldn't imagine it being Michelle's lover.

There was no verbal reaction at all, so Charlie decided to carry on the conversation one-sided. "Okay, this is what we're going to do. I'm going to take you back to my house, then sort out those cuts and bruises. I think a nice warm cup of tea is in order too unless you prefer something stronger. Then you are going to snuggle down in a nice warm bed and get some rest."

Charlie waited a few moments for the words to sink in. She knew they had when a single tear formed at the corner of Michelle's good eye and trickled down her cheek. Charlie thought it said a lot about Michelle's state of mind when she couldn't muster enough energy to wipe away the tear.

CHAPTER SIX

CHARLIE PRESSED THE remote control on her key fob and closed the garage door with some satisfaction. She always did. For some unknown reason, she always equated her car's safety with her own personal safety. She was sure some wise shrink somewhere in the world would have an answer to the conundrum. She didn't care. It was just the way it was. However, given the circumstances, Michelle's and her own safety seemed to transcend even the Audi's tonight, a thought extremely worrying to Charlie. It was almost as though something deep within her brain knew the situation with the bastard was not at an end.

Michelle stood at the side of the Audi, a stunned look transcending her face. What a beautiful face, temporarily scarred by a moron's hands and bad humour. Charlie needed to get her injuries looked after as quickly as possible and see where Michelle wanted to go from there. The police would be Charlie's choice, but she could understand if there was some reluctance to follow the police route. Even with changes in the law with regard to domestic violence, there was sometimes reluctance on the police's part to perhaps take the situation more seriously.

Charlie had seen a horrendous television programme not long ago where a girlfriend had been stalked and brutalised by her boyfriend. The ending had not been good and, of course, the girl's parents had placed the blame squarely at the door of the police. On the other hand, the police had to get the woman in any of these cases to agree to press charges—and it wasn't always an easy task. However, it wasn't Charlie's call to make. She knew nothing of Michelle's history with this man, but she was going to do everything in her power to find out what the hell was going on! He looked dangerous to her.

She walked round the car, took Michelle gently by the shoulders, and looked deeply into her eyes. They were so expressive. She could see hurt, disappointment, and confusion staring straight back at her. "Michelle," she said with true concern in her voice, "you need to come with me, and we'll have a look at those injuries properly. Let me see if you trust me enough to practise my Florrie Nightingale on you." Charlie smiled in the hope of receiving one in return and although the corner of Michelle's mouth began to move, it was obvious every muscle used to smile hurt—a lot!

A look of pain shot across the bruised face and went straight to Charlie's heart. She had never believed in love at first sight—until now, but she couldn't come up with any other explanation as to why she was taking this situation so personally. It was almost as though the abuse had taken place in Charlie's mind and on her own body.

The thought of love worried Charlie. Perhaps she was mistaken. She hoped she was. She wasn't sure she was ready for anything so deep and meaningful, and she chided herself for the thoughts she had had earlier in the evening. It was an eerie feeling to suddenly feel responsible for someone else.

Charlie had only ever had herself to consider, although she liked to think she hadn't gone through life being so insular she hadn't thought of other people. She was sure she had. Still, it didn't mean to say she wasn't a spoiled brat. Perhaps, for now, it was just safer to say she was bewitched.

"Come with me. Let's see what we can do." Charlie disabled the alarm and then took Michelle's hand, leading her through the access door into the kitchen. She realised she was going to have to suppress the great anger she was currently feeling and try not to influence Michelle in any way with regard to the man. It occurred to Charlie this situation might run for quite a while, and her mind was suddenly filled with all kind of doubts. She didn't know how she was going to keep Michelle safe and away from him. She only knew she was going to try. If Michelle would let her.

***

WITH THE SCRIPT playing softly in the background, Michelle sat safely ensconced on the sofa with a mug of tea in her hand. Charlie stared at her from the oversized easy chair on the opposite side of the room. She had her feet tucked up beside her—her own mug of tea in hand.

She had used antiseptic in warm water to bathe the cuts, and then put on antiseptic cream and gave Michelle an ice bag wrapped in a tea towel to put on the swollen eye. Those things were as much as she could do for the time being. She was still waiting for Michelle to begin a conversation, but so far, it had been yes and no answers or silence. Charlie was learning a new life lesson—patience. She had never had any and never thought she would, but Michelle had a positive influence. Eventually, though, she caved in.

"What's his name?" she asked. It wasn't something Charlie really needed to know, other than to substitute bastard, arsehole or idiot in her own mind.

"Martin." The reply was delayed and weak, but a reply nonetheless. Michelle proceeded to retrieve a gold cross and chain from her neck beneath a polo neck sweater, then she began to run the chain through her fingers in a very nervous kind of way.

"Is he your husband?" Charlie asked.

"Yes." Silence accompanied by a single tear and the constant rubbing of the chain.

"Does this kind of thing happen often, Michelle?"

"No, of course not. I don't know what's come over him. He's normally the sweetest, gentlest of men, and I don't like your implication he's some kind of habitual abuser." Her voice held a hardness Charlie couldn't understand given the circumstances. The good thing was at least the facial expression now held something more than the downtrodden female look. A spark of fire glinted there in the unclosed eye for a second or two, but Charlie spotted it and was relieved to see it.

"It's not what I'm suggesting at all. I'm just trying to think of the best way to help here, but I need to know where to start. All I have to go on is your husband screaming at you and beating you up in an alley. If you don't want me to help, then just say so. It's none of my business. I just can't stand by and watch a woman get hit, especially by a guy his size. He could do real damage without even realising it."

"I'm sorry, Charlie. It's all come as a bit of a surprise to me, too. He's been particularly bad today, for some unknown reason. Would you believe it all started because of the paper boy?"

Michelle's eyes drifted off to some middle space, leaving Charlie in no man's land. There was suddenly a very uncomfortable atmosphere in the space between them.

"What on earth did the paperboy do to cause Martin to get so riled up?" Charlie took a sip of her tea in order to give Michelle time to get back from wherever she was in her head.

"He got the papers wet, that's all."

"I'm not surprised. It was pissing down this morning."

"Not acceptable as far as my husband is concerned." Michelle drank her tea, and then continued to look in the cup. "A lot of things aren't acceptable to him lately."

Charlie made a quick decision not to drive the conversation any further. She could sense Michelle drifting further away, going somewhere acutely painful, given the look on her face.

"I'll tell you what. How about we call it a night if you're sure you don't hurt anywhere else. Nothing needing hospital treatment, I mean."

"I'm okay."

"Come on then. You follow me, and we'll get you tucked into bed as I promised. I'll even put the electric blanket on for you."

Charlie was now beginning to put everything together, and given the conversation in the last few minutes, it would seem this last beating was not the first Michelle had suffered at Martin's hands today. Hence, where Michelle must have got the welt on her neck. Martin must have done it this morning. Charlie made a pact with herself as she considered all she knew about the situation. She was determined if Martin wanted another piece of Michelle, he would have to go through her to get it.

CHAPTER SEVEN

CHARLIE DECIDED TO give Michelle the double en suite bedroom nearest to her own, thinking if Michelle needed any help during the night, she would be right next door. She provided her with a nightdress, dressing gown, a new toothbrush, and towels, and waited for her to get ready for bed. She was worried when she was taking such a long time in the bathroom, wondering if Michelle was having trouble getting undressed. Charlie was on the verge of asking if she needed any help when she came out.

"Would you like me to wash anything for you?" enquired Charlie, thinking she could throw Michelle's clothes in with her own.

"No thanks. I have some washing to do at home, so I'll do them all tomorrow."

Charlie was horrified Michelle was contemplating going back home so soon. She was sure she would get the backlash from Martin for what Charlie had done to him.

"Michelle, do you think it's wise to go back tomorrow? I mean, he's really going to be pissed at me, and I'm not going to be there. I think he's going to take it out on you, and I couldn't live with results. Please, stay a few days. Give him a chance to calm down and see the error of his ways." Charlie couldn't believe the words coming out of her mouth. She could see no way he was going to calm down. She was trying to give herself some manoeuvring time. On the surface, she seemed calm and relaxed. Underneath, she was panicking like hell! The chasm of responsibility was getting wider.

Charlie looked across at Michelle and hoped she would see some sense. She looked helpless and forlorn as she stood there with her battered face cuddling a heap of clothes. "Can I see what I feel like tomorrow?" she asked in a pleading kind of way. She was oblivious to the fact Charlie probably couldn't have denied her anything she asked for.

"Sure, if that's what you want," agreed Charlie—but her stomach lurched at the thought of Michelle taking another beating because of her actions. "My dad always said I would end up getting someone into trouble for something I did, and I think the day has arrived. I seem to be incapable of keeping my thoughts and actions to myself. It never mattered at the gay rallies or the union marches, as long as I kept away from the police lines. This time, it's personal, and I don't want you to get hurt."

"Charlie, please don't get upset. I'm just grateful you were there to help me. At some stage, I will have to talk to Martin to find out what on earth is happening because I have to admit…I'm floundering." Michelle took a handful of damp hair and pushed it behind her ears. The dark welt stood out, as though proud of itself.

"I have tried to go over things I might have done or said to see if there is some pivotal point which would have sent him over the edge causing him to lose his temper so badly, but I just can't think of anything. The only way to find out is to ask, and it will have to be done soon. I don't want to leave it too long."

Charlie's head was beginning to fill with all kinds of pictures as she imagined Michelle talking to Martin and none of them looked good. She was roused from her deep thinking by Michelle's voice. "Charlie, I want to thank you for what you did tonight. I'm not sure my body could have taken much more today. I want you to believe I don't know what I did to upset Martin. He wasn't even supposed to be in town. It looks as though he changed his mind about having a weekend away with the boys. I shouldn't have told him what pub we were going to, but hindsight is always twenty-twenty."

Her face took on the most incredibly sad expression, as she retrieved the cross from the cleavage peeking from the V of her nightgown neckline. She stroked the chain and cross mindlessly.

Charlie thought Michelle might cry. Charlie knew she would weep buckets herself later.

"Can I ask you something else?" She looked hopefully in Charlie's direction.

"Anything. Ask away."

"Will you stay with me tonight?"

Lights flashed and bells rang in Charlie's head, and she could feel her face flushing, embarrassed at the involuntary way her body was reacting. If only Michelle were saying those words in any other circumstance, Charlie would have been turning cartwheels, but it wasn't. "Of course I will. You hop into bed and get yourself comfortable. I'll go get a quick shower and be back shortly. Would you like the TV on or some music, perhaps?"

"No, I'm okay, thanks. I have a thumping headache, so best not aggravate it." She tried a weak smile, but it still looked a painful process as she grimaced shortly after.

"I'll bring you some painkillers, too," Charlie said as she walked through the door.

Charlie did cry buckets as the warm water cascaded over her face. She hoped there wouldn't be any trace when she returned to the guest bedroom. She desperately wanted to avoid Michelle getting any idea this experience was affecting her so deeply. She couldn't explain herself—to anyone at the moment—least of all Michelle.

CHAPTER EIGHT

CHARLIE COMPOSED HERSELF after her shower and made sure there were no tell-tale signs of her weeping session by checking in the full-length mirror in her bedroom. No puffiness or red rims were evident around her eyes, so she was confident there would be no questions asked as far as Michelle was concerned.

She re-entered the bathroom while brushing her hair back from her face, hoping just to take a little moisture out of it before going to bed. She really didn't want to do a Phyllis Diller impression before she had her morning shower. There was nothing worse than a bad hair day before your morning coffee. She brushed her teeth with determination. She wasn't sure why. It's not as though she was on a date or anything.

There was this nagging seed at the back of her mind, and she hoped a good impression might help their situation grow into something wonderful. It might be some way down the line, but more likely, it would never happen at all. She felt like crying again, but for a completely different reason. *A love lost before it was even found. Crikey,* Charlie thought, it must be time for me to get my period. A brief fit of depression followed.

Dressed in her new pyjamas and sporting rarely-worn slippers on her feet, Charlie stopped short of entering the spare bedroom. She could feel the trepidation beginning to kick in and she trembled. *I have to stop thinking about her in a sexual way,* Charlie thought with more hope than she actually possessed. Just the thought of Michelle in the spare bed, not even her own bed, was enough to make Charlie break out in a cold sweat.

The thought of those eyes on Charlie as she wrapped her limbs around Michelle's body, succumbing again after hours of unrelenting pleasure, made Charlie go weak at the knees. If it was like this in her, albeit vivid imagination, what would it be like with accompanying sight, smell, and taste, (*oh, yes! the taste*) of Michelle's body for real? She hated herself for thinking this way, it just wasn't right. She knew better. Her hand shook slightly as she reached for the door handle, and she paused for a second, took a deep breath, turned the handle, and walked into the room.

Michelle was fast asleep. Her chest beneath the duvet rose and fell with deep, even breathing. In a way, Charlie was glad she felt so comfortable and safe that she could sleep so peacefully in her home. On the other hand, the opportunity for further conversation had passed. It would now have to wait until morning. With great stealth, Charlie went to the en suite and got Michelle a glass of water to accompany the two painkillers Charlie had retrieved from the medicine box. She placed both on the bedside table in case Michelle needed them during the night. Charlie then pulled out the knitted blanket from the bottom of the wardrobe, curled up in the easy chair at the side of the bed with her feet on the footstool, and covered herself with it. The idea crossed her mind it might be a long night.

***

THE SCREAM PIERCED her subconscious, breaking into her own dream as a knife was about to puncture the skin on her abdomen. She woke with a start, expecting to find Martin in the room, holding the knife and coming to take a second pop at her. In her dream, he had caught her off guard. She had been dreaming of making love to Michelle, and he had walked in on them while they were in bed.

He moved with the speed of lightening, first stabbing Michelle, and hurdling Michelle's body, pinning Charlie to the bed. She had found herself paralysed as she tried in vain to reach out and gouge his eyes or push his nose back into his skull. She had feared he would rape her, but he slowly raised the knife, ready to plunge it deep into her body as Michelle's blood dripped from it. A weird thought had crossed Charlie's mind. What if Martin had been unfaithful and Michelle's blood was carrying some gruesome disease? This thought was closely followed by a voice in her head screaming at her to wake up.

Her eyes opened into a wide stare, but only sparkling lights greeted her. She could feel a thin film of moisture covering her forehead, her body obviously having its own reaction to her dream. As she tried to pull her thoughts together and wait for her vision to clear and adapt to the darkness, she could hear a loud racking sob coming from the direction of the bed.

"Michelle," said Charlie in a calm voice, which belied her true condition, "are you okay? Are you in pain? Do you want me to send for a doctor or an ambulance?" With each question, Charlie's voice rose higher in pitch, trying to convey the gravity of her perceived role.

"Charlie, I've only had a bad dream. I've still got a headache though."

"Thank goodness." Charlie sighed heavily, conveying every bit of the 'thank goodness' she felt. "I put a couple of painkillers with some water on the bedside table earlier. Can you see, or do you want me to put the lamp on?"

"No! Please don't turn the lamp on. It will only make the headache worse. I can see well enough to take them."

Charlie suspected the reason for keeping the room in darkness had more to do with Michelle's marked face than the headache, but just nodded her head in agreement, not wanting to survey Michelle's face herself. It would only add to her anger and overload. She desperately needed rest. Anger, she had found, zapped her strength just as much as anxiety. The combination of the two was doubly debilitating.

Charlie pulled the blanket up around her ears, but the charged silence was broken by Michelle's soft voice. "Charlie, can I ask you a favour?"

"Of course. Anything."

"Would you come and lie with me. I feel really lonely and scared. I know you are only there, but..." Her voice trailed off as though her mind was off to visit the same faraway place.

"I don't mind at all. It's probably better for me to be horizontal anyway. I don't sleep well propped up. I tried doing it for many months before my grandma passed away and never did get much rest."

Charlie surprised herself. Not one sexual thought had passed through her mind as the offer of sharing the bed seeped into her addled brain. Either she was really tired or she was missing something here. For once in her life, had caring for another person superseded her own needs and wants? This was new territory for her, but it felt good.

She discarded the blanket on the chair and slipped into bed beside Michelle. She didn't touch her but quite happily laid on her back, staring at the ceiling, taking in the smell of her own shampoo drifting across from Michelle's hair. She could also detect the smell of the shower gel Michelle had used, wafting up the gap between them, from the heat being produced by Michelle's body.

Was Michelle hot because of the dream or because Charlie was so close to her? Could she only hope Michelle was having those kinds of thoughts in her current condition? Charlie knew she wasn't surveying the situation correctly. A married woman in an abusive relationship was not going to be having those kinds of thoughts about her. If ever.

Michelle's mind was probably in flight mode, and Charlie wouldn't have blamed her. Goodness knows what would have happened in the alley if she hadn't happened to be in the right place at the right time. Charlie had a lot to thank Gavin for—she would remember to buy him a drink. *Oh, it makes us even,* she thought with a smile.

As Charlie's eyes finally began to close, she heard Michelle mumbling in her sleep. The sound of her breathing increased a little and for the briefest of moments, Charlie thought another nightmare was on the way. Instead, there was a little incoherent mumbling and Michelle flipped over on her side and threw her arm over Charlie's midriff. A wry smile appeared on Charlie's face as she gently placed a hand on Michelle's arm. She drifted off to sleep with the thought of how knights in shining armour come in all shapes and sizes...and both sexes.

CHAPTER NINE

CHARLIE WAS STRUGGLING to breathe as she fought off the shadow of heavy sleep. She opened one eye and lifted her head a little off the pillow. The early morning light cast dull grey shadows around the room. She recognised her guest bedroom. The fitted wardrobes with built in vanity area were definitely hers, but her mind struggled to fill in the rest of the blanks. Who the hell did the arm belong to that was pinning her so successfully to the bed? Her chest felt as though it had a boulder on it.

The realisation came like a bolt from the blue. Oh My God! Charlie's mind flew into turmoil mode and it only got worse as she realised her legs were pinned, too. She could feel bare flesh against her midriff—what the hell was the other thing poking at her? A nipple! She gulped at the air and swallowed hard. She didn't know what to do. If she started moving limbs, Michelle might wake up and think Charlie was touching her up. *Oh, hell.* Charlie could feel her temperature rising and another cold sweat breaking out on her brow.

What the hell! Charlie spoke sternly to herself in her mind. *Michelle was the one who asked you to share the bed. You didn't invite yourself. You were only there for her sense of comfort. She knew you were a lesbian when she invited you into bed. Given the conversations, which took place in the pub, she must have realised. People move around when they sleep. Stop getting wound up, you silly bitch. Just move her arms and legs and go to the bathroom. That's it. Done.*

Charlie took some comfort in the fact she had beaten herself into submission. She suspected Michelle had a lot more firsts to come today and waking up in bed with her body wrapped around a lesbian was going to be the least of her problems.

She was just about to grab Michelle's arm when she felt movement. The arm moved first, then the left leg, followed quickly by the nipple. There was moaning and some shuffling of clothing. Charlie suspected this might be a normal routine for Michelle.

Charlie still hadn't looked at her, and if truth be known, she really wasn't looking forward to it. Very slowly, she shifted her eyes to the left and took a long look. Michelle's face looked awful and, of course, she had to open her good eye just as Charlie gave her look of horror. A hoarse whisper escaped Michelle's mouth. "Spectacularly good, eh?" in a tone almost predicting what the answer was going to be before Charlie spoke.

"I'm afraid so. Michelle, I'm so sorry." Charlie felt as though she was about to burst into tears at the sheer impotence she felt regarding this whole situation. "You're not going to be fit for anything for a few days. I think you can safely say work won't be an option for a couple of weeks."

A look of concern passed over Michelle's face. "Jeff is going to sack me. I haven't been there long enough to accrue any holidays and calling in sick is not an option for me. I need the bathroom." She dismissed the conversation and Charlie with a swift turn of the head and headed for the bathroom. It was only then Charlie noticed the blood in the bed.

Charlie found Michelle some of her clothes and placed them on the bed before Charlie made her way to her own bathroom.

***

"I'M SORRY, CHARLIE. I think I started my period. There is blood on the sheets. Can I pop them in the washer for you?" Michelle said as she walked into the breakfast room, her manner just a little deflated. She wasn't walking quite right, but Charlie couldn't put her finger on what was wrong. Perhaps she had missed some part of the assault and it was affecting Michelle's legs in some way, or perhaps her period was making her lower back hurt.

"No, just dump them on the floor of the laundry room. I will put them in after breakfast. What would you like to eat? I can tempt you with a cooked breakfast, cereal, yogurt, or I even have some croissants in the freezer. Juice, coffee?" she said as she looked for some kind of answer.

"No to the food, but coffee would be perfect." Michelle at least managed a weak smile, which is more than she could do the day before.

As they both sat at the table drinking their Costa Rican blend coffee, Charlie had time to survey Michelle's face properly. The two cuts, one on the eyebrow and one on the lip, had both begun to form scabs, but the light blue bruises around them stood out on the chin, eyelid, and forehead. The eyelid was swollen, effectively closing the eye shut, and no amount of forcing would open it, as Charlie knew from past experience. Getting the wrong side of a hockey stick would do the same damage. Even though the sticks weren't supposed to get so high—they did.

Charlie was mostly worried about the cheekbone. It seemed to have a ridge running around it. She was tempted to ask Michelle if she could touch it, just to see if the damage were to the soft tissue or if the bone had cracked but decided against it. "You really should go to the hospital and get them to check your cheekbone and to make sure it isn't broken, Michelle." Charlie tilted her head to one side as if the action was going to increase the concern in her voice.

"NO!"

Charlie reeled back in surprise at the ferocity in Michelle's voice.

"No hospital and no police. I would like to deal with this on my own."

"Okay. If you want your face to look like a boxer, then it's entirely up to you, but it would be a shame to spoil such a pretty face." Charlie smiled in hope the light-hearted comment might get Michelle to change her mind.

"I really think it will be okay in a few days, or else I would go get it checked out. Honestly, Charlie. Thanks for the nice comment, but you really don't need to boost my ego. I'm fine really. I want to thank you for all you've done for me, a complete stranger really. You've been absolutely great. I don't know what I would have done without you. Thank you for last night, too. You made me feel safe. You have a kind heart and a beautiful soul." There was a brief silence and then, "I really should go home. I can't hide out here forever."

Charlie's heart skipped a beat. She couldn't keep Michelle a prisoner here in her home, as much as she wanted to for Michelle's own protection. There must be something she could say or do to make this obstinate woman see sense.

"Look," Charlie took a deep breath. "Please don't take this the wrong way, but I think your husband has lost the plot. He's doing a good impression of a psychopath at the moment. I honestly don't think you'll be safe. I do have a Psychology degree, Michelle—I do know what I'm talking about." Charlie dragged her fingers through her hair in exasperation. She stared at Michelle with an intensity she knew was needed to drive home the point.

"He will hurt you. There is no doubt in my mind. He will hurt you because of what I did to him, and I honestly don't think I could handle it."

Charlie could feel her eyes pooling with tears. This woman had such a weird effect on her. She could bring out a fierce protectiveness Charlie hadn't known was even in her psyche while, the next minute, reducing her to tears just at the thought of what might happen to her. Charlie questioned her own motives. Did she really believe Martin would hurt Michelle or did Charlie just want her and was now trying to manipulate the situation in her favour?

No. She truly believed Martin would hurt her.

She had been in his space, experienced his hatred first hand, and felt the darkness surrounding him. Calculating and ruthless. A really bad combination to be carried around by a man his size. He could inflict a great deal of harm with very little effort. Was she out of her mind doing what she did to him last night? Charlie had no doubt, she had been very lucky to get away with it.

***

DURING THEIR SECOND cup of coffee, Charlie noticed Michelle absentmindedly playing with the cross and chain around her neck. "Was the cross a gift from someone?" Charlie asked trying to open up the conversation and get Michelle to tell her something—anything.

Michelle nodded her head absentmindedly. "A wedding present from Martin. I think having to attend church services for a few months before we got married, then the reading of the banns of marriage had a profound effect on him for a short while. Neither of us is particularly religious, but I just hankered after a white wedding in a church with a lych-gate. From being a child, I'd always pictured having one after seeing a flower covered gateway to a churchyard in a fairy tale book. The thought seems a little silly now, but Martin made it happen for me."

She played with the cross and chain some more. "He gave me this at the reception. He put it around my neck, fastened it, kissed the cross, then he told me he would love me forever." Her voice began to tremble. "I don't know what happened, Charlie. We had a perfect life up to a few months ago." The tears began to fall, unfettered.

Dramatic mood swings and a flaring temper coming from nowhere must be awful to live with, thought Charlie. *Not knowing whether you were going to get a hug or a punch in any situation must be like existing inside a nightmare.* The next snippet of conversation brought Charlie out of her contemplation.

"Then he wonders why I've gone off sex. He goes for ages not showing any interest then when he does he's not performing right, if you know what I mean. Sorry, you wouldn't know, would you? I mean, you're into women and..." Michelle's eyes dropped to study the top of her coffee.

Obviously, still not comfortable with the lesbian aspect of the situation, thought Charlie, so she answered in what she hoped was a light-hearted reply.

"I had a life while trying to come to terms with my lesbianism, Michelle. I was asked out on dates and everything. I actually had rampant sex a few times, too. Well, I was rampant." A smile broke out on Charlie's face and she was pleased to see Michelle was trying one for size, too. Charlie felt better when faced with the smile and it would help to get information if Michelle were more relaxed.

Something was nagging at the back of Charlie's mind, but she just couldn't quite get the fishing line in there far enough to hook the thought. "What do you do for a social life, other than go out pub crawling with your co-workers, that is?" Charlie decided to try to keep the conversation as light-hearted as possible.

"We used to go the cinema quite a lot. We would always go see the new releases. We used to sit in the back row and hold hands—even if it was empty. A bit childish, but it's something we've always done." A look of great sadness swept across Michelle's face, but her eyes sparked with a look of betrayal. Charlie had to stop herself from wanting to fall into those pools, to reach out and caress the bruises and the cuts, to stroke this woman's hair and hold her in a tight embrace.

"What else?" Charlie asked, more for her benefit than Michelle's.

"We were gym addicts. We were both members so we could go whenever we liked. Normally, we would do an hour or so after work, three or four times a week. I did circuits, but Martin preferred weights and boxing."

"Crikey, he doesn't look as though he needed any help with the weights. He's a big, strong man." *Brute, more like,* thought Charlie but kept the thought to herself.

"He never used to be so big. When I say big, I mean bulky. The weight training must have done it, although why he needs such a physique just to hit a golf ball around a course or to sell computer software is beyond me. He's always been competitive though. I suppose it's just a side effect of being under pressure at work in the early days. There was always a bigger company moving faster or catching up or something." Michelle's eyes fell to look at her coffee again.

"Look. I have to go fill the car up and get some fresh milk from the filling station. Why don't you go have a nice long bath? There are lots of toiletries along the side so just take what you need. All the towels are in the closet at the top of the stairs. While I'm out, I'll see if I can find us something tasty for lunch."

"What a wonderful idea, Charlie. Thank you so much for all this. I don't know what—"

Charlie raised her hand in a stop sign. "You have to stop thanking me, really. You just enjoy your soak and I will see you in a little while."

It was only when Charlie was halfway to the filling station did her brain actually engage—the fishing line finally landing on its target way back in her brain. "Steroids!" she shouted as she looked skyward and banged her fist on the steering wheel. "Sorry," she said to the car. *What are you doing?* Charlie thought to herself. *It's only a car.* The thought worried her.

CHAPTER TEN

MICHELLE LOWERED HERSELF carefully into the warm water and let it gently enfold her lower half as she got used to the temperature of the water. She let out a low, satisfied moan. *Oh, it feels so good,* she thought to herself, a lopsided smile passing across her lips. She carefully pushed her legs forward followed even more carefully by her rear. She was glad of the glide given by the very expensive bath crème Charlie had allowed her to use, feeling no resistance as she slipped slowly into the water.

Charlie was the most generous, thoughtful woman on the planet. There was just something about her… She must have a little bit tucked away being able to afford such luxuries, but at this moment in time, she threw away the thought, not caring to think too deeply about anything. She just wanted to wallow and rest. Her body felt as though she had gone five rounds with a heavyweight boxer. Actually, it had gone two rounds, which was more than enough. She continued to slide until she was up to her neck in bubbles. They were so close to her ears she could hear them popping.

She closed her eyes and listened quietly to them. They had a soporific effect and she could feel the good eyelid getting heavier. She took a deep breath and lifted her knees to enable her to slip her head underwater. She could feel the warm water creeping over her face, the feeling of relaxation beginning to engulf her. She held it there as long as she could as she felt the heat seeping through her skin, gently caressing the tired, aching muscles. She moved her jaw gently from side to side, just checking for some improvement and there certainly seemed to be.

As she lifted her head and readjusted her body, she checked to make sure none of her skin was visible. It suited her not to be reminded of the worst of yesterday's events. Not yet anyway. For the moment, it suited her not to think of the near strangulation, the near suffocation, and the rape.

It was still too much to take in, yet a tear escaped. She could feel another pooling at the bottom of her eye, but she was determined this would be the last one. In her mind, she wanted to retreat, just for a little while, to the sun-kissed beaches of the South of France. The warmth of the water and the scorching heat of the sun. Bliss.

She had gone with her friends at the end of her gap year, soaking up the sun during the day, and then in the evening, after a quick shower in the shower block, they picked up cheap bottles of wine and took them down to the beach. They had made the trip by coach and were staying on a caravan site, but they had all agreed when they booked—they might not have had much money, but the sun shone the same on everyone—rich and poor alike. So they decided they would do what they could afford and just relax for the whole ten days.

There was one day in particular, Michelle remembered, when they arrived at the beachside cafe for their usual breakfast of strong coffee and croissants. She stood on the raised deck, looked at the azure blue water, and thought for a moment—this must be what heaven would look like. Her gaze swept around the cove to the local town two miles away by beach, and she couldn't see another human being.

When a visit to the beach cafe came at lunchtime, there was still nobody in sight. The same order was bought every day. Four Pan Bagnat sandwiches, each wrapped in a thick white paper serviettes. Michelle's mouth began to water at just the thought of it. The large, round, crusty *pain de campagne,* drizzled with olive oil inside, and stuffed full of lettuce, thickly sliced tomato, sliced hardboiled egg and topped off with tuna, drizzled again with olive oil and then liberally scattered with sea salt and cracked black pepper. It had tasted wonderful as they gazed at the water mirroring the colour of the azure sky, feeling the hot sun as it bronzed their skins. Their little piece of heaven on earth.

The day had stayed with her for another reason. Janice, the quietest of the four of them, came out to them that day. Michelle remembered her words as if they had been spoken yesterday. On the beach, as the sun was going down, Janice suddenly sprang to her feet and turned to face the other three. "I want to tell you something," she said—and then bent down to pick up her wine glass. "I'm a lesbian."

She waited for some reaction before carrying on. There was none, only a silence having made the air around them still.

"I've wanted to tell you for a long time, but there was never the right moment. Now is the right time. I want you to understand something. I don't fancy any of you. You're my friends, and I love you, but not in any sexual kind of way." Her eyes moved from one to another, looking for a sign, any sign of disgust or dissent, lingering for just a fleeting moment longer on Michelle. She found none.

Keri, always the joker in the pack, jumped straight in.

"Well, thank goodness for that. I have enough trouble fighting the men off." There was a slight pause, and then everyone erupted into laughter. Everyone assured Janice it didn't make any difference to them. She was who she was, and no further discussion seemed necessary.

Following Keri, they all raised their glasses.

"To Janice," she said, "our only gay friend!" They had clinked their glasses in unison and kissed her on the cheek. Janice looked mightily relieved.

Michelle was always of the opinion you couldn't help who you fell in love with—no matter what the gender or combination of gender. Love was love. It didn't mean it would be there forever. She mused as to what had happened to the three girls she thought she would be in contact with forever, but heavy university schedules and busy social lives soon helped to gently sever the ties.

She and Janice had found themselves alone later the same night on the beach. Drunk as skunks. Keri and Linda had called it a night after the fifth bottle of wine and gone back to the caravan, but Janice and Michelle had said it was a shame to waste number six.

"Let's go in the water," Janice said, and they both quickly stripped down to their bikinis. "I've always wanted to do this. Be in the sea at night in the dark, just feeling the water against my body. Do you think I'm weird?" she had asked, tottering a little and slurring her words.

"We've had a lot to drink, so we should be careful," Michelle had answered, cautious as ever.

"Come on. Nobody experienced anything good by being leery." She had held out her hand to Michelle and they ran, full tilt into the cool sea.

Michelle's body had immediately formed goose pimples from head to toe, her nipples stiffening and feeling extremely sensitive, and the water brushed against her bikini with each new wave. On thinking about it later, she thought it was probably what got her on the sex trail. They stood hand in hand, feeling the cool water bathing them from their shoulders down. An odd gentle wave, trying to go slightly higher as they instinctively rose in the water to avoid it.

"I'll miss all of you," said Janice as she pushed back her head and looked into the cloudless sky.

"You've been my friend forever, and I don't know what I'll do without you." Her voice was carried out to sea on the next wave.

Michelle never broke her gaze from the sea set on the imaginary horizon. However, she sensed an energy emitting quietly from Janice—she was crying. Desperate to comfort her, she held back—her body stirred unusually—like a longing ache. The curious pull made her afraid. Afraid of herself…afraid of Janice…afraid of the precipice and jumping off.

"Janice, you'll be fine. Really, fine…we are all going to different places. We'll all be in the same boat. Okay? Come here." Michelle turned and reached for her friend and pulled her into an embrace. At first, Janice rested her head on Michelle's shoulder and sobbed in the way only alcohol can induce.

"I really will miss you," Janice said. It touched Michelle's heart softly, slowly, and tenderly.

"I'll miss you, too." Out of the cloak of the starlit night, Michelle lightly kissed her on her warm, soft, salty lips. Tentatively at first, then with an intensity coming straight from her toes. She wiggled her feet to get more purchase in the wet sand under the water. She had just meant it to be a kiss.

She wouldn't have known what else to do—but Janice did. She brought both hands to Michelle's breasts and began to massage. The water was cool, but the heat from Janice's hands burned straight through the material of her bikini top, searing like a hot iron. Suddenly, Janice stopped what she was doing and grabbed her by the hand.

"Come on," she said, suddenly sounding sober. "Come with me."

Janice guided Michelle away…the soft music receding with each step to where the beach was silent and then she pulled her down to the sand.

"I don't want you to say anything," she said in a voice so firm it was almost a command—her gaze steady and defiant.

Michelle lay with her eyes looking at the stars in a cloudless, moonless sky—like diamonds scattered across a dark blue velvet throw, the stars shimmered. Her head was now clearing of the alcohol rush, her skin cold and clammy at the front, but her back drying as the parched sand sought out the moisture on her skin.

Michelle could feel Janice's fingers trailing over her legs. It wasn't a tentative touch—she was experienced and deft. Michelle was surprised at the realisation Janice, unknown to the three of them, must have had some kind of an experienced lover—or maybe just naturally gifted.

Janice lay beside Michelle, propped on her left elbow, and began to touch Michelle's midriff, circling the belly button and then Janice bent forward and kissed it. She began to lap around the edges, occasionally dipping the tip of her tongue in fully, filling the void.

Michelle began to squirm. Not because it felt uncomfortable, but because she found it pleasing—her kisses were magnificent. In fact, they were driving her wild, beyond her limited experience—beyond everything.

Janice began to snake her tongue around Michelle's midriff, down the side until she was almost touching the sand, finding a particularly sensitive spot on Michelle's side. Michelle closed her eyes. Not because she couldn't look at her friend, but because she was trying to imagine what was coming next.

The pleasure was becoming excruciating. Her bikini straps were being lowered, exposing her breasts to the cooling air. She thought for a fleeting moment she might object, but the thought was dumped like rubbish in a bin.

She felt a breeze across her breast and thought for a moment the wind had picked up until she smelled the alcohol from Janice's breath. Her nipples had been erect before, but this simple action made them feel as though they were about to pop off her body completely.

Also, this was the first time Michelle had felt the direct connection between her nipples and her crotch. No boy she had ever been with had done this to her. A spark of electricity ignited from one area to the other with lightning speed. She knew the wetness was flooding out of her. She thought she should feel ashamed allowing her friend to seduce her this way, but she didn't—not for a moment.

Then Janice's mouth was on her breasts, circling and swirling, flicking at the top of the nipples so quickly it almost felt painful. The suck was astounding— strong like a vacuum sending Michelle's body several feet in the air without leaving the ground.

Janice's hand began to snake down her body, leaving a heat trail behind until finally, it was between her legs, pushing up the top of the bikini bottoms with the back of her hand. She was slow and deliberate as she eased through Michelle's pubic hair. Each root wired sexually.

The second Janice touched her clitoris Michelle's world exploded into space. Her orgasm began at her core and sent her whole fabric skyward.

One touch—then it was all over.

Not another word was spoken between them during their journey back to the campsite, and Michelle had regretted not making the acknowledgement, but she hadn't known what to say. Confusion, embarrassment, and the close proximity of their mutual friends had helped to delay the conversation, which never did take place.

Out of all her friends, she most often wondered how Janice was faring in the world. She must see if she could track her down via one of the social network sites, once all this drama with Martin was passed. She wondered why she had only thought of Janice.

Perhaps it was because of the experience they had shared, although she had met Martin shortly afterwards and had never consciously given their night another thought. Janice had never mentioned another word about being gay on the holiday, and everyone treated her the same as they always had, but in hindsight, Michelle wondered if not mentioning it had been fair.

Janice might have wanted to talk about it, the reason she had shared her erstwhile secret. It had only been a few weeks before they all went to University, nearly fifteen years ago now. Janice could have kept it to herself had she wanted to and nobody would have been any the wiser. Twenty-twenty hindsight is a wonderful thing, Michelle thought, in more ways than one.

CHAPTER ELEVEN

MICHELLE STOOD IN front of the full-length mirror naked, just staring at her body. The tears she had been storing during her long soak in the bath were now being shed with abandon. She looked a mess. The puffiness on the eye had receded slightly so Michelle could open it a little, and her vision seemed unimpaired.

She cursed the size of Martin's hands because the impact of the blow had been both above and below the eye. How her lip had become split as well, was a mystery to her. The nick in the eyebrow was now beginning to bruise around the outside, as was her lip and they were both beginning to turn a light blue.

Her cheek was the most painful and she prodded at it. She didn't know what she was feeling for, though. She just hoped he hadn't broken her cheekbone. She didn't think so.

The hand mark on the side of her neck was now a deep blue-black, but the most horrendous bruising was on her inner thighs. Large areas were now joining together, giving very little remaining pale flesh showing between her knees and genital area. The bites on her breasts were numerous but not too deep and didn't look as though they would leave any lasting marks.

She sobbed as she took in the full picture. What had she done to deserve this? Again, she began going over the same things in her mind, rehashing every situation in which she might have upset him. In her mind, she couldn't think of anything. Obviously, Martin's mind was being affected in some way, by something, but she couldn't for the life of her think what it could be.

Michelle couldn't bear to look at her body a minute longer and threw on the robe Charlie had provided for her, trying to gather her thoughts and assess the situation she found herself in. She needed to be practical, but her mind seemed to grope around in the ether for something to cling on to, like a fallen tree in the rapids. Her cheek was throbbing mercilessly. It jerked her mind into the here and now.

She wandered into the bathroom to see if she could find painkillers and then she remembered Charlie had retrieved some from the medicine box in the lounge. She made her way to the lounge as she pulled the dressing gown tighter around her, wanting her bruised and battered body to be shielded from unseeing eyes would judge her.

Charlie had left the medicine box on the windowsill, and as Michelle reached out her hand to grab it, she shuddered. A premonition told her Martin was close. She raised her head slowly not wanting to look up for fear the warning was true. She felt her body go cold—hands and body shaking uncontrollably.

She blinked several times hoping beyond hope her vision was now playing tricks on her. The vision remained. There, parked across Charlie's drive, was Martin's Volvo. He sat in it—watching her every move.

She heard the buzz from her mobile and went to retrieve it from the table. She opened the message.

You can't stay in there forever—she read over and over again.

It was too much for Michelle. She just managed to get her rear end on the seat by the window before the stars appeared in front of her eyes and she passed, thankfully, into oblivion.

***

AS CHARLIE TURNED the corner from the main road, she noticed some idiot in a Volvo V70 parked across her drive. *Wonderful,* she thought. *They send these reps out in their flashy car with satellite navigation and what happens—they get lost.* She could see the driver crouched over, as though he were looking at something on the passenger seat. *Probably decided to look at a road atlas instead,* thought Charlie as a smile crossing her lips.

However, as the driver lifted his head, his upper torso following, she realised she knew of only one person who would be able to fill a window with so much body. Martin had caught up with them. Charlie's stomach did a huge roll and her mouth became suddenly very dry. She didn't know whether to stay or just keep driving. She saw him glance in his rear view mirror, and she knew the option of fight or flight had been taken away from her. She now had no option. He'd seen her.

Okay, thought Charlie. *Let's see how good your mobility is today, you bullying piece of shit.* Her blood began to run cold as she thought of Michelle. Had he somehow managed to already get into the house and harm her again? She revved the Audi then took her foot off the accelerator and coasted to a stop behind Martin's Volvo. A saving thought popped into Charlie's mind. Perhaps he didn't know where Michelle was, although Charlie had no idea how he had even found her house.

As she got out of her car, Charlie's legs felt weak. She was frightened to death. She used the car to stop herself from falling down. As Martin unfurled himself from the driver's seat, his intimidating size spooked her. Charlie didn't remember him being quite so enormous, either in the pub or in the alley. She did notice he was putting very little weight on his right leg, and he too was leaning on his car as a means of support.

She could see his left hand balled into a huge fist. Charlie swallowed involuntarily. She stopped short of his car, thinking it would be a good time to open up the conversation before he got within striking distance of her.

"What do you want?" she asked, as she looked him straight in the eyes. She took in how much he resembled Dolph Lundgren, the actor. He was ruggedly handsome and she could understand what Michelle had seen in him.

"What do you think I want, you daft bitch? I've come to get my wife. Don't deny she's here, because I've already seen her, showing herself like a whore at your window. I thought I was in Amsterdam. I suppose old habits die hard. I wish I'd never come to this fucking town." He banged his palm on the car's bonnet.

Charlie flinched. "Martin, Michelle hasn't done anything wrong. It's all in your head. You aren't thinking straight. Have you been taking something?" Charlie had taken a leap of faith and hoped it would have a positive outcome.

"You have no idea what you're talking about! Now go tell Michelle I've come to take her home." Charlie could see the knuckles on his left hand turning white.

"I think the damage has already been done, Martin. Michelle is still very hurt and in pain, so I suggest you leave it a good while before you contact her." Charlie couldn't believe she was so calm about this awful situation. She saw a change in Martin's face. It was becoming contorted with rage again, as it had been in the pub. Charlie slowly began to move backwards towards the driver's door.

"When did you become a fucking oracle? You have no right to interfere in my marriage! Don't think I've forgotten your part in all this, bitch. I will be coming back to teach both of you a lesson, and the best part is, you won't even see it coming. In fact, it's already started."

His voice had taken on a very low, almost whispering tone. The threat was out there. Not wrapped up in some fancy monologue of veiled dialogue. Right there in Charlie's face.

The hairs began to stand up on Charlie's neck. "Really? Well, do your worst because, for my part, I intend for you to never lay another finger on Michelle. Ever!" The last word she spat out with as much venom as she could muster.

He laughed and then sneered. "Oh, it will give me the greatest pleasure to give you what I gave her yesterday, and I don't just mean a good hiding. It sounds as though you need to be put in your place, woman, whether you like it or not—you frustrated cow! I've made myself a promise. I'm going to have sex with whoever I want from now on, whether they like it or not. I'm sick of women thinking they can fucking do what they like and it never having any consequences. Now, I'm going to do the same."

He threw his head back and let out a demented laugh. It rooted Charlie to the spot. His words seared into her brain. She truly believed she had crossed the path of someone with evil intent—something she thought she would never do again.

He made his way to the car, never taking his eyes of Charlie the entire time. He lowered himself into the Volvo and Charlie noticed as he gave some assistance to his right leg, almost lifting it into the car. He slammed the door with unnecessary force, and as he reached out his hand to turn on the ignition, he glanced at her through his rear view mirror. Charlie shuddered and suddenly went cold.

His eyes were cold, but at the same time held a menacing, murderous look. It worried Charlie enormously. The ignition fired, the engine revved and he drove off—wheels spinning. She watched him drive to the end of the cul-de-sac and negotiate a three-point turn.

As he drove past her, he waved and put his thumb up. To any passer-by or casual onlooker, it looked as though she had just helped a rep find his way to his next client.

Very clever, Martin, Charlie thought to herself.

This was getting serious and she needed not to underestimate Martin's guile or innate natural intelligence. He was a very clever man, she had no doubt, and she also knew—he wasn't finished.

CHAPTER TWELVE

EVERYTHING SEEMED TO be in order when Charlie entered the house. Nothing was out of place in the kitchen, certainly no signs of any struggle. "Michelle," she called out quite loudly as she had no idea where in the house she was. She waited for a reply as she placed the groceries on the counter. Nothing. "Michelle, are you here?" she shouted even louder, just in case she had fallen asleep in the bath.

As Charlie strained her ears to listen for a response, her heart stopped as she heard a slight groan coming from the lounge. She rushed as fast as her feet would carry her to the lounge at the front of the house. In those few short seconds, every conceivable situation had flooded her brain. She almost didn't dare go in for fear of what she might find, but the strength of her feelings for Michelle was an overwhelming sensation. She was becoming her pulse, each beat driving her forward towards the edge of a precipice.

She rushed over to Michelle and briefly glanced at her just to make sure no further damage had been done. "Michelle, look at me. Are you okay? Has Martin been in here? Did he hurt you again?" *It's already started* came flooding into her brain.

The reply when it came was weak. Michelle's eyelids began to flicker. She opened her undamaged one. She tried to focus.

"No, he hasn't been in the house. I saw him parked outside, then I started to shake, then he sent me a text message. I fainted, I think." She looked extremely pale, and Charlie could still detect the slight quivering of her body.

"Did you have anything to eat while I was out? Just a slice of toast or something?" Charlie asked, thinking Michelle's blood sugar was probably running on low.

"No, I haven't had anything but the coffee this morning. I was in the bath and I had a headache. I saw him when I came to get the painkillers from the medicine box. He didn't do anything to you, did he?" She took hold of Charlie's hand as she waited for a reply.

"No, he didn't," she replied, "but he did say some things I didn't understand. So you and I are going to have a chat while we have some lunch and a cup of tea. Let's see if some food will make you feel better." Charlie forced a smile, which held no emotion behind it, in the hope it would put Michelle at ease. There were a few tough questions coming her way.

Cheese on toast topped off with a little chive always did the trick, Charlie thought to herself as she put the two slices on a plate. Michelle's hand still trembled a little as Charlie handed her the plate. Michelle lifted a half slice to her mouth and began to eat.

"Try to drink the orange juice as well while the tea brews, just to raise your blood sugar quickly. See if it will help the shaking. It might not all be due to the shock. We haven't eaten as we should have these past few hours, and I think it's beginning to catch up with us both. Gavin would have a fit if he knew I'd missed breakfast. 'Most important meal of the day,' he always says. I think he's been taking lessons from my grandmother. He acts like her too, most of the time. Is the cheese on toast okay for you? I can make you something more substantial if you'd like."

Charlie gazed across the table at Michelle and thought how perfect this situation would be under different circumstances. Charlie felt as though she was perpetually on the edge of the abyss ready to fall off when she was in Michelle's company but realised she wouldn't want to be anywhere else.

She gave the pot on last stir and then began pouring the orange liquid into the mugs.

"Charlie, it's perfect. I hadn't realised how hungry I was until I started eating. I could eat a scabby horse between two bread vans." Charlie laughed aloud at the comment. Michelle added, "Northern saying." Michelle tried to smile but obviously found the thought of the impending conversation difficult.

"I need to talk to you about Martin, Michelle. Is it okay?" Charlie asked. They needed to get this topic out of the way before they could move forward.

Michelle lifted her eyes mid-bite and nodded her head very slowly as if half agreeing. "What do you want to know?"

"Can you remember when Martin's temperament began to change? Was it after he started to go to the gym?"

Michelle contemplated the question as she slowly chewed her food. "No, not straight away. I would say perhaps six or seven months afterwards," she answered with a quizzical look crossing her face. "Why? Is it important?"

"Do you remember anything happening around the same time? New friendships, new staff, friend changes of any kind?"

"Yes, there was as a matter of fact. He swapped from circuit training to weights and boxing and changed his trainer. What are you trying to get at, Charlie?"

"I think Martin may have been using anabolic steroids to increase his muscle bulk. The problem is, they have some very nasty side effects including behavioural changes.

Everything you've told me about his change in personality and a bodily change fits in perfectly." Charlie took a big bite of her food. "Not to mention the lack of sex drive. I'm sorry I have to mention things like this. It must be very upsetting."

A look of intense sadness passed over Michelle's face, and she grabbed for the cross that hung around her neck. Charlie couldn't help herself as she reached over the table and gently stroked her cheek, carefully caressing the swelling with her thumb. "I'm really sorry, Michelle. I didn't mean to upset you."

Charlie was surprised as Michelle tilted her head and leaned into her touch. It caught Charlie off guard and she took her hand away—quickly. What she really wanted to do was hold Michelle's head in her hands and kiss her—with all the passion swelling inside her, like a tidal wave building up to its full force. She needed to remove herself from this situation as soon as possible—but she didn't know how. The thought of abandoning Michelle seemed an alien concept, but it just wasn't going to work and she needed to be selfish—just for a change. Charlie could feel her insides clench at the thought, but it was going to have to be that way. The situation was getting well out of hand. For Christ's sake, she had only known the woman for twenty-four hours!

Just as Charlie was beginning to feel like a complete bastard, spooky music from her ringtone filled the room. Gavin—again. Michelle jumped in her chair, and as Charlie moved around the table to pick up her mobile, she put her hand on Michelle's shoulder. She just couldn't help touching the woman and it would have to stop. "It's okay," she said, gently. "It's only Gavin."

"Hi, Gavin. What can I do for you? No, I don't have the TV on. Hold on, which station? Charlie grabbed the handset from the table and quickly turned on the portable TV she kept in the corner on the counter in the kitchen. The picture showed a building with giant flames leaping high above the roof, shrouded in a thick black smoke.

It took a moment for both of the women to register what they were seeing. As the camera zoomed out, the women's faces changed to an identical look of horror as they saw the sign for Bamber and Brooks Ltd attached to the iron fence, and they realised they were looking at their place of work. Charlie was brought back to reality when she heard Gavin gently weeping into the phone.

"Charlie, I'm so upset. I don't know what to do. Poor Jeff was beside himself when they were interviewing him earlier. He was crying and shaking like a leaf. His whole world gone up in flames. He built the company from scratch. I can't believe old George has gone." There was a giant sob leaving Gavin's throat when Charlie interrupted him.

"Gone. What do you mean, gone? What's happened to George?" Charlie closed her eyes as she waited for the answer, secretly dreading what it might be.

"He's gone, Charlie. He's been killed. He wasn't killed in the fire though. They found him in the night watchman hut. They aren't giving out any more details yet." Charlie went cold and found herself rooted to the spot like a tree on shifting ground, legs quivering.

"Gavin, I can't talk now. I'll phone you back later. Thanks for letting me know." The numbness was creeping down from her brain, enveloping her body.

She shook her head, not only in disbelief, but also to clear away the horrifying images circulating in her mind. George hadn't died in the fire, so how had he died? Charlie couldn't believe what she was thinking, but she never did believe in coincidence.

Chapter Thirteen

CHARLIE DIDN'T REMEMBER sitting down at the table. She didn't remember Michelle making her the cup of tea steaming on the table in front of her, either. She didn't feel much at all except—numb. Charlie had never really believed in the devastating after-effects of a shock, even though she had a Psychology degree. For all the Freud, Jung, and Adler she'd read and absorbed, she had always thought it just a little weak of people to accept the offer of counselling. 'You wait until life really bites you on the bum. See what you feel like then,' one of her friends had said to her, completely unaware of the ordeal Charlie had already endured.

She had always wondered if the trend for counselling had gone over the top elevating trauma and grief to a status they didn't deserve. Too much responsibility being passed over to an outsider to sort out. The grieving and healing being hindered instead of helped. Her peers had thought her harsh and a little heartless—today she agreed with them.

After her experience as a child, Charlie never had counselling, just her father and mother asking her, '*How are you feeling, darling?*', '*Is there anything we can do for you, sweetheart?*', '*What can we get you to make you feel better?*'. Charlie only remembered feeling horrifically afraid of the dark, which she never did before the kidnapping. They didn't do anything to ease her suffering.

She had no doubt the event had shaped her personality—hardened her. Being alone, tied to a bed in a cold, dark garage with no sense of time, knowing your life was at the mercy of the two men, was bound to shape your thoughts on life.

Now she felt like the previous version of herself—weak and vulnerable. She had no control over the tears as they cascaded down her cheeks. All for an old man she had known for a long time yet still barely knew, but liked beyond reason.

She wanted her Uncle Lenny.

Her uncle had been the one who had been good for her after the kidnapping. 'My dear little Charlie,' he had said, as he took her in his arms and hugged her like a mother bear with its cub. 'You must realise although the world has bad people in it, you just unlucky to have come across two of them. Let's hope this is the only time you see the harsher side of the world. If you ever have cause to worry, go to your mum or dad and tell them how you feel. They will understand.'

Her reply, she was sure had shaken him—the look of surprise on his face evident. 'I think I'll come to you if you don't mind. All mum wants to do is give me things, and dad, well…' She didn't trust her dad to do the right thing anymore.

Her uncle had been her rock; taking her out of the house, distracting her, the fleeting moments of pleasure at the zoo or seaside with him becoming longer as time progressed until finally—she could go for days without thinking about her ordeal. She needed him now, as she believed another evil deed had crossed her path.

Charlie suddenly felt warm. She could feel a warm body pressing into her shoulders with arms draped over her front crossing over her collarbone, wrapping her up like a warm blanket against a cruel wind. It made Charlie feel good. Every now and then, she could feel a warm kiss being placed on top of her head and soothing words being spoken. The repeating of Charlie's name brought her back to her senses. "Charlie, are you okay?" Michelle asked in a voice so low it was barely audible. It held in its soft chocolaty tones concern and disbelief, and for the first time, the faint hint of a Geordie accent.

"Yes," replied Charlie—but the answer held no conviction or belief. Her mind was trying to process all the new information. The images of the flames dancing above the building, mesmerising in their various shades of colours from light yellows to dark amber oranges. Licking at the sky in their eagerness to escape their confines of being bound to the building by their tendrils. Charlie imagined she could smell the acrid smoke as it hugged the building in its tight embrace. *Dancing. Dancing on George's grave.* Charlie coughed.

She wanted to be there for her friends, for Gavin and Poppy, but she couldn't string two coherent thoughts together. She hated Martin—one thought. This is what he meant when he said it had already started. "I think I'm just having a little trouble processing everything. It's not every day you see your place of work go up in flames and a wonderful old man you've known for years dies at the same time. I have this awful feeling he's been murdered, Michelle—and I think Martin did it." There. Charlie had said it. Her belief about the matter was out in the open, and she was past caring whether Michelle liked it or not.

At the mention of Martin's name, Charlie felt Michelle's body stiffen, and she released her from the hug. She moved opposite Charlie at the table. She began to play with the cross and chain around her neck. Charlie had the sudden urge to rip it off her neck and throw it a far as she could—if possible, straight into hell.

"Charlie, that's a bit of a leap. Okay, I can understand you don't like him after what he did to me, but to accuse him of murder and arson is a bit far-fetched. His mind may be a bit messed with steroids if what you say is true, but murder? No, I just can't and won't believe it!'

Charlie could feel the blood pressure rising and the red mist descending.

"Michelle, have you listened to one bloody word I've been saying? You didn't see him or hear him out there. He was like a man possessed. He is cold and he is calculating. And I believe he means every damned word that comes out of his mouth!"

"Charlie, that's my husband you are talking about! The man who buys crosses and flowers and makes love to me in the gentlest of ways." Michelle was waiting for some reasonable response. Charlie just wasn't capable of giving her one. Charlie kept going over the things Martin had said outside. Each comment pounded in her brain. She needed to clear her mind. She looked at Michelle, still trying to draw in the threads to weave something coherent.

Charlie cleared her throat, not wanting to lose her temper, but she could feel herself drawing so close. Most of it was her own frustration at not being able to find the words to convince this obstinate woman of her husband's deadly intent.

"Michelle," she said, looking suitably befuddled as she rested both her elbows on the table and placed her head in her hands. "How much do you believe in coincidence?" She lifted her head and looked at Michelle—waiting for an answer.

"I do but not much. Why?" Michelle seemed confused at being thrown such a question.

"Because we have a situation here and it seems to be beyond the bounds of coincidence, yet you don't seem to believe it!" Charlie could hear her voice rising. "We have your husband's strange behaviour beginning after a change in trainer at the gym and his sudden increase in body mass. Then he goes off sex or can't perform or whatever, and then starts using you as a punch-bag and subjecting you to God knows what other horrors."

Charlie brushed her hands through her hair at the thought, and then she continued. "He has mood swings. Next, the place where you work burns down, the place he thinks your lover also works and a defenceless old man is killed. Then, lo and behold, he turns up here looking for you, and I'm still at a loss as to how he found us. Now which bit of coincidence don't you understand?"

The response from Michelle was swift. "All right, Charlie, you've made your point. It all does seem a bit too much to be a coincidence—but he's my husband." She took a large gulp of her tea.

Charlie was on the verge of losing it. "If you're trying that out as a mantra, it doesn't work for me."

Michelle glared. "As for finding us, he only needs a phone number and he would be able to trace everything from the information the computers hold. Then he can trace the numbers rung and numbers that have called. Just like the police can." Her eyes widened into a wild look. "He can't be using my mobile I wouldn't think because I haven't answered him. But I can't be sure. There isn't anything he can't seem to do on his laptop. Damien, his boss, even had his car modified so he can use it on the move, too." Michelle looked slightly embarrassed to be passing on this information. It sounded as though she was extolling his virtues.

"You mean he can trace people's names and addresses—all from interaction with my phone?"

"Yes, and, of course, when he has their home information..." Michelle dropped her gaze and looked sheepish.

"You mean he's a hacker?" Charlie couldn't quite believe what she was hearing.

"I've seen him hack into police systems for fun. You have to understand, Charlie, when systems are set-up, modified, or integrated, they sometimes have to be repaired. The experts sometimes leave a back door open so they can get in easily for repair purposes. He hasn't always been out on the road."

Michelle took a deep breath and then drained the remnants of the tea in her mug. "He spent years devising and developing different systems, both here and abroad. He was right at the top of the tree." Michelle walked to the sink and rinsed her cup, refilling it with water. Charlie wanted her to use a glass but thought herself churlish for the thought. Actually, she wanted to wring Michelle's neck for bringing this shit into her life and the lives of everyone she knew.

"Very little is out of his reach, believe me. I've seen him in action. But murder? I really don't think he has it in him, Charlie, I really don't." Although the words were coming out of Michelle's mouth, Charlie didn't believe she was a hundred percent convinced by them.

"Jesus Christ, that's all we need! Someone with those kinds of skills on our tails. Let me play Devil's Advocate, just for a second." Charlie looked at Michelle with a stone-cold stare, trying to convey the seriousness of the situation. "Suppose he has done the things I suspect him of...just follow my thinking here. Would it be possible for him to track things like credit cards, car details, and mobile phone usage, even abroad?" Charlie was worried.

"Anything digital, I suppose it would be possible. Certainly, police and government I know he can do. They are supposed to put safety measures in on these systems, but they always leave a back door open somewhere, because it's easier to access the systems if something goes wrong." Now, even Michelle looked worried. "Charlie, don't get ahead of yourself here. We don't know he did anything yet."

"Well, he certainly did a number on you, didn't he?" Charlie was sorry and ashamed of the words as soon as they tumbled out of her mouth. She hoped she would be forgiven for uttering them.

At the same time, she was glad what she truly thought was out in the open. The sooner she was out of this situation, the better. Charlie's stomach was flipping—she was anxious. She wasn't sure, if she and Michelle split up, who he would come after first. One thing she realised as she was having the conversation with Martin was neither of them would be safe until he was locked up. Charlie didn't care where—whether it be a mental institution or prison—as long as he was secure behind a lock and key.

Charlie's mind was now working like it never had before, thinking of different situations and what solution she could come to for each one. Michelle had been taken out of the equation. She wasn't thinking clearly and with what she had had to endure, Charlie could understand it. It irritated the hell out of her, but she could understand. She still wasn't sure she had heard the full story but was confident she would be told the details when the time was right.

When Charlie looked up, Michelle was looking straight at her. Her eyes were wide with disbelief. "Yes, I suppose you could say he did a number on me, Charlie. But it was me—not you. This is not your situation—it's mine! He's still my husband, and I remember what he used to be like before all this—this crap! He was kind, gentle, loving, and generous. He just doesn't have it in him to commit murder. I admit something, and it may be steroids, have had some effect on him. It's blatantly obvious, even to me…but murder…" Her eyes found something on the wall to stare at as her voice trailed off.

"Look, Michelle, I truly am sorry. Not for what I said, because I believe it to be the truth, but because you had to hear it and because you had to go through whatever it was you went through. Something happened to me when I was a child and for a long time, I didn't want to talk about it either. But do you know what? In the end, talking about it to my Uncle Lenny helped. I was only thirteen, so there is a difference, but still…"

It was time for Charlie to stare off into the distance, forcing away images from the past. Not because she couldn't face them again, but because now her mind had to be focused on the task at hand. Keeping them both safe. If Michelle wanted it.

In the heat of the moment, Charlie crossed the short distance between them. She stood square in front of Michelle until she looked her in the eye. "Michelle, I don't know why, so I can't explain myself, other than to tell you what I feel. I need to keep us safe. Call it instinct, gut feeling, intuition or premonition. Quite honestly, I don't give a shit. I only know we are not safe here because Martin knows where we are. Now, are you prepared to trust what I'm saying or not?"

She looked at the spot on the wall again. Charlie could tell she was considering all her options. She went to bite her lip but got a sudden reminder of her injuries. The pain seemed to tilt the balance in Charlie's favour. As much as she wanted to extricate herself from the situation, she desperately wanted to keep Michelle safe

"Okay, Charlie. I do trust you. I just can't seem to get it into my head things have got so bad so quickly. I'm sorry for doubting you."

What happened next was like a paragraph from a romance novel. Michelle bent forward to kiss Charlie on the cheek, but in the same moment, Charlie turned to speak to her, and the kiss landed firmly on Charlie's mouth. It seemed to take forever to register what was happening, given Charlie's mind was busy elsewhere—trying to keep them alive.

Charlie expected Michelle to pull away. But Michelle didn't. They kept their lips firmly together. Charlie could smell her own bath crème and shampoo, but it smelled so much nicer on Michelle. Everything feminine Charlie tried in the perfume line ended up smelling like cat pee. Michelle's lips started to move and as much and as hard as she tried not to—Charlie's did, too. Her mind was screaming *no,* but her body wasn't listening. The kiss was just on the point of deepening fully when Michelle's mobile sounded a text message arrival.

Charlie thought, when the kiss broke Michelle might have started mumbling an apology or worse still, start making excuses for her actions. But she didn't. She just turned and picked up her mobile. Her hand began to tremble as she touched the screen, then a look of horror crossed her face. She handed the mobile to Charlie whose face showed shock and horror as she read those seven little words...

From Martin: I am going to kill you both.

She needed to speak to Uncle Lenny, Gavin, and Poppy. It was time to make plans.

CHAPTER FOURTEEN

SHE PUNCHED IN Poppy's name on the contact list and waited for her hand's free to connect. Poppy answered straight away. "Charlie, isn't it just awful? Poor, George." Charlie swallowed hard.

"Yes, Poppy. It's downright diabolical, but I don't have time to talk about it right now. I need to meet up with you and Gavin. Can you arrange to pick him up and then meet me at Fletcher's Garage as soon as possible? I need to talk to you both."

Poppy's voice quivered. "Charlie, you sound weird. Is everything okay?"

"The honest answer, Poppy, is I have no bloody idea. See you in a while."

Charlie didn't know what the hell to do next. It felt as though she were trapped, as the saying goes, between a rock and a hard place. She desperately wanted to help Michelle but felt as though she was treading water.

The police were the ideal solution. She could drag Michelle there, but she couldn't make her talk. If she wouldn't report the assault, then Charlie couldn't hold a gun to her head and make her do it. One thing she had learned about Michelle in just a few hours was she was stubborn. Very stubborn. Almost to the point of stupidity. But Charlie realised she wasn't Michelle, and it wasn't her problem as she had quite rightly been told—even if it did feel as though it were. She was hoping her two dearest friends could see something she couldn't because, at the moment, Charlie felt as helpless as she had in the dark garage all those years ago.

***

GAVIN LOOKED UPSET—eyes red-rimmed and under his nose appeared to be full of white speckles where the tissue had caught in day-old stubble. Charlie was in awe of his handsomeness, even in his current state. The chiselled features were arranged in such a way causing eyes to be drawn to him like they would be to a fine painting—mesmerising and stunning. His face's only flaw, a small scar running up from his top lip toward his left cheek—worn like a badge of honour from his early days in Glasgow and fighting to protect his early sexuality. The scar merely enhanced his attractiveness. His body was tall, lean, and muscular—not from any strenuous workout sessions, but from efficient genes.

The need for him to expand his horizons had driven him south, initially training in law and then he arrived at Bamber and Brooks to lick his wounds when he realised he would never make the grade as a solicitor. His black hair and Italian dark eyes were not out of place with his surname—Conti.

"O–M–G! Charlie, are you completely mad? What do you mean, helping her? In the same breath, you are telling me you suspect her husband is loco and he burnt down our place of work, not to mention killing George." Gavin began to weep gently. "I can't stand this. You need to go to the police and tell them everything you know. They appear clueless, and you should be giving them some clues."

Charlie looked suitably ashamed as she screwed up her eyes and wiped her hands over her face. "I hear what you're saying, Gavin, but you haven't seen her. She's been absolutely pummelled and the damage was only from a slap. There is a big welt on her neck where it looks as though she's been grabbed or choked." Charlie reached out her right hand and placed it on Gavin's throat. "The marks are under here, under her ear." She squeezed where she had seen the marks.

Gavin put his own hands where Charlie's were on his neck. "Jesus Christ—"

Poppy piped in. "He's not going to help. I tell you, we are a bit short in the miracle department of late."

Charlie flashed her eyes at Poppy in the rear view mirror. "I saw her yesterday at lunchtime after I spoke to you, Gavin. She was in the loo with a polo shirt collar up high around her neck, trying to hide the mark. She is walking in a weird way, too. I don't know if he's kicked her on her legs, but she's definitely not walking right." Charlie sipped her coffee as the wheels in her mind began to whirr, engaging into gear.

"O–M–G. Do you think he raped her?" Gavin closed his eyes and covered them with his hands.

Charlie cringed at the thought although she believed Gavin had it right. "I don't know for sure. But what do you think will happen to her when he gets a hold of her after what I did to him? I might I have crippled him, but worse in his eyes, I belittled him and made him look a fool. I know he's not going to take it lying down—he would probably kill Michelle. Retribution, Gavin. Retribution." Charlie shook her head in disbelief as if realising for the first time what she'd done.

"Plus, what exactly do you want me to tell the police? 'Oh, yes, officer, this guy has beaten up his wife, and I think he might be responsible for burning down where we work and killing the night watchman.' Can you hear how that sounds, Gavin? They won't believe me! They won't—" Charlie wiped her face with her hands again in frustration.

Gavin shook his head from side to side in disbelief. "O–M–G! Charlie, how horrible. Fancy sharing your home with the worst kind of brute. I wonder how long he's been subjecting Michelle to those particular horrors." Gavin's voice trailed off and he turned to stare out the window. Charlie thought the shock of the incident was creating a cumbersome weight on Gavin. *Could he take it?*

Poppy, after taking a few swigs from the takeaway coffee Gavin had brought them, shifted her position in the back of the car where she was folded like a piece of origami. "It's going to be pure speculation at the moment, Gavin. Knowing Charlie's luck, they will probably arrest her for wasting police time, thinking she's just a lesbian trying get her toaster and to protect her new recruit."

"New recruit?" Charlie almost choked on her coffee.

Poppy ignored it. "It will make it even worse if Michelle refuses to say anything, and my bet is she probably will. Charlie, I'm really sorry I gave him your phone number. What an absolute bastard. His story just sounded so plausible. He came into the pub and knew we were from Bamber and Brooks, and he knew your description. He said he'd seen you with his wife and needed to send her a message but her phone was off. In my defence, I was drunk and he sounded so desperate. I'm really, really sorry."

Charlie turned around to put her hand on her knee. "Poppy, you're right. I thought the same thing about the police. Except Michelle is not a recruit for anything. She just needs help keeping away from her bully of a husband. Don't worry about the phone number. It's done now. I will simply get a new one."

Gavin let out a big sniffle. He then raised a voice of concern, "But, Char, why does it have to be you? I really think you might get hurt. You don't know what he's really capable of doing. He could end up wanting to kill you both if he doesn't already." He wiped his nose as the snot began to dribble—he still looked handsome as he picked at more bits of tissue on his stubble.

Charlie smiled at him, trying to be reassuring, but she had a feeling no matter what she said, it wasn't going to convince him of anything. She reached over and wiped away the tears from his cheeks, feeling the outline of his beard growth.

"Gavin, I will be fine, really. If we have to run away until the police find enough evidence, then we will." Charlie pressed her hands into the leather grip on the wheel and leaned forward.

Between gulps of coffee, Poppy spoke up from the back of the car. "Charlie, does she really mean that much to you when you hardly know her? I didn't even know of her existence until we had a chat in the pub. I have to say, she seems a nice lady. She's only been at the company a few weeks—"

Gavin blew his nose. "Right."

Poppy took a quick sip. "I didn't know Jeff was even hiring a company secretary—for God's sake—but, of course, since he floated the company…now that I think of it, it's a good thing Gordon invited her to come out with us, or I still wouldn't have known about her. Jesus, I think I'm losing my touch." She snorted a laugh through a dribble of coffee at the comment.

Through the rear view mirror, Charlie noticed, despite the laugh, Poppy's light hazel eyes looked sad as she gazed out the window looking for answers, looking for something. Each time Charlie was with Poppy, she was reminded of Jessie J, the singer. Everything about her was the same—height, weight, body shape, except the face, which had the familial look of a cousin rather than a sister. Sometimes, Poppy could act like an airhead with no common sense whatsoever, but Charlie knew she had a brain as sharp as a razor blade when applied, the observance of a hawk and the perception of a cold reader.

"I don't think you are losing touch, Poppy." Charlie caught Poppy looking at her in the mirror—connected. "Nobody else at Bamber and Brooks opens their mouths about anything. They are so wrapped up in their own little worlds. Even if Jeff gets the company up and running again, I'm not going back. I'm sick of it. I need a change and now would seem to be the perfect opportunity. Fate has dealt me this hand for a reason, so I'm going to make the best of it. As for Michelle, she needs help and that's enough for me."

The silence hit the car like a sledgehammer.

Poppy was the first to break it. "Charlie, don't you think you're overreacting a little bit? I know it's come as a shock and you're gutted about George like we both are, but it's your livelihood. What else would you do? There are hardly any jobs going out there at the moment and let's face it, you've been there like—forever."

"Don't worry, Poppy. I still have some of the money my grandma left me, so it will keep me going for a while until I can find a new job." Charlie looked out through the windshield hoping to avoid more questions. With Gavin and Poppy as her companions, she stood little chance of avoidance.

Gavin turned his head and peered into the side of her face to see if he could get her to turn round. "How much are we talking about here, Charlie? Do we need to start helping you look for a new job now, next month, next year, next reincarnation?" She hated lying to him, but it really was none of his business. She smiled. He looked stone faced.

"A few months should do it. I have enough to cover the essentials." Charlie blushed.

"Your mortgage must be a fortune! Are you sure you're going to have enough to last?" asked Poppy, genuinely concerned. Charlie finished her coffee before answering.

"I'll be fine. I'm a big girl now. Will you two stop worrying about me? I came here looking for answers and all

I'm getting are more questions. You've given me something to think about anyway."

"I should bloody well hope so," said Gavin, wiping his nose for what appeared to be the last time. "You don't seem to have thought this through to the end."

"Gavin and I have to go to the police station for interviews on Monday. I've already phoned a few people to pass on the information. Have they been in touch with you yet?" asked Poppy, slurping her dregs.

"No, not by mobile anyway, although I haven't checked my answering machine. I suppose we will both be on the list, although they won't have Michelle's mobile number unless someone else gave it to them. It's a good excuse to get her there so I'll drag her along. What facts can we tell them though? None at all. If Martin did do all I suspect, I would have to hand round one to him. He may have won the battle, but the war is still raging. Look, I'm sorry for getting you more wound up than you were. Go enjoy the rest of the weekend as much as you can and perhaps we can get together on Monday after the interviews. I think we will give our shopping trip a miss, Poppy. I better keep my money for any essentials." Poppy nodded in agreement.

"Okay, it sounds like a plan I can go with," said Gavin, grabbing all the empty cups, "and Charlie—be careful."

"I will, Gavin. Both of you—try not to worry."

As Charlie watched them drive away, she wondered about her last words to them. Did they really have a reason to worry so much about her? She hoped not, but she couldn't be sure. Martin was certainly a man out of control and she could only hope he came to his senses fast because the alternative didn't bear thinking about.

CHAPTER FIFTEEN

WHEN SHE RETURNED to the house, Charlie immediately went to the window, drew back the curtains to look for stalkers or prowlers of any kind. The note on the table said Michelle had gone to lie down. She sighed. *What's next?*

Charlie went over to the answering machine and noticed the number two light was blinking in red so she pushed play. The first message was for replacement windows...delete. The second one was spoken by a beautifully enunciated voice. "This is Detective Inspector Paul Brett from the Walden Police Station. Because of the incident at Bamber and Brooks on Friday night, we are asking all employees to come in to make a statement on Monday morning. If you can reach out to your colleagues to inform them as well, we would be grateful. Thank you very much, Miss Reinette—I hope to see you on Monday."

Her stomach dropped and she wiped her brow. It wasn't her place to tell the police anything—it was Michelle's place. It was up to Michelle to shed the light on the change in Martin's behaviour and to shed the light on the assault. Michelle had the insight on the most recent cataclysmic shift in Martin and the internal demons he was struggling against. The recent history had been a violent turnaround to the person he used to be. The police needed to know about his insane jealousy and his belief Michelle's lover worked at Bamber and Brooks. They needed to know—everything!

Charlie busied herself gathering the ingredients she needed for dinner. A simple rustic dish of tomato sauce, finished with fresh basil tossed amongst a liberal helping of spaghetti, finished with a generous grating of parmesan cheese. She selected and opened a bottle of Chianti so it had time to come to room temperature.

The meal wasn't rocket science, but it looked appetising and taste tests proved wonderful. Just the thing she and Michelle needed to ease out of a stressful day. They both needed a brief respite from the bubbling cauldron.

As Charlie added the chopped tomatoes to the sautéed onions and garlic, she heard shuffling behind her. Her heart quickened and she smoothed the seams of her trousers. An inner pulse drew a smile on her face as she glanced at Michelle. A dishevelled pale and bruised woman stood before her, yet radiance outlined a sultriness exuding from her pores.

"I thought I smelled cooking. What are we having? I'm starved." Michelle pushed a hand through her chestnut coloured hair and stretched. She eyed Charlie and then eyed the steaming pan.

"It's a surprise so no peeking. Would you like a drink while you're waiting? I just opened a bottle of red, but it won't be properly warmed yet or I can make you tea or coffee. There is also juice in the fridge if you prefer."

Michelle smiled, grateful for an easier subject than what lay underneath her robe.

"Goodness, Charlie, it's like living in a hotel. I think I'll have a small glass of not yet warm enough wine." Michelle smiled and held Charlie's gaze. "I'll get it though. You carry on cooking—whatever it is. It smells delicious. Can I get you something?"

"I will join you with the Chianti. A small glass for me too, please."

"Even though it hasn't warmed up yet?" Michelle gave a hearty laugh, which completely disarmed Charlie.

"Enough of that, young lady, or I shall send you to bed with no supper. The first rule—do not disrespect the cook."

"Oh, you're a cook amongst your many other talents." She made a slight bow.

Charlie laughed, suddenly having the urge to pull Michelle close and kiss her. "I like to think I can survive if I have to. I have a few dishes of choice I like to feed my guests. This is one of them—plus it's quick and easy."

Michelle poured two small glasses of wine, placing them both down at the side of the cooker. Michelle then dragged over a stool from the kitchen island and sat to the side of where Charlie was standing. "Is it okay to watch?"

"I don't think you are going to be able to avoid it sitting there. So much for the surprise."

"Martin does most of the cooking in our house, so I suppose I better learn something quickly." Michelle's face took on a faraway look.

Good, thought Charlie.

Charlie smiled at the thought of sharing her first dinner with Michelle.

If only it were a real date.

Michelle sat back in her chair, pushed her plate away from her, and blew out her cheeks. "Charlie, that was absolutely delicious. I can't believe something so simple to make tastes so good! Wonderful." Her whole face, including the half-closed eye, lit up with a smile and Charlie was in awe. Those lips issued ripeness to her beauty.

"I'm embarrassed—it must be the wine." The heat rose to Charlie's face.

"Don't be." Michelle raised her glass and took a sip. "Red is a good colour on you."

They laughed. A happy levity had replaced the gravity of their situation for the time being.

Charlie refilled their glasses, sharing the last of the wine in the bottle.

"Warm or not, the wine was fabulous," Charlie said, glancing at the label as she placed the empty bottle on the table.

"Thank you for the lovely meal, Charlie. Thank you for allowing me to stay and mostly, thank you for looking out for me. I could have run to Newcastle, but he would have found me. I didn't want to worry my mum and dad. They are elderly now and really don't need any aggravation, although it would certainly please them to have me back living with them." Michelle stroked the cross dangling from the chain. "I think it was what they had planned all along—for me to finish uni and go back. They need a quiet life now though. They don't need Martin thundering around with his bad temper. He doesn't like them very much so it would be a good excuse for him to go off." She took a large gulp of wine.

Charlie didn't want to put a damper on the evening, but it was Michelle who had brought up the subject of Martin, so she thought she would try to encourage her to open up. "Was that what you meant when you said he saved you?"

Michelle held her wine glass close to her chin and nodded. "He felt he'd saved me from a life of drudgery with my parents. He thought they had planned it all along— to have a child late in life so the child would be there to support them in their old age." She took another sip of wine while considering what to say next. "I don't think that's the whole truth, but I think there may be some truth there—perhaps their efforts may have been a little delayed and then proved unsuccessful. I have to believe them when they say I was unexpected, and they had been trying since they were married. Otherwise, it makes them cold and calculating—for years, I couldn't stand the thought—I don't think it's true anyway."

"Do you fancy watching a film before we turn in?" Charlie asked, changing the subject completely, not wanting to get in too deep at this time of the evening. She didn't want to spoil the ambiance they had built up during the meal and certainly didn't want tears.

"Great idea! Do you have, Pretty Woman?"

"Do I? One of my all time ever favourites. You go and get it from the rack, and I will make us coffee. Would you like a liqueur with it?"

"No thanks, Charlie. Just coffee and you can stop trying to get me drunk." Michelle laughed.

"Oh, no! My plan has been foiled." Charlie held Michelle's gaze and pointed towards the espresso maker on the counter. "Coffee," was all she said.

Michelle went to bed as soon as the movie was over. No mention of Charlie joining her for the night, so she didn't ask. They had both laughed and both cried, but at different parts of the film. Was there always going to be this chasm between them?

Charlie had been left to her thoughts and realised they were still in a precarious position. Hovering between friendship and...what? Her thoughts would take her no further into the void of the uncertain future. Her thoughts saw sense—even if her ego wouldn't.

Charlie checked the window again for any sign of Martin's car and had the thought it might be better to spend the night downstairs. Her inner voice spoke to her. *What are you going to do if he shows up, Charlie? You won't have the element of surprise on your side this time.* The thought made her shudder. He was more than capable of killing anyone with his bare hands and probably had. The thought of George taking on Martin brought tears to her eyes—yet made her determined. *I am going to bed tonight and I'm going to sleep.* With determined inner thoughts of peace, Charlie went to bed and fell right to sleep.

CHAPTER SIXTEEN

MICHELLE LAY IN bed trying desperately to sleep. She had only managed an hour or two, and now it was light again. Alone in bed last night, she had wondered why Charlie hadn't offered to keep her company. Perhaps she no longer thought she needed protection or the comforting feel of another body close—within touching distance.

It must have been the accidental kiss. She had only wanted to kiss her cheek to thank her—then she had turned. She'd enjoyed the softness of Charlie's lips on hers and wanted it to deepen into the kind of kiss you remember as the first time you really kiss someone with meaning. Like Janice's had been all those years ago. She felt as though she was being unfaithful to Martin now, though—the old version of him, anyway.

She had known Charlie such a short time in real terms—yet it felt like a lifetime already. Their souls had conjoined—connected in a profound way, in the pub as they passed each other. There couldn't be any other explanation for it. She wanted the kiss again now but knew she wasn't brave enough. Her life was complicated enough without it, and she severely lacked inner strength and backbone.

She needed to rid herself of the constant headache pounding deep beneath her skull. She was cursing herself for drinking red wine, which had only added to her woes. The headache constantly beat in rhythm with her heart. *Bang. Bang. Bang.* The same heart that thought she would probably never recover from this time in her life. How had her life gone so askew in such a relatively short space of time, she wondered. A few months ago, she had been married to the most wonderful man. Although she tried not to—she smiled at the thought of him.

She remembered the cross he had placed so tenderly around her neck after they were married. His kiss on top of it, so warm and gentle. Every visit to the cinema when he would scurry to the back row, dragging her behind him, as though they were school children ready for their first kiss.

She remembered the flowers he used to bring her from the garage on the way home from work, as he would push them forward into her hands wearing his cheesy grin and always adding, 'Flowers for my lady.' They were usually a little jaded by the time they got to her, the edges of the roses turning a little brown and the leaves on the stems wilting badly through lack of water, but Martin had gone to the trouble of stopping to get them. It proved he had been thinking about her while he was away from her. It proved he had loved her...then.

He would always take her head in his hands and kiss her tenderly, telling her how much he missed her during the day, then he would wrap her in his arms and hug her, but with such gentleness, as though she was the most fragile object in the world. When he said she was his entire world, she believed him. Now she felt like the leaf on the stem. Wilted.

***

CHARLIE MADE HER way upstairs, with a small amount of trepidation. Her mind was in constant flux although she found herself in too much turmoil to be afraid. She tapped quietly on Michelle's door and waited for a reply. "Come in, Charlie," Michelle answered quietly.

Charlie closed the distance between the door and the bed with some consternation. She put out her hands holding the coffee mug at arm's length—like an offering. And it was—a peace offering, although Michelle didn't know it yet. Charlie had done some deep thinking when she awoke in the early hours after a short but refreshing sleep.

She sat on sentry duty at the window, eyes wandering from one house to another—alert to any movement, seeking out shadows. She was wrapped in her grandma's shawl hoping it would give her some otherworldly insight as she stared at her quiet neighbourhood thinking of Martin, thinking of Michelle, and thinking the best route of keeping one from the other.

They had no strength if she and Michelle separated, so they had to stick together, like it or not. They had no way of knowing where Martin was or what he was planning to do. The only way he was prepared to tell them anything was by text messages on Michelle's mobile. Other than his one face to face with Charlie—texts—always texts.

They would have to stay ahead of him.

"Good morning. How do you feel today?" Charlie asked in the brightest voice she could fabricate.

"Would you like the stock answer or the truth?"

"Always the truth. So—how do you feel?"

"Like shit. I've hardly slept, my banging headache has come back, and I'm worried about Martin." Before Charlie could speak, Michelle held up her palm facing Charlie. The universal stop sign. "Don't say anything, Charlie. It won't help. I know how you feel and you know how I feel. We don't agree on this, but you're my friend and I don't want a fallout with you. We'll have to get over it—both of us. Agree to disagree."

Charlie sat down on the chair knowing Michelle was right. They were never going to agree on the subject of Martin.

He was always going to be a thorn in her side. Digging away in her ribs. She looked at Michelle's lips as she put them on the rim of the coffee mug—full and sensuous.

She could still feel the pressure of the inadvertent kiss on her own lips. Should she bring up the subject or let it be? Had Michelle forgotten it had happened at all—after all, it was an accident. The kiss was, but the lingering definitely wasn't. The pressure she had felt wasn't an accident either.

It didn't look as though Michelle was prepared to discuss it though. She'd had many opportunities the night before while they were both in a genial mood, but it didn't look as though she was even tempted to bring the subject up.

Charlie would let it lie—for now.

Michelle looked deeply into her coffee mug, obviously not in the mood to be disturbed or to have any deep, meaningful conversation. Charlie stood and stretched out her back, feeling the after effects of spending a good portion of the night in the chair.

"Tell you what. You finish your coffee, have a rummage through my wardrobe, and find some clothes that nearly fit. Then grab yourself a shower and meet me downstairs when you're ready. We need a quick chat, and then we are going out."

Charlie couldn't believe she had formulated a plan in her state of confusion last night—but she had. It was all about delaying tactics, timing, and trying to keep Martin away from them for as long as possible.

Michelle came downstairs dressed and looked ready for action. She had chosen a pair of Charlie's jeans and a thin T-shirt, which fit better than the jeans did. She looked fresh from her shower, her hair still a little damp— showing its tendency to curl. "I don't suppose you have any hair straighteners, do you?" she asked, although once she'd glanced at Charlie's hair, she laughed. "What a silly question!"

"No, I'm afraid you're out of luck in this house, but I promise I'll get some for your next visit."

Michelle smiled. "Okay—deal. Now, what do you want to chat about?"

Charlie smiled a benign smile. "Martin." Charlie jumped in before Michelle could speak. "Now, I agree with what you said about us never agreeing about him and that's fair enough. I have to bow to your superior knowledge of him because he's your husband. Please, just bear in mind what I've said too, especially about the coincidences." Charlie could feel her mouth going dry. "I don't know what you are going to tell the police in the morning and it's none of my business, but I'm working on the premise you won't tell of any suspicions—just facts about Bamber and Brooks."

"Police? What?" Michelle was focused on Charlie, demeanour blazing.

Charlie reached out with both arms to the air in front of her and patted. "No, I haven't called them. I forgot to tell you. We have to go to the police station to give statements in the morning. They left a message on the answering machine."

Charlie looked out the window when she saw Michelle nodding through the reflection, dreading what Michelle's reaction was going to be to the next suggestion, so she decided to put the ball in her court first.

Fresh coffees in hand, seated and looking at each other across the room. "Michelle. What do you want to do?" Charlie just looked at her—seriously.

The question obviously threw Michelle a little. Charlie could see it by the look on her face.

"I have no earthly idea, Charlie. I think it would help if I knew what frame of mind Martin was in. Then I could make a decision of some kind." She paused and looked at her coffee before taking a healthy swig.

"At the moment, everything is just up in the air. I think I should just go home and face him. It would give me the opportunity to say what I need to say to him. Everything has been one-sided since Friday. He doesn't know what I'm thinking or feeling."

Michelle began to drift off into a daydream.

Although the mention of Michelle going home frightened Charlie, she still needed to remind her of the true nature of the situation.

"Michelle, have you looked in the mirror? Do you really think he gives a crap what you think or feel?" Charlie took no pleasure from having to point out the obvious. "He has the disposition of a madman at the moment. Please, can't you at least see this? I don't believe in coincidences, and if I'm reading this situation right, he's killed one man and committed arson. He has the capacity to find you via anything electronic—me too, for that matter. I'm worried about you. I'm worried for me and everyone else we've been in touch with by phone."

Charlie took a mouthful of the cooling coffee. "I know I've brought this situation on myself by sticking my oar in, but what was I supposed to do? Stand by and watch as he beat you to a pulp? From what Martin said, it doesn't seem to have been the only thing he did to you either. So please, will you just see sense."

As she reached forward and put her mug down on the coffee table, a tear dropped from Michelle's eye onto her cheek. She bowed her head trying to hide it from Charlie. She hugged herself as her body shook, racked with deep guttural sobs. *Finally,* thought Charlie—*the message was getting through.*

Charlie's heart went out to Michelle, her mind transported back to the time she had been rescued from her captors. She had the same reaction to her trauma, functioning numbness until her uncle had broken through. Though she was barely a teenager, the capacity adults possess for refusing to believe the truth had already kicked in.

She closed the distance between them—Charlie tentatively reached down for Michelle and brought her to her feet. After the kiss, she was reluctant to make any physical contact. She didn't want Michelle to think she was taking advantage of the situation. On the other hand, she didn't want her to think she had been abandoned either.

Charlie realised she was treading a fine line. On one hand, her feelings for Michelle were deepening by the minute, but on the other, she wanted out of this situation because she knew how dangerous it could be taking on a man like Martin, given his frame of mind. Things had gone too far now. She couldn't and wouldn't abandon Michelle, but it didn't mean she had to be happy about it.

"Come here." She spoke tenderly as she drew Michelle close and enclosed her in a warm embrace. She gently rubbed her back through the thin T-shirt in a comforting gesture. She was sure Michelle must hurt in places she couldn't see. She knew other things had happened to her and there was certainly other damage to her body, but until Michelle told her everything, she only guessed what the damage could be.

Michelle pushed her body forward and snuggled her head into Charlie's neck, as the sobs began to subside. Charlie could feel her warmth through the material of the T-shirt and as their breasts moulded to each other, she could feel Michelle's erect nipples.

Charlie began to panic. It would be so easy just to turn her head and start planting delicate kisses on Michelle's forehead and lift her hand to begin to caress the back of Michelle's neck—but no!

She pushed Michelle slowly backwards and spoke in a gentle voice, ready to reveal the next part of the plan. Charlie took a large gulp of air.

"I think we should take off."

CHAPTER SEVENTEEN

"WHAT?"

"I THINK we should get out of the country—and pretty damn quick. He has us cornered here. He knows where you and I are and where the people are we've been in contact with. We have no work to go to and quite frankly, his frame of mind has me spooked. I think the more distance we can put between him and us the better. If he does pick up our trail later, then at least he's leaving the people we care about here, alone. What do you say?"

"I think you're completely crazy."

"No, that would be your husband." The joke was feeble—Michelle didn't smile. "Try to think clearly, Michelle. I'm not trying to force you into anything, but you better make up your mind fast before he does something or tries to do something to us—or the people we love."

The look on Michelle's face showed confusion, but Charlie refused to say another word to her, in case later she would be accused of forcing Michelle to do something she just didn't want to do. Charlie was itching to get a move on, but she just waited moving from one foot to the other in her anxiety.

"Okay, Charlie. I'll go along with it for now. But, and it's a big but, I can change my mind if I want to, at any time. Is that fair?"

"Good enough. Right, it's time we make a move. We have some work to do. Can I just ask you a question though? If you had a choice of going anywhere in Continental Europe, where would it be?"

Michelle answered without hesitation. "I would go to a little place in the South of France called Cavalaire. I had gone there with some friends after my gap year before I started university."

"Then Cavalaire is where we're going." Charlie smiled, and she believed she saw a smile creep slowly across Michelle's face. "I need your name as it appears on your passport."

***

"HI UNCLE LENNY, how are you doing?" Charlie smiled just at the mention of her uncle's name.

"Well—hello, Charlie. It's good to hear from you. I'm doing all right. You don't often phone at the weekend. Is everything okay?" His voice was tinged with an edginess she could detect quite clearly.

"Okay? Well, I've had better times. Actually, I have a problem, but I don't want to bother Mum and Dad with it. I need your help if you're able to give it." She crossed her fingers in the hope the response would be a favourable one.

"If I can, I will, you know that. Now come on—out with it."

She proceeded to tell her uncle the whole tale from beginning to end, and she could hear deep sighs at various points, but he kept silent until she had finished her story. He had always been a great listener. She waited for his response.

"Charlie, I have to tell you, I'm not very happy about this." Charlie's heart lurched. "It's against my better judgement because I think you have bitten off more than you can chew. I will only help if you promise me one thing."

"Of course, what is it?"

"You must put the police on speed dial in your phone."

"Consider it done."

"All right, Charlie, what do you need?"

"Cash and your car," she said quickly, in the hope he would agree before he had a chance to appreciate what she had actually said to him.

"Is that it or would you like to add a kidney to the list as well?"

Charlie chuckled despite the dire circumstances. "Do you think you could get me three top of the line mobile phones, pay as you go, one with Euro capability, please? I think I will have to top up with Euros when I get there. Plus, could you get them delivered to your house by midday tomorrow? I know it's asking a lot, Uncle Lenny, but it really is important. I wouldn't ask if there was any other way, you know that. If I had time, I would release some of my own money, but since it is Sunday afternoon, I have about as much chance of doing that as plaiting fog."

"I understand, Charlie. It's not about the money or even my car, or any other 'thing'. They can be replaced—you can't."

Charlie took a deep breath in order to try to control the emotion building within her. "I know, Uncle Lenny. What happened all those years ago still affects me too, but I can't let it rule what I do in the here and now and what decisions I make. Michelle needs help, and if I can, I will help her."

"She better be worth it, Charlie. It's all I can say. Right, money. How much and what currencies?"

"What have you got?" She looked up to the heavens and thanked goodness her uncle made a lot of his diamond deals in the privacy of his own home. He had a safe, which would have rivalled a high street bank.

"I have…umm, twenty thousand in sterling and fifty thousand in Euros. I can always wire you some more if you need it."

"No. No, you can't, Uncle Lenny. I explained."

"Oh, damn it, Charlie, I forgot."

"Well, try not to forget what I told you again. Oh, damn it, I forgot, too. I need tickets to the Continent. Will you see if you can get me to France late tomorrow? It will be better using your information to book. Just make sure my name is on one ticket. The other ticket will need to be in the name of Michelle Jane Bailey. If you could make sure your tank is full of petrol, I would be grateful. Thanks, Uncle Lenny. I will make it up to you, I promise."

"I don't want you to make it up to me, Charlie. I just want you to promise to come back in one piece."

"I will—I promise. I will be with you as soon as I can after the interviews tomorrow."

***

CHARLIE PULLED THE Audi around the corner onto Michelle's road, and Michelle began motioning with her hand for Charlie to slow down. "It's just here on the left, Charlie." Charlie was impressed. A lovely detached house with a beautiful lawn and beds of what would eventually be roses when the warmer weather had done its job. "Are you staying in the car?"

"I am until you tell me Martin isn't inside. I know his car isn't here, but it doesn't mean he isn't. Until then, I'll turn the car around and keep the engine running. Please don't take too long with your packing. The main thing you need is your passport. Anything else we can buy on the way."

Michelle's eyes widened. Even the swollen one was now making a little progress, but both began to pool with tears.

"I don't know if I can do this. I don't know if I have enough courage to run."

Charlie grabbed her arm and gave it a firm squeeze. "Michelle, I don't know if I can protect you here, and we have to think about the others. It's not just me and you, is it?"

Michelle's face was reflecting some fear as it had crossed her mind. Charlie suspected it was thoughts of her mum and dad. Threatening tears began to flow. "I am so fucking angry with him! Why is all this shit happening?" She banged the dashboard with her blanched fist.

"Because he's been very stupid and selfish. Michelle, we need to get a move on."

"Yes, okay. I'm going. I'll tell you if it's clear." She left the car with her head hung low and her feet slurring along the ground. She was not in a good place, so Charlie decided she would make it her role in life to help Michelle find a good place.

Michelle seemed to be taking a long time, and Charlie began to fidget. She imagined all kinds of horrors going on in the house. The wait had only been a few minutes—it seemed like a lifetime. She couldn't wait any longer. She was not going to wait for any all clear signal. She was going in—now.

Michelle had left the front door ajar, so Charlie pushed it open just a little further. She stuck her head across the threshold and turned her head to try to improve her hearing. Facing her was a mirror on a vestibule wall. Charlie jumped as she saw her own reflection, and then admonished herself for being so jumpy.

All she could hear—was silence. She opened the door fully and entered the house, all the time listening for any giveaway noise to prove Martin was in the house. Nothing. As she looked through into the lounge, she saw Michelle sitting on the settee, her elbows resting on her knees, her head in her hands.

The room looked as though the proverbial bomb had hit it. Furniture that could be broken with bare hands had been. There were pieces of dining chairs, a coffee table, and a bookcase strewn in pieces across the floor. The dining table had one leg pulled off and was tilted on its side.

Books with pages torn from their spines had been thrown haphazardly across the floor. DVDs and CDs lay at the bottoms of the various walls into which they had been hurled with great ferocity—leaving short stripes or small holes at random spots. The ceiling had them too, but for the life of her, Charlie could not understand how he'd done it.

The large screen TV had not escaped. The screen had shattered when a mini hi-fi system had been lobbed through the front of it. The beige carpet was watermarked, and when Charlie followed its trail, she saw the bottom half of a giant vase with the remnants of tiger lilies in it—the heads of them had been ground into the carpet spreading orange pollen marks looking vaguely like some alien species of blood. The small chandelier that had hung in the middle of the room was now on the floor beneath its original hanging place, most of the crystal shattered from the impact—wires dangling dangerously close to the floor.

Charlie checked out the next room. Her mouth agape, she entered, belief momentarily suspended. She waded into deep glass shards, broken plastic and smashed crockery. Cupboards had been emptied and ripped off the wall—their contents joining anything else breakable on the floor. Charlie had seen enough.

She went back into the lounge, taking Michelle by the arms and lifted her to her feet.

"Charlie, I am so sorry for doubting you. I can't believe he's done all this." She motioned around the wrecked room with her hand. "My poor home. Just as I was getting it in some kind of shape. Look at it! In absolute shambles!" She wiped tears from her cheeks with care.

"You know what?" she asked with a little more grit in her demeanour than Charlie had heard of late. "The bastard can rot in hell as far as I'm concerned. Come on, let's go."

She headed for the stairs at the far side of the room, her gait still with a certain amount of caution in it. Charlie followed her, just in case there were any surprises waiting upstairs, but the silence hung like a pall in the building.

The trail of destruction continued with pictures ripped off walls and small broken ornaments in tiny pieces on every step. Martin had really done a number in the master bedroom—Michelle's clothes torn to ribbons, littering the floor. An ankle length black leather coat lay on top of the bed. When Michelle saw it, a look of horror crossed her face and she raised her hands to cover her mouth. There was a trace of dried semen across the front of it. She looked embarrassed as she looked straight at Charlie—as though she would have the answer to everything.

Grasping, Charlie said with a slight shake of her shoulders, "I think he may be having a psychotic break. It wouldn't surprise me. Just grab your passport and let's go."

"I hope to goodness he hasn't touched the safe. I'm not sure he would have remembered the combination. He never took any notice of anything practical I would tell him." She kicked all the clothes on the floor out of her path to the wardrobe, opened the door, and knelt in front of the safe anchored to the floor. With more agility in her fingers than Charlie would have thought possible given the circumstances, she sent the tumbler flying like an acrobat until finally, there was a pronounced click. Michelle reached in and rifled through what papers were in there until she finally held up her passport. She gave a brief smile. "Got it!" she said triumphantly.

As they were ready to leave the house, Michelle grabbed her bag off the settee. Her bag began to vibrate and the familiar sound of the message alert hung in the air. The women looked at one another as Michelle retrieved it from the bag. Michelle looked at it and then passed it to Charlie.

From Martin: Are you coming out or do I have to come in and get you?

The message made Charlie shiver.

"He thinks we're in my house." Charlie was worried.

"That's good though, isn't it?"

"Not when he finds out we're not in there. Christ only knows what he'll do next." Charlie's mind was racing.

"What should we do?" Michelle seemed to be picking up the seriousness of the situation.

"I have no bloody idea."

"Well, in that case, give me the phone."

Charlie passed Michelle the phone and she began texting. The message was only two words long—and the second word was *off*.

CHAPTER EIGHTEEN

THEY HAD TO decide quickly where they would go to hide for the night so they chose a cheap hotel. They needed to get off these streets quickly and hide the car as best they could—perhaps in some back street—close by. Charlie had a feeling the car would be what Martin would focus on looking for. It stuck out like a black kitten in a litter of white. For the first time in her life, Charlie wished she owned a battered, fourth hand, Nissan Micra—such would be anonymity.

They couldn't go back to Charlie's house—that much was obvious. Even if Martin had left by now, there was nothing to say he wouldn't return. They couldn't stay at Michelle's house for the same reason. If he had Uncle Lenny's details, he could even look there—there was no point going there until they had to—tomorrow after the interviews. They didn't have enough money to stay at a decent hotel and buy clothes for tomorrow. Inwardly, Charlie was beginning to panic. She had never been without access to money before. It wasn't a feeling she enjoyed very much. It was beginning to feel like being on the high wire—with no safety net.

Charlie was doing something she had never done before—walking through the doors of Walmart They needed a change of clothes. Basic toiletries they could get from the hotel, but nothing more. They had a total of three hundred and fifteen pounds and forty-three pence between them in cash when they left Michelle's house and most of which had been Michelle's contribution.

Their room at the budget lodge cost them thirty-five pounds. They knew they couldn't use their debit or credit cards to draw any extra cash—Martin would be alerted to their location. She knew there was money waiting for her at her uncle's, but it didn't help her current anxiety. Deprivation was the overwhelming sensation. Charlie knew it belonged in the past—in the garage. But the wave of despair was beginning to resurface.

As they wandered in and around the vast aisles of clothing, trousers, shoes, underwear, Charlie quietly slipped into dream mode. The lost hours of sleep and the tension were both debilitating and making her patience short and her mind whirr. She felt like a volcano ready to blow and Martin's image was fuelling the magma.

Again, she wondered if it was all worth it. She could just tell all she knew to the police tomorrow and get it over with—but to what end? She glanced at Michelle currently rifling through the vast array of yellow…orange…red tops—a shopper in heaven—oblivious to anything else. Zoned into the task at hand, hiding behind a pair of Charlie's old sunglasses.

Michelle stopped abruptly and pushed the sunglasses up, looking at Charlie.

"Charlie, will you please grab something to wear for tomorrow, and then we can go and get something to eat." Michelle's voice brought her back to planet earth—in the here and now.

"Yes, sorry. I was miles away." Charlie looked at Michelle again and took in the bruising and the weariness. Sunglasses were atop her head now; she was still using them as though she was fooling anybody. Michelle might have temporarily tuned out of the situation, but her face said it all—hidden deep was the tension and worry—she knew. She knew he was out there looking. Hunting his prey. She knew he was scouring the planet so he could quench his lust for revenge. She knew he was after her.

Could I leave her in the hands of that man?—Not a chance! Charlie had made her choice.

An hour later, they sat in Burger King finishing their meal. Charlie felt Michelle tap her lightly on her shin with her foot as Charlie stared at her empty container.

"A penny for them," said Michelle pushing away the remnants of her meal as she placed her two elbows on the table, cradling her head in her hands—her dark brown eyes with gold flecks sparkling—alert.

"Is there something wrong? Specifically, I mean."

Michelle glanced skyward and swallowed loudly, trying to lubricate her throat.

"I know there is nothing right about this whole situation. Do you want to give up? You can take off at any time. You do know that, don't you, Charlie?" Michelle took a large gulp of her coffee as she waited for Charlie to reply. "This not your fight, you know. You don't owe me anything. I'm just grateful you've got me this far." Her head dropped and Charlie looked at her.

"Michelle, it became my fight the minute I stuck my nose into your business. I have no intention of giving up. Together, we stand a chance. Individually, we have none. There is nothing wrong. I'm just tired. One thing does worry me though…"

Michelle pushed her elbows forward and moved closer to Charlie. "What's that? Is there anything I can do to help?"

"No, not really." Charlie moved her face closer to Michelle's and spoke to her in a low, quiet voice. "I have to tell my sister I've been to Walmart"

Michelle's movements were as quick as a cat's—as she threw the empty packet of fries at Charlie's head.

***

THE MORNING AFTER, Charlie sat leaning against the Audi in the car park of Walden police station. For the first time since she'd stopped smoking in her mid-twenties, she wished she hadn't. She was edgily nervous and looked at her watch—again. It was three minutes past ten. Three minutes later since the last time she looked. They had arrived at ten past nine and it already seemed like twenty-four hours ago.

What the hell was keeping Michelle?

Charlie's interview had been brief. They had asked questions about routine, dodgy looking strangers and George. This was where she had been able to help them most, filling them in about his character, background and his love of his betting on the horses. Nobody else had known him as well because nobody had taken the trouble to find out. It hadn't stopped her from beating herself up, thinking she should have known more.

To most of the people who worked at Bambers, he had merely been the night watchman. The man who turned up at four forty-five, just before they were leaving work. The one who would wave and touch the black, shiny peak of his cap as they drove from the car park. To Charlie, he had been more than this. He had been her confidante—her support when she felt as though she were wandering aimlessly through life—a direction giver. Her main father figure after her Uncle Lenny, but she felt it had been one-sided.

What a shame her father didn't possess the qualities of both Lenny and George. Her father had always showed his love in monetary terms—not in ways to show he cared for a girl who was living in a world with flaws, where she felt his money could have made a real difference—but he did nothing with it.

He laughed at her attempts to bring up conversations about the homeless, animal rights and equality, where his love and support would have been appreciated.

"Oh, Charlotte, for goodness sake! Why can't you be more like Jessica? Go shopping for the day instead of sitting in front of the TV watching those God-awful programmes about animal abuse. You know they only upset you. You are only one person. You can't save the world," he would say, his face like thunder.

"It doesn't stop me from wanting to try, Dad," she had screamed back at him in frustration. That had been one of their typical encounters. It had made her both angry and sad but more importantly—isolated.

Michelle pushed the sunglasses down on her face as she walked through the doors of the police station, making her way quickly across the car park towards Charlie.

"So, how did it go?" asked Charlie eagerly, hoping Michelle had given some indication Martin may have been involved.

"Actually, I could have swung for the pimply youth who interviewed me. Abraham. He seemed more bothered about my cuts and bruises than a murder and a major fire." Her aura reflected her anger.

"What did you tell him?" Charlie asked, eager to know if Michelle had told the truth.

"I told him I'd had an accident at home after I got back from the pub and went to stay at your house because Martin was away." Charlie's face changed, taking on an angry scowl.

"Look, Charlie, I told the truth about what I knew concerning the fire and George—which wasn't much. Anything else is none of their damned business, and if they start asking questions about it and insinuating anything different, I will tell them so."

"You've just dragged me into a lie, which may or may not be pertinent to their case. I'm not happy about it, but we don't have time to argue now. We have some shopping to do before we get out of this damned country so get in the car and let's go."

Charlie got into the car and closed the door with a loud bang. When she looked, Michelle hadn't moved an inch. She pressed the button and lowered the passenger-side window. "Are you coming or not?" Charlie bristled, turning on the ignition and swearing to herself that she wouldn't wait. As she engaged first gear, a scowling Michelle got into the passenger seat. Charlie popped the clutch without waiting for Michelle to click her seatbelt on.

CHAPTER NINETEEN

THEY ARRIVED AT Loundon Road, St John's Wood, London, just after eleven in the morning. The leafy suburb was bathed in watery sun and the vibrant green of the newly opened leaves infused the air with its own iridescence. *It's good to be in England in the spring,* thought Charlie. This kind of spring—not Walden spring. Only an hour and a half away after hitting the motorway, yet it was like another world. Gone were the gloomy dark clouds and intermittent rain—Charlie believed she even felt a little warmth coming through the windshield of the Audi and also a little warmth from Michelle, too. Her spirit lifted a little. Perhaps their infinite tale of doom was beginning to look up.

Parking was horrendous in London. In her uncle's location, most people worked so Charlie knew she had a good chance of parking close to his Range Rover and as she turned the corner into Loundon Road—there it was—a space behind his car—vacant for the time being.

"Keep our fingers, toes, and everything else crossed the traffic wardens have already been round. We don't want them entering our number plate into their little machine. No tracking us, please!" Charlie said with a hope and a prayer.

"Will just my fingers be okay? I will probably need everything else." Michelle smiled, lifting up her crossed fingers in front of her face, which eased the tension between them a little.

"I guess it will have to do then. Come on. Let's see if we can beg a cup of tea before we start our buying spree and hauling stuff around." Charlie smiled but noticed a look of doubt as it travelled swiftly across Michelle's face.

She doesn't think I can pull this off—but she's wrong.

As they both got out of the car, Charlie pressed the lock button on the ignition fob and the indicator lights flashed wildly. She pointed to the tall, shiny black gate in the high, sandy stone wall. "This is it," she said in a proud fashion. "I just love my uncle's taste—in everything."

Her uncle had left the gate open as he promised. As Charlie turned the loose, round metal handle, the gate swung wide open. She heard Michelle gasp as she was afforded her first full view of the house. "Oh, Charlie. It's magnificent." Charlie closed the gate behind her and pulled the latch.

Michelle stood open-mouthed at the end of the path looking towards the pristine, white, Georgian frontage. The A-shaped portico was held aloft by four Doric columns—the whole building a juxtaposition of straight lines. It was showing itself against the startling blue sky, doing itself the most justice.

"Yes, I think so, too. I've always loved visiting this house. It was a wreck when Uncle Lenny first bought it and over the years, he's not only restored the outside but also the inside, to its former glory of Georgian England. It has a lovely calming effect and the furnishings—well, I'll let you see for yourself."

As they approached the door, it was opened with a flourish. Lenny stood there—grinning. He stood on the threshold and with a great sweep of his arm—cavalier like—he spoke. "Welcome ladies, do come in." After he had closed the door behind him, he swept Charlie into a tight embrace. "How are you, my darling girl? I hope you didn't take too much of a grilling from the police."

"Well, it—" Charlie started.

"Oh! Where are my manners?" Lenny interrupted. He turned toward Michelle. "I'm sorry—you must be Michelle. It's a pleasure to meet you. You must forgive me. It's been a while since I saw Charlie. She is by far my most favourite relative!" He smiled as he held out his hand to Michelle and as she began to shake it, he placed his other hand on top—as if giving a blessing of some kind. Charlie thought it a lovely touch.

Michelle replied with a very sheepish, "Pleased to meet you, too." She held her eyes downcast. Charlie inwardly hoped Michelle wouldn't spend the whole meeting being so down in the mouth.

Charlie looked at her uncle's tall, willowy figure dressed in his grey chinos and white Lacoste sports shirt with its little crocodile logo—smiling. She saw no hint of disapproval in either his voice or his demeanour—at the moment. He had developed deeper lines around his eyes of late but wearing well for a man just into his fifties. He was her mother's junior by twelve years, but Charlie classed him as a generation apart—younger somehow. Perhaps it was due to his carefree attitude, which was much easier to adopt when children were not part of the equation.

"Before I forget, I will give you these." Charlie held out her car keys. "Please be gentle with her." She looked at him seriously for a second, and then bared her teeth in an ear-to-ear grin.

Lenny took them and turned around to take down a set of keys hanging on a hook behind him, placing Charlie's in their place. As he turned back, he spoke with concern in his voice. "Here are mine and the same thing applies. You do know I would have been more willing to give up a kidney, don't you?" They both laughed aloud and Michelle looked thoroughly confused. He simply said, "The Reinette and Stern families both endowed with auto maniacs," and then he laughed heartily.

They settled in the lounge waiting for Lenny to bring the tea. Charlie watched Michelle as she scanned mouth agape around the room—stunned by the design, style, and décor of the interior. "I don't know much about the Georgian period, but most of this furniture looks genuine to me. Does he always buy from the right period?"

Charlie could enlighten her on some of the purchases. "I know he gets a lot of his stuff via Sotheby's and other auction houses, and he does have lots of friends in the trade—so that must help. I do know he had the wall coverings especially made and they cost him a packet." She glanced around the room as if taking in her uncle's achievements for the first time. "He has totally done this building justice inside and out. He always told me if a job is worth doing, then it's worth doing well."

Michelle arose from one of the two luxurious chaise lounges, which brandished shiny walnut frames. She meandered toward the wall at the back of the room and ran her hand over the deep gold brocade covering the walls. On the way, she pointed at the writing bureau and the table beneath the window. "Charlie, are all those pieces of furniture walnut?"

Charlie nodded and smiled. "My uncles pride and joy—his walnut!"

"They are beautiful..." Michelle looked in her element. It warmed Charlie's heart just to survey her. As she gazed, a rope slowly untethered from her armour and the lure of the mystery woman enticed her heart. Seeing Michelle in her world, Charlie knew she fit. She just knew she would.

As if on cue, the door opened and Lenny came in pushing a low, ornate silver trolley adorned with teapot and all the other paraphernalia associated with real English teatime—even if it was so soon after their late breakfast. A two-tier silver cake stand was full of slices of Battenberg cake, cream cakes, and coconut macaroons, which he knew were Charlie's favourite.

He wheeled it to the side of the walnut coffee table with its inlaid jade top and placed the silver tray with the cups and saucers on it, in front of the two women. "I think Charlie can be mother," which immediately designated Charlie to pour the tea. "I thought you might appreciate a little something in your tummies. I think shopping was mentioned." He smiled joyfully as though his long lost chick had returned to the nest. "Now come on you two—tell all!"

Michelle jumped in as Charlie passed out the cups and saucers. "There's not much to tell in all honesty. They just wanted to know if we'd seen anyone suspicious lurking around the office on Friday. Had we spoken to George at all on the previous few nights, that kind of thing. According to the others who were there, they were asking everyone the same questions."

Charlie could feel a lump forming in her throat. "I had taken him his usual coffee, but he didn't say anything out of the ordinary to me. He said he hoped I had a good night out." Charlie felt a tear on her cheek. "While we were out having a good time—he was being murdered!" Lenny moved closer to Charlie and pulled her close to him. A sob wracked her throat.

"I'm sorry, Charlotte. I know you thought a lot of him. Now you know what I tell you about bad people in the world. You have to be very unlucky to run across them. You've been unlucky—twice, Charlie, but these things have a way of evening out. Try not to worry, sweetheart." He squeezed her shoulder and lowered his brow.

Michelle leaned across and squeezed Charlie's wrist to add to the comfort, but all it did was kindle the little flame sizzling at the back of Charlie's mind. The look of concern in her gaze was obvious.

Michelle took up the story again. "They also wanted to know what we were doing on Friday night, too. Luckily, we were all together in the pub, so we could all vouch for one another. Even later in the night, everyone had someone with them from what the other's said." Michelle had a sheepish look on her face again.

Lenny, for the first time since the women arrived, didn't look pleased. Charlie knew it was coming—it looked as though it was going to be now. For although her uncle was mild-mannered, she knew he possessed a fierce temper when riled.

"Why haven't you told the police about your husband's assault and your other suspicions, Michelle? Surely it's relevant," Lenny asked, looking directly at Michelle—his brow furrowed.

Michelle put down her cup and saucer with a clatter. Charlie was sure it was an indication of her nervousness rather than bad manners.

"I think it's up to me whether I report an assault to the police. There are complications I just can't process at the moment. Martin hasn't told us anything about George or the fire. He could have been miles away as far as we know. He was supposed to be going away with his friends for the weekend. He may have—we don't know anything for sure."

Michelle lifted the cup, minus the saucer and took a drink of tea. It irritated Charlie. "It's only Charlie who has assumed these things happened. We don't know anything for sure. I haven't stopped Charlie from telling the police what she thinks. That's up to her."

Lenny looked from one to the other, but his gaze rested on Charlie. "Why haven't you said anything, sweetheart?" His voice had taken on a softness, which sounded as though he was questioning a child.

Charlie took a drink of tea and continued to stare deep into the contents before she answered. "Because I don't have any solid evidence. If I go mouthing off about what I think, they may start enquiries, but it's not going to be enough to get him locked up. I can't do anything to lead them to him. It's not my story to tell. It's Michelle's story." She looked past her uncle's shoulder, focusing on her words. "We are going to be left high and dry, and the police can't be everywhere. I can't see their budget allowing twenty-four-seven protection for us—can you? Even if they could hide us away somewhere, they will need a forensic paper trail, and that will mean records and computers..."

Lenny rubbed his hands over his eyes and let out an *ummph*. "I suppose you're right. At least this way you will have the jump on him. Perhaps some distance is a good thing right now. It might give him some time to calm down. Let's hope so. Come on, let's finish with the tea and cakes, and then I will get the paperwork and money sorted out with you."

Michelle looked distraught. "If you don't mind, I'll excuse myself and go and use your restroom if I may. I desperately need to freshen up," she said, running her fingers through her wayward hair. She looked frazzled.

"Not at all. Follow me and I'll show you the way, and perhaps on the way back, you would like to have a wander around the house. Charlie, I'll see you in the library."

***

THE LIBRARY, A corner room of grand proportions with windows from two walls bathing it in natural light, gave the duck-egg blue paint a surreal glow. The plaster was smooth, like a baby's bottom. It looked resplendent with the other two walls covered in walnut bookcases from ceiling to floor and its walnut writing desk sitting proudly by the front window, flanked either side by deeply upholstered wing chairs in a slightly deeper shade of blue.

Row after row of books on display, spines in all different colours encouraging someone to reach out and sample the goods. Charlie would have loved to indulge herself, as she

121

and her sister had many times in this room—holding on to a real book. E-books were good for a voracious reader, but they just weren't—tactile. They didn't smell like a book!

Charlie sat in a chair by the window, waiting and wondering what her uncle really thought of her plans. Did he suspect the strength of her feelings for Michelle? If he had, it hadn't stopped him from getting angry.

Her uncle made his third and final trip from his desk to table and laid out the documents and currency on the oval table before her. Charlie shivered. She wasn't cold but attributed the reaction to the thought she was about to leave the safety—of her family—of Poppy—of Gavin.

She reminded herself she must talk to Gavin and explain again, why she was running. Poppy she knew would understand and she could just imagine her trying to calm Gavin down. Charlie knew Gavin's rants of old, but he really did have her best interest at heart, so she couldn't be too annoyed with him. Okay, she had to concede, using herself and Michelle as bait wasn't ideal, but deep down, Charlie had convinced herself it was right. Time would tell if she was right or wrong.

"Are you all right?" her uncle asked as he ran his hand down her forearm, flattening the gooseflesh having formed there. Concern hung heavily in his voice. He stared at her—his good-looking face with its deepening crease lines and brows beginning to furrow. She was crestfallen—knowing she had contributed to them.

"Yes, thank you. Just a little tired, but nothing serious." She hoped her smile convinced him—but she feared it hadn't.

"It's not too late to change your mind, you know. Nothing is written in stone, Charlie—even though you think it might be. My darling girl, you could always hole up here. I could get twenty-four hour security." He looked hopeful and Charlie thought long and hard before she decided she had to burst his bubble.

"Uncle Lenny, do you trust me? My judgement, I mean," she asked.

"Well, you've always been on the money with the important issues. I have no reason to doubt you."

"Good. Then I need you to understand. I believe this man to be dangerous. Really dangerous. All the more reason to run—not less. I can't put anyone else in danger because if something bad happened, I would end up a basket case. I'm not prepared to risk it. I need to help Michelle and try to keep her safe. Her parents are elderly and vulnerable, and she has nobody to help her. She has only been in Walden a short time so hasn't really developed any friendships." She looked at her uncle hoping he would understand her thinking. She couldn't choose any other words.

"I'm it."

Lenny smiled at her with tenderness. "Charlie—always supporting the underdog. I can tell you care for her, Charlie. I'm not blind. I just hope she proves worthy of your friendship and your love. Come on, let me get all these papers and money sorted with you and then you can be on your way." He pulled his niece into a bear hug and held her for many moments.

The library door opened just as Charlie loaded the last of the money into her bag. Sterling on top for the shopping, Euros underneath for when they reached France, e-tickets with their passports in the front section for the ferry and Border Agency staff, should they need to see them. Car details in the inside pocket. She put her new phone with all necessary details entered in her jeans pocket.

"Uncle Lenny, would you give Gavin his phone sooner rather than later? I would be grateful. I don't want him to be out of the loop long. He worries like a mother hen as it is. It's a wonder he's not on tranquilizers with all that's going on. I'm not happy about leaving him, but he has responsibilities here. Oh, and remind him not to use it for phoning Poppy." Charlie's unhappiness was reflected in her face.

"Tell him we are both thinking of him," Michelle said, blank-faced.

"I'll have a run over to Walden this evening and hand it to him in person—then there will not be any trace of the new phone on his calls or my old one. Just put his address and postcode in the new phone for me, will you, sweetheart?"

Charlie beamed, picked up Lenny's new phone from the table, and entered Gavin's details. "Thank you, that's a great weight off my mind. I will phone you when I get to France." She tilted her head to one side and her eyes began to pool with unshed tears. "I don't know what I'd do without you. Would you keep an eye on Mum and Dad, and Jessica, too? I know they are not your responsibility, but…"

Lenny nodded and closed the distance between them, looping an arm around both Charlie's and Michelle's shoulders. "You—both of you—concentrate on keeping yourselves safe. I'll look after everything on this end." He took his arms from around them both and dipped his hand into his trouser pocket. He retrieved a small brown pouch held together by a drawstring top, which he pulled apart until it opened. He placed his palm on the open top then tipped and shook the bag until the contents landed in his palm. It held a cut diamond of quite some size. It shimmered and reflected colours of blue, orange, and green off its intricate facets.

"You remember Louis in Nice?" he looked directly at Charlie and she nodded in confirmation. "If you start running low on funds, take this to him. I'll let him know you may be coming. He will give you a good price."

Charlie began to speak. "Uncle Lenny, you don't have to…"

He cut her off mid-sentence as he replaced the jewel and pulled the drawstring closed. "I know I'm not obliged to do anything. I couldn't help you last time—but I can now. Off you go now and good luck!" He pulled her close and kissed both her cheeks as he pressed the small bag into her hand.

Charlie pulled away from the curb and waved one last time to her Uncle, who suddenly looked lost and forlorn—his hands pushed deep into the pockets of his chinos—head and eyes downcast. Michelle also waved at Lenny, and as she turned and looked out of the front window, a tear left the corner of her eye. "What a wonderful man," she said, genuinely overcome. "You are so lucky to have someone like him in your life, Charlie."

"You have no idea how lucky," was Charlie's reply as she eased quickly into the London traffic.

CHAPTER TWENTY

CHARLIE ENTERED THE shopping mall in a daze. She couldn't remember where she had put the list of items they would need for the trip she had made the previous night but feared it was still on the bedside table at the hotel. She checked her pockets again and still couldn't find it. "Damn and blast the bloody thing! I can't find the shopping list. I think the best thing to do is start with what you'll need, Michelle," she said tersely. "By the time we've finished, perhaps I will have remembered. I really am not in the bloody mood for this—I hate shopping under pressure."

"Oh, stop being such a grouch. It's got to be done—unless you want to spend the rest of your life in those Walmart clothes." Although Michelle's voice was admonishing—her face held a smile.

"Good point." Charlie's face creased as it began its familiar smile. She looked at Michelle and wondered how this woman, who she hardly knew, could know her so well. Then Michelle's face took on a serious look.

"Charlie, before I spend anything, I need to know where the hell you are getting your money from. You are not going into debt for me, I won't allow it—and I won't allow

Lenny to do it for me either." Michelle lifted up the sunglasses still adorning her since she left the house and perched them on top of her head.

"Trust me, Michelle. I am not going into debt. I don't think I could get into debt if I tried."

"I'm sorry, I'm not with you?" Michelle tilted her head.

"I have a substantial sum of money thanks to my grandma. The family business has always been diamonds, and she built up quite a bit of money during her lifetime. I got half of it when she died—bless her. My parents have always had more than enough, so she left them out completely in favour of my sister and me. We have enough to last several lifetimes. Lenny is her son and as you can probably tell, he's not doing too badly either—hence his semi-retirement."

Charlie's smile was rueful as she thought of her grandma and the special place she kept for her in her heart. She wondered what her grandma would have thought of her running off to the South of France with Michelle. Charlie thought she would have agreed wholeheartedly.

"*Charlotte*," she had said to Charlie in one of her more lucid moments, "*the world, it seems, refuses to see the error of its ways. Bullies the world over continue to impose their will amongst the poor, the downtrodden and the less well educated. Sometimes, even people just going about their daily business are caught up in the miserable fury of a stronger person's will. It should never go unchallenged—never—by anyone.*"

"You know, Michelle, Grandma's good friends from her youth had been murdered when Hitler's men invaded Holland in 1940. After this, she told me the underdog always had to be protected—especially from bullies."

Michelle said, "Almost sounds as if your grandma's ideas are coming to fruition now."

Charlie stepped toward Michelle. "You need not worry about the truth here or the money."

Michelle pushed her hands through her hair. "Can I give you half of the total? How much are we talking about?" Michelle asked.

Charlie couldn't think of a reason not to tell her. "Seventy thousand in Euros and sterling. We can't use our cards, remember."

"Hell fire!" A look of panic and fear crossed Michelle's face.

"Look, I told you not to worry and I meant it. Think of it as a holiday treat. I can afford it, honestly." Charlie looked at Michelle and waited for the information to be processed. As she feared, Michelle had reservations.

"I'm not sure I can let you do it, Charlie. You hardly know me and..."

Charlie lifted her hands as a sign to stop. "I know enough." She placed a finger lightly on Michelle's lips in order to silence her. She felt their softness and tried to fight the feeling where she would imagine those lips—softly caressing the different parts of her aching body. How she hankered for this woman to touch her. A fluid sensation drifted between them, thickened air—energy—something. For a split second, Charlie wondered if Michelle caught the unspoken drift.

"I am worth, in total, sixteen point eight million pounds, so I'm telling you not to worry. Let's go and buy what you need. I have the cash." Charlie smiled at Michelle smiling back at her and it felt good. No—it felt terrific!

"Charlie, you are so full of it," Michelle said with eyes rolling while tapping Charlie on the arm. "Sixteen point eight million and working at Bamber and Brooks. Why wouldn't you?" She laughed gently shaking her head to herself.

Charlie turned on her heel as though she hadn't heard the comment. If she explained why she worked at Bamber and Brooks, she would have to explain what had happened to her as a teenager, and she wasn't quite ready to share the private part of her life. Not yet—the time wasn't right. It would seem they had reached an impasse, both holding secrets close to their chests like cards at a poker game—not quite ready to reveal all. Charlie hoped the revelation would happen in the fullness of time because, without it, there was no hope Michelle would fall in love with her.

***

MICHELLE CHOSE A popular high street shop to do her shopping, filling first one basket to overflowing and then another which Charlie carried for her. Every so often, she would glance at Charlie as if looking for permission to add yet another garment to the overflowing basket to which Charlie would just widen her eyes and nod. With every conceivable weather option covered, they left the store and continued to a small boutique Charlie had spotted a little further back.

"Oh, Charlie, just look at this top," said Michelle as she perused yet another railing in the boutique handing over an off the shoulder, burnt orange affair Charlie would never have thought of buying—not her style. Michelle held it up across Charlie's chest and glanced up into Charlie's eyes. "It really does suit you, but I suppose you'll be the one wearing it, so it's up to you."

Charlie looked at her reflection in the full-length mirror and she liked what she saw. "Actually, I quite agree with you. I am going to buy it, and I'll wear it the first time we have a civilised dinner—how's that?" Charlie threw the top across her arm with her other prospective purchases.

"Are you inviting me out to dinner, Ms Reinette?" Michelle asked in a low, sexy voice, heavily laden with lascivious questioning. Her eyes were expressive and for a moment, Charlie thought she detected a flash of wanting—then it was gone.

Charlie pushed her hand through her short hair. "I am, Michelle—are you accepting?" Their fervent gaze was unbroken.

"I am, Charlie." Michelle gave a radiant smile, which nearly knocked Charlie off her feet. There was no scabbed lip or the semi-open eye or the bruised cheek and neck, in her eyes. She saw wanting, knowing, and more than a hint of trepidation.

Charlie felt her core begin to heat. The wheels of sexual arousal were beginning to engage, finding traction in Charlie's furtive imagination. She realised she must shake loose from these wild imaginings before the primal urges took too firm a hold. "Let's pay for this lot and get on our way. It's time to go and get holdalls and the damned camping equipment. The civilised dinner is looking a long way off!" Charlie laughed because she didn't know what else to do.

Michelle patted Charlie on the back and smiled again. "I'm following you."

"First to the car to drop these off then to the camping store." Charlie smiled back at her and then rolled her eyes.

Charlie knew if they stayed in a hotel in France, they would have to surrender their passports for all relevant details to be recorded—then details would be handed to the police. It was something they did—daily. She couldn't risk Martin tracking them through the French system, so the only solution she could come up with was to use a tent and pitch it in a field somewhere suitable. On the upside—she would have Michelle to herself for the camping duration. Charlie almost found a smile.

Suddenly, Charlie froze in front of the camping store. The window displayed tents, cook stoves, and mountain bikes. Her heart thundered in silence.

Michelle grabbed her arm and pulled her along. "Oh, come on Charlie, lighten up!" Michelle said as they walked through the doors of the camping store. "Camping's not too bad!"

Charlie swallowed hard. "Easy for you to say. You haven't been cosseted most of your life. Even the Winnebago that my dad used to borrow had a five-star toilet. I know I have to cope—it doesn't mean I have to like it." Charlie grimaced—inside she was smiling.

The guy in the camping shop must have been on commission and thought it was his birthday. Under strict instructions from Charlie, they should have everything they needed when they left the shop—he covered all the bases, although Charlie was at a loss as to why they would need the small shovel he loaded into the top of the trolley.

As he motioned with a wave of the hand for them to follow him to another area of the store, he stopped abruptly. He turned and asked to neither of them in particular, "Would you like two one man tents or one two man tent?"

Michelle answered without hesitation, "One two man, please," then turned and said to Charlie, "I hope you don't mind. I wouldn't feel safe on my own. So if you have no objection…"

"No, that's fine," Charlie replied, a reassuring smile crossing her face. *It must be my birthday too,* she thought to herself.

***

CHARLIE LOOKED AT her watch again as she fought to ease her panic. They waited in line to board the ferry at Dover's Eastern Docks—still twenty minutes to sailing time of a quarter to twelve midnight ferry. As she edged closer to the ramp, her undigested dinner of veggie burger and chips began to make its way up her gullet. Charlie could feel her heart beginning to pick up its pace. Would she make seventy-five minutes?

Michelle looked across and took in Charlie's obvious discomfort. "You okay, Charlie? You don't look so good. Do you get seasick?"

Charlie just shook her head vigorously from side to side with her eyes closed and head down. She was trying desperately to keep her food where it should be. Although she loved being on the water—she didn't like being on a vessel so huge. She was not good with heights, and as she lifted her head and gazed upward through her side window, the top decks looked well beyond her tolerance level. She decided she would hide as much as possible during the seventy-five minute crossing. "No, I'm just not good with heights and those top decks look a long way up from where I'm sitting. I'm trying not to be sick. Oh, great! Our turn to load. Timing is everything."

The car was put into drive and they followed the loading marshal's wave as they proceeded up the ramp. He pointed to their spot in the dimly lit interior, and Charlie duly parked their car. She could already smell the fuel and oil embedded in the deck and could feel the heat generated by the newly parked vehicles.

Charlie began taking in huge gulps of air as the anxiety attack began to worsen. "I think I will have a shower and change clothes. It might liven me up a little and take my mind off things. We have a long way to go, and I don't want to feel uncomfortable."

They exited the vehicle both clutching their newly purchased hand luggage. Charlie immediately made a quick dash for the stairs. "Thank goodness Uncle Lenny booked us a cabin," said Charlie as they clambered up the metal staircase from the car deck. "Let's find out where it is," she said as the ship began to fill with a low, gutsy rumble and an infinitesimal vibration.

The engines had started and they were beginning their journey towards continental Europe. Away from everything

British and the aegis of family and loved ones towards—Charlie gulped—towards—the unknown.

***

THE CABIN WAS compact and comfortable and Charlie felt refreshed from her shower. With her panic duly subsided, she was ready to take on the long, tortuous journey that lay ahead. "Michelle, do you want anything from any of the shops or cafes? There will be a duty-free for sure, coffee shops, restaurants."

"I don't want anything from the shops or food, but I could definitely do with a coffee. How about you? Do you still feel sick?" Michelle was concerned and looked a little fretful.

"I feel okay now, thanks. A coffee would be great though. I'll have a large latte with two extra shots, please. That should keep me awake an extra hour." Charlie took a small brush from her bag and began brushing her hair vigorously. "I might even get my hair dry before we get off."

"Why wouldn't you—you've hardly got any!" Michelle laughed at her own comment and Charlie feigned a hurt expression.

"Are you trying to say you don't like my hairstyle?" She began to move her bottom lips in a quivering motion. "I'm genuinely hurt."

"Oh, stop being a baby! If your feelings get hurt so easily, you will be in hiding the entire trip." Michelle laughed—loud and long.

Charlie couldn't help but smile. At last, she felt as though she was getting a glance at the real Michelle Bailey. Putting the English coastline behind them seemed to be working—feeling both the emotional turmoil and the physical upheaval easing away. "I have something for you." Charlie grabbed for her large shoulder bag she used instead of a handbag—she loathed handbags. Michelle waited patiently and

Charlie fussed inside the bag. She then lifted her head and handed Michelle a fistful of Euros. "There's some currency to use. When you start running low, let me know."

Michelle lifted her head and looked at Charlie—surprised, eying first the Euros and then Charlie again. "What the fu—"

"Look, Michelle, it just stops me having to keep going through the bag. Same money so what's the difference. What's mine is yours."

"Charlie, there is over three thousand Euros here," said Michelle as she riffled the money, "and you're acting as though it's peanuts." There was silence for a moment, the air heavy and expectant. Michelle stared at her—mouth open.

"It's true, isn't it? About how much money you have." Charlie merely nodded. "Bloody hell, I know someone with money." Michelle began to laugh then stopped—abruptly. "This doesn't make any difference, you know. I'm still going to pay you back. I don't want you to think you're keeping me. It's merely a loan. I have money. I just can't get to it." Michelle was serious and looked tragically sad.

"And I told you it was my treat. Now, are you going to get those coffees—or am I doomed to die of dehydration?"

"I'm going now," she said as she stowed the Euros in the wallet she'd retrieved from her handbag. "Don't forget…it's your turn to buy next time." Michelle closed the door behind her, and Charlie could still hear her laughing as she walked down the corridor.

As Charlie gazed out of the cabin porthole, blackness stared back at her, broken only by the reflection of the internal lights and her vague reflection. Her heart felt heavy again—even though she and Michelle were on the same wavelength to a certain degree—the happy banter helping them here in the present. She always felt as though she was doing the right thing, but on this occasion, so many close to her were questioning her decision. The seeds of doubt were growing, watered by her own insecurities. Even Michelle wasn't really convinced and had threatened to pull out if she felt things weren't going right. Loneliness suddenly enveloped her. The same thought from earlier ate like a worm into her brain—time will reveal all.

***

DRUMMING HER FINGERS on the steering wheel as they sat in the car waiting to disembark, Charlie steeled herself at the thought of the long drive ahead of her. It was a thousand miles from the Channel coast and the port of Calais to the Cote d'Azur, but she had promised Michelle should she begin to feel tired, she would pull into one of the AutoRoute services and grab a nap. Although the weather was chilly at this end of France, as they neared the south, it should begin to warm. She felt tired now despite the shower and the extra shots of coffee—goodness knew what she would be like after a few hundred miles.

She had looked at the satellite navigation again for total distance. One thousand sixteen miles according to SatNav. *Not all in one go*, she thought. Certainly doable over a couple of days. The only blip she could think of was the Périphérique—the Paris ring road—one of the busiest roads in Europe no matter the time of day or night. It was possible to be bumper to bumper at four o'clock in the morning.

Charlie retrieved her phone from her jacket pocket, entered her uncle's name, and then pressed call. As the phone rang, doubt again resurfaced. She let out a sigh as the phoned was answered. "Hi, Uncle Lenny. We are just about to disembark."

"My darling girl, how are you? Are you feeling okay to drive? It's been a long day for you."

"I'll be fine. I've promised, Michelle I'll pull over into a service area the minute I start to feel tired." She hated having to tell him a little white lie, but she didn't want him to worry. "I promise to phone again in the morning, and then you can tell me about Gavin. I don't think we have time now." She heard her uncle laugh and it elevated her spirits.

"Does Lenny sound okay?" Michelle asked as Charlie ended the call.

"Yes, he seems fine. I think he's had the Gavin experience if his laughter was anything to go by. I'm giving him a ring in the morning, and then he can tell us all." Charlie and Michelle chuckled at the same time.

***

FROM THE MINUTE they left the harbour, Michelle was fast asleep. Charlie was content just to have peace and quiet. Driving on the other side of the road was bungling her nerves. But, all she needed was a few miles under her foot and orientation to the other side, and she would be okay. She had done it countless times before—often going with her father to Holland, France or Belgium to meet clients where she had been more than happy to act as his chauffeur. No business for her—all pleasure.

As they reached the outskirts of Paris, Michelle began to rouse from sleep. She looked surprisingly refreshed; although Charlie noticed her eye was still only half as wide open as the other. She could still see the bruising quite easily, even in the blue hue of the night mode of SatNav. It didn't stop Charlie's heart quickening its beat or the heat from slowly rising to her neck and face.

Charlie didn't want Michelle to notice the effects of the emotional charge she was having. She frantically rubbed the seam on her jeans. *Stop it*, she thought. She didn't want her to think Charlie was applying any undue romantic pressure—so Charlie began checking and re-checking mirrors—trying to avoid facing Michelle at all costs.

Charlie heard Michelle's seatbelt release with a resounding click. A light flashed on the dashboard and a muted bell began to sound. *Bing. Bing. Bing.* Charlie looked at the glowing red flash of the seatbelt symbol. Her heart pounded suddenly. She turned, needing to warn Michelle she should fasten her seatbelt—her lips were greeted with a kiss. It was soft, it was warm, and it was tender—hopeful. Sweet surprise.

Although it pained her to do so, Charlie turned away and trained her eyes on the road. Her body reaction was full on—the pulse between her legs quickening, setting up a resounding throb. Her body glowed as the heat overtook her, melting away her reservations. She ached to stop the car, take Michelle in her arms and kiss her with so much passion it would shake her to her boots. Instead, she just asked feebly, "What was that for?"

"That was for helping me. I don't know of any other stranger who would go to all these lengths to protect somebody they barely know. You're my heroine." Michelle smiled with her eyes and her beautiful face lit up. Bruises, cuts and all.

"Well, thank you, and you're welcome," Charlie replied with a calmness she certainly didn't feel. She wondered if someday, Michelle's answer would be, "Because I love you."

CHAPTER TWENTY-ONE

AN HOUR AFTER Paris, Charlie could feel her eyelids drooping, beginning to slowly close, intense concentration taking its toll. The clock showed four-thirty a.m. She was grateful of the lightness of the traffic, only an odd car passing every now and then—a workweek. Nevertheless, she decided it was unsafe to go any further. The complete and utter darkness wasn't helping. No wonder they called this stretch of road the black hole.

Her tired bones ached. She'd been awake nearly twenty-four hours and her body was screaming *stop*. Had she been ten years younger, she would have grabbed a cup of strong coffee and told her body to keep going—but she wasn't, so she pulled into the service area, so brightly lit, it broke into the night's penetrating darkness like a beacon.

"Michelle," she called gently, not wanting to break her from her sleep or alarm her. Charlie waited a few seconds. No reaction. Charlie called her name again—louder and stronger. "Michelle. Loo break."

Michelle mumbled and grumbled in a low voice and then Charlie watched as she opened her eyes, blinking as she did so at the same time trying to focus on the clock. She stretched her arms, pushing her breasts forward and arching her back. Charlie had to look away—*those breasts are just too close,* Charlie thought to herself.

"What time is it?" Michelle asked as she scrubbed her face with her hands.

"Just half past four. We'll have a quick loo break and grab some drinks. I need a few hours' sleep before we hit the road again. I'm bushed." Michelle nodded, grabbed her coat off the back seat, and climbed out of the car. Charlie saw her shiver as she placed it around her shoulders. "It's really cold now, Charlie, and looks as though we might get a bit of fog, so probably best we do have a break."

She slammed the door and walked towards the light of the bathroom symbol, which glowed brightly in the dark, handbag swaying beside her, hugging her coat close to her body. Charlie climbed from the car and followed wearily behind, thinking to herself how she would never get used to a hole in the ground instead of a toilet—but any port in a storm.

Staring at the inside roof of the car, Charlie reclined the seat as far back as it would go. She wanted to have a deep, meaningful conversation with Michelle about their running away and the kisses. They had shifted the tone between them. The last kiss still lingered on her lips. Again and again, she felt it and relived it. A thank you would have sufficed—but no. Michelle had used a kiss instead.

The breathy signals Michelle put out both confused Charlie and excited her. The thought made Charlie's stomach clench and a smile crossed her face. Now was not the time, but it would have to be soon.

Like a veil, sleep covered her, and she drifted and drifted, imagining her and Michelle next to each other on a beach somewhere exotic—hands searching for each other's sexual secrets, which would yield to arouse and inflame them bliss. Awakening for a moment, she glanced across at Michelle to see she had succumbed to sleep, too. Charlie's eyes closed. All she could see was Michelle. Michelle was all she wanted to see. Her mind and her heart and her whole body trembled into a sleepy oblivion.

***

CHARLIE COULD FEEL her arm being squeezed.

"Charlie?"

Charlie opened an eye to see the object of her last dream. *Michelle*. She was exhausted and her body was soaked in ache. She tried to turn over, but the armrest dug into her ribs—making her wince. She wondered how many times she had done the same thing during what was left of the night. The day had dawned grey, miserable and foggy, as they sat in the lowlands. Not a trace of green anywhere. It enveloped the car in its damp shroud. She blinked to clear her vision. How she hated being awakened before she had had a full nights' sleep. Michelle's voice interrupted her jumbled thoughts. "Charlie, are you awake?"

"I am now," said Charlie with an edge to her voice. She realised it wasn't Michelle's fault, but she was just so damned tired.

"I'm sorry to wake you but your phone keeps ringing. I'm surprised you didn't hear it."

"When I'm in a deep sleep, it's like trying to wake the dead. When did it ring?" Charlie asked, blinking and brain fogged, remembering it was a new phone so the ring might not have registered deep down in her brain.

"It's been going on and off every few minutes, so obviously, it's urgent. It's your Uncle Lenny. I looked at the display," said Michelle in a timorous voice.

The sound of her uncle's name brought her back to the land of the living with a bump. "It must be urgent because I asked him not to ring unless it was. I better phone him back." Charlie could feel her hand trembling as she grabbed for the phone off the dashboard at the same time bringing the seat up to her driving position and rubbing the sleep from her eyes. Uncle Lenny answered on the third ring.

"Charlie, it's so good to hear the sound of your voice, sweetheart. I need to tell you something. Are you sitting down?" Every unthinkable thought rushed like a tsunami into Charlie's head—every thought concerning someone she loved. She felt a wave of nausea begin to register deep in her gut, making its way slowly to her stomach.

"Until a few minutes ago, I was asleep, so yes, I'm sitting down. What's wrong?" Charlie tried to keep the concern out of her voice but knew she was fighting a losing battle. She plucked at the stitching on the edge of the armrest with her fingernail, her anxiety building by the second.

"Charlie, I've had the fire brigade and police phone me and both apologised for the lateness of their calls. It appears they are having issues with their respective computers systems." Charlie heard Lenny take a breath and let out a long sigh. Charlie knew he hadn't missed the significance of that particular nugget. She just knew she wasn't going to like the news. "I hate to be the bearer of bad news." She heard her uncle take another deep breath and his voice held a distinct quiver. "Your house has burned down. They are treating it as suspicious. I'm so sorry, sweetheart."

Charlie could feel her head begin to swim, and the little colour noticeable in her face was being drained away by the force of gravity. She grabbed for the steering wheel as the shell of the car began to spin around her. Her world was literally being turned upside down. She closed her eyes and took a deep, calming breath, trying to ground herself. After a few moments, the feeling settled—but it seemed to Charlie to take forever.

A look of horror transcended Michelle's face—she could obviously hear both sides of the conversation. She turned her head to look out the window and began to stare into space. The news made her freeze.

"Charlie, can you hear me?"

Charlie was shell-shocked. Silence and a deep-rooted terror. Her eyes widened and bile rose in her throat accompanied by hatred she had never felt before. *Martin was really racking up the points on his death wish,* Charlie thought.

The call ended.

Charlie put a hand on Michelle's shoulder and squeezed lightly. "First, it was George, then Bambers, and now this. He's not going to stop the madness, now is he?"

Michelle turned and looked at Charlie. With tears in her eyes, she spoke. "No, he's not. We have to run, Charlie. We have to run."

***

FIFTEEN MINUTES LATER, with a paper cup of strong French coffee in her hand, she phoned her uncle back as she watched the fog slowly begin to lift. After synchronising her phone with the SatNav, Charlie could hear his voice coming from the speakers in the car. He sounded miles away—then Charlie realised it was because her thoughts were drifting. She tried to focus on what he was saying as she took a large gulp of coffee.

"I've told the police the whole story, including your suspicions. They said they would pass all the information along to their superiors. I know Michelle wanted to keep her husband protected from any police involvement, but I think we have passed the point of no return. He needs to be caught quickly—if it's he causing these fires." He broke his conversation. Charlie had a suspicion he was smoking one of his cigars. "I don't believe it's a coincidence and I don't think you do either. I'm sorry about your house, sweetheart. Is there anything you want me to do after the police and fire people have finished their investigations?"

Charlie was still numb. She fumbled for her words. "Ummm…it would be helpful if you could find my grandmother's jewellery and anything else personal if there's anything left." Charlie stopped in the disbelief at the words tumbling from her mouth.

"Thanks for the help, Uncle Lenny. I don't know what I'd do without you. Hopefully, they will catch him soon, and then we can all go back to normal." She was grasping at straws. She had a feeling it was Martin who had burned her house to the ground. He was that kind of person now—vindictive to a fault.

"I've actually been a little lenient with the truth. I told the police you had gone on holiday for a couple of weeks with a friend and left your mobile with me because you needed some peace and quiet. That's why I'd answered your phone. I told them I thought you had gone to Germany camping—but I didn't know for sure. I hope I've done the right thing."

"You did absolutely the right thing, and if they ask again, tell them I haven't been in touch. When they ask me about Germany, I'll just tell them we changed our minds. I'll see if I can stay away from them, at least for a few days. No doubt they will track me down eventually." Charlie felt a wave of guilt wash over her at dragging her uncle into their mess.

"I did give them details of my car, I really had no alternative." Her uncle sounded tired, an edge of sadness to his voice.

"Please don't worry. I'll just have to make sure I don't get caught speeding or something. As for the other, I might have to tell a few white lies myself. I'll be in touch again soon. I will have to give Gavin a call. He will be worried about me. How was he when you saw him yesterday?" Charlie wasn't sure if she really wanted her uncle to answer the question.

"Worried to death…as we all are. He phoned Poppy and let her know what was going on. He doesn't know about the house yet, I haven't told him—but I will. Charlotte, are you sure you will be able to handle this? This man's deranged behaviour is escalating. I need to know you are okay. I couldn't bear to think…"

143

His voice trailed off and Charlie picked up his thought and ran with it. The use of her formal name always made her think of being a little girl—but not anymore.

"Uncle Lenny, I'm not thirteen now. The teenage part of my past is over. I'm a grown woman and I'm capable of fighting back!"

Michelle turned and looked at her. Frown lines appeared above her eyes in a quizzical fashion. Charlie shook her head and shot her a warning look in return, which said—*not now.*

"I'm just glad no one was in the house." Charlie gripped the steering wheel and moved her head forward to still her mind.

Lenny's voice was quiet. "Well, if you're sure. You know what to do if you need me. I'll be right here—waiting. I love you dearly, you know."

Charlie choked back her tears. "I know. I love you too."

As the minutes ticked by after ending the call, Charlie was aware Michelle hadn't spoken for quite some time.

"Michelle, are you all right?"

"Me? Me?" Her voice began to increase in volume. "What about you, for Christ's sake? After everything that you've already done for me—you lose your beautiful house. Then, to top it all—my husband is trying to fucking kill us! No, Charlie, to answer your question, I am not all right. I am far from all right!"

"Look, things can be replaced. It doesn't matter whether it's a paperclip or a house. They are just things. We can't be replaced. You and I have futures. Every moment we are on the earth, we're leaving footprints in the sand. I don't know about you, but Martin is not going to erase my footprints or stop me from making new ones. He is a cowardly piece of shit, and I will see him put away."

Michelle considered her reply as she stared out the window. Finally, after what Charlie considered an eon, Michelle replied, "Fuck him!"

Even given the seriousness of the situation, Charlie grabbed hold of Michelle's arm and roared with laughter. "I think that means it's time for breakfast!"

***

THE AUTOROUTE WAS flashing by in a deep green colour now the white fog was beginning to abdicate its hold over the earth. Trees rose tall as they clung to the edges of the carriageways creating an eerie hue relaxing on the eyes. Charlie yawned, stretched her spine up and back, and shuffled in her seat. She missed her Audi.

Charlie was dumfounded at Michelle's capacity for sleep. Asleep again after only thirty minutes back on the road. Charlie mentally compared her to a pig that after pigging out would sleep. Charlie chuckled and decided she wouldn't share her thought.

The break from the conversation did, however, give her time for reflection. Current events prompted action.

The fact the fire had taken place the previous night meant Martin was still in England, and now the police had become involved—providing they put all the pieces together correctly—the chances of he getting out of England to go anywhere were slim. Charlie breathed a small sigh of relief. Did she trust the police to connect the dots? She had no reason to given the fiasco of her own rescue years ago.

Michelle stirred and reached with her arms above her head in a long stretch. Charlie glanced over from time to time and watched as she slipped her sunglasses from her head onto her face and yawned loudly.

"Was that a power nap then?" Charlie smiled as she turned to her.

"Of course. I need to be alert, though and keep you awake, especially since the driving rules are different here than at home."

"And you're going to achieve such a thing by being asleep, are you?" Charlie laughed heartily, knowing this comment would probably wind Michelle up.

"I'm doing my best here, Charlie. I'm under pressure just like you. I'm just reacting to it diff—" When Charlie began to laugh, Michelle punched her playfully on the arm. "Oh, you..."

"You are so easy. I'll tell you what. You keep me awake by telling me a little about your past. I know more about your husband than I do you. Fill me in on the things I need to know. I know you're Jeff's Company Secretary—tell me about it." Charlie wanted to know everything about Michelle. No detail was too small or insignificant.

"Well, okay. I have a BA Honours Degree from Strathclyde University in Accounts and Business Law." Charlie raised her eyebrows indicating she was impressed. Michelle's response was a smile. "From there, I got a job with Lynchpin— the architect people. It's a huge company, and I was lucky to get a chance with them. I was the company secretary's deputy, and I learned enough with them for Jeff to give me a chance. I think I would have eventually got the job with them, but—"

"Whoa! I thought secretaries typed and stuff like that. Aren't you a little over-qualified?" Charlie asked, genuinely confused and for a moment, ruing she hadn't taken more interest in her father's business.

Michelle laughed. "No, Charlie, it's not that kind of secretary. We send information to the stock exchange, Companies House, directors and shareholders. Advising stockholders and directors of their legal responsibilities is another huge part of the job." Michelle retrieved a water bottle from the glove box and screwed the top off. After she had taken a huge gulp of it, she continued. "That's why I need to know about law." Charlie could tell she was pleased with her own achievements. Then she added as an afterthought, "I can also type a hundred words a minute if I have to." Charlie's admiration level was raised another notch. "I hope this conversation isn't going to be all one sided—what's your story?" Michelle took another gulp, and Charlie could feel her eyes on her.

Charlie cleared her throat. "I have a Psychology Degree from Cambridge. My mother and father thought I might help them in the family business—I declined their offer."

"So rather than work for the family, you chose to do inputting work at Bamber and Brooks. Have you worked for them the entire time since university?" Michelle's face had question marks painted all over it.

"Well, I am a director of the family firm but in name only. It has its perks, as you well know." Charlie glanced through the side window and noted some horses galloping freely through the lifting mist. Running free. Spurred on, she pressed on the accelerator and felt the turbo engage.

"Yes, it does. Quite a few," Michelle added.

"After university, I just wanted a mundane job for a while, just to help my brain calm down, but I liked it at Jeff's, so I stayed."

Michelle offered water to Charlie. She shook her head.

Michelle put her feet on the dash. "Don't you find it boring? I mean, you seem a very intelligent woman. How do you feel fulfilled every day doing the same repetitive tasks?" Michelle put the bottle in the cup holder and put her hands on her knees.

"It suited me and my situation. I don't know what else to say. Well, that's how it used to be. I've told Gavin and Poppy I'm not going back."

"I'm glad to hear it. You're wasted there, in my opinion," mumbled Michelle as she drifted off to sleep—again. Her right leg opened as she relaxed.

Charlie never thought deeply about it before, but now she did. She had enough of everything to do what she wanted—enough cash—enough investments—enough property. She was beholden to nobody. Although she hadn't earned a fortune, she had enjoyed her job at Bambers and the pay had been enough for month-to-month living. Plus her director's benefits topped up her income nicely. Bambers had been good for her self-esteem. Years to build her self-assurance. Now, it was time for a change.

She'd always felt uneasy and unworthy of her grandmother's fortune. Touching the goods she had never earned felt like robbery. She didn't deserve it. She hadn't earned it. She didn't want it. Now she needed it.

A management company ran her portfolio, including what had been her grandmother's home. The bank took care of everything else—a perfect arrangement. But now her situation called for a future—a future worth pursuing. *Transfer some money into the working account.*

In no time, Martin would track them down. When he did, she wanted to have the money and she wanted to run far away to a place he could not find them. He wouldn't have enough money to follow them, anyway.

He was a wily bastard. This much Charlie had learned and they would both have to be alert—just in case he slipped through the police net. There should be an all points out on him by now. But it depended on his location when they released it. He could even be on the Continent. Chasing, chasing, chasing! Charlie bristled at the thought. Now she knew how foxes felt.

The unknown was beginning to get to her—control freak. She knew she was.

Fuel indicator laid low on the red line. Charlie glanced at Michelle as they hurtled down the long, straight stretch of the AutoRoute in the fast lane. An awareness emanated between them as Charlie's gaze seemed to awaken Michelle.

She turned and lifted her sunglasses onto her head and looked in Charlie's direction. *Her face, which was expressive in its glorious beauty, was as much so in her overwhelming sadness.* She felt her throat tighten and a well of water rise in the basin of her eyes. She looked to the open road. "We need diesel," Charlie said as she wiped her nose.

"I don't know what to say—except I'm sorry. If I'd gone straight to the police, perhaps he wouldn't be going to these lengths now. Charlie, I am so, so sorry you've been dragged into this when you were only being kind."

"Where's this coming from? Have you been dreaming? I thought we were supposed to be filling each other in on our pasts. I'm sure I asked you not to apologize again. It doesn't matter who did what to who and why. We have a situation. Let's just spend our energy resolving it—shall we?" Charlie didn't mean to sound sharp, but she did.

Charlie glanced and could see tears in Michelle's eyes. Beaten. Completely. It broke Charlie's heart. "Michelle, I'm sorry if I sounded terse." Charlie reached out and placed a hand on Michelle's forearm, squeezing reassuringly. 'I just don't want us to get distracted.'

Michelle looked directly into Charlie's eyes, her eyes still holding the pooling tears. 'I'm sorry. I'm just a big baby who worries and cries about anything.' Michelle's eyes hooded and from beneath them came—a look.

In a matter of moments, Michelle's demeanour had changed. Charlie suspected there was an energy building inside her and it was about to burst through the surface. An epiphany. A realisation she could feel safe, protected and loved by a woman—a dawning of contentment was crashing through the immenseness of the current state of affairs. Charlie knew it wasn't the time or place to be venturing down that particular avenue.

She could feel the air between them alive with their chemistry—she knew Michelle could feel it, too. Charlie so much wanted to reach out and caress Michelle's face, but she held back—not wanting to add to the pressure of their plight.

"Michelle, crying won't help. Self-recrimination is the last thing we need right now. I shouldn't have stuck my nose into your business, but I did. So, no more crying over spilt milk. Let's get the hell on with it and get to the coast as soon as possible. The sooner we bury ourselves in the tent— the better. Now, I'll drive while you start singing a hundred of bottles of beer on the wall, to keep me awake. Or, you could put the Pink CD on full blast. That might do the trick, too."

Michelle obliged and slipped the CD into the player. "You're right, Charlie. You drive and I'll look for services."

Pink's CD only kept Charlie alert for the next ten minutes. As her eyelids began to wander south, she decided a thorough rest was called for.

"Okay, here is the service area, and I'm pulling off. We are getting a room and I'm sleeping until I wake up—that's it! Hopefully, Martin will be heading toward Germany. Even if he isn't, it should be tomorrow before the hotel gives the visitor information to the police. Enough leeway for us, I think."

"You're the boss," said Michelle through a loud yawn. After checking in, Charlie was asleep before her head hit the pillow.

CHAPTER TWENTY-TWO

IT WAS TUESDAY morning, cold, wet, and depressing. The slate grey sky with black intermittent rain clouds reminded Detective Chief Inspector Ian Winter of December—and he hated it. Late spring wasn't supposed to be like this. Where were the bright early mornings? They seemed to have been invaded by dark, heavy clouds and were delaying a real dawn by hours.

His pounding headache wasn't doing anything to lift his sagging spirits. Spirits—he knew when he had had his fifth double dark Jamaican rum last evening he would pay for it and he was—dearly. It was a habit he needed to rid himself of quickly. If the brass got a whiff of his drinking habits, his career would be shorter than that of a Bond girl. When the pharmacy assistant began saying, "The usual, sir?" as she handed over his painkillers, bells had started to ring.

He liked his new job; he just didn't like Walden. The worst move he'd ever made, but the only move he could make if he wanted his career to move upward. He'd already sacrificed so much for his career, but women were most unforgiving when it came to police pressures. While there was a mobile telephone, his life would never be his own, and the women he'd had relationships with just wouldn't stand for it. The kudos of the job lasted a nanosecond.

He slammed his car door so hard it was in danger of falling off its hinges, the loud bang reverberating off the glass frontage of Walden Police Station, as it sprouted from the untidy car park like an unwanted weed. *What a sixties monstrosity it is*, he thought, glancing up at the building as he tried to shake off the raindrops from his shoes. "Steady there, Gov. You'll have to use the car later," came a voice from the other side of the small car park.

Detective Inspector Paul Brett had a smile on his face—as always. The minute he turned the corners of his mouth upward, his whole face lit up with a beam. DCI Winter thought Brett's face looked like a full moon stuck on top of a business suit. Dark blue today with a lilac shirt and a dark purple tie. DCI Winter had never seen shoes as shiny as Brett kept his—black leather you could see your face in. Water had an uphill struggle clinging to the wax; it just paid a brief visit on its way to the floor.

He envied Brett's dress sense. In comparison, he felt as though he was dressed in sackcloth. His grey suit needed cleaning and his white shirt was now tinged with unhealthy grey. His pink tie had a couple of small yellow grease marks at the bottom. Takeaway curry—his downfall. He looked up from his water-stained brown brogues to see Brett surveying his appearance.

"I have a blinding headache this morning, so not in the mood for funny quips or sarcasm. Shall we get on with it?" Winter said as though a stinging tone would make up for his shabby appearance.

DI Brett stuck out his tongue and smiled as his boss's back as he took loping strides towards the front door. *In for a good day*, thought Brett as the glass door swung shut in his face.

***

DCI WINTER WALKED out of his office straight into the squad room. He found the inside of the building much the same as the outside—depressing. Magnolia paint covered every paintable surface but over the years, every wall had succumbed to scuffing, damp patches, and even odd splatters of blood, which had left brown smears after careless wiping. The windows were worse than useless. North facing giving no light whatsoever even on the sunniest of days. *Awful bloody place*, he thought to himself.

His assembled squad were several and varied. Although most of them he knew would spend hours behind a desk checking and re-checking information, there were a few notable, very talented bodies. DI Brett, currently joking with two of his constables, was like a dog with a bone when he got a whiff of a case. "For Christ's sake, Paul. Who dressed you this morning? Purple? Who told you that colour was allowed in the police force?" Laughter rang throughout the room. Paul Brett laughed with them.

Tenacious was a word often used by his peers, but they were wrong. He was more determined than tenacious. Then there was his nose. Not the one on his face, but the one that could sniff out a wrong'un at a hundred paces. DCI Winter knew he would go far, and although he didn't often show it— was happy for him. The only female in the squad was recently promoted Detective Sergeant Laura McCarthy. She was an import from somewhere in the North, and if her previous bosses had been correct in their assessment she was another who would go a long way. He suspected her career would not be interrupted by boyfriends and babies—but he could be wrong. Bright as a button, and although her dress sense was much like is own, a little awry—and he was kind—in a way, it seemed to help her in the job. Nobody took her very seriously—which was a terrible mistake to make if you were a villain. From what he had seen, she had a way in the interview room and would twist a suspect into several knots, until they wouldn't know which way was up. An art form in itself—God given.

DS McCarthy had become aware of his presence and coughed loudly into her hand. "Gov's here," she muttered. As if by magic, the room began to quiet down as he took his place by the whiteboard filled with lines with arrows, pictures, and scribbled lines of texts. All assembled took a seat. "Thank you, ladies and gentlemen. I do believe we have some work to do here. Shall we begin?"

***

DCI WINTER RAISED his voice to be heard above the crowd after the assignments had been passed out. "Will you lot just keep your complaints down to a dull roar. You can't always have what you want. Those of you who have crap now, will not have crap the next time. That's how it works. Leedham, are you still griping?"

The loud voice of Bob Leedham was suddenly quiet, after a sheepish, "No, Gov."

"Glad to hear it." A quick glance in DC Leedham's direction said it all. "First things first. I got the report back from the Fire Chief. There was definitely accelerant used which makes it arson. Bambers was torched, no doubt about it. When the report is back from the lab, he will let me know what kind of accelerant. He strongly suspects petrol and given the man has a nose like a bloodhound, I have no reason to doubt him. Next—George Mason was definitely a murder victim. He took a severe beating to the body, but the death blow was blunt force trauma to the head and the pathologist thinks it was done using fists. You attended, Laura. Anything of special interest?"

Laura McCarthy shook her head, her green eyes glassy as though covered with a film of water. As she tilted her head forward to glance down at the piece of paper in her hand, the fringe of her short, black hair fell forward. "No, Gov—nothing special—although he did mention it had all the hallmarks of excessive rage. He said, quote, 'Anger doesn't even come close.'"

Winter nodded, acknowledging the fact excessive rage was something to be remembered. "Anything in the background?"

Laura shook her head. "Nothing at all. Fit and healthy. Retired at sixty from engineering, then his wife died unexpectedly during the first week of his retirement. He got the job at Bamber and Brooks a couple of years later. From what I can gather, he liked his work and got along well with everybody."

There was silence for a few seconds while DCI Winter took a large gulp of his now cool tea. "Bob, you did the background check on Jeff Bamber. Was there anything of special interest we should know about?"

Bob Leedham spluttered on the question he wasn't expecting in his eagerness to reply. "No, sir. No reason for the arson, he's quite a rich man, as it happens," he said as he wiped some errant coffee drips from under his nose. "He employed George Mason well past retiring age and they got on very well. George used to give him tips on the horses. His alibi is solid, too. He was at The Grove with his wife and two daughters celebrating the young one's eighteenth birthday. She certainly had one to remember, poor girl." He swiped his fingers through his short grey hair, the look on his round face pensive. He was perturbed by the situation. Winter could tell. It expressed a gamut of emotions for an experienced copper.

Winter nodded his agreement at the young lady's plight. "Now then, yesterday's interviews. Anything of note come out of those?" Laura raised her hand. "Yes, McCarthy. Did you find something?"

"Just a bit of history, Gov. After a lot of digging through old stuff, I found Charlotte Reinette was involved in a kidnapping. When she was thirteen, she was kidnapped by two of her father's employees. She had a pretty torrid time by all accounts. Locked away in a disused garage in the middle of nowhere for a week."

The room suddenly hushed. "The bastards had tied her to a bed and kept her on bread and water—when they thought about feeding her, that is. During their interviews, it turns out, on one occasion they skipped a couple of days because each thought the other one was doing it. If they had brains, they would be dangerous," she said, although her face didn't reflect the pretend levity.

Bob Leedham piped up in his baritone voice. "Is she from well to do then?"

Laura replaced her mug of tea on the desk in front of her. "Her family are diamond traders based in London. Richer than God himself and a little bit more than you, Bob." Most people in the room laughed, including Bob Leedham. "In the end though, the two villains gave it up. Although Charles Reinette kept up dialogue with the two, because of the tittle-tattle going on inside the house, they knew he wasn't going to pay up."

"So why didn't they just leave her? It seems she was pretty well hidden away." DC Jon Abraham leaned forward on his desk, as though implying the case had suddenly become interesting.

Laura looked directly at Abraham, her face a picture of blankness. "They couldn't take the chance just in case by some miracle she was found. It never occurred to them to cover their faces so they knew she would give them up. It does show it wasn't planned—not well, anyway. The fact they handed themselves in helped as far as sentencing was concerned."

"What?" Bob Leedham's voice thundered through the room. "They were a couple of imbeciles who put a girl through hell for a week, feel sorry for them, and don't throw the key away. What a load of bollocks!" Bob Leedham spit out the last word with disgust

Laura continued, "They each got twelve years and they served every day of it—no remission. Dalton, the chauffeur lives in Cornwall with his sister and has a job as a cellarman in a pub in the town. Granger is unemployed and moved back to his hometown of Forfar. I've asked both the locals to check out alibis, just in case. In all honesty, though, Gov, I can't see it's related in any way. It's been eight years since their release, and we've not heard a peep out of them."

DCI Winter rose from the isolated chair facing the group and perched himself on the corner of the nearest desk. "Good work, Laura. I remember the Reinette case. In fact, I was involved in the investigation. I was a very young constable with the Metropolitan Police. We turned London upside down looking for the poor girl. It turns out she was in the countryside somewhere in Kent. In all honesty, things could have turned out very nasty if they hadn't told us where she was. No one would have found her by accident. She would be dead."

Laura was staring down at her desk playing with a paper clip. "Downright awful," she said in disgust.

Bob Leedham wouldn't let it go. "Gutless!"

"Yes, they might be, Leedham, but she survived and they got their just desserts and served every damn day of it. If I were she, I would have been more annoyed with my father. Her father could have afforded the ransom of half a million many times over, but he wouldn't pay it." The DCI stood looking down at his shoes pensively. Suddenly, his head shot up and he faced his team. "Now, to the case in hand, any word on the closed-circuit television, Paul?"

Brett adjusted his tie, although none was necessary. "I've phoned the lab, chasing it up. They have all the ones from the surrounding buildings and are trawling through the footage now. None survived from Bambers. They will let us know if they spot anything."

"Thanks, Paul. Offer them some help from here if they need it. Another pair of eyes won't do any harm." He took his last gulp of the cold tea. "Anything else of any note?" He glanced around the room, hopeful.

Jon Abraham raised his hand from the middle of the room as the others in attendance shook their heads. He stood to make his announcement as his colleagues looked at the ceiling, out the window, and anywhere else but at Abraham himself. They thought him a gilt-edged prat—putting it simply, an idiot.

"I don't know if this is of any interest or not, sir. A lady I interviewed..." He reached and grabbed a single sheet of paper from his desk, "a Michelle Bailey, looked as though she'd been in a car wreck. Her face was really cut and bruised. She said she fell down the stairs at home, but her explanation was all wrong. It just didn't add up."

"A likely story—probably a domestic," piped up Laura.

"She said she was out with a group from work because it was First Friday, then went home and had the accident—didn't go to the hospital but instead, went to friend, Charlotte Reinette's house. It just seems a strange thing to do if that's what happened. She said her husband was away for the weekend with a group of friends and didn't want to worry him. She gave Miss Reinette's address for contact as well, sir. I find that very telling."

DCI Winter nodded in agreement. "I agree, Abraham, it does seem a bit odd, but if it was a domestic and she chooses not to report it, there isn't much we can do. Did she look edgy when you asked about the fire?"

"No, sir, not at all. In fact, she was quite calm throughout." Abraham stuck out his chest, as though he was about to receive a medal. None was forthcoming.

"Before we leave, did anyone we interviewed come up with any tales of woe about previous employees? Anyone sacked or mistreated that they thought capable of revenge?" All about him shook their heads as they glanced hopefully at one another. "Okay, ladies and gentlemen. Back to the assignments and if you come up with a glimmer of an anomaly about anything, I would like to know, please."

Back in his office, DCI Winter began to worry. At the moment, they had nothing. Nothing on the night watchman George Mason, nothing on the owner Jeff Bamber and nothing on the employees. Two exceptions—an old case from twenty years ago and a probable domestic violence incident, as yet, unreported. Winter thought, *this murder and arson can't go unsolved.* His unblemished career wouldn't go astray now. *Not now.* He was married to his career. There was nothing else. This awful bloody town would not be the ruination of him—he would make sure of it.

CHAPTER TWENTY-THREE

THE EARLY WEDNESDAY afternoon through the Maures was beginning to turn into a pleasant ride. Just south of Lyon on the A7, the grey clouds hanging defiantly above them—reflecting their mood—began to clear, and by the time they reached Valence, the full sun's reflection was bouncing beautifully off the majestic Rhone. It was incongruous such a beautiful sight of the fast flowing river full of its eddy's and occasional pools of stillness be set partly amongst the heavy industry of the area. *Very much like Michelle and her present situation,* Charlie thought in passing.

Now, the further south they went, with the A7 and A8 behind them, the more their moods lifted skyward away from the anguish Martin had inflicted. The conversation had changed, now much lighter in content after they had finished the end of each CD they had sung their way through—at the tops of their voices. Mary Chapin Carpenter was a revelation to Michelle. She sat up and took notice as Charlie blasted her way through a succession of songs.

"Why have I never heard of this woman before?" Michelle asked at the end of the *Stones in the Road* album. "Her voice is so mellow, and the lyrics she writes are great."

"Uncle Lenny introduced me to her a long time ago. He said I needed to calm down." She chuckled loudly and her shoulders bounced up and down, just to exaggerate the point. "But, as usual, he was absolutely on the money. I did find her music calming. Even the kick arse songs." Charlie found herself smiling. "Just lately though, she's gone a bit more folky and reflective. I like that even more." Charlie thought how it mirrored her own life in so many ways.

"Well, I shall certainly be listening to more," said Michelle as she read the lyric booklet.

Charlie thought of the time her Uncle had a heart to heart with her about her wild ways. She rolled her eyes at the thought of how much alcohol she must have consumed throughout that time, and how many women she had slept with. Michelle had come into her life at just the right time, but Charlie thought to herself, *the Universe knows everything about timing.* She just hoped Michelle's Universe was talking to hers.

***

THEY STARTED DROPPING down into the foothills on the coast side, passing the fields of budding grapevines buried in their furrows—standing to attention like soldiers on parade. Silence. The music stopped. Then Michelle started to shuffle in her seat. She leaned forward resting her folded arms on the edge of the dashboard, straining herself against the tension of the seatbelt, gazing contentedly out of the windshield—a slight smile turning the corners of her mouth.

As Charlie glimpsed at the furtive smile, she turned and gazed at the slight gaps between the wooded hills. Then she caught the briefest glimpses of the Mediterranean Sea. She smiled and a gentle, weird sensation drifted into her chest. It was the same vision, the same sea as she had witnessed descending into Nice airport a few times when accompanying her father. Now, it was different—changed in her sight, in her mind and in her heart. She felt the release of something locked deep inside, some emotion she hadn't tapped into for many years—happiness.

"The sun knew we were coming," Michelle idly remarked. "It's like my long journey from the past—a long way to come."

She brought Michelle close to a place she loved and she was proud of herself. All she had to do now was keep her safe. Charlie took a big swallow as she thought of the next job on the agenda . . . the tent. She had never been camping in her life and the thought, for some obscure reason, troubled her. Was it somehow linked to the garage? Some little detail having slipped her memory? What was it?

Her parent's idea of camping was to take a Winnebago her father had borrowed from a friend for a week and to then dump it in a field. Her parents would dine from their hampers and drink champagne from flutes while she and Jessica made their own entertainment—playing pooh sticks and board games and reading copious amounts of books. *No obvious links. It had to be something.*

No doubt the experience under canvas would help her transcend, help her find her memory and break into one of the neat little boxes in her head. A box where she filed all the unpleasantness away. Camping, canvasses, unopened boxes— she hated it already.

When they finally reached seaside resort of Sainte-Maxime, Michelle was nearly off the edge of her seat as if waiting for some miracle to happen. Charlie couldn't contain herself any longer. "Michelle, what are you waiting for? Are you expecting something? You've been shuffling around on the edge of your seat for ages now." Michelle turned to look at Charlie and gave her one of those mysterious, heart-flipping smiles. Her whole face lit up, and it was obvious the soreness from the beating was beginning to recede.

"You just wait and see. It will only be a couple of minutes." Mystery was there in the voice, but it was a light-hearted reply.

Charlie shook her head and continued to follow the traffic on the St Tropez road until finally, Michelle let out an excited squeal. "Charlie, just look to your left," she said, pointing vigorously with her index finger in the direction of the white apartment blocks lining the edge of the sea.

Charlie did—and was left breathless. As the gap between buildings opened up, they found themselves on a road bridge crossing over what looked like a wide stream, the colour of green tourmaline and, as she followed with her eyes downstream, the colour seemed to fade and transmute into the colour of the azure sea.

Charlie reached across and placed her hand briefly on Michelle's shoulder. "That's one hell of a sight, Michelle. Absolutely glorious." Charlie's smiling eyes went back to the road and for once, she was happy there had been a slight build-up of traffic, making their progress across the road bridge slowly.

"I don't know why, Charlie, I just knew you'd like it." Michelle let out a contented sigh.

Charlie's eyes were once again drawn downstream. A miniature version of the Tyne Bridge appeared in her line of sight—painted white—seemingly joining the two white apartment blocks on either side, the picture framing the stream's entry into the Mediterranean where its colour had taken on the shade of azure blue for which the sea was famous.

With the sun on its downward arc in the western sky, the bridge was framed against the darker sky blue. It gave one of those magical visions that set itself in a person's mind forever. It had obviously done so for Michelle all those years ago. She turned to look at Charlie, her eyes filling with tears of joy, her face imparting a serene, angelic look.

The perfect moment was shattered when the text alert sounded on Michelle's phone. She looked furious, dragging her gaze away from Charlie as she snatched the mobile from the top of her bag and looked at the caller display. Before Charlie could get the words out to not open it, Michelle had. Charlie slowly closed her eyes and muttered, "Shit!" under her breath.

Michelle put her hand to her mouth, realising the moment she had done it exactly what she had done wrong. She stared at the text message and turned the screen so Charlie could see what it read—*Sorry to have missed you.*

Charlie realised Martin was talking about not having burnt them to a crisp in her house. She was beside herself with fury and slammed the side of her fist on the steering wheel. She was furious about his arrogance, his viciousness, but most of all, his wanton destruction. People and property meant nothing to him now as he wreaked his acts of vengeance.

Charlie wanted to lower the window and throw the phone on to the road so it would be shattered and crushed— annihilated, by the next passing car or better still, a large truck. Her bad temper was about to burst its banks like a river swollen by floodwater. She knew Michelle needed to keep the phone active because of her elderly parents, but she was beginning to hate the sight of it.

Michelle had explained to them she was going on holiday and not to ring unless it was important, but as she had reiterated to Charlie, more than once, they were elderly and accidents happened. Charlie understood—but she was fast running out of patience with both Michelle and her phone.

"Christ, I am such a bloody idiot!" Michelle cried in anguish as she began another journey on the road of beating herself up.

Charlie bristled with irritation and didn't contradict the statement. "Look, it's not the best thing that could have happened, but now this changes things. We just have to be a little more careful. Your GPS isn't on, so the only thing he knows for sure is which tower the signal was bounced from—the tower could be anywhere—and so could we."

Michelle screwed up her eyes and ran her hands over her face, albeit gently. "He knows exactly where I am."

"How did you work that one out?" Charlie asked in desperation.

"It's on my Timeline on Facebook—as my favourite place. I said so when I uploaded some photos from the holiday. " Michelle dropped her head in her hands and began to sob.

Charlie didn't know what to do or say. On the one hand, she wanted to scream to the gods to stop having a laugh at her expense; on the other, she was close to losing it with Michelle. So, instead of saying or doing anything, even consoling, Charlie just carried on driving, losing herself in what was her biggest pleasure. She refused to think about the situation any more until she was rested, fed, and watered.

As they approached the outskirts of Cavalaire, the palm trees having lined their route terminated their escort as buildings began to be more prevalent, a sure sign they were approaching civilisation. Charlie decided she'd better ask Michelle where she wanted to go. She didn't want to break the silence because she was in her comfort zone—but she desperately needed a rest. Her body seemed to be suffering the same effects as jet lag. "Any idea where we can park up just for an hour or so? I really need something to eat and drink."

Michelle looked at Charlie hopefully, recognising she might be at the end of her patience. "Yes, I think I might know just the place." A huge smile crossed Michelle's face—normal conversation had now been resumed. "Just go to the next roundabout and turn left. There is a parking area that leads to the beach. It shouldn't be busy at all because it's only used by the locals on weekends. It's normally deserted during the week."

Late afternoon found the beach quiet as a grave. There were three other cars in the car park—not a person in sight.

Charlie pulled as far down the lane as she could, toward the large umbrella signifying a cafe. A brightly coloured sign, all the colours of the rainbow announced, "Bloup. Bloup." Charlie's immediate thought was the name belonged to a seafood restaurant. She didn't care. Her hunger and thirst were threatening to overtake her thoughts. She felt starved. They had drank water and eaten sandwiches from the service area. Now it was time to relax and have a cafe meal.

CHAPTER TWENTY-FOUR

BRETT'S MOONY FACE appeared in the small pane of glass of DCI Winter's door. Winter was watering the two orchidees on top of his filing cabinet at the side of the only window, as Brett tapped softly on the glass. Winter waved for him to come in as he dribbled the small amount of water into the second plant pot. He gazed lovingly at his two plants as the flowers of one pale pink and one pale yellow cascaded down, making them top-heavy to the point of bending the supporting stems in half.

He stroked the leaves lovingly, and then turned towards Brett, who was sporting his ear-to-ear smile.

"Next time we are out and about, Paul, remind me to get some canes for the plants, will you? I've been trying to remember for a couple of weeks and failed miserably. Now, what can I do for you?"

Brett held up his hand and waved a memory stick in the direction of his boss. "You better have a look at the footage they've sent through from the lab, Gov. Very revealing." Brett went around the front of his boss's desk and inserted the memory stick into the side of his computer. He brought up the relevant file just as his boss reached the desk.

Winter settled into his big chair and looked at the screen. "What have they found then? It better be good after three bloody days."

Brett beamed as he continued to click. "Oh, it's good."

Winter stared at the screen—hopeful. The opening showed footage taking in the gate of the factory opposite, the road and the fence, the gate of Bamber and Brooks plus George Mason's hut. At the rear, across the car park was the main entrance of Bamber and Brooks. "By hell, Paul, that's a good shot. Please tell me it's a stationary camera."

Brett smiled at his boss while pushing his Windsor knot a little closer to his Adam's apple. "It is, Gov. Plus, the resolution isn't bad. The set-up must have cost them a pretty penny and for it, we are eternally grateful." He let out a low chuckle. "This is where it gets interesting."

Winter leaned closer to the screen, making an oath to visit an optician soon. As he stared at the screen, he saw a car pull up close to the entrance of Bamber and Brooks, headlights on full beam, causing a slight flare on the footage. The driver's door opened and a huge man extracted himself from the driver's seat and made his way to George Mason's hut. The man was dressed in all black, including a hoodie with the hood up.

While facing the camera, he had his head down.

"He knew the cameras were there, which means he's done a reconnaissance. I would bet my bottom dollar there is more footage of him and or the car recently. Ask one of the constables to see if they can get ahold of more footage from about Wednesday and run it through looking for the same car or any foot traffic. This chap is huge, so he should stick out like a sore thumb. We might get lucky."

The footage continued as the large man attracted the attention of George, who could be seen through the small window, putting on his security man's cap. "Looks a sprightly man for his age, George does."

"Yes, Gov. He was an active man by all accounts. Had his own allotment. Grew vegetables and flowers, which he shared with his neighbours. The ladies were particularly fond of him. In fact, they are organising his funeral. He only has a brother, and he's two years older and not a well man. I'm sure the ladies will do him proud." Brett's face had taken on an ashen hue and it wasn't missed by DI Winter.

"Don't worry, Paul. We'll get the bastard responsible for this mess. I think we should send a contingent, just to show our respects." Brett nodded his approval.

The footage remained playing, and DI Winter watched everything unfold before him. After a short conversation with the big man, George unlocks the gate to Bamber and Brooks and lets the man inside. Winter wanted to scream *No!* at the top of his lungs, and he would have if it could have changed the outcome. It was now written in indelible ink in the books of history. George was gone and no amount of screaming would bring him back. He shook his head in his mourning.

The action moved to George taking the man to the front door and unlocking it. "What on earth could he possibly have said to make George let him in? Did I notice a slight limp there as he crossed the car park? Just rewind it will you, Paul?" Brett did as he was asked. "There, look. He is definitely limping on his right leg."

Brett nodded. "Good spot, sir. I missed that." He added the note in his notebook that he retrieved from his inside pocket.

Both men disappeared from view on screen for a few minutes. Winter grabbed his chin and rubbed at his stubble. The next action horrified Winter and Brett. Brett narrowed his eyes as if not really wanting to watch and Winter focused his gaze. The large man emerged with George tucked under his arm like a rag doll, legs, arms and head dangling grotesquely.

"He must have knocked him out inside. Poor bugger wouldn't have known what hit him." Winter had disgust oozing from his voice. The footage continued as George was thrown into the hut disappearing from view, but they could see the top of the big man through the window as he reached down and grabbed George's clothing with his left hand reigning blows to the inert body with his right fist.

"Jesus," said Brett, screwing up his eyes even more. "It doesn't get any better the second time watching, either."

The large man was then seen shoving George back to the ground, continuing to assault him using his feet. Each kick left the two men in the room wincing. Suddenly—the assault stopped, stone dead. The man walked coolly out of the hut to the rear of the car, opened the boot, and took out a petrol can. He then walked calmly to the front door of Bamber and Brooks and disappeared inside.

"Well, at least we have something. All we have to do now is find out who this man is. I have a bad feeling about this case, though. This chap is brutal and brazen. I think he's on a suicide mission." The idea did not sit well with Winter, but he knew in his heart it was the truth. Death by Cop—the modern way to fame.

Brett nodded. "I get the same feeling, sir. Although he's covered his face, I don't think he's worried about getting caught. I think it's just a delaying tactic until he gets the job done. Whatever the job might be. I hope we get to him first."

The man had completed his covert mission. He was back in his car and away before the first flames began to lick their way onto the outside of Bamber and Brooks. "So," said DI Winter, "anything on the car? Or is it too early?"

Paul Brett looked at his boss and shook his head. "Bob Leedham thinks it's a Volvo, but we don't know the model yet."

"Ask the team to drop everything else they're doing. Get them to go through all relatives and friends of the employees and track down anyone who owns a Volvo of any description. You can ignore all the older models, start with the newest first, and find out where they all were on Friday night." Winter closed his eyes and inserted a thumb and forefinger in each socket, rubbing slowly, massaging his eyeballs. He hoped he might rub away the images of the deathblows—he couldn't.

Paul Brett looked heartsick, yet his face held a look of grim determination.

"We can't hang around on this one, Paul. I need those alibis checked—sharpish! You can pull Bob Leedham off the team and get him to work on finding out where this guy bought the petrol. Get a uniform to give him some help. Hopefully, this hasn't been planned for weeks, so he'll need footage from early Friday morning from every petrol station in the area. Start at the nearest to Bambers and work outwards. You can tell the team overtime is available, and I would like everyone there unless their mother is dying. Any other excuse won't wash. I think we are dealing with a clever bastard here, Paul. Let's nail him before he does any more damage."

CHAPTER TWENTY-FIVE

THE THREE WAITERS were busy playing a game of cards as they entered the café—obviously a quiet afternoon. Charlie couldn't see crockery or cutlery that had been used by customers or anything else out of place. A waiter came to them immediately, notepad in hand, and showed them to a table near a large, open window about halfway down the outside wall and in between the newly painted stucco walls. The decor was rustic, and the style reminded Charlie of a rural cantina she had visited in Mexico.

Michelle couldn't contain herself, and she reached the small table, covered with a red and white chequered tablecloth and a dainty bone china cruet set and the salt and pepper keeping each other company near the wall. She reached over and placed her hand on top of Charlie's, smiling with glee. As Michelle opened her mouth to speak, Charlie shuddered.

"Are you cold?" she asked sounding quite surprised glancing out the window to see if there had been a change in weather.

"No, someone just walked over my grave," said Charlie, not wanting Michelle to know the true cause of her discomfort—Michelle's touch.

"Don't say that, Charlie! It's a horrible saying. I want to be in a happy mood—in my happy place and with hopefully, a happy friend. Thank you so much for bringing me. I can't tell you how much it means to me. I want you to have a taste of what I feel. It makes me feel calm. I know I shouldn't be, given the situation, but I can't help myself. Now, I just want to walk along the beach and watch the sunset. With you."

"Not before we've eaten, you don't." Charlie smiled because she couldn't help it. There was a maniac chasing them, and they had travelled the length of France trying to avoid him. He had killed a lovely old man, burnt down their place of work and her lovely home, and yet, here they were, sitting in a cafe in Cavalaire, without seemingly a care in the world.

Michelle picked up a menu with her free hand and began to scan it as the waiter shifted his weight from foot to foot. "I don't even know why I'm looking. I know exactly what I'm having." She passed the menu over to Charlie.

"Which would be what, exactly?" asked a very hungry Charlie.

"A Pan Bagnat." Michelle began to laugh when she saw the look on Charlie's face. "I gather you don't know what the hell I'm talking about." The waiter scribbled as Michelle held up two fingers to indicate they would both have the same, and then he made his way towards the kitchen whistling a happy tune.

"You would gather right. French, the language, culture and everything to do with it, is a mystery to me. I can't say I haven't been before. I have, with my father. You don't learn much though when you are ensconced in a hotel most of the time. So, I am in your capable hands." At the mention of the word hands, Charlie looked down and realised Michelle still had one hand over hers. It felt good, like a well-worn glove on a cold day. Michelle's excitement was palpable.

"You leave everything French to me. I'll handle it."

Charlie had never felt so relieved.

As they waited for their food, the waiter brought them both small breadsticks with their glasses of local wine. Michelle took a tentative sip and then smiled. Charlie smiled, too—just because she could. "Something I should know or is it a deep, dark secret?"

"No, nothing like that. The last time I had local wine here, it was horrendous, but I was young and it didn't matter. The campsite we were on had some lovely people visiting, and one night, we decided to have a corned beef hash party." Michelle looked at the breadstick she was holding in her fingers, then broke off a small piece and placed it in her mouth. Charlie looked on—contentedly.

"We all made our own version— and believe me— there are plenty. We took out the large cool boxes and mixed them all together. It tasted wonderful." Michelle let out a hearty belly laugh as Charlie grimaced at the vision in her head. Michelle's face broke out into a wide smile as she recalled the memory.

It didn't matter somewhere on her face were all the colours of the rainbow, as some of the bruises had begun to fade while others were still dark and angry. *She looks beautiful,* thought Charlie. She was—inside and out.

Michelle continued with her tale, excitement mounting in her voice. "After the meal, when the children went to bed, one of the men decided he would go to the camp shop and get some wine for us to drink while we were playing Trivial Pursuit." She took a small sip from the glass in front of her.

"He came back with the biggest flagon I have ever seen, and we all started drinking the local rough red. It's only now I realise how bad it was, but we should have had some idea when we spilled some on the melamine tabletop and couldn't get the stain out. It didn't matter what we tried, even bleach wouldn't shift it." She laughed again, with the same gusto as before. It was then Charlie realised it wasn't necessarily the place that attracted Michelle back to this area, but the good memories it held for her at this bad time in her life.

Charlie glanced around the small cafe while they were nibbling on the breadsticks, her eyes scanning every corner with interest. The blue painted ceiling had been covered with drooping fishing nets, and on each wall, given pride of place, was a ship's wheel, the centre of which held discreet lighting effusing a soft glow around the room.

At the side of the cash register on the dark brown counter sat a sextant on one side and a large conch shell on the other, the pale shell ridged with swirls of taupe. The windows had rolled up rattan blinds sitting above, on the inside the hinges for the shutters opened outwards. It took Charlie a moment of staring to realise there was no glass at all.

Apart from its rustic appeal, it held a quiet elegance—all the crockery being the same fine bone china as the dainty cruet set, the outside shutters had been left open to bring the outside world in and was hewn from the same kind of dark wood as the counter. It was definitely welcoming and unhurried, the various waiters walking around doing their duties with genuine smiles on their faces. What was not to love?

Suddenly, Charlie's attention was taken by the sound of chirping behind Michelle. Charlie looked past her, to see a little sparrow perched on the edge of the sugar bowl on the table behind. Nobody rushed to shoo it away—the sparrow intent on getting a little sugar before bedtime. This showed the true nature of the little cafe and Charlie felt relief. No health and safety here. She had been transported back to the years where common sense ruled and the nanny state had not yet impinged on the daily lives of the populous.

***

"IT'S A SANDWICH!" Charlie proclaimed as the waiter served the Pan Bagnat, a small smile crossing her face and that of the waiter, knowing full well she was in for a quick retort.

"Do—not—say—another—word! If you do, I will not be responsible for my actions." Michelle's face was like stone.

"Oh, yeah, and what are you going to do—shorty?" Charlie's grin broke out into a full-blown laugh. Michelle stuck out her tongue as she grabbed a quarter of the very large sandwich. "Very grown up, madam."

Michelle wrapped her mouth around the food in her hand, closed her eyes and let out a very loud, "Mmmmm."

Charlie closed her eyes as the fantasies began.

Michelle was looking completely relaxed as she finished off her coffee, just a small amount of bread crust left on her plate. Charlie was the happiest she had been in years. It was at this defining moment, as she gazed across the table staring at Michelle, Charlie realised she was totally and hopelessly in love. She didn't know if any feelings she possessed would be reciprocated and she didn't care. She was high on the feeling and she loved it.

As they talked about their childhoods and families—Charlie could not yet share her innermost turmoil. Once she realised it wasn't the time or place, yet again, she was worried she might be avoiding the issue. No, she realised, she wasn't doing any such thing. She just didn't want to spoil the moment. She knew though—one day she would.

Michelle looked her in the eye and Charlie began to melt. She so much wanted this woman but knew it would likely end in disappointment.

"Charlie, would you mind if we go for a walk on the beach? Perhaps we could call in for a nightcap on the way back. Looks as though it will be in the dark though. Do you mind?"

"Not at all. It would be a pleasure after spending so much time sitting."

Charlie wedged the money to pay the bill and a generous tip under her empty coffee cup. She was delighted to see Michelle wave to the waiter, who had provided his service, in a way of thanks, so Charlie followed suit. It was obvious Michelle felt at home in this part of the world. Charlie was fast joining her in her joyous feeling.

The ease of conversation continued as they began their stroll along the beach, the sun low in the indigo sky and the waves lapping endlessly on to the beach, beating out the rhythmic tidal tattoo. The arid sand seeped into the sides of their shoes as their footprints were covered by the fluid material washing into the impressions they made. Charlie thought about Martin and how he was trying to do that to them. Wipe them out.

Although it would have suited Charlie never to have the name of Martin mentioned, ultimately it was unavoidable. He and Michelle had been a couple for a long time, and he was, and continued to be, a big part of her life. She had told Charlie he had been her saviour, her rock and she thought her lifelong companion. Charlie mused on how life could change in a heartbeat.

When they were a good distance from the café, Michelle stopped walking and turned to face the sea. She wrapped her arms around herself and shivered slightly as if picking up the slight movement of air rolling in with each wave. It was barely noticeable. Charlie walked up beside her and placed the sweater she had tied around her waist around Michelle's shoulders. Charlie then stepped back a little to let her have her moment of reverie in peace. Charlie glanced at the scene in front of her. It was a beautiful sight as the dark blue blanket covered the light blue sky, quickly turning day into night—the sea would soon be the colour of black ink.

Charlie could see the lights of the town at the other end of the bay. The white lights from the shops and homes, twinkling like bright stars; the coloured ones from the attractions nearer the water, the walkways, and awnings of the cafes and restaurants, and the lights edging what looked like a marina. She could make out poles from a jetty protruding into the sea and also the edging of some kind of building—perhaps a boathouse or something similar.

The water lapped onto the shore only a few feet away from their feet, bringing a peaceful feeling to Charlie's psyche. It felt good.

Suddenly, Michelle took a couple of steps backwards and let her small hand slip effortlessly into Charlie's hand. This time, Charlie realised there was no other reason for this, other than Michelle just wanted to do it. The action scared her a little, as all the complications with Martin came flooding into her mind. She suddenly had the impulse to run—to leave this woman far behind in her wake. Charlie took her hand away and moved into a new space, standing in a self-imposed silence.

"I'm sorry," said Michelle, after what seemed like hours to Charlie, a noticeable quiver in her voice. "You have been so good to me, Charlie. it's not right I should come to you for emotional comfort as well. I'm so confused. I feel something for you. I just don't know what that something is. You have given me a lot, and I'm so grateful for everything. I don't know how I will ever repay you and your family."

"Michelle, you don't owe me or my family anything. A situation has come up and we're dealing with it—that's all. I don't want to see any harm come to you. Pretty soon though, we are going to have the authorities to deal with, one way or the other."

Michelle stood as one moment after another drifted into the enveloping silence.

"He raped me and nearly choked me to death. He was vicious and unrelenting. I thought I was going to die as I began to suffocate. He pushed my head into a pillow as he assaulted me from behind then turned me over and choked me from the front. He was out of his mind. It wasn't my Martin who did it to me. I didn't recognise anything of the man I married."

Charlie was stupefied.

"I don't know how I'm going to be able to tell anyone else. I want to run, but it will only stay with me. The hurt—the humiliation—it will never go away."

Charlie let out some sound deep inside. She wasn't sure if Michelle had heard it or not. She closed her eyes and took a deep breath to calm herself. She could barely speak as she stepped towards Michelle and gathered her in her arms. Tears flowed from them both and mingled as they stood cheek to cheek clinging ever tighter in the embrace.

"You told me and you're going to tell them. I will be there with you to support you and see you through this. You need to unburden yourself because carrying this forward into your future will do you no good, Michelle. Take it from someone who knows."

Michelle moved away walking slowly back towards the café, the sound of, "How could you possibly know?" lingering in the air behind her. She stopped every now and again to take in the darkness, not acknowledging Charlie's presence.

The silence was back, no doubt fuelled by the suggestion Charlie had made, although this time it was edged with an anger coming off Charlie in a groundswell of emotion. She would make sure Martin paid for what he'd done... one way or another.

CHAPTER TWENTY-SIX

CHARLIE HAD SUSPECTED the rape from what Martin had said to her outside her house. Even Gavin had nailed it. However, suspecting and knowing for sure were two completely different animals. Charlie was not prepared for the way she felt as the words had tumbled from Michelle's lips.

Charlie began to feel panicked. Pure and simple. She wanted to run away and hide, castrate the bastard, hold Michelle close and get on the first plane to the Bahamas—all at the same time. Castrating the bastard won out. Her head was out of control, thoughts somersaulting around like stones on a riverbed. She wanted him to suffer and was sure there was a place booked to the nether world for men like him. Disgust rose from deep within her. The bile made her gag. She wanted to vomit.

Michelle broke through her thoughts by speaking into the rush of the tide. "I can't say any more. I'm sorry. The thoughts just hurt too much." Tears began to cascade down Michelle's cheeks again and she stood, sobbing, looking so desperately alone.

Charlie couldn't stand it. "I know the feeling," she said, almost in a whisper. She walked forward and opened her arms again in a gesture of comfort. Michelle turned to face her and walked into them without looking Charlie in the eye. Charlie didn't care about anything else—she just wanted Michelle to feel wanted—protected—loved. Charlie could do all of those.

As Charlie's arms enfolded around this beautiful woman, she thought she detected some kind of reaction from Michelle's body, and it caught Charlie completely by surprise. Michelle pushed so close to Charlie, she was like another skin, her aura invading Charlie's pores. She could feel the body heat searing its way through her clothing, warming Charlie in the process. The cadence of her heart sounded as though she had run a marathon.

Suddenly, a light appeared on their patch of beach. Charlie wondered where the light had come from, and as she turned, she found them bathed in the light emanating from the café's deck area. They were back where they had started. There were no voices to suggest they had company. Charlie was glad. It wasn't a moment she particularly wanted to share.

The voice of reason in Charlie's head was screaming *NO!* Michelle tilted her head and looked at Charlie's lips and inched forward—then stopped. She looked into Charlie's eyes—Michelle's own pupils so large, they had almost taken away the iris—mysterious—deep—seriously seeking permission.

Charlie ignored her inner voice and answered by moving those last few millimetres, gently touching those soft yielding lips with her own. Charlie was sure she heard a gasp followed by a sensuous throaty moan. Charlie's body began to respond internally—preparing—lubricating.

Michelle pressed on harder, ignoring the injury to her lip and Charlie responded in kind. She could taste coffee and wine, a curious yet pleasant combination, which reminded her of the chocolate liqueurs her family used to pass around the table at the end of Christmas meals.

Michelle moved away from her—just a fraction, then she felt the tip of Michelle's tongue gently caressing her top lip. As their chemistry began to mingle, Charlie began to feel her body mechanism propel into overdrive. She opened her lips and their tongues touched, soon caressing, challenging for position.

Charlie jumped as she felt a strange sensation in her feet. Cool and wet. She looked down at her feet to find they were surrounded by tidal water. The tide was coming in—in more ways than one. They looked at each other and began to giggle. The moment was over—but at least they'd had a moment.

The waiter looked at them and the wet footprints they were leaving on his clean floor. He just smiled, shook his head, and then looked at Michelle for her order. She ordered two cognacs and some antipasto for them to nibble on. Charlie didn't really feel hungry—she felt enervated. The travelling, irregular hours, and high emotional content over the last few days had left its mark on her. Completely and utterly spent.

The drinks and food arrived quickly. Michelle devoured the contents of the little china bowls on the table in front of her. In the largest bowl were large green olives, coated with herbs and stuffed with pimento. Michelle placed one between her lips. When she began to suck, Charlie thought she would have a stroke. The look must have been evident because Michelle started to giggle.

"Sorry," she said, although the timbre in her voice revealed otherwise

"Yeah, right," replied Charlie, face implacable.

Michelle continued to suck on the olive and twirl it around, using her tongue to take off the bits of herbs, then, as she wedged the olive between her teeth, she began to suck at the pimento in the middle. Anything but eat it. The more she sucked and rolled the olive on her tongue, the more Charlie could feel her blood pressure rising—imagining steam billowing out from the top of her head in big white clouds.

Charlie was helpless. She could only roll her eyes and give the impression she had been in this situation before—she hadn't. In her mind, she was substituting the olive for every bit of her anatomy she could give a thought to—it was very erotic. Charlie stared and smiled at the display. She had the sneaking suspicion Michelle knew exactly what she was doing.

The brandy had been smooth and warming and was beginning to have a soporific effect on them both. "I think I need to close my eyes for a few minutes," said Charlie, her eyes almost closing a she walked to the car. She couldn't believe she felt so tired when she had slept away last night and a good portion of the morning.

"Me, too. I think the last few days have finally caught up with me. It's too late and dark to start pitching a tent now. How about we look for some out of the way rest area for the night?"

"Sounds like a plan, but I still need a few minutes."

***

CHARLIE WAS ROUSED from a deep sleep by the sound of voices from outside the car. She jumped when she saw the sight of a policeman's uniform. Michelle was shaking her head and showing her passport and Charlie was beginning to panic when suddenly, the policeman turned around and began to walk away. Michelle got in the car and let out a heavy sigh. "Charlie, let's go. Just drive, anywhere, and I'll explain in a minute."

Charlie didn't argue. She raised her seat, put on her seat belt, started the engine, turned the headlights on, and began to drive towards the main road as Michelle finally locked her seatbelt in place. At the end of the lane, she saw the policeman leaning against his car, pencil in hand while writing something down in his notebook.

"Hells bells," said Charlie, rolling her eyes and banging the heel of her hand on the steering wheel. "Now we are up a shit creek without a paddle. The first thing the nice little policeman is going to do when he gets back to his nice little station is enter the information into his nice little computer. When are we ever going to get some good luck? I'm getting pissed off with this." Charlie smacked the steering wheel again with the heel of her left hand. Tiredness and frustration. Charlie had visited this place before.

The ensuing silence was deafening—it was then Charlie realised what she'd said. "Michelle, I'm sorry. I didn't mean you, this place, or anything like that. It's just we seemed to have been dogged by bad luck from the onset. It just goes to show how much our lives have become digitised. It's pathetic really, and yet I don't know how I'd exist without my laptop and mobile, so I shouldn't be bitching really. I am sorry."

"Charlie, don't you realise it's my fault you're in this position? It's me who has brought all this down on your head. I think my middle name should be Jonah. Anyway, according to our little French friend back there, we are breaking some kind of bylaw sleeping there in the car. I explained we had had a long drive and were only napping before booking into a hotel. I'm not very good at telling lies." The smile was a weak one, but it was a smile, and it gave Charlie hope.

"Well, I'm not sure about you, but I don't feel inclined to run. If we have to make a stand anywhere, then I think we should make it here. We could keep running all over the globe—but do you know what? I don't want to give Martin the satisfaction of chasing us—I think it's giving the creep a hard on. I for one do not intend to aid and abet his weird fantasies. We will keep our heads down for a few days and see what happens. I have no doubt we will be tracked down by the police, but we shall just plead ignorance. What do you think?"

"I couldn't agree more. My body and mind need time to recover. I can't think of a nicer place to do it."

In a weird kind of way, Charlie was elated. The onus of responsibility had now been lifted from her shoulders, albeit because of a *fait accompli*. Plus, the necessity for camping was now over. She let out a huge sigh of relief. It's not as though Charlie had anything against camping per se, she didn't. Something was nagging at her and she couldn't snag the thought. Her version of communing with nature would continue to be from the safety of a five-star log cabin with all mod cons…for now.

She pulled the car into the most convenient spot, which just happened to be a petrol station.

"I'll fill up with diesel, and when I've finished, I'm going to get our accommodations sorted out."

"I thought we were staying in the car tonight and then looking tomorrow to find somewhere to pitch the tent for tomorrow night."

"There's no point doing it now. The information is going to filter through soon enough. Plus, you told the policeman we were going to find a hotel. We need to know we have complied if we need their help later. When Martin catches up with us, I want plenty of people around as witnesses. Plus, I really don't want to do camping." Charlie put the most pathetic look she could muster on her face. Michelle laughed.

"Oh, Charlie, you must be the bravest person I know. Then you wuss out of camping." Michelle tilted her head to one side and pulled down the corners of her mouth. "Poor baby." In an instant reaction, Charlie stuck out her tongue. "Very grown up, Miss Reinette. What's the alternative then?"

"Have you any idea how much disposable income Martin has access to?"

"No, sorry, I don't, not completely anyway. He has a work credit card and a personal one, plus the cash from our bank account. His limit on his personal credit card is five thousand, plus we have around six thousand in the current account. All the other money is tied up in long-term savings and investment. The work credit card is the joker in the pack though. It could be for any amount of money."

"Well, eleven thousand isn't going to last him long down here, for sure, so we shall simply outspend him. We will hide ourselves away as much as possible, but we will do it in style." Charlie smiled inwardly. She realised this little escapade might cost her a bundle, but she also realised it might show Michelle a part of life she had never experienced before, and that was worth all the money in the bank.

CHAPTER TWENTY-SEVEN

GRATEFULLY, THE ROAD into St Tropez was quiet. Normally, it was a frenetic negotiation of cars—a foreign place even with the aid of a SatNav, where the locals drove in your boot, horns blaring, drivers yakking into the air. Charlie's patience would have been tested. Absolutely shattered. Luckily, the road bequeathed silence. Now, the long drive from the Channel had taken its toll. Her eyelids closed and opened in an opaque lull. Her head began to roll. She was at the point of being dangerous.

Her phone acted like a goddess, it even provided a postcode. A five-star hotel—yes! Charlie prayed for a room, any room, just a place to rest their heads. They both needed a shower and to get out of the clothes they were wearing. At this juncture, Charlie's clothes were ready to walk to the laundry on their own.

The wide well-lit road of the Avenue du Quinze announced the approach to La Residence de la Palmier. Charlie could make out the wall in front of what she assumed to be the hotel building, so she slowed the car passing a wall of rectangular shaped stones which gave the outside a rustic Provençal kind of look. She pulled the car through the gateway where the black, wrought iron gates had been pushed back. They passed through a small avenue of six trees coming gratefully to a halt. The journey—over. She had delivered Michelle to the area where she wanted to be. Tomorrow, they would relax and plan a move, a move forward—toward their futures, wherever they may lie.

"Michelle, just wait here and I will go see if they have a room." Charlie pushed her fingers through her gritty hair. She glanced at Michelle. Silence. She was fast asleep.

"Okay then. You just wait there until I get everything sorted out, your ladyship. Don't you worry your pretty little head about anything." Charlie's sarcasm was tainted by her tiredness. The tension was beginning to get to her. Her head flashed an image. Once. Twice. Three times. Martin could be around the corner, any corner. She didn't feel safe. She felt exposed. She felt war torn.

She rubbed her eyes.

Charlie tilted her head to one side and let out a large sigh, her hands running over the seams of her jeans. She studied Michelle—chestnut hair framing delicate skin, a small French nose, a slight dimple. Her high cheekbones gave her an oriental look at times and an olive complexion was due to a Mediterranean influence in her gene pool. Then there were those lips. The full, sensuous, highly kissable lips. Charlie let out a sigh. If only she could reach across now and kiss Michelle lightly on those same lips and wake her in the manner of all good fairy tales.

With the same thought running very quickly through her mind, she left Michelle asleep, got out of the car, and entered the building. The entrance had mood lighting absorbed by the matte, muted colours and giving the serene, luxurious feeling only the best hotels could provide. Charlie was ready to throw herself on the mercy of the night receptionist if she had to. They would take the broom cupboard or a lounger by the pool—if only they could get some refreshing, satisfying sleep.

The sound of her approaching footsteps alerted the gentleman who had his head bowed, his fingers rifling through a stack of paperwork. He lifted his head and smiled in recognition of a potential new customer—although, in a split second, Charlie realised what a sight she must have looked. If he saw anything wrong with her appearance, it definitely didn't show on his face. As his lips moved to speak, Charlie jumped in first. "Do you speak English?" she asked, slight concern showing in her voice.

"Of course, madam. My name is Claude and I am the night manager. How may I be of assistance?" he said, in a voice that sounded as though it had been ironed. The smile, she assumed, had been achieved by plastic surgery or the overindulgence of Botox.

"Marvellous. The French speaking half of the duo is asleep in the car." Charlie pushed her fingers through her hair, hoping it would make her look at least a little more civilised. "Please, come to my rescue and tell me you have a room available for a few days. I'm sorry I can't be more precise. We're not sure of our plans yet." He nodded his head in a military fashion then began tapping on his computer keys with his eyes gazing at the monitor.

Charlie noticed how French his clothing appeared. Immaculate, grey pinstriped suit and sparkling white shirt with a lemon tie. She didn't know how it worked, but it did. He looked like a French fancy, topped off with hair she was sure had once been red, but now turned a wiry salt and pepper.

"We have one Standard Sea View with any of our offers. All our rooms have super king-sized beds that can be separated into singles by housekeeping, on request." He looked at her with his smile fixed as though she should know what the heck he was talking about, as regard the offers.

"We'll take it with the best in the offer range, and I'll let you know as soon as possible as to the length of the stay. If you could ask housekeeping to separate the beds tomorrow, I would be grateful." Charlie squeezed her platinum credit card and the hundred Euro note in her hand.

"Very good, madam. The computer is informing me the room is available for the next eleven days so there is certainly no hurry." The smile was beginning to make Charlie irritable. "I shall just need to take some details and also a copy of both your passports."

"Before we go to the room, could I possibly explain something to you? It really is a rather important but delicate matter, and the rest of your staff will need to know, too." Inside, Charlie was longing for some help to ease the burden. They needed someone on their side. Being awake twenty-four seven and expecting to be alert to the danger Martin could present, wasn't an option.

"Yes, madam, how may I help?" Claude leaned forward on the desk. He was obviously into subterfuge. Charlie got an overpowering whiff of second-hand garlic.

"My travelling companion, Mrs Bailey, has had some problems with her husband of late. She is not in a good way and needs some thinking time as to how to solve her problems. I have brought her here to allow her the space and time she needs. However, her husband seems intent on trying to influence her with his presence. I need to keep her husband away from her. Do you think you could help me with this, Claude?"

The smile still adorned on his face.

"Why, yes, of course, madam. The hotel is more than willing to help. If you could leave Mr Bailey's details with us, I will inform all staff this man is not to be allowed on the premises. I think we should be able to avoid any confrontation. We have very efficient security staff available day and night."

Charlie breathed a heavy sigh of relief. "Thank you, Claude. Mrs Bailey and I are both extremely grateful." Charlie hated the stilted version of English she was currently using, but it seemed effective with Claude. Charlie offered up the hundred

Euro note along with her credit card. Claude accepted them with a deep bow of the head and a slight click of his heels.

***

MICHELLE WANDERED WIDE-EYED around the room. Charlie sat on the edge of the bed and watched, wondering if Michelle's gorgeous eyes would ever fully return to their sockets. The car had been taken for valet parking, and the luggage delivered to the room. Now, it was the two of them in a room in St. Tropez and if not for the quasi-craziness of the situation, it was all quite beautiful.

"Charlie, it's wonderful. I could never have imagined somewhere like this, never mind staying here. Just look at the place, it's so impressive." Michelle walked to the centre of the very large room and turned full circle, pointing out various items in the room as she did. Generally, Charlie didn't give two monkeys for décor and the like, but she had to admit it certainly made a good impression on her.

The room was painted white, except the alcove where the headboard fit, which was painted a cheery yellow. The room furniture was all white with the essential edging trimmed in gold. On either side of the round white coffee table were two dark blue upholstered easy chairs.

The large patio window was covered top to toe in net curtaining with a heavier curtain in pale green pulled to one side and fastened with a gold braid. The whole thing was brought together by the striped bedspread covering the king sized bed, including all the colours in the room. The lighting in the bed alcove came from two reading lights on the wall either side of the bed and gave the room a cheery glow, but Charlie noticed there were other small lamps, again white, with gold stems and bases, at various points in the room. Very impressive.

"Do you want to use the shower first, or shall I go?" Michelle asked, unbuttoning the brass button on her jeans.

"You go first. At least you have some clothes unpacked. I haven't started on mine yet," Charlie answered wanting to get Michelle out of the room as quickly as possible. She wasn't sure she could watch Michelle get undressed and keep her hands to herself. She berated herself for the thought. Michelle was still very badly bruised on her face and goodness knows what damage the rape had done to her internally. The blood in the bed at home was likely a result of the assault rather than Michelle beginning her period. What could she say to convince Michelle to visit a hospital?

Charlie's musings were broken suddenly—

"Charlie—come in here..." Michelle's voice called to her from the bathroom. Charlie's heart leapt in her chest in a panic—what the hell could be wrong? All thoughts of Michelle's modesty left her. Charlie grabbed the door and flung it open. The hinges were spring loaded and it flapped back as quickly as she had opened it. Just in the nick of time, Charlie used her forearm to protect her face. "What the...?"

Michelle jumped. She lifted herself out of the sunken bath in surprise. Charlie was treated to a view of her naked upper torso, breasts, in particular. As Charlie had suspected, they were marked with bruises and bites. The sight sickened her.

Michelle lowered herself into the water and surrounded herself with the bubbles. Up to her neck, covering every blemish on her body with the creamy white foam. She stared at the wall opposite and spoke to Charlie in a voice devoid of emotion. "Sorry, Charlie. I didn't mean for you to see. I just thought if you wanted a shower you could have one now if you don't mind me having a soak while you carry on. The shower is behind, so it's okay, I can't see you."

Charlie was suddenly overcome. As tears were threatening to fill her eyes, she swallowed the emotion gathering in her throat. Not emotion of anguish, but of anger and frustration. She walked across the room and knelt down beside the bath. She trailed her hand in the water until Michelle looked at her.

"What?" Michelle asked in an aggressive defensive tone.

The tone of her word cut over some of the last nerves Charlie held onto. An irritant. Charlie was trying very hard not to lose patience with Michelle, who was pushing her buttons without even knowing it. But, the time had come.

"Listen, Michelle." Charlie swallowed hard. "Let's get some things out in the open here. You have been beaten and raped by your husband. The damage he's done is unknown because you won't go to the hospital or see a doctor. You won't report him to the police for the assault and rape, and I, for one, am struggling to make any sense of it!" Charlie's voice had reached shouting decibel level. "So, you explain to me why you won't do all the things you should be doing before I completely run out of patience with you. I'm right on the point of saying to hell with it and climbing on the first available flight to the fucking Bahamas!"

Charlie knew Michelle would cry, but if that's what it took to get her to see sense, then so be it. "Come on—tell me!" She gave Michelle the hard stare—not a trace of emotion showing on her face.

Michelle looked directly at her, eyes narrowed in determination. "Because he was my husband a long time and I loved him, but most of all, like I told you before because he saved me."

***

AS THEY BOTH climbed into bed, Charlie steeled herself. She had forgotten about the conversation she'd had with Claude.

"I'm sorry about the bed situation. A king size was all there was to offer when we booked in. Housekeeping will come and change it into singles tomorrow."

Michelle had merely waved her hand to indicate it didn't bother her in the slightest as she lay on her back at the far side of the bed, eyes closed. "It's fine," were the only words issued from her mouth.

Charlie believed her but wondered if she would still feel the same once the tiredness had worn off and she'd finally had a reality check. The good thing was the bed was so big contact would be minimal, if at all. All Charlie had to do was to try to keep her mind off Michelle's body. She needed Morpheus to grab her and drag her under—quickly! Michelle had not indicated once she had wanted to return to their 'moment' on the beach. No hand holding, no comfort needed—no nothing.

They'd had no more meaningful conversation regarding Martin either. Charlie realised she would pay for her loud outburst. She was convinced the cold shoulder treatment she was now receiving was only a taster. No doubt, she had sounded like Martin—like a bully. Charlie felt so hurt she was beginning to show signs of being what she detested most in life—then reminded herself she only had herself to blame. She had been the one who decided to interfere.

Michelle had not influenced her in any way, and her only contribution to the whole thing was to come up with a destination. Charlie had done this because of Michelle and the feelings she held for her.

"Goodnight and sweet dreams," she said softly, suspecting Michelle was already asleep, as she turned off the light above her head. The room was plunged into darkness. Charlie drifted off to sleep to the sound of the sea rolling on the shore and thoughts of Michelle.

Chapter Twenty-Eight

As DCI Winter walked through his office door into the team room. All he could see were faces illuminated by computer screens giving each of his team an eerie glow. They all looked suitably absorbed—some of the stress revealed itself with the occasional hand sliding through hair or a fist pressed to a cheek as they tamped on the keys looking, searching—finding something, anything marked by a lead.

Shit! Fucking delays. Bloody Thursday already and no further forward. There were too many in the last few days. The loss of the computers at the DVLA has knocked them sideways. He couldn't understand how a Government run organisation could lose its computer systems—then it happened to them! The case was bitten by bad luck. He knew better but swore someone had laid a curse on them. Six days with nothing concrete to work on. He crossed his fingers. *Something has to give.*

He could have done without being summoned. The Superintendent was getting edgy because of the lack of progress, so sooner or later, the Deputy Chief Constable was going to get involved. He wasn't particularly looking forward to his nothing-to-show-for meeting with the Superintendent and DCC. The whole of the meeting—him defending things which were beyond his control and moving his head like a nodding dog on the parcel shelf of a moving car. 'Yes, sir.' 'Of course, sir.' 'Three bags full, sir.' These were the highlights of the meetings.

The Deputy Chief Constable might not want the shit landing within his smelling distance, but it wasn't shit caused by Winter or his team. He would 'yes' all the Chief wanted, but he wouldn't accept responsibility for someone else's crap. Computer failures, un-returned phone calls, dodgy license plate recognition…not his fault. The Superintendent was worse than useless. The man never had his back. He was too busy covering his own arse.

His hand was on the outer office door when Laura McCarthy let out a shout from behind her computer. "Gov, before you go anywhere, I think you should hear this. We've just had notification from the Fire Service of a fire out in Vale—8, Vale Crescent to be precise." She paused briefly and smiled. "That's Charlotte Reinette's house. It got torched on Monday night."

Winter slowly turned to set his gaze upon his detective.

The bodies in the room became suddenly still as heads lifted from their computer screens—aware of the significance of the information. They breathed a communal sigh of relief. There was—at last—a break in the case.

Laura stood. "They've had a problem with their computer system, so there's been a lag in the information getting passed along." She abruptly re-checked and scanned her computer screen for any more updates.

"What the hell is going on? Can't people get off their arses and pass information along any other way? What's wrong with their bloody phones? Jesus Christ! Is this bloke fated to get the run on us?" Winter shot his eyes skyward in the hope a bolt of lightning would descend with all the answers written on it. "Either that or he's the luckiest bastard walking. Bob, could you please get in touch with the locals who attended the scene and get copies of all statements taken at the time."

"Yes, sir." Bob Leedham nodded in confirmation and loosened his tie, seemingly invigorated by the thought of some action.

"Any news on the petrol purchase yet?" asked DCI Winter, currently on a roll in the good news department.

"No, sir, not yet. It certainly doesn't look as though it was anywhere close to Bamber and Brooks, but once we have the home address of a suspect, I can start from there and work my way back towards Bambers." Bob Leedham slowly grinned—like the smile on the face of a tiger—prey just edging into sight.

Winter buttoned his coat. "That would be grand, Bob. Thanks. See if you can get the statements first though. They would be useful to have before the meeting I'm going to call later."

Jon Abraham lifted his head to look over his computer screen. "Sir!" he said, excitedly. "I think we may have found a link here. You know I told you Michelle Bailey was staying at Charlotte Reinette's house? Michelle Bailey's husband drives a Volvo." He paused, in the hope of applause. There was none forthcoming, so he carried on talking. "A company car owned by Comso D Limited. The company is in computer software and owned by a Damien Richard Bettinger, Head Office— Newcastle. Still gathering information, sir. Do you want me to stay on it?" Abraham looked like a puffed up turkey cock in his black jacket, white shirt, and red tie, with his chest sticking out. He was almost sitting to attention.

Winter clenched his fist at the news and punched the air. "Yes, I do, Abraham. I want every 't' crossed and every 'i' dotted, and I want it a fast as humanly possible. I am on my way with the Super to see the Deputy Chief Constable. It will take me forty minutes to get there so I would be very pleased if you will send me any information you get up to that point.

There will be plenty of brownie points in it for you." Winter smiled, but there was no warmth in it. "Thank you for your efforts, ladies and gentlemen. Now, can you share the load and follow up on the leads as quickly as possible?"

Winter could finally relax his shoulders a little. "Laura, could you organise a meeting in the conference room for two o'clock, please."

Laura glanced his way. "Two o'clock. Yes, sir—no problem."

Winter smiled. "Thank you. Make sure everyone has what they need and bring all relevant footage and information I need to add to the murder book. It's time to make sure everyone is singing from the same hymn sheet. Thanks. See you all later."

DCI Winter left the building, making his way across the car park to his car, his demeanour now a little more relaxed. It was about time they had some decent leads on this case. They were well overdue and the case had seemed dogged by bad luck from the beginning. They needed some justice for George Mason and any other victims of this maniac. It wouldn't do any harm to pass on some decent information to the Chief Constable, either. Good fortune was beginning to come his way, and he would ride it like a wave all the way to the Chief Constable's door.

***

THE CONFERENCE ROOM was hot, sweaty, and airless, with no windows and only one effective door. The magnolia colour of the walls had taken a battering during the days when smoking was allowed in buildings—the room now bearing witness to its past with its yellow dinginess.

Winter wanted to know which imbecile had decided to call this rabbit hutch a conference room. Even though big enough to hold a large table in the middle of the room, there was hardly enough space to manoeuvre around the chairs without brushing against the wall. The other door he knew had extra chairs from all over the station piled up against it in the corridor on the other side of it. They would be moved when the next Health and Safety inspection was due, then returned to where they'd been, rendering the door unusable once again—making this room an airless death trap.

His mind, however, was eased a little by the outcome of his earlier meeting with the Chief Constable. He had acknowledged that the blame for the delay and disruption was beyond the control of Winter and his team, and their response had been to bring in high-level government fixers. As multiple agencies had been targeted, an enquiry was being initiated, the main suspect—Martin Bailey.

The sixty-inch LED screen television was wall mounted at the side of the unusable door and was just showing the last of the assault on George Mason, accompanied by looks of horror on the faces of the assembled group with odd gasps and sighs thrown in for good measure. DCI Winter could tell his team were aghast by what they saw—as was he. Paul Brett was right. Seeing it a second time didn't make it any easier to watch. Suddenly, the viewing ended and the screen turned blue.

Winter stood and looked around the table at his assembled team. He closed his eyes for a few moments, just to let the horror seep in and also, a little time to pay homage to George's memory. It was Bob Leedham who broke the stillness. "I've seen some cowardly stuff in my time but that takes the biscuit. The suspect must be six-four, six-five, or something close and George must closer to five-six. Hells bells, talk about a playground bully."

Paul Brett, for once not the trace of a smile on his face, spoke up. "I feel physically sick each time I see the footage. Poor fella."

"Not bad, Bob." Laura McCarthy glanced at a sheet of paper in front of her. "George Mason was only one point six eight metres—five-feet-six in old money. The suspect, according to my calculations based on the height of the gatepost is one point nine eight metres, which is six-feet-six inches. Plus, he's built like a brick shithouse. Let's not forget that." Although Laura meant this comment as a joke, nobody laughed, so she shuffled papers to hide her embarrassment, her face colouring red. Winter thought the lack of reaction reflected the gravity of the situation. It didn't take policemen long to develop their gallows humour.

"So, ladies and gentlemen. Anybody else with comments as to what you have just seen. I know it's hard for you to contain your anger, but please—try. I don't want this man walking away from these crimes amidst screams of police brutality or evidence fixing." All Winter could hear was whispered mumblings. "I can't hear you," he said sharply, awaiting a response.

There were various responses of, "Yes, Gov," "Understood," and "Yes, sir." Winter nodded appreciatively.

"On to the leads. DC Abraham has some news for us, I believe."

"Yes, sir, I do." Abraham shuffled his huge wedge of different coloured papers and computer printouts. "I've been checking out Michelle Bailey's husband, Martin. All information gathered so far is on this sheet." He waved a sheet of paper and proceeded to hand out the rest of the copies.

"Now, although the techs couldn't get the plate number of the car we saw on the video, we do know it's a black V70. It has tinted rear windows and it's built on a sports chassis. That's why it looks so close to the ground." He availed himself of the glass of water from the table in front of him and pulled his shirt collar away from his skin. "The most important detail is this—it runs on diesel—not petrol. So, if we can get footage of him buying petrol—wallop! Nailed the bastard!"

Winter interjected while making a calming motion with his hands, as if patting Abraham on the head. "It won't do us any harm, Abraham. Anything else?"

Abraham replied with a nod. "I spoke to his boss, the owner of Comso D, a Darrel Richard Bellinger. He was a little reluctant to speak to me—kept edging the questions. I got the feeling he might be good friends with Martin Bailey. In the end, he said he had a meeting and could I possibly ring back tomorrow. I wasn't happy and told him so, but he has us over a barrel. He has the information we need."

Laura McCarthy laughed. "Oh, he might think so, but I think we have ways of making him cooperate." She smiled knowingly.

Paul Brett, in an angry voice, added his thoughts. "What does he thinks this is? He is supposed to be helping the police with their enquiries in a murder investigation and he has a bloody meeting! Couldn't he delay it for a few minutes? Send his apologies and cancel? Why are we at the bottom of everybody's bloody list until they need us? It makes my blood boil."

Winter was nodding in support. "I share your anger and frustration, Paul, but it always seems to be the way. I would bet my life on the fact he's on the phone warning Martin Bailey." Winter turned to avail himself of the water and poured himself a glass from the carafe.

"I have some news to add from the Fire Chief," Winter said after his first mouthful. "The accelerant used at Bambers was petrol, but it will be a few more days before the lab can come up with the forensic analysis. So it's a waiting game as far as this aspect is concerned." Winter rose from his chair, took off his jacket, and placed it on the back of his chair.

He continued. "As for the Reinette house, according to the statement I've read, a black car was seen just before the fire. It also says it's the second occasion it's been seen. On the first, the driver was spotted speaking to Charlotte Reinette. The neighbour thought it was someone who was lost so didn't take any notice of the plates."

Winter loosened his tie. The heat continued to be oppressive—thick and cloying. "Laura, could you organise Bailey and Reinette to come in again as soon as possible for some more interviews, please?"

"Could be a little awkward, sir. I put the additional information received on a sheet in the bundle," she said with trepidation in her voice and a look of awkwardness on her face.

"Why? Why is it a problem?" Winter was trying not to rush her.

"They've taken off on holiday, sir. Both the uniforms who took the fire call and the fire brigade say they spoke to the uncle, Leonard Stern, who answered Charlotte Reinette's mobile. He says she's left her mobile with him so she could get away from it all. Michelle Bailey is with her."

Winter was busy rubbing his eyes in disbelief in what he was hearing. "Didn't the people who interviewed them warn them not to leave town?" The room went deathly quiet.

Jon Abraham was the first to speak up. "No, sir, sorry. I didn't think Michelle Bailey would be going anywhere the state she was in." Abraham could see Winter's face going puce as he waited for fall-out.

He was saved by Paul Brett speaking up. "I just forgot. No excuses. I'm very sorry, sir."

"You will both be bloody sorry by the time I've finished with you. Every shitty job that comes down the line, you two will get it. Have we any idea where they might have gone?" Winter looked at McCarthy for more information. "Her uncle said Germany was mentioned...camping. But didn't know for sure."

"Did you speak to...," Winter glanced down at the sheet of paper he had liberated from its bundle, "Mr Stern personally, Laura?" asked Winter, his face still coloured bright red.

"Yes, sir, I phoned him the minute I had the information. I asked him if he spoke to them to explain that they must come back as they are part of a murder enquiry. Or, to go to the nearest police station and hand themselves in. I did mention protective custody. I hope that was the right thing to say, sir. I would have checked with you first, but you were with the CC."

Winter nodded to show she'd done the right thing. "And there's been no contact since they left?"

Laura McCarthy shook her head. "Leonard Stern says no."

Winter looked at each of his officers and shook his head. "I'm not inclined to believe a word any of them says. I think they are just frightened to death of Martin Bailey's proclivity for violence. Right, let's see if we can track them down before Bailey catches up to them because I have no doubt that's what he's trying to do. Jesus! Why is this room so bloody hot?"

He finished what water was left in his glass and poured another one, leaving the carafe empty. "DI Brett, can you please get all the necessary warrants with regards to phones, computers, etcetera. We need to know if they will give us any clues as to where they are. Concentrate first on the Bailey phones and computers, laptops, tablets, the usual rigmarole—and Reinette's phone. Get that from her uncle and see what information it gives us. Hopefully, they will supply us with what we need. Did you try Michelle Bailey's number Laura?"

"Yes, Gov, several times. No answer," she said, shaking her head. She pursed her lips and grabbed a paperclip from her desk. "I'll try a couple of more times, then I'll text her, asking her to get in touch."

Leedham interjected, "Do I get on with the CCTV from the garages working from the Bailey house then, sir?"

Winter nodded at Leedham with a smile. He knew Bob loved to get his teeth into something solid. "Great idea, Bob, thanks. Right. Laura—could you organise the other DC's to gather background on Martin Bailey? Get a forensics team to go over the Bailey house with a fine-tooth comb. If there is any link with the arson, we need to know. Ask them to send any information to us ASAP. I'm not in any doubt he's our prime suspect at the moment." He reached for his water again, after a mouthful, twirled the glass around in quiet contemplation in front of him.

The next thought struck him. He looked at McCarthy again. "Plus, Laura, see if the team can find a link between Charlotte Reinette and Michelle Bailey—it would strengthen the suspicions we have. Also, any previous hint of domestic violence in the Bailey household? My gut tells me it will be in the mix somewhere. Advise the other arson team for now we are combining the two cases." Winter's mouth was as arid as a desert. In contrast, his back was soaked with perspiration. He took a large draught of his water.

"As Senior Investigating Officer, I think I can make a decision for all of us. If I know their SIO, I don't think it will worry him at all. I'm sure it will allow him to put in an extra round of golf. I don't think we have much choice on the matter—the link looks obvious to me."

He glanced round the room at the team, speaking to nobody in particular. "Will one of you try to track the movements of Reinette and Bailey? Get any information you can off the uncle about what time they left, and then at least we'll know where to start with Eurostar and the ferry companies."

DCI Winter put down the murder book he was holding, the thick pile of papers making a resounding thud. He looked at DC Abraham with a determined scowl. "Jon, get yourself home at close of play tonight and pack yourself an overnight bag. I'll pick you up at seven. We are going to have a nice trip up the M1 to give Damien Bellinger a surprise first thing in the morning. It's about time he started taking us seriously. I'll phone the local Superintendent to clear it."

Paul Brett lifted his head from his paper bundle, "I'd pay to see that." He smiled a knowing smile.

CHAPTER TWENTY-NINE

CHARLIE WAS SURE she could hear a noise, but she was so comfortable she didn't want to move. She loved the feeling of the bed as the mattress gently embraced her. She also had a feeling of déjà vu as she felt the weight of limbs strewn across her chest and legs. Michelle's gentle snoring invaded her hearing and she could feel her warm breath on her neck.

What a great way to wake up, she thought, disturbed only by the intermittent irritating sound of Michelle's message alert on her phone. She lost her smile when she realised who the message was probably from. Would it harm to leave it another couple of hours? She knew, however, Michelle's phone would just go on giving the alert, whereas hers gave up after a couple of attempts. She decided to give in.

"Michelle, wake up. You have a message on your phone. Michelle!" Raising her voice a little louder seemed to do the trick. The arm across her chest tightened and the legs roped her even closer. She thought Michelle was still asleep.

"Charlie, throw the phone into the sea," she replied, her eyes still tightly closed.

"Would you like me to do it from here, or should I go out on the terrace?"

"After I've had my two cups of coffee, you can do it from wherever you like."

Charlie giggled at the quick retort. "A room service call then? I would need at least my right arm to do that." The arm across her chest closed in, clamping Charlie's arms even tighter.

"I am so comfy. Please don't move. Can't you do it by telepathy or something?"

"No, I'm afraid not. I promised my mother I would stop using telepathy when I was a child."

There was a slight pause. "Oh, go on then," Michelle said with a bit of the grumbling grouch and rolled over onto her back. As Charlie rolled over to pick up the phone to contact reception, she noticed the time on the alarm clock.

"No point trying to get breakfast now. It's one thirty. I'm so glad I put the 'Do Not Disturb' sign on the door. What would you like with your coffee? Some antipasto and a tray of sandwiches okay for you?"

"That sounds lovely. Thanks, Charlie."

"You're welcome, ma'am," said Charlie with a smile, "Now, read your message."

The message glared from the screen and hung in the air like a storm warning.

It was from Martin: Lovely morning in Cavalaire Sur Mer. Why don't you join me?

It screamed at them from the screen.

***

THE PATIO OUTSIDE the room was shaded from the fierce heat of the afternoon sun by the yellow canopy extending from above the patio door. Push button controlled from inside the room—Charlie was impressed. They had decided they were not going to skulk around the room like terrified prisoners of war, but would have their brunch in the fresh air as they took in the sights and sounds from the surrounding area.

It certainly was a beautiful setting amongst palm trees and tall ferns fluttering in the light breeze coming off the sea. The ferns were dancing like ballerinas as the wind twisted them from side to side. Beautifully arranged, they obscured the views of the numerous paths and the car park from the visitor's eyes, yet afforded a small view of the beach and the slim jetty prodding its way like a finger into the sea. Charlie could see two dinghies moored there and wondered if they belonged to the hotel. She smiled deciding an outing might prove to be a worthwhile escapade at a later date.

Each room was separated from the next by beds of border plants, smaller ferns and numerous bits of greenery— interspersed with succulents and tall lavender plants on the verge of flowering. The beds lay perpendicular, running away from building's brickwork in scalloped billows, at the end of which lay a pot with a shaped box shrub that looked like a lollipop. It was a feast of delight for the human eye.

"Well, at least we know where he is, Michelle. You were right. He must have headed straight for Cavalaire," said Charlie, breaking herself away from the view, hopeful to lift Michelle's mood. Knowing Martin was not in St Tropez should be a fact worth knowing. Charlie took a bite of roasted tomato on a slice of toasted baguette, and then popped in a black olive just to give an all-round flavour. She smacked her lips in appreciation.

Michelle was scowling. "I don't give a stuff where he is. He makes me want to throw up. I hate him. I hate what he's done to me and to George, and I hate the man he's become. Honestly, Charlie, you wouldn't believe what he used to be like, so gentle and caring. The true gentleman." Michelle gently caressed the cross as it hung loosely from her neck. "He saved me from a life of sanitised boredom with my parents. They expected me to go live with them after university, to settle down in their terraced house, and be the good daughter." She looked sad as the thoughts took her away in the gentle breeze. Bereft.

"I wouldn't have had the strength to say no to them. Mum always said it was such a shock when I came along. She was always reminding me how much they had given up in order to keep me at school, and it's true, they did. The weekend work and paper rounds did help towards paying for the food though."

Charlie was confused and stared intently at Michelle until she picked up her gaze. "You mean you went out to work in your free time to earn your keep? You didn't use it for your spending money?" Charlie knew her face was showing frown lines as her brow furrowed in displeasure.

Michelle shook her head in reply, as it began to drop in a defeatist attitude. She was staring at the table. "Martin didn't like the idea either. I would have gone back to them if he hadn't come into my life because I felt so guilty. He was strong on my behalf and I loved him for it. He told my parents, in no uncertain terms, there was no way I was going back to live with them because we were getting married. He hadn't even proposed to me." She drained the last of her coffee and uplifted her eyes to ask Charlie to refill the cup.

Charlie obliged. "Cream?"

Michelle nodded. After a long moment of contemplation, she tore viciously at the cross and snapped the chain in two. The cross lay in her open hand as the chain links dripped from the side.

"Now he's probably done all those horrendous things, and for all we know, he's trying to kill us, too. He thought we were going to be in your house, didn't he?" she asked with a definite tremor in her voice, her hand shaking as anger seethed within her.

Charlie nodded her head in affirmation.

"If he does anything to cause harm to you, Charlie, I'll kill him myself." She stood quickly, raised her arm above and behind her head, then swung it with all her might, launching the cross and chain as far as she could towards the beach. It landed in the bushes that shielded their view. She flopped into her chair, breathing heavily as she recovered from her fit of pique and the physical effort.

"We are not even going to go there, Michelle. We are going to have a day trying to relax and enjoy the pool and this beautiful weather. Later, perhaps we can work out this awful bloody mess."

Charlie was pleased by Michelle's comment of killing Martin herself, but let it go unmentioned as she poured a little more cream into her own coffee cup. She didn't want Michelle to get the impression she was attaching too much importance to what could have been a throwaway comment. She picked up Michelle's mobile from the table, eyeing the screen.

"I gather you've had your phone on silent. You've had some missed calls. Have you checked the numbers?"

"Yes, and I don't know who they belong to, so I'm not phoning them back."

Charlie nodded in agreement. "I am going to have to get in touch with Uncle Lenny and Gavin to see what's going on in England. I'll give them both a ring, and then we can move to the pool and take in some of these wonderful rays. I didn't expect it to be so warm or sunny this time of year." Charlie began to drink her coffee with a smile.

"Give my love to both of them when you speak to them, will you, Charlie? They have both been so kind and supportive. I don't know either of them really. I've never even met Gavin. If it hadn't been for you and them, I would have been in this mess on my own..." Her voice trailed off and Charlie knew her mind was replaying old memories and new scenarios.

Charlie felt guilty about Michelle and Gavin. Michelle would be horrified if she'd known how much Gavin had been against this plan—and the others too if she were honest. She couldn't control what Gavin thought, or Poppy or her uncle. She had to do what she thought was right. They could either support her decision or not.

Her gaze lingered on Michelle as she sat in the chair at the side of the patio table, a vision in her light blue bikini. The memory of the kiss from the beach came flooding into her mind, starting up the familiar tingling warmth inside her sexual core. What she really wanted to do now—this instant—was to take Michelle's head between her hands and kiss her—strongly and deeply. A kiss conveying how she felt about her, the depth of the love she was feeling, even though their acquaintance had so far been brief. It didn't matter to Charlie how long. It was just the way it was.

Instead, she banished the thought from her mind, picked up her mobile and coffee cup, and then walked inside, leaving Michelle nibbling at the food, drinking her coffee and staring aimlessly at the water in the swimming pool.

**

"HI UNCLE LENNY. It's Charlie." Charlie took a sip of coffee, knowing a long conversation was about to ensue, needing to keep her drying throat lubricated.

"Charlie. It's so good to hear from you. How are you and Michelle managing?"

"We are fine, thank you. We've found a lovely hotel, and the staff, so far, have been very obliging."

"Hotel? What happened to the camping idea?"

"It's a long story, Uncle Lenny. Suffice to say, it didn't pan out. How are you?"

"Gavin and I are just fine."

Charlie felt her face flush a little when she heard Gavin's name mentioned. "Gavin is staying with you?" she asked cheerily—although, for some reason, she did not feel at ease knowing. It seemed strange for him to involve someone else so closely, when he was normally such a private, guarded person.

"Yes, well, it seemed to make sense. We didn't want Martin to divide and conquer. This way someone can be awake at all times. I also have a protection team outside and my shotgun inside. I won't be frightened to use it either, should Martin Bailey come for a visit." Charlie could tell he had resolve in his voice.

Suddenly, Charlie was overcome with guilt. At the end of all this was her uncle going to be facing a murder charge? There had been reports in the news where homeowners had defended their homes and families and paid the price of prison for the culprit dying. She was not sure her uncle could do it. He would wave his shotgun, she was sure, hoping it would be enough of a deterrent, but actually pull the trigger—she doubted it and sighed with relief. He couldn't even do it to birds on a shoot. Her uncle was a gentle soul and she wanted him to remain as such. For the first time, she was glad Martin was in France.

"What other news is there?" Charlie asked, hoping to change the subject.

"Martin, it would seem, is somewhere in France. They have circumstantial evidence linking him to both the incident at Bambers and at your house, so be careful." Strain was beginning to show in her uncle's voice. "The police want you to go to a police station and hand yourselves into protective custody. They want you to come back here so they can use you as bait!" Charlie heard fury in his voice, which she had only heard one other time—after her kidnapping. He had been furious with Charlie's parents for not paying the ransom. She didn't think he had ever fully forgiven them.

"We know he's here, Uncle Lenny because he sent us a text message this morning from Cavalaire, but we haven't heard anything since. We knew the police would catch up with us at some stage. We just complicated the situation for them being in another country."

"I don't care how much of a complication it is, you stay there, and you keep your heads down. Leave it until the maniac is behind bars before you do anything, please, Charlie. It's not I don't trust the police. It's just sometimes circumstances move faster than they do. I don't want anything happening to you. I didn't then, and I don't know now." Charlie was sure she heard a tremor in his voice as he tried to keep his emotions in check. "I…" She heard the phone land with a bang on something solid.

The next voice she heard was Gavin on the other end. "Hi, Charlie. It's me."

"Hi, Gav. Is Uncle Lenny okay?" Charlie wiped a thin layer of perspiration from her brow.

"Yes, he's gone for a cigar to help him calm down. He's very worried about you, Charlie. You know he thinks of you like the daughter he never had. He's such a lovely man. So warm and caring. No wonder you think so highly of him." Gavin's voice sounded normal. No affectation, just normal. Something Charlie hadn't heard in a while. She wondered what had made him so calm.

"So, you're holed up with my uncle then? Are you looking after one another?"

"Yes, we are eating right and getting some sleep. It's in chunks of two and three hours. It's not ideal, but it's working for now. He's worried sick for you and Michelle."

"Tell him not to worry and tonight, make sure you both go to bed. Martin is here so you have a night free of worry. Even Superman would be hard pressed to get back there tonight. Is there anything else you can think of that we need to know?"

"Lenny has put some discreet security at your mum and dad's place, and Jessica's too, just in case. Poppy is up with an aunt with an unpronounceable name in North Wales. By the way, you have some explaining to do when you get home, madam. Richer than Croesus and working at Bamber and Brooks. I shall want explanations, young lady!" Charlie smiled at the thought of one of Gavin's diva performances, arms flying in all directions when he was told the news of her wealth. Her uncle obviously hadn't realised she still had some secrets.

She was glad they both had some support though and that her family was also being looked after and Poppy was safe. It was a little less worry for her.

By the end of her conversation with Gavin, a single tear was running down Charlie's cheek. She suddenly felt very alone.

CHAPTER THIRTY

THE WATER IN the pool felt cool against Charlie's skin. She was drifting on her back, eyes closed, allowing the sun to paint the inside of her eyelids pink while she tried to drift away into nothingness. She felt light as air as the water supported her weight, and she could feel the tension ebbing from her body. Had it not been for the predicament they were in, it would have been heavenly.

Charlie opened one eye and glanced around. From the surface of the water, her view was perfect, creating an optical illusion—the pool was an extension of the sea and the sky and gave Charlie the feeling she could drift in perpetuity. Just what she needed to calm her mind and clear the bad thoughts nagging away—tugging—unrelenting. She made a mental note to have a word at reception and ask them to stay vigilant, because as sure as eggs were eggs, Martin would have no problem tracking them down now they had decided not to hide away.

Hiding had done them no good. While Michelle was intent on keeping her parents in the picture, they didn't really stand a chance. She had checked the display every time it rang, checking to see if it was her parent's number, but she hadn't answered it once. However, you could never anticipate the parental tug. It was too much of a personal experience. Michelle thought of her parents all the time, even though they hadn't been at all kind, it would seem. Making your child work to pay for her own keep. It was very cruel. To endow a child with so much guilt, just for existing, was unforgivable.

Charlie's parents rarely crossed her mind. The thought saddened her, but she doubted it saddened them much. Perhaps they had used up all their emotions during her kidnapping, although if she were honest, she didn't have much of a relationship before the event. Charlie could never work out when it happened or how it happened—she only knew it had. They hadn't even broken stride when she told them she was gay. Her sister was still very close to her parents, and she envied her a little, but not much. Charlie had always felt like an alien in their environment. She had learned to distance herself from all of them, except Uncle Lenny. She still loved him more than words could say.

Charlie's thoughts were interrupted. At first, she thought they must have been having a shower of rain as she felt one or two spots of water touch her face. Then suddenly she was hit with what seemed like a wall of water that completely covered her face and chest. The shock of the cool water where the sun's rays had previously been made her eyes fly open— half choking on the rivulet that had made its way up her nose and down the back of her throat. She tracked down the source of the interruption.

Michelle was stood beside her, up to her shoulders in water, ready for the next onslaught. Both her hands shot out in front of her, palms facing Charlie, as she pushed the surface of the pool. A great wave covered Charlie. She was slow to react and was only just in the position of lowering her feet to the floor of the pool. The cool water covered all her warm flesh, went up her nose, in her ears and in her eyes. She sucked in her breath and then blew it out in a splutter.

"You will pay for that!" said Charlie in a nasally diatribe as she shook her head trying to clear her ears.

Michelle laughed loudly as she waited for the reaction. "Just as I suspected...all southern yap and no bottle," she said in an accent worthy of a true Geordie, trying desperately to provoke a reaction. Pretty soon, she got one. Charlie leaned forward, grabbed her by one wrist, and reached down to grab hold of the nearest calf. Charlie half lifted before ducking down and getting her full body below Michelle's, then springing upwards from the bottom of the pool lifting Michelle clean out the water— throwing her as far as she could manage across the pool. She had heard a squeal of delight before Michelle hit the water sending spray and wash everywhere.

Michelle surfaced, water dripping down her face, which she quickly pushed away, taking her hair with it. For the first time, Charlie got a good look at Michelle's face, without sunglasses or hair impeding it. Charlie thought she was perfect—even though the bruises were still evident. The swelling of the eye had receded. It looked as though the initial ice treatment had worked—although the bruise was now turning yellowy pink. The lip had lost its scab, but the deep coloured welts around the neck looked as though they were fading a little less quickly, showing more direct pressure had been applied, rather than a glancing blow.

Michelle's breasts had bite marks and bruising, although they didn't appear to be very deep and were healing well. Charlie had been shocked when she saw Michelle's legs when she came to get in the pool. She hadn't been privy to seeing those before. Large areas of rainbow colours running from just above her knee to the top of her inner thigh.

Each new bruise she saw, the more her gut reacted. She wanted to harm Martin. What she really hated more than anything was the fact Martin was making her something she truly wasn't...a believer in violence. She didn't even harbour those kinds of feelings towards the two men who had kidnapped and held her prisoner.

Charlie laughed aloud as she saw Michelle approaching for the next attack, twisting her shoulders to propel her legs through the deep water. As soon as she was within reach, Charlie brought her hand out of the water and threw a handful straight in Michelle's face. "Oi! It was my turn!"

"Turn? Turn? I wasn't aware there were any rules about water fighting. Every woman for herself," and with a flick of her hair, Charlie launched herself out of the water to catch Michelle square on the shoulders, pushing her down and giving her a quick dunk.

Before Michelle could recover, Charlie had swum to the side of the pool, hauled herself out, and was sitting under the white and yellow sunshade. "Fancy a drink, shorty?" she asked as Michelle stood in the middle of the pool, water dripping with her head tilted questioningly to one side.

Champagne, thought Charlie.

***

THE VEUVE CLICQUOT, La Grande Dame, had arrived chilled to perfection to the small dining table on the terrace, the elegant dark shaped neck sticking out of the top of the silver ice bucket. Michelle and Charlie, now covered in their beach top and shorts, their bikinis draped over the backs of the other two chairs.

"I'm pooped," said Michelle, half closing her eyes and stifling a yawn, head tilted to one side. She looked relaxed and was beginning to pick up a tan from their time spent in the water. Her skin glistened with a deepening olive glow. The sight of the smooth skin and the tops of the full breasts peeking out of Michelle's top brought a surge of desire to Charlie, the now familiar tingling beginning between her legs. It would soon begin the pulse. She wasn't sure how long she could contain herself. The wanting was becoming harder to endure.

"Then you will have no chance keeping awake after you've had some of this," remarked Charlie, passing her a flute, three-quarters full of the champagne, the barely coloured liquid issuing its unrelenting fizz.

"I will do my best. No point leaving all of it to you. We are in this together—remember? Everything—including the good stuff. " Michelle lifted her glass in a toast and Charlie leaned forward and clinked her glass with Michelle's glass.

"To survival," said Charlie, looking deep into Michelle's eyes.

Michelle answered with, "To us and thank you," as she drank through the hum in her throat. "This is absolutely delicious, Charlie." Her face was picture perfect in its smile. "You're not trying to get me drunk again, are you?"

"Would you care if I were?" she inquired as she began to quaff the cold champagne.

"Not in the slightest." Michelle looked directly into Charlie's eyes as if she were trying to discover some hidden agenda. "But you don't have to, you know."

Charlie was caught off-guard by the remark, and decided to use levity to ease the tension she was beginning to feel, caused by the slight warming sensation of her lower lips. Her toes began to curl upwards...always a bad sign if she was trying to avoid having a sexual encounter. Thoughtlessly, she ran her fingers down the seam of her shorts.

"You mean I could have gone down the liquor store and got a bottle of cider, instead?" Charlie's eyes narrowed and her lids became hooded with desire. "You should have told me."

Michelle roared with laughter, shaking her head from side to side, as she leaned forward and grabbed Charlie's forearm. "You really are the best friend anyone could have, Charlie."

The statement killed Charlie's amorous thoughts—stone dead! She and Michelle were not in the same mode of thought. "Tell me I'm a friend when all this mess is over."

"I don't need to wait. I can tell you now. I don't know anyone, other than my family, and not even most of those, who would have done for me what you have. You are the sweetest, kindest, most considerate person I have ever known." Michelle took a mouthful of champagne and rinsed it round her mouth as she made a humming noise. As she swallowed, she put her glass on the table, leaned back, and closed her eyes.

Charlie knew she was deeply in trouble. She was awash with raw emotion. She wanted this woman more than words could say, but she didn't want Michelle to capitulate because of gratitude or drink. She wanted Michelle to want her because of love, and she wasn't sure if it would ever happen.

The thought saddened her and she tried to swallow the lump of emotion tempting to come to her throat. Gavin's wise words came back to her...*Keep away from married women. They are bad news!* Charlie wasn't sure Michelle would get involved with her romantically no matter how much she flirted and teased. Charlie had a feeling she was doing it because she thought it might bolster Charlie's ego. She couldn't know how much it ripped Charlie apart each time there was any kind of physical contact. She was merely grateful for Charlie's help.

The temptation might be there for a quick roll in the hay, but the awkwardness it would bring would be self-defeating. They both needed to be aware and on their guard as much as possible—not distracted by feelings of guilt or self-loathing, and those were both possible, for both of them. Charlie looked at the glass of champagne in her hand and wondered now if drinking was a good idea. She took a long pull on the liquid and smiled as the bubbles danced on her tongue and excited her taste buds.

What the hell. She needed it.

***

As Charlie walked through the corridor towards the reception, she glanced through the windows admiring the mature palm trees as the top leaves wavered in the slight breeze. She considered the sights they must have seen over the years, reflecting on how badly some people with an endless supply of money could behave. She had seen some awful things happen in the guise of high spirits and playfulness, and she had wanted none of it. Gone were the days of watching people throw up from too much drink, and sometimes, even in a state of collapse because of illegal substances.

Hearing bad words coming from people's mouths, only to be denied later when the reality of sobriety kicked in, just made her angry. It had taken her a long time to get from there to here, and although things could be better, she wouldn't change it for anything.

She hoped later she wouldn't hit the deck with a big bang, but it was a chance she was willing to take. She'd had her heart rule her head before, but nothing this strong had ever taken hold of her. It was a piece of heaven created by the devil. Now she had to hope it would still be there when the devil was gone.

A glance towards the outside wall brought Charlie's world crashing down around her as she caught the head and shoulders glimpse of the man she had come to loathe.

Martin Bailey was here!

Her mind went into meltdown as scenario after scenario coursed through her mind. He had found them—she knew he would. Now she had to hope the hotel security were as good as Claude believed them to be.

As Charlie neared the reception, she saw the front door begin to swing open. She quickly turned, retracing her footsteps around the corner from where she had come, not wanting to face Martin until she had a plan worked out in her mind. So, her strategy for later—scuppered.

He hadn't found them quite as quickly as she would have presumed and the thought troubled her. What had he been doing in the meanwhile? Charlie felt as though she was going to sink to her knees as a quick rush to her spine indicated she was about to succumb to a panic attack. Her legs began to tremble and her heart was now beating a tattoo in her chest. She struggled for breath as it came in short, ragged bursts. A weakness overcame her, quickly stripping her of the strength in her limbs. She put her back against the wall for support and looked skyward. She wanted to flee but couldn't.

His voice thundered down the corridor like an underground train. His anger reverberated from every wall, and Charlie was sure she could see the very expensive light fitting vibrating as the power of his voice began to escalate. She closed her eyes and wished to be anywhere but in this particular hotel at this moment in time. She felt exhausted. She knew it wasn't lack of sleep because she'd had plenty. Ergo it must be the tension.

"I want to see my wife...NOW! I know she's here. Look it up! Her name is Michelle Bailey. LOOK!" he shouted at the tiny receptionist who cowered with fear, not even a little restraint showing in his tone. "I know she's here so I suggest you phone her room and get her out here before I start smashing—up—the—place!" Yelling at the receptionist, he banged his fist hard on the desk at the end of every word.

Charlie took a quick peek around the corner, hoping and praying Martin was looking in any direction other than hers. The peek revealed he was now leaning heavily on the reception desk, the top half of his body inclined as much as possible to get closer to the receptionist. The woman was slender and could be no taller than five-foot-two. Charlie thought she looked about twelve.

"I'm sorry, monsieur. I cannot reveal the names of the patrons. It is company pol—" Her well-rehearsed patter was interrupted by the sound of the front door swishing open, the low muttering of male voices invading the air.

She heard Claude issue the opening salvo, and she again peeked round the corner, only this time she carried on watching, revealing as little of her head as possible. "Monsieur. We do not appreciate strangers coming into our hotel issuing threats and orders. Now I suggest you leave before we call the police and get you formally removed. The gendarmes will not be gentle, I assure you." Charlie thought Claude a very brave man as Martin stood at least head height above him.

Martin turned on his heel and for the first time, eyed all three of his opponents. Claude had nowhere near Martin's bulk, and Martin spent very little time surveying him. He obviously posed no threat. The same could not be said of the other two men. Although an inch or two shorter than Martin, both were equally as bulky. The thought flitted through Charlie's mind questioning if they had achieved the results of their physiques the same way. She doubted it. Martin ran his eyes slowly over each man, lingering briefly over their chests and biceps straining the material of their light blue polo shirts. Charlie was more impressed by their quadriceps as they tugged at the legs of their matching shorts.

"Why don't you two just run away and fucking play in the sandbox and leave the grown-ups to get on with business." Both men eased forward a fraction as if ready to pounce. Claude lifted his hand to indicate they should stay where they were.

Charlie braced her legs with her hands just to keep herself from falling over. She knew she had no chance of running anywhere if Martin got past the security men. Terror was ruling her emotions.

"Monsieur, I will not ask again. We will not give out guest information, so you are wasting your time here. Please leave my hotel—now!" Claude raised his voice to a level Charlie didn't think he had in him.

The receptionist grabbed for the phone, looked first at, Claude and then Martin. For the next few lingering moments, all participants could have been playing statues, everyone standing their ground. Charlie waited, still staring, not daring to take a breath. The deadlock was broken by Martin. His breath was fragmented and his voice, wavering, held contempt and anger.

"I know my wife is here. If you think your pathetic excuse for security will keep me away from her—think again. I am not leaving this fucking country without her!" As he pushed the two security men out of his path, he started muttering oaths and expletives that made Claude's face contort. The door swished closed as Claude pulled the cuffs of his shirt slightly below his jacket sleeves.

"Thank you, gentlemen. I don't think I will will need you again for a while. Please stay vigilant in the grounds and ask the rest of the teams to do the same. May I suggest one man on the gate and the others around the beach entrance?"

"Oui, Monsieur," both said in unison as they made their way out of the door.

CHAPTER THIRTY-ONE

BACK IN THE room, Charlie stared at the large glass of brandy she held in her hand. She still held the last sip she had taken in her mouth, tasting the strong flavour as it warmed. She swallowed slowly, tilting her head allowing the liquid to trace all the way to her stomach, radiating heat as it slid slowly downward. The previous sips were now doing their job of relaxing her. It had taken a long time for the panic attack to subside and for her strength to return.

"How do you feel now, Charlie? You looked like death warmed over when you came back," Michelle asked as she squatted in front of Charlie, her hands resting on Charlie's knees.

"I've just had a bit of a shock with Martin turning up out of the blue. Scared the living daylights out of me, even though I was half expecting it." Michelle began rubbing Charlie's knees.

"We need to come up with some kind of plan, Charlie. We can't keep running, although it does seem like a good option right now." Michelle stopped stroking but kept her hands in place and stared at Charlie intently. Charlie could feel the heat spreading up her legs towards her crotch. She could feel her concentration slipping as the fingers of her left hand glided down the seams of her leisure trousers.

"I doubt whether we could get out of France now. The police in England should have dragged the French into it by now. I doubt whether we would get past their borders without being held for questioning at the very least." Charlie felt downcast, her head hung low. The emotional rollercoaster was beginning to take its toll on her. Tears were not far away. In a rare moment of anguish, she could feel her mind considering their situation hopeless. The idea did not sit easy with her.

"Any ideas welcome. About now would be good…" Ideas were as rare as rocking-horse droppings.

"When the manager comes calling, and he will, we will have to play dumb. We need him to believe we didn't know Martin's behaviour would be so atrocious. We only thought he would come enquiring might be the way to play it. If he realises for a moment how bad Martin's behaviour can be, he will ask us to leave, Charlie, and I for one am not ready to go yet." Michelle's face held a rueful look, but at the same time, her eyes were showing fear.

"I think by the look of your bruises he may already suspect how bad Martin can be."

Michelle nodded in acceptance. "Now, to change the subject, may I suggest dinner in the restaurant, surrounded by as many people as we can find. I do believe you have a top you promised to wear. We shall have to hope the security is as good as you said they looked."

Charlie phoned reception to book a table for dinner, greeted by the familiar tones of Claude on the line. Before she could say a word, Claude began to speak. "Am I speaking with Ms Reinette?" His tone sounded serious.

"Yes, Claude, this is Ms Reinette." Michelle stopped her task of assembling her outfit for dinner on the bed and looked up at the mention of Claude's name.

"Miss Reinette, I wonder if I may come to your room so I may speak to you and Mrs Bailey on a very important matter." Claude's voice held a grim determination, which Charlie knew she wouldn't be able to sidestep.

"Yes, of course, Claude. Come along when you're ready."

"Thank you, madam. I shall be with you shortly."

The gentle tap on the door made them both jump, although they had been expecting it. Waiting for Claude's visit had made Charlie's nerves fray as she continually looked at the clock. Fifteen minutes they had waited. Michelle just continued to get ready for dinner although the fear was showing in her eyes as they darted around the room at any little noise. The television being turned up loud in the next suite had nearly sent her into a meltdown as she clutched her hands to her breast. "Jesus Christ! I don't think there was any need for that," she said as daggers from her eyes flew in the direction of the adjoining suite. Michelle was jumpy—no doubt about it.

Claude's voice called her name quietly from behind the door. "Ms Reinette. It is Claude. Madam, are you there?"

"Yes, coming, Claude," called Charlie. She was trying to sound as calm as her voice would allow. As she rose from the chair, she looked at Michelle, who sat on the end of the bed. She put out both hands palms down patting the air, indicating for Michelle to stay calm so they could appear united in their acting performance.

Charlie opened the door with a smile and brushed her arm towards the room. "Come in, Claude," she said as she followed him into the room, "What can we do for you?" she asked, wide eyes open and enquiring.

"I have some unpleasant news that I must pass on, Mesdames," he turned to face Michelle, lips pursed and hands clasped together in front of him. Charlie felt as though she was standing in front of the headmaster, ready to face his wrath. "Your husband made a visit this afternoon, madam. He was not..." he began but broke his sentence with a manufactured cough emanating from his throat, "happy."

Charlie was expecting him to ask them to leave, but was surprised by his reaction.

"This hotel does not like being held to ransom and his demands, when met with the hotel resolve, resulted in—threats. I have spoken to the manager this evening on the matter, just to clarify our position. We will protect you to the best of our ability, madam, given the limited resources we have. We shall concentrate our efforts around the perimeter of the hotel and also around your room, especially during the night. I can appreciate how much in danger you must feel. It cannot feel good, and I am sorry you have to go through this terrible experience."

Charlie could have cried. Michelle did. Both of them breathed a sigh of relief in unison.

"However," he said, as Charlie got an instantaneous sinking feeling, "we would advise you to speak with the police. He does seem a dangerous man." He shot a look from one to the other, as though expecting some answer to his suggestion.

It was Michelle who spoke first, as she dried her tears on a tissue. "I'm sorry, Claude. It's just not an option at the moment, for reasons we can't explain. I'm truly sorry."

A trace of understanding crossed his face, and he nodded his head in reluctant acceptance. "Very well, madam, but you must understand, should the hotel suffer any damage or loss, we must involve the gendarmes. This is, I'm afraid, hotel policy, as is the payment for any damages. I am sorry."

Charlie jumped in before Michelle could answer. "Of course, Claude. I understand completely and accept responsibility although we hope that no further visits are forthcoming. I'd like to take this opportunity to thank you for your help and the protection of the hotel." Charlie went to her bag and retrieved a yellow two hundred euro note. She passed the note to Claude, who clenched it in his hand.

"Merci, madam. Rest assured we will do our utmost."

"Thank you, Claude, much appreciated. Could you book us in for dinner when you return to reception, please?"

"Why, of course, madam. It would be a pleasure. Would eight o'clock be satisfactory?" The ironed smile was back.

Charlie smiled and nodded.

***

THE RESTAURANT WAS a large, low room annexed on the west side of the hotel, the wall opposite the entrance discreetly housing heated units Charlie suspected were used at breakfast time or for carvery meals. The area was hardly visible at this time of evening, the lighting for the room coming mainly from the low-level wattage of the wall lights and the candles lighting each occupied table, giving the patrons eating a sensuous glow.

"I love they've used candles," remarked Michelle as they followed the waiter to their table. He looked magnificent in his stiff, high-winged collar and black eveningwear.

There was only a handful of diners and Charlie noticed none of them turned to stare as they were shown to their table. Another habit of people who used expensive hotels. They minded their own business and expected the same courtesy from others. The waiter pulled out each chair so they could sit and flicked out their swan-shaped napkins and placed them on their laps. A moment later, he handed out menus without saying a word and then faded into the background, allowing them time to take in the ambiance and to decide on their food before ordering their accompanying drinks.

"Would you like me to order?" Charlie asked, not sure whether Michelle had even seen a menu so complicated. "Given you picked the Pan Bagnat, I think it's my turn..." Charlie tilted her head to one side and her face broke into a broad smile. She felt a slight tap on her shins as Michelle kicked out.

"You behave yourself. Showing off in your new top. I must say, you look stunning." Michelle looked very pleased with herself, her eyes sparkling in the candle's glow, eyes focused solely on Charlie. "Yes, I would be honoured if you would order. Thank you." Her smile was warm and admiring. "The burnt orange colour really suits you, Charlie. Have I mentioned it?" Michelle began to giggle, but it was cut short by the approach of the waiter.

Charlie ordered quickly. "Chicken Liver Pate and Fruit de Mer for both of us, merci. Just one bottle of wine, I think." Michelle nodded in agreement. "Would you ask the sommelier if he could choose for us? Merci." The waiter nodded and made his way to the kitchen. He was replaced a few moments later by the sommelier. He came through from an entrance opposite their table carrying an intricate metal stand and ice bucket he placed beside the table.

"I hope this will be satisfactory, mesdames," he said as he retrieved the bottle of Chablis from the ice and showed the bottle to both of them. He took a corkscrew from a holder at the side of the stand and removed the cork with a loud pop. He very gently poured out a small amount into Charlie's glass, which she sipped, letting out a low hum of appreciation.

"Wonderful. Thank you." The sommelier nodded, turned on his heels, and went to stand at the side of the entrance, gazing around the room, no doubt waiting for a raised hand calling for his attention.

As they tucked into their pate with wafer-thin Melba toast, they eased gently into their conversation, appreciating the large distance between the tables. Conversations would not be overheard.

"I can't believe how Claude has come through for us. I think we can safely say he's on our side." The thought warmed

Charlie, feeling as though the cloud of doom had thinned a little.

"It's because he's a romantic at heart. He thinks you ran off with me."

Charlie stopped mid-chew, mouth agape. The thought had never occurred to her.

"No. He just feels sorry for your predicament. You heard what he said." Charlie was shaking her head. She was sure Michelle was wrong in her assumption.

"Charlie, does Claude give you the impression he's efficient?" Michelle gazed into Charlie's eyes, not giving any clue as to her train of thought.

"He is efficiency personified, as far as I'm concerned, and he can be in my corner any time. Why does it make a difference?" Charlie was puzzled, but it didn't stop her eating the pate.

"We can assume he told housekeeping to come and change the king-sized bed to two singles then?"

Charlie put her hand to her mouth, nearly choking on her mouthful of pate. "I completely forgot about the bed! Why didn't you say something? I would have chased it up. It slipped my mind." Charlie could feel her face beginning to colour.

Michelle laughed a quiet laugh. "Charlie, the colour of your face is clashing with the top. Which, if I may say, was an excellent choice on my part. The contrast brings out the colour of your eyes." The laugh changed into a grin. "The point is, Claude would not forget, he just didn't make the order. He thinks you've run away with me. He thinks we are lovers."

Charlie shook her head in disagreement. Instead of carrying on the conversation, she finished her first course, wondering whether she should order more wine.

Michelle was impressed with the Fruit de Mer, her eyes widening in disbelief when she caught sight of it. The huge three-tiered dish arrived delivered by two waiters, along with small pots containing various dips and bowls containing lemon water for cleansing their fingers. The lobster, crabs, and oysters were placed on the lowest tier, interspersed and decorated using samphire, parsley and wedges of lemon. The uppermost tiers were filled with oysters, langoustines, prawns, mussels, scallops, and clams. The amount of food looked enormous. Michelle's eyes were out on stalks.

"How the heck are we supposed to eat all this food?" she asked, looking first at the food and then at Charlie. "It's never going to happen, is it?"

Charlie laughed and then looked around to see if anyone was listening. "The idea is you talk, eat, talk, and eat until it's all gone or you are too full to eat anymore. It can take hours."

"I don't want to eat all night, Charlie. At some point, I would like to go to bed and go to sleep." Michelle pushed her hair behind her ears and stared at the food—mouth agape.

"Then can I suggest you begin eating?" Charlie grabbed a langoustine and began de-shelling it on her plate. She ate with gusto.

On the return to the room, Charlie quickly released the button and zip on her black, silk slacks. She felt too full. "I hope I'm not going to be sick. I shouldn't have eaten that last oyster."

Michelle rubbed her stomach. "I was full an hour ago. I don't know why I carried on eating, other than it tasted so good. Thank you, Charlie. It was wonderful."

"You're welcome, but tomorrow, it's a pizza from room service." Charlie turned on her heels and flopped down heavily onto her back on the bed, made a cross with her arms, and left her feet on the floor. "I don't want to move. I could stay here forever." Charlie closed her eyes as she felt her body being enfolded by the mattress.

"I hate to burst your bubble, but we have to talk, Charlie. The problem is Martin is still rearing his ugly head."

"I know, Michelle, but I just need to rest for a while. I think the Martin discussion will be better once we have had a good night's sleep and a hearty breakfast."

Michelle groaned loudly. "How can you think of food now? I feel as though I'm about to burst."

Charlie smiled as she continued to stare at the ceiling. "It's because I'm English, and I'm always thinking about a good breakfast. A nice, greasy fry up…"

Michelle's aim from the other side of the bed was true as the pillow hit Charlie full on the side of the head. "What did I tell you about food? Stop talking about it!"

Charlie sat up and began to laugh. She turned to Michelle, her eyes twinkling with defiance. "Now there's something new to add to the list. 'Michelle Bailey has a short fuse and is prone to episodes of violence.' Not a very nice trait, shorty."

"It is not violence, merely playfulness." To reinforce the point she tipped her head to one side and painted her face with a false smile. "Now, would you like the bathroom first, or shall I, before you start pushing any more of my buttons?"

Charlie's mind and eyes immediately flew to Michelle's breasts, which at the moment were encased in pink, silky, lacy material underneath an extremely attractive pink summer dress. *Now there are a couple of buttons underneath there I would like to press.* As she battled with her inner voice, the only thing she could come up with was, "I'm okay. You go right ahead."

Coward!

CHAPTER THIRTY-TWO

SITUATED ON THE outskirts of Newcastle, the building's edifice was radiant. Ironically, it housed a suspicious person of interest—Bettinger. It would seem that Bettinger was not only Martin Bailey's employer, but also a friend and ally, and this was his lair. Winter gazed at its art deco style frontage and turned to survey its setting. Green fields and an occasional clump of trees rather than the built-up areas of the city centre. He despised the desperate city of Newcastle and the frenetic road crossings, but this building stood apart from the melee.

Once inside, the reception area was more than acceptable with its high glass frontage and its partial ceiling suspended in seemingly thin air. He found himself nodding in appreciation and Abraham stared at him—bemused. "Have you had a thought, sir? You seem to be nodding at something."

"Only the building, Abraham. Don't you find it relaxing being in such a space? I envy the workers here." He continued to look around the room—still nodding

"I doubt whether the workers would agree with you, sir. To most people, the place they work is just a building. A place they go to, do eight hours and go home again." Abraham looked at his watch. "I wonder where our Mr Bettinger is. It's a quarter past ten already. An hour and a bloody half waiting for him, albeit in the car." Abraham rose to his feet and looked at the door as if this action would shorten their wait. His lanky frame held on to his blue suit—but only just. Winter noticed, although his shoes were shined, they were not as shiny as Paul Brett's were.

"Abraham, sit down! Your staring at the door is not going to make him rush his coffee. Long gone are the days when someone told our Mr Bettinger what to do. If ever, in fact." Winter smiled a knowing smile and began looking once again at the architecture. "Patience, man, patience."

DC Abraham flopped into the chair like a teenager who had been refused a top up on his allowance. The receptionist glanced over and smiled at the display given by the young detective constable, who looked as though he still belonged in a school uniform.

Obviously used to waiting for her boss to arrive, thought Winter. *You should join the police force if you want more practice.*

The almost silent whoosh of the automatic door caught both the policemen's attention at the same time. As they turned to look, they were faced with the approaching figure of who Winter assumed was Damien Bettinger. A small, elegantly dressed man holding a slim briefcase was nothing like the picture Winter held in his head. They both stood. The receptionist sat up to her full height, and Winter realised that both he and Abraham were at attention also. The air was thick with power. Bettinger's power.

"Ah, the police, I assume," he said, a smile appearing from nowhere now fixed on his face. "Angela, could you arrange coffee for three in the conference room, please..." The receptionist nodded at his request. "And if you gentlemen would like to follow me, we shall find somewhere comfortable for our discussion," he said, showing his back to Winter and Abraham. Winter was not amused. Abraham cleared his throat—noisily.

***

NOW THIS IS what I call a conference room, Winter thought as he looked appreciatively around the room. The high ceiling was the main feature, taken up to the second floor to allow spotlights to be equidistantly spread—embedded into the walls. The windows were the same size as the reception area, but heavy dark blue drapes were folded neatly between each one to allow the area to be turned into a blackout room, although why it would be needed he couldn't imagine. The room did have a spectacular array of home cinema equipment, but blackout—a little over the top.

However, he didn't appreciate Bettinger. He thought he was a smarmy toe-rag who needed a boot up the backside, but he realised his attitude wasn't going to get him very far. If they wanted Bettinger's cooperation, then they were going to have to work for it. Winter glanced at Abraham and hoped 'the look' would convey what he needed him to do. Right on cue, Abraham reached into his pocket and retrieved his notebook.

"Gentlemen," said Bettinger, clicking open his briefcase, "you have me at a disadvantage."

Abraham approached the table in front of the plush, light blue chairs that formed an arc around it. Abraham gave a look of feeling small and isolated in this position. Winter realised this was exactly what Bettinger wanted—the upper hand.

"I'm DCI Winter from Walden police and this is DC Abraham." They both held up their warrant cards together. Bettinger took first Abraham's then Winter's. Winter bristled inside. He didn't understand why this small gesture made him angry. It just did.

"Ah, DC Abraham. I remember you calling yesterday. I apologise for not being able to spend more time answering your questions. I had an important meeting to attend."

Abraham smiled. "There I thought you were late for your round of golf, sir."

Winter could have slapped Abraham on the back in congratulations. Instead, he spoke to Bettinger. "Well, I hope you have time now, sir. We need information in a murder enquiry and also an arson enquiry, and they need to be dealt with now. It's very important we locate Martin Bailey. Yesterday would have been better."

Bettinger looked very uncomfortable and loosened the top button on his pristine white shirt.

"There must be some mistake. I can't see Martin having any involvement with something so unthinkable. Just lately, he has been showing some signs of stress, but murder? I just can't see it. There must be some mistake—there must be." Bettinger shook his head.

Winter stared at Bettinger, who did look genuinely shocked at the prospect of his employee and probably a friend, being involved in something so heinous. "Could you fill us in on a little background information, Mr Bettinger, regarding Martin Bailey's employment? Plus any other information you may hold. DC Abraham got the impression you may be friends with Mr Bailey."

Abraham was just nodding in agreement when the door was opened by a middle-aged lady dressed as a maid, complete with frilled cap and white apron, pushing a tea trolley bearing a large cafetiere, cups, saucers, milk jug and sugar basin. Winter could see a look of relief pass across Bettinger's face as he began to stride down the room towards her. *Distraction won't make the task any easier*, thought Winter. *Time to spill your guts, Mr Bettinger.*

Once they were all seated around the table, cups of coffee at the ready, Abraham placed his notebook and pen in front of him, hoping it would give Bettinger the hint it was time to talk. He squirmed in his chair and began fingering the collar of his shirt. "Now, gentlemen. I'll start at the beginning, and then you'll know everything I know. After I've given you this information, I won't be able to help you further. I have a business to run, and I can't keep taking huge amounts of time away from clients. Apart from which, I will have to find cover for Martin temporarily."

Winter, not wanting to give Bettinger the chance to make up the rules, answered straight away. "We'll see, Mr Bettinger. Now, if you would be so kind..."

Bettinger took a gulp of his coffee. "Martin came to work for my father directly after he had finished university. We'd had the nod from one of the professors Martin would be an asset to the company. He knew computers like the back of his hand—an extremely bright young man. He started at the bottom with programming, in his spare time inventing new business software, which he was only too pleased to share with us. Needless to say, he didn't stay at the bottom of the ladder very long. He was promoted within a matter of months."

During the disclosure, Winter noted Bettinger was staring at the table, as though reliving past moments he shared with Martin Bailey. He continued. "Over the years though, he seemed to get a little distracted with the job. We tempted him with bonuses and more money than we probably should have, but we were a growing company and a lot of the growth was due to Martin's input."

Abraham interrupted. "So why did he stay then if he was so unhappy with the job? I think if it had been me, I would have been away on my toes. Just find a job with more challenges."

"I think he would have if it hadn't been for Michelle. She was a Geordie through and through, despite her lack of accent now. Martin arranged for elocution lessons for her. He said people could be biased where accents were concerned." Bettinger played once again with his shirt collar—allowing himself thinking time.

"Martin had issues with her parents though. He believed they had planned to have Michelle late in life so they would have someone to care for them in their dotage. Also, because they were elderly, she wanted to stay close. He wasn't happy about her parent's influence. However, whatever Michelle wanted, she got. I for one am grateful for his thoughtfulness towards her. Our company was not in a good place when Martin joined us—now it is." He drained the last of the coffee from his cup. "Along the way, it has also made Martin quite a wealthy man. I don't think Michelle knows though. She thinks he's just on a salary the same as everyone else. He always said it would be a nice surprise for her when they retired, which he planned to do at fifty."

"So what did this work entail over the years, Mr Bettinger?" said Winter, cringing at the bitterness of the coffee.

"Programming, installation, integration of systems for large companies, corporations, and governments both here and abroad. There was no job too big for Martin. He was diligent and reliable—just what you need in a worker. Plus, Michelle was always supportive of him. Never once did I hear her say, she wished he wasn't travelling abroad or that he was spending too much time at work. She was very gracious. My wife and I are very fond of her. We were sorry to see them both leave Newcastle."

"So you knew her well too, then?" asked Abraham, as he looked up from his notebook.

"My wife and I spent time with them both at social events—family birthdays and Christmas. We didn't have children either, so we sort of gravitated to one another. Martin and I are also members of the same golf club and over the years, we acquired the same group of friends. It just seemed to happen coincidentally." Bettinger suddenly looked haggard, as though the seriousness of the situation had suddenly hit home.

Winter decided to turn the screw a little tighter. "What prompted the move to Walden then? Michelle didn't want to leave her parents and Martin didn't want to leave her—yet they both left Newcastle. Why?"

"Martin had a run-in with one of his clients. Actually, our best client. He had a meeting in London with Mr Yamamoto of BRC Honshu. Things got a little heated, and Mr Yamamoto swears Martin pushed him. Martin said he only got hold of his arm to emphasise the importance of a point. I'm inclined to believe Martin. If Martin had pushed him, they would still be digging Mr Yamamoto out of the wall." Bettinger smiled a hollow smile. He knew things were beginning to look bad for Martin Bailey—and it showed.

Winter maintained the pressure. "When did you last speak to Martin, Mr Bettinger?"

"Last Friday morning. A group of us were supposed to meet up at a spa in the Midlands. We'd planned a golfing weekend, but Martin never showed up. I tried to reach him on Friday evening, but his mobile kept going to voicemail and there was no answer on his landline." Bettinger began to play with the collar of his shirt again. His pressure release.

"Have you tried to reach him since you spoke to DC Abraham yesterday?"

"Yes, but he didn't answer. I tried his number a few times. Don't forget, Inspector, he has one of our company cars. If he's walked off the job, I need it back." Bettinger sounded very angry, as though someone had stolen his most treasured toy.

"And as a friend, of course, you would have told him the police were looking for him and to go to the nearest police station and make them aware of who he was." Winter lifted his eyebrows to emphasise the point. "We need him to know, Mr Bettinger. Do you understand?" Winter began a staring contest.

Bettinger was only too happy to oblige and stared straight back. "Yes, of course, Inspector."

Abraham ceased writing, and much to Winter's surprise, he began to speak. "Before we go, I'd just like to ask you a question, Mr Bettinger. Do you know if there were any instances of domestic violence in the Bailey household?" Winter was impressed with his Detective Constable and smiled inwardly.

"Definitely not! Martin would never do such a thing. I know him. Although he has a bit of a short fuse, and more so just recently, he would never hurt Michelle. I have never seen two people more suited and they absolutely adore each other. I just couldn't see Martin doing anything so vile. It's just unthinkable!"

"Well, it looks as though someone has used her face as a punching bag, so I thought I'd ask."

"It can only be someone else or an accident maybe." But there was doubt shining like a beacon in Bettinger's eyes, and it's wasn't missed by either Winter or Abraham who looked at each other—recognising a breakthrough. A crack.

Winter stood and offered his hand, which Bettinger shook, limply. "Thank you, sir, for all the information. If we need anything more from you, we'll be in touch." Winter reached out and placed a business card on the table, all the time waiting for Bettinger to object to their getting in touch further.

"Should you get to speak to Mr Bailey, please ask him to visit the local police station, or contact me direct. Both my numbers are on the card. Thank you for your time, sir." Winter and Abraham gave a slight nod in unison. Bettinger responded by opening his briefcase and extracting a laptop.

A light went on in DI Winter's head. "Oh, I almost forgot, Mr Bettinger. How does Martin use his laptop from his car and what would his e-mail address be?"

Bettinger looked at Winter with contempt. "He uses PCI LAN Card and a sim card for any telecom services he needs. He also has some modifications, such as an extra battery inside the car. His e-mail address is Bailey at Comso dot mail. Now, will there be anything else?"

Winter, a tad confused on the computer lingo, looked at Abraham, who was noting the information in his notebook. He expected the younger man to at least have some idea what Bettinger was talking about. Abraham closed the notebook then looked at Winter with his eyes opened wide. Winter looked blankly at his DCI.

Winter exhaled. "No, sir, that will be all for now. Thank you again for your time."

CHAPTER THIRTY-THREE

THE TRIP BACK to Walden had proved horrendous. The M1 was littered with road works, speed restrictions, breakdowns and three lanes of bumper-to-bumper traffic. The usual Friday afternoon fare. Winter's early lunch sat uneasily in his stomach, the meat and fat grinding, trying to ease its way through his digestive system—failing miserably. Each time they hit another back up, his throat and mouth filled with stomach acid and a reminder of what he'd eaten—so he grabbed for another couple of Tums.

As Winter began to chomp on the tablets, his mobile on the consul sprang to life. "Take the call, will you, Jon. Thanks."

"DCI Winter's phone, DC Abraham speaking." The DCI could only take glances at Abraham as he ummed and ahhed in response as to what was being said. "Okay, I'll pass on the information, sir." Abraham was quiet as he ordered his thoughts.

"Yes," said Winter, the silence beginning to irritate him

"It was DI Brett, sir. The Bailey house has been trashed—totally and utterly. Not a thing in the house remains in one piece. Forensics are going to have a tough time. However, they have retrieved a petrol can from the garage and from what they are saying it smells as though it's been used fairly recently. They are trying to get an initial match."

Jon Abraham scratched his head, as though retrieving more information. "There is no record of domestic violence in the Bailey household, either here or in Newcastle. Plus nobody can find any kind of link between Bailey and Reinette previously. Oh, and Mr Stern has phoned. Apparently, he forgot to mention he was the one who booked the ferry for the two women, so we at least have the ferry information. Looks as though Bailey is our man, sir."

"I bloody well hope so, Abraham. We don't want to start all over again at this stage of the game."

"Will you phone, DI Brett back and ask him to get on to the Gendarmerie Nationale. See if they can track the movements of the car from the ferry. Thanks, Jon." A worried furrow creased Winter's brow as he took two more Tums out of the bottle.

"I don't think you are supposed to take them quite so often, sir," offered Jon Abraham

The reply, when it came, was a low growl. The rest of the journey was completed in silence.

***

AT HALF PAST four, Winter strode purposefully into the team room, not stopping to meet or greet any of his colleagues. He opened his office door and slammed it purposely behind him, walking straight to his orchidees and began stroking their leaves and caressing the flower petals.

He dropped into his chair and turned on his computer. He'd hated the trail to Newcastle because a stupid man had misplaced loyalty. He wanted to punch Bettinger's lights out, get rid of his stomach acid, and then sit down to nurse a nice large Jamaican rum. Instead, he reached into his jacket pocket and retrieved his bottle of Tums, popped the top, shook two into his palm, then put them in his mouth and crunched them between his teeth. He stared at his desk whilst waiting for his computer to come to life.

He could hear a soft murmur coming from the team room. No doubt, they were pumping Abraham for the information gathered from the trip. It would save him doing it—for the time being, anyway. Soon, he would have to go out and address a brief team meeting, once Abraham had typed up the information Bettinger had given them. He wondered how much extra help Bettinger was giving Bailey without their knowledge. No doubt, in time, all would be revealed and he would make damn sure Bettinger paid for it. The lesson would teach him not to mess around with the police. The DPP would probably want to give Bettinger a slap on the wrist. He intended to go for the jugular.

A discreet knock on the door roused him from his pensiveness. "Come in," he called, knowing full well who was on the other side.

Brett entered, holding a mug, well away from his smart, grey, three-piece suit. Light pink shirt and darker pink tie rounded off the outfit—very smart, but Winter didn't know why. "I thought you might appreciate a decent cup of tea, sir," he said, offering the mug and a smile.

"Thanks, Paul, much appreciated," replied Winter, taking it but not sure whether it would aggravate his acid attack. "How have things been going here?"

"Before I answer, I have a message for you. Can you please ring the Chief Constable's office?"

"What?" said Winter, unsure he had heard Brett correctly.

"Can you please ring the Chief Constable's office, sir? It's urgent." There was no smile on Brett's face. Winter knew he was aware of how serious the request might turn out be.

Winter was struggling with the implications. He didn't think he and his team were doing badly with the case, given the obstacles they had faced. "Okay, Paul, I'll do it now."

Brett nodded and left the room, leaving Winter to contemplate his future and the impending phone call to God.

***

THE TEAM ROOM, though busy with their enquiries and the chasing down of clues, hushed the minute Winter opened his door. Everyone now knew of the phone call and each of them had their own idea of what was going to happen. Instead of leaving his office, he popped his head around the edge of the door and called, "Brett, McCarthy, and Abraham, my office please."

The three turned and looked at each other with slightly panicked looks on their faces. Two of them knew they'd made mistakes in the case. McCarthy hadn't a clue what she had done wrong.

***

WINTER SAT BEHIND his desk, his guts growled as he made a steeple of his fingers in front of him. He contorted his face a couple of times, moving his eyebrows upwards and his lips sideways.

"It would seem someone has a direct line to the Chef Constable. He didn't say who—but I can hazard a guess. Paul, how are you fixed for taking control of the team for a few days?"

"Oh, sir, I'm really sorry if I've done anything to land you in the shit. Yes, of course, I can do it, no problem. Eva is in control at home and the twins are not causing any problems, so a few extra hours here wouldn't be a problem. How long is the suspension for? Did he specify?"

"Oh, I haven't been suspended, I've been ordered to go to the South of France. Babysitting!" Winter's face began to redden.

Brett and McCarthy looked stunned. Abraham did not.

"St Tropez, sir?" Abraham smiled as if he knew some secret Brett and McCarthy were unaware of. McCarthy wanted to put a boot up his rear.

"No, but close, Abraham. Not far from Nice."

"I just wondered because Charlotte Reinette has used her credit card to secure a hotel room in Saint Tropez. She has a platinum card." He beamed, as though he knew her personally.

Paul Brett shuffled from foot to foot and looked at Abraham. "When exactly were you going to share the news, Abraham?"

"Sorry. It only came through a couple of minutes before we were called in. The information was left overnight. I was just getting the other information from the internet." He looked suitably ashamed. McCarthy thought he was just after extra brownie points and gave a quick glare.

"So why do you want to see me and Abraham, sir?" asked Laura, barely able to keep the anger from her voice.

"Because, Laura, the Chief Constable has asked me to take a DS and a DC with me. We may need twenty-four hour cover, depending on what the French have in mind as assistance. Now, do either of you have any objections? Sick cat, shopping, piss-up down the Fleece?"

"No, sir, I don't have any plans," said Laura McCarthy, her face expressionless. Winter suspected inside, she was doing a happy dance.

"Jon, what about you?"

"Yes, sir, I can come with you. Nothing on at all." A broad grin crossed his face, and surprisingly, Winter smiled back.

DCI Winter retrieved a piece of paper from the top of his desk and glanced at it. "We are booked on British Airways flight BA2024 from Gatwick leaving just after one tomorrow afternoon. I need you to meet me at the main entrance at no later than ten-thirty. Check online for baggage allowance. I should imagine the weather will be changeable over the next few days, so bear it in mind."

Winter took a swig of his cold tea and grimaced. "I don't want either of you to think this is an easy option, you know. This man is dangerous and we have to be alert at all times."

Laura McCarthy motioned with her hand to attract Winter's attention. "Excuse me, sir, but can I just ask…are we officially on the job. It just seems a very strange assignment."

"Good question, Laura. Yes, we are officially on the job, but we have no jurisdiction. We are beholden for what the French will allow us to do—if anything. We are extra bodies if nothing else. Europol in Nice have been sent a request by the Chief Constable and he is awaiting a reply. He'll send us all the information and I'll take my portable fax machine."

Winter reached out for some more papers and cleared his throat. "Do you have anything else to ask before you go?" Both McCarthy and Abraham shook their heads. "Okay then, off you go and see you tomorrow. Any hiccups, you let me know straight away. Paul, if you could hang on a little longer, I would like to run through the operations with you for the time I am away. Overtime for this weekend has been allowed."

As they left the room, Winter gathered the information for the trip and put the loose sheets in his briefcase. He stared at the door and wondered about his companions. McCarthy was a tried and tested officer and had been in stressful situations before. He considered her more than reliable. Abraham was an unknown quantity. Eager—yes. Quick on the uptake— yes. Ability to work under stress—unknown.

Winter's guts grumbled. He had a feeling by the end of this assignment, the question of Abraham's true ability would be well and truly answered.

***

THE FAX MACHINE in the Europol office began chattering just as Florian Bissette stood and was about to put on his jacket. His mind wasn't on his job, but miles away in Chamonix where he was going to spend seven glorious days with the woman of his dreams. He had tried everything to tempt Marie to go on holiday with him in the past, but always fallen short. Now she had agreed and he couldn't wait. His heart fluttered in anticipation and he began whistling a happy tune.

When the chattering stopped, he took the sheet of paper and placed it on the edge his desk without a second glance. It would be up his replacement to deal with the requests while he sat in the sun outside the hotel with Marie and enjoyed a bottle of wine.

With a great flourish, he removed his jacket from the back of the chair creating a quick, swirling movement of air. The edge of his jacket caught the paper as Florian rushed for the door and the air lifted the sheet gracefully off the desk, wafting from side to side as it made its way to the floor. It slipped noiselessly under the drawer section of the large solid desk the fax machine sat on by the window. Out of sight from anybody in the room.

***

"VINGT-CINQ MILLE. Blanc, EDF, gare dans le parking situe a deux pas d'ci, dans la rue principale," his contact said, as he dangled the van keys in front of him.

Martin put the twenty-five thousand in euro notes on the table, and the ugly man snatched them quickly with a gnarled hand. "A pleasure doing business with you," replied

Martin, knowing full well the man could not understand a word he was saying. Martin could speak perfect French but didn't see why he should make the effort.

He pulled the keys from the man's hand and looked around the room. He couldn't see anyone else making a move in his direction, so he stood on wobbly legs and made his way through the main room to the exit.

Martin Bailey exited the bar on the back street in Marseilles, temporarily blinded by the late afternoon sun. He made his way towards the sea front and the car park where the vehicle was parked.

He whistled a tune nobody had ever heard, a collection of random notes made up in Martin's addled brain. He opened the back of the van and looked inside. Everything appeared to be there.

He sat in the driver's seat and stared vaguely in front of him. Whatever it was he'd been smoking in the back room while he was waiting for his contact had been good stuff. His head was swimming, thoughts now unconnected and random. He waited until the right one appeared in his head.

Michelle! What was he going to do? Oh, yes. He remembered. That's why he was here.

CHAPTER THIRTY-FOUR

THE SILENCE BETWEEN Michelle and Charlie was palpable. They'd had silence at dinner, too. Neither had been interested in what they'd ordered or what they'd eaten, their minds wandering, plagued by what-ifs. The week, which had intervened since Michelle's fate had been sealed, was weighing heavily on their minds. Another joyful morning by the pool had quickly trailed off into long silences and imagined slights.

Now in bed, both staring at the ceiling, both feeling lost and threatened, it was Michelle's voice that intruded into the uncomfortable dead air. "Charlie, are you awake?"

"Yes."

"Will you talk to me?"

"What about?"

"I don't know. Anything to fill this awful silence. I hate it when we are not talking. Are you thinking?"

"Of course. Don't you think I should be?"

"I'm sorry. It's all my—"

"Do not say you are sorry again. I could quite easily lose my temper at this point. This situation is what it is, and I'm trying to think of a way of getting us out of it. Everything I think of has us coming out of it in a body bag. I'll let you know when we don't!" The silence interrupted them again, uncomfortable and strained.

Again, it was Michelle who spoke first. "Why do I want us to make love?" Her voice was low, husky, and needy.

Charlie thought she had fallen asleep and was at the beginning of some erotic dream, which started with her ripping all Michelle's clothes off. She remembered the olive in Michelle's mouth and she began to feel a little warm. "I'm sorry. What did you say?"

"I said... why do I want us to make love? I understand I find you extremely attractive. I thought it would have been obvious to you by now. I like everything about you, body, mind, and soul. I feel as though I've known you forever. I understand it all, but what I don't understand is why I want us to make love. Right now, this very minute. It seems though it should be the last thing on my mind, but it's not. I'm struggling to think of anything else. Why now, Charlie?"

Charlie cleared her throat and tried in vain to get some moisture back in her mouth. She passed the tip of her tongue over her teeth, hoping her lips would stop sticking to them. "Errr, it could be because of the stressful situation. People often have the urge to make love after a death, for instance. It's a release from the stress and also helps to reaffirm life. You are probably feeling your life is being threatened, which I have no doubt it is." The last sentence made Charlie take a big swallow, bringing a huge dose of reality to her door. She realised Michelle must have been doing a lot of thinking about her. It made Charlie want to smile.

"Will you help me reaffirm my life, Charlie?"

Not waiting for Charlie to answer, Michelle sat bolt upright and began to take off the silky top of her pyjamas. She crossed her arms and took hold of the hem on each side of her top. Charlie could see the dark purple as it shimmered in the light from the lamp at the side of the television, which was illuminating the room in a subtle diffused light. "I gather from the silence that you are not going to help? You are allowed to speak, you know." Michelle's voice was low and throaty.

"I think if I speak I might wake up, and I don't want to wake up."

Michelle began to giggle and Charlie rolled onto her side so she could see the show more clearly. Michelle continued to ease the fabric upwards. As the material crumpled into the folds, Charlie gasped as the top began to slowly reveal Michelle's smooth, tanned midriff, and as it began to lift higher and higher, the dip beneath her breast revealed.

Charlie had a quick intake of breath. She could feel her breathing rate increasing, becoming deeper and more deliberate—a flush crept from her neck upwards. She knew she was blushing with acute embarrassment. She was sure she was bewitched by this beautiful woman.

At the first sight of Michelle's nipples, Charlie let out a gasp that quickly turned into a moan. A slight touch from Michelle at this moment and she would have an orgasm right there and then. The lack of self-control worried Charlie—this wasn't like her at all. Then, in one movement, the top was over Michelle's head, revealing for the first time what Charlie had been fantasising about for days. The dark brown nipples stood erect, the areola already puckered, ripe for grazing with her tongue. Charlie instinctively licked her lips, her mind choosing to ignore the after effects of Martin's violence.

"I'm new at this, so you'll have to teach me what I need to know," said Michelle, sounding almost coy in her statement.

"By the look of you, it won't be much. You are doing okay at the moment," said Charlie, breaking into a fit of the giggles. "It's a long time since I had a virgin," said Charlie, trying not to sound too cocky, although she did love to be in the driving seat, and now she had her chance. A look appeared on Michelle's face and then was gone just as quickly.

Charlie flipped over on her knees and edged across the bed towards Michelle, who was now holding the top of her pyjamas in front of her. Charlie noticed the searing look of sexual tension in Michelle's eyes—the wanting—the needing—and she let out another gasp, turning immediately into a deep, throaty growl.

"You really turn me on, and you haven't done anything yet. Michelle, I can't believe you are here with me—wanting to make love. I don't know why I'm so attracted to you, or why it happened so fast. It just did, and I'm more grateful than you will ever know."

"Circumstances have forced us together, Charlie. I don't care what the future holds, as long as we are both healthy and together. Now, am I going to get a kiss or what?" Michelle smiled and her whole face lit up, putting the lamplight to shame.

Charlie grinned, lifted her knee, and placed it on the other side of the bed, straddling Michelle's legs. She eased herself down as gently as possible, not knowing to what extent Michelle was still hurting. "If I hurt you, you need to tell me. I never want to do anything to hurt you."

Michelle nodded in affirmation as Charlie reached up with the back of her hand and gently stroked, first her cheek and then her lips. She leaned forward and began to kiss the places she had stroked, and then moved on to her forehead, then downward, covering Michelle's whole face in light, feathery kisses. When she reached her lips, they instinctively both leaned forward and the kiss, so gentle at first contact, began to have an added pressure from both of them. Michelle placed her hand on the back of Charlie's head and pulled her closer. Charlie could feel herself beginning to produce the moisture, which on previous occasions had taken an age to generate. She wanted this woman so badly it hurt.

Their lips parted in unison—Michelle started on one side of Charlie's mouth and began to gently nibble and pull on her lips, moving from one side to the other, first top, and then bottom. Charlie could not believe how erotic this simple gesture was, and she could feel it gently binding them together on a different plane. It made Charlie's head swim and her mouth produce a moan, and she realised her body would belong to this woman, now and forever.

Charlie noticed Michelle's body was beginning to shift position. At first, she thought she was hurting her, but then she realised Michelle was just trying to get closer to her. The movement made Charlie want to cry. This woman, who had been through so much physically and mentally, was willing to give her whole trust to Charlie. It filled Charlie with some kind of energy, which she just wanted to show Michelle in a physical way.

She leaned forward, took Michelle's head in her hands, and began to kiss her with urgency. Deep, fulfilling kisses and duelling tongues, touching tips and penetrating thrusts, the thrill reaching all the way down, making Charlie's toes curl. She glanced back to see the same happening to Michelle's toes. It gave her a warm feeling inside—and put a smile on her face.

Michelle looked deeply into Charlie's eyes. "I don't know about you, Charlie, but I don't work well with clothes on. What do you say we get rid of these things and get more comfortable?"

"It works for me," Charlie said, not even trying to conceal her smile. It didn't matter what this woman wanted, Charlie was prepared to give it to her. Charlie began undoing the buttons on her top when Michelle's hand reached out and stopped her.

"Let me do it for you," said Michelle, her dark eyes smouldering with passion.

"I think I may have had trouble. My hands are shaking." Charlie giggled and looked coy.

"Then it's a good thing I came to your rescue." Michelle began at the bottom and each time she undid a button, she planted a kiss on Charlie's mouth. With two buttons left to go, Michelle reached over and kissed Charlie deeply. Her hands worked their way up inside Charlie's top and as Charlie gasped, Michelle kissed her again.

During the kiss, her hands reached Charlie's breasts and Charlie felt her circle them slowly from the outside, inward, in ever decreasing circles. Finally, she reached the nipples, taking both of them between her fingers and thumbs, starting with a gentle pressure, then moving to their tips, gently stroking and then using her nails, raking them with a bit more panache. The result was electrifying. Charlie's body went into meltdown and the crotch on her pyjama bottoms soaking wet. It was time to get out of them.

"I need to take off these bottoms, they are getting wet," Charlie said, rather sheepishly.

"Mine, too. I will if you will," said Michelle, letting out a hearty laugh. They both climbed out of bed and began to take off their pyjama bottoms. There was no offer of help this time. Urgency had entered both of them with the need building quickly. Charlie felt distinctly overdressed with her top still on, so she took that off, too. She was not sure she would hold out much longer if Michelle continued to come up with little tricks like the last one.

The floor was now littered with clothes and the need to be in bed for any reason had diminished. As they stood there naked, facing each other in the lamplight, taking time to survey each other's bodies, there was no embarrassment, no furtive glances, and no trace of unwillingness. "Perfection," passed Charlie's lips.

"Charlie, you are absolutely stunning. You have the most wonderful body." Michelle took a step forward and began touching Charlie's breasts again. She laid the palms of her hands on her breasts so the erect nipples were rubbing into each palm.

"Ah, we have a breast woman," said Charlie with a smile, as she arched her neck and looked skyward.

"And what would your preference be?"

"Come here, and I'll show you," was the reply in a strong, husky voice.

Michelle took a step forward. Charlie didn't give her chance to say anything. She pulled her close, their bodies moulding together. Seamless. Charlie kissed Michelle's full lips with a passion she had only just discovered. The heat in her own lips needed to be quenched by the smoothness of Michelle's own mouth. As she pulled on the back of Michelle's head so she could not escape her passionate kisses, she slipped her fingers between Michelle's legs.

A gasp came from Michelle, and Charlie was sure it could be heard in reception. She accessed the dripping folds, as slick as silk, they ingratiated themselves around her eager fingers. Wet. Charlie didn't go for the gentleness she would have preferred, but indulged in a hurried fervour she just couldn't contain any longer.

As she placed her thumb on Michelle's clitoris and gently stroked her fingers back and forth through Michelle's wetness, she felt Michelle's body drop, going weak at the knees. Charlie shifted her hand from behind Michelle's head to round her waist, supporting but caressing along the side of her waist, her mouth dropping wet kisses into the crook of her neck. The movement elicited a loud moan from Michelle, aroused further by the movements.

The bud grew against Charlie's thumb with each pass as if straining to leave its sheath completely. Charlie decided not to enter Michelle's body. Some instinct told her Martin had probably done damage and would take time to heal. As Charlie continued to slide amongst the slickness of the hot folds, she heard Michelle start to moan and then suck in a sharp intake of breath.

Charlie sensed Michelle was beginning her orgasm, so she increased her pressure on Michelle's clitoris having now grown to such a size Charlie thought it might burst. As she grabbed either side of it and began to coax, Michelle shuddered. Her legs stiffened as she threw her head and shoulders backwards, and then took in one almighty breath. After what seemed an age, Michelle brought her head forward, knees weakening and looked at Charlie with such tenderness, it made her want to weep. Their connection was complete—minds melded. She placed her head on Charlie's shoulder and kissed her gently on the neck.

"Thank you," she said, in a sleepy kind of way. "I will never forget this experience—ever."

"It was my pleasure, and I think now we should get some sleep. You look kind of sleepy to me."

"But Charlie, I wanted..."

Charlie placed a hand on Michelle's lips to silence her. "There will be other times, I hope. Right now, sleep is more important. We need to be ready."

***

CHARLIE'S PHONE BEGAN to ring as she left the bathroom and hurried across the room to retrieve it from the table. She glanced at the display as she pressed to answer. It was her Uncle Lenny.

Before she could speak, her uncle had launched into a diatribe, giving instructions with fervour. At the end of what only could be described as a one-sided conversation, Charlie said goodbye and climbed into bed.

"Who was that?" asked Michelle, voice heavily laden with sleep.

"Uncle Lenny. He and Gavin will be here tomorrow. With three policemen. We will need to check out." Charlie couldn't believe her own words.

"What the hell is he thinking?" Michelle scrambled to a sitting position and rubbed her eyes with purpose. "I can't believe he's doing this."

"He thinks it's the best call. He knows we're determined to make a stand and he doesn't want us to be alone. I'm sorry. I can't stop him."

"Okay, I can understand him and Gavin, but why the police? He doesn't have the right, Charlie." Michelle lowered her head, obviously distraught.

"But he does have the right. He's doing it to protect me." She knew the time had come.

"When I was a teenager, I was kidnapped by a couple of household staff. The gardener and the chauffeur." Charlie gulped, knowing if she stopped talking now, she would never speak of it again. "They took me to an isolated garage and tied me to an old bed. I was gagged, blindfolded, and left for days sometimes, without food and water." Charlie glanced at Michelle and saw tears pooling in the bottom of her eyes, in a face holding a look of horror.

Charlie's face was blank. "The worse thing was if I needed to go to the toilet, I just had to go where I was." Charlie let out a wracking sob and her body convulsed as the floodgates opened, spilling forth years of shame and embarrassment. The tears came with each new thought.

"Oh, sweetheart, come here," Michelle said as she scrambled to the other side of the bed. Charlie could feel herself being enveloped in Michelle's arms.

"I remember the gardener saying they should have pitched a tent in the middle of nowhere because then they wouldn't have to deal with the smell being so bad."

"No wonder you're averse to camping. Have you only just remembered?"

Charlie sucked in a breath and nodded vigorously. Suddenly, her body began to relax, she was glad she had said it...glad she had told Michelle, glad she had, at last, remembered.

Charlie lay with her head on her pillow snuggled into Michelle's shoulder, sleep approaching fast. She felt loved, wanted, and safe. The safe part was debatable, she knew, but now, with help on the way, she felt buoyed. They would pick Uncle Lenny and Gavin up at four o'clock tomorrow afternoon from Nice airport, and hopefully, spend some quality time with each other while trying to find a solution to the problem.

Charlie knew she was too tired to deal with their predicament any longer. Perhaps something would come to her in her sleep because they certainly still needed help from somewhere. Whether it was the police or not, time would tell. She kissed Michelle's cheek and breathed in the smell of her shampoo, then very slowly drifted off into an unwilling sleep.

Chapter Thirty-Five

As the car rounded the bend on the Moyenne Corniche, Charlie leaned into it, wishing she were driving her Audi. Uncle Lenny's car was okay, it had a turn of speed, but it didn't have the low centre of gravity or the sleek lines that made the corners so easy to take. She certainly wouldn't be applying the brake all the time. Why couldn't she go any faster? Hurry up, you piece of crap, she thought to herself, as she rounded the next curve.

Glancing in her mirror, she could see Martin catching up with her, with every metre—the closer he came. Her heart hammered in her chest and she could feel the perspiration beginning to form on her brow. She felt hot and sticky. Why the hell wasn't her air-conditioner working? As she came out of the curve, she slammed her foot down hard on the accelerator, but instead of picking up speed, the car began to slow.

She looked at the fuel gauge. Empty.

No, you bloody fool! She screamed in her head as the car slowed to a complete stop. She looked in the rear-view mirror and could see Martin clearly as he approached, the most murderous look crossing his face. Her heart rate was now at its limit as the blood whooshed through her veins.

She looked for some indication he was slowing his car—but there was none. Oh, my God! He's going to smash straight into me. He's going to kill me! She closed her eyes and waited. Waited for the impact, which had now become inevitable.

There was a thunderous roar as the grinding of the twisting metal echoed inside the car, the sound reverberating around in her head. She heard the breaking of glass as the windows began to shatter. Then her head shot forward as if in slow motion, toward the steering wheel, and she felt the impact as it connected with her cheek. She felt pressure on her neck and realised she was being strangled by the seatbelt, but something didn't feel quite right. She could hear Michelle screaming, but she hadn't been in the car with her, so how could that be?

A dream! She opened her eyes to the sight of a fist travelling towards her. Although she tried to move her head out of the way, it connected with a glancing blow on the other side of her face from where she imagined the steering wheel had cut into her. She could feel the blood running down the side of her head from a wound and could clearly now feel why she hadn't been able to move her head. Martin had her pinned to the bed by her throat, knees either side of her, but the give of the pillows beneath her head and the mattress was allowing her a little manoeuvring room, but not much.

Charlie thought she was going to lose consciousness as her vision began to take on a pink hue and bright spots began to dance in front of her eyes. She could feel the bile from her stomach beginning to rise into her throat, mixing with the pressure from Martin's hand. The choking sensation overwhelmed her and she began to panic. Martin had a blank look on his face as he began to raise his fist again. In a very low, controlled voice, he leaned forward and whispered, "You really should learn to keep your curtains closed, you dyke bitch. I got a good eyeful of your performance this evening. I found it very exciting though—you might say." He laughed as he leered and lifted his other hand to show he had masturbated. Charlie wanted to kill him.

"There I was looking for a man, and all along, she'd swapped sides without me knowing. What did you think? I would let you walk away with my wife. Hand her to you on a plate, no questions asked? Time for you to learn your lesson, I think. Don't say I didn't warn you."

Charlie began to struggle, knowing exactly what Martin had in mind. She would rather let him beat her to death than rape her. She was sure she would rather die than give him any satisfaction. She tried to work her body so she could at least try some self-defence moves, but he was just too heavy and too powerful. Charlie could hear Michelle above the thunderous hissing in her ears, whimpering and pleading with Martin to let Charlie go, but he was oblivious to anything apart from the infestations of his warped mind. Charlie could feel his erection as it pressed into her body as he leaned forward. It made her feel sick.

He began applying more pressure to her neck, and although she was trying to punch his arms and shoulders and prise his hands away from her throat, nothing was working. Her vision began to turn from pink to red. Her eyelids began to close and the hiss in her ears got louder.

A loud, thunderous crash was the next thing Charlie heard as she was on the verge of losing consciousness. Martin's hand eased on the pressure, and suddenly, he fell forward on Charlie, his immense weight pushing all the air from her lungs. She gasped for breath even more, and then she saw movement at the side of her.

"Try and push up, Charlie," she heard Michelle say, and she tried to pull Martin's unconscious body off her. "Come on, sweetheart. I can't do it all by myself. He's a dead weight."

Michelle managed to move him enough so Charlie could take a full breath and relieve the pressure on her chest.

She nodded towards Michelle to show she was ready, and then pushed with all her might as Michelle pulled him from the side. He rolled, unceremoniously off her and landed on the floor with a loud thud. Charlie took in a huge lung-full of air and tried to order her reeling senses. She pushed her way to sitting and swung her legs over the bed. She tried to get up, but her head felt as though it was about to explode. Her hand reached out and pressed the switch for the lights at each side of the bed. Dazed, cut and bruised, she surveyed the scene before her and tried to take in what had transpired.

The floor was strewn with broken glass and torn net curtaining. A chair from the patio lay tipped on its side at the bottom of the bed. The earthenware pot from outside had broken into large pieces, but the lollipop-shaped box plant had survived its ordeal. At the side of the bed was a broken lamp from the chest of drawers near the bathroom—shattered into pieces with blood splashes standing out vividly against the snowy white of the porcelain.

Michelle's voice had a tremor so bad she could hardly speak. "Do you think he's dead? I might have killed him, Charlie!" She looked so forlorn and so emotionally beaten and helpless. Charlie just wished she could hold her. So she did. There was no love lost for Martin, and Charlie, quite honestly, couldn't give a toss whether he was dead or alive, except for the fact that she didn't want Michelle to have to go through a trial for murder.

Charlie took Michelle in her arms and held her close, swearing to herself no harm would ever come to either of them again. "What I want to know is where the hell security is? Idle bastards! You grab the bags and I'll check him out," Charlie spoke in a hissing croak. Charlie pointed to the unconscious Martin. "We'll go to the car park from the poolside and avoid reception. We'll phone them once were on the move. Go on now. We'll talk later." Charlie gently pushed her away.

Charlie wiped the blood from the side of her face with the back of her hand, aware of the pain making her teeth ache, and she cursed Martin for what he had done to Michelle and what he had now done to her. Whatever he thought he was going to achieve, he had failed miserably and Charlie, for one, was glad.

As Michelle looked around the room and just threw things into the bags, Charlie walked over to Martin and looked down at him.

You don't look so tough now, do you, you prick.

Charlie couldn't believe how much she loathed this sorry excuse for a man. As she bent over to feel for a pulse in his neck, her head felt as though it was building with an enormous pressure. She bent her knees and squatted. The different movement eased it some.

Charlie reached out her hand and she saw how it trembled, but spoke harshly to herself saying it had to be done. They had to know—it would change everything. She felt a beat under her fingers and realised he was still alive and the wound on his temple seemed to have stopped bleeding, but there was a small pool at the side of his head. She looked over at Michelle, who stood, bags around her feet, hands wringing—waiting.

She wasn't taking a breath, her eyes like saucers. Dressed only in her nightwear, as Charlie herself was, she looked small and lost.

"He's alive," Charlie pronounced and immediately, Michelle's face registered relief. "The pulse is steady and fairly strong. It's time to go."

They jumped in the car and exited the car park, just managing to squeeze through the gap left by one gate being open. Charlie breathed a sigh of relief as they sped up the road. She didn't care where they went as long as it wasn't here. She was feeling woozy and sick so she didn't want to drive far. Just far enough to find somewhere safe where she could tend her wounds.

Charlie glanced at the illuminated clock of the car. Three thirty. With any luck, the police would have Martin in custody within a few minutes, and then they would be free to go home and face whatever needed to be faced. At least they would be facing it together.

***

CHARLIE LOOKED AT Michelle with a total look of disbelief on her fist-marked face. "What do you mean he's gone?"

"Claude said there was no sign of him when security got to the room. The police were afraid he'd carted us off, but given the lack of belongings, and there was no sign of our car, they decided we'd probably made a run for it. Claude confirmed it because he saw us leaving the car park. Claude said the police are advising us to go in, Charlie." Michelle stopped to take a deep breath but looked frightened to death.

"The hotel doesn't want to press charges because you're paying for all the damages. Of course, they want to preserve their reputation. The police have left a number with Claude. Do you think we should go to the station and let them help us?"

"No, I bloody don't. Martin will have access to their computers just the same as he has with our police, so what's the point? He'll find out where we are regardless. At least we can keep moving this way. He'll have a bit of a headache for a few days I should imagine. Perhaps he'll rest up. I don't know anymore. I'm so tired and confused, I don't know which way is up." Charlie tried to regulate her breathing as she began to feel the panic begin to start its tingling at the bottom of her spine.

"I didn't thank you for saving my life. I am truly grateful. I'm sorry I wasn't there to hit him over the head when he was hurting you. I know it was horrific. Did you think you were going to die? I sure as hell did. Then you rescued me." Charlie felt a lump catch her sore throat and a tear form in her eye. Both of her eyes were so swollen though, they couldn't escape.

Michelle reached to stroke Charlie's cheek. "I have never felt so helpless, and then so enraged in my life. I just couldn't stand the thought of him hurting you. I knew words weren't going to work. It was as though he just couldn't hear me. Then I saw the lamp, unplugged it, and then hit him with it as hard as I could. I think I caught him on the temple as he turned. When I think about what he said about watching us, I was livid. How dare he, the twisted bastard?" Michelle continued to stroke Charlie's swollen face and gave her a weak smile.

"Since it happened to me, I often wondered why he didn't kill me, but do you know what? I think beneath all the bulk and power beats the heart of a cowardly shit. I wasn't going to let him hurt you. I love you."

Charlie tried to smile but couldn't so she reached out and took Michelle's hand. She could feel both sides of her face swelling to the point of bursting, and the pain was becoming more and more unbearable.

"Charlie, pull over somewhere out of the way and let me have a look at the damage. You may have to go to a hospital."

"Like you did, you mean?" Charlie snapped, with more venom than she intended. "I'm sorry, Michelle. It's just I feel worn out, and my temper is getting the better of me. I feel violated, even more so than..." As Charlie's mind wandered through the past, finding a point to settle, Michelle's face showed a grave concern.

"Charlie? Charlie, are you okay? Are you thinking about the garage?" The urgency in Michelle's voice jolted Charlie back to the present.

"Yes, sorry. My mind was just wandering a bit."

"Will it help if you talk to me about it? I'm a good listener, you know." Michelle squeezed Charlie's left hand and gently stroked the webbing between the thumb and forefinger with her own thumb. Charlie gripped harder with her right hand on the steering wheel. The touch was such a small gesture, but it made Charlie's hand feel as though it was on fire. Charlie stole a quick glance and she could see the concern written all over Michelle's face.

"Maybe another time. I have plenty to keep my mind occupied in the present without dragging the past up, too." Charlie tried another smile, but it didn't work. It only increased her pain to the point of distraction.

"Charlie, up there, look," said Michelle, raising her arm and pointing towards a rest area off to the right. "You should be able to pull in there a fair way. Then we will hardly be visible at all."

Charlie pulled the car off the road. She could feel every pothole—even through the very good suspension of the car. Her ribs hurt, as did her pelvic area, but there again it would with someone of Martin's weight using it as a trampoline. She knew she was going to feel even worse as the time progressed, but she would just have to keep it together until they could find somewhere suitable for their needs. Where the hell the bolthole would be, she had no idea, but she had a feeling her uncle might.

Once they were dressed in their day clothes, Charlie felt more alert—although what her clothing had to do with it, she had no idea, but they couldn't stay in their nightwear, as tempting as it was. She loved the feel of her hipster jeans normally, but they were just nestling on a sore muscle, and movement made her wince every time she had to turn. The T-shirt would suffice as well, as the softness of it enveloped her tender upper torso.

Michelle had cleaned up her face as best she could with tissues and water, being patient and gentle as she eased away the dried blood from Charlie's face and the back of her hands. She had managed very well in the torchlight, Charlie thought, as she reached out and stroked Michelle's face to show her appreciation. "Thank you," she said softly, which Michelle answered with a smile.

"My pleasure, honey. I will have a proper look in the morning unless you think you need to go to the hospital now, which is the option I would prefer."

"You mean the same hospital with all those nice little computer terminals? No, I think I'll take my chances, but thanks for asking. The only thing I need now is two painkillers and as much sleep as I can manage before I'm disturbed. I long for a week in bed."

Michelle chuckled. "Would your choice be alone or can I tempt you with some company?"

"Tempt away, but I can't promise anything at the moment. I'm just a tad sore."

"All I'm offering is company, Charlie. You just let me know when you're ready for anything else."

Given the situation, Charlie couldn't imagine why she would find humour in anything Michelle said, but she did. "What are we talking here? Tango, quickstep?"

Michelle chuckled again. "Only if it's the horizontal version."

Charlie wished she could have smiled at the comment, but instead, she replied with a half-strangled laugh. Her throat was beginning to swell.

"Come on, temptress, let's bed down for the rest of the night. I have a feeling it might be a long day ahead." Charlie washed down three painkillers—just to make sure, with a swig of water. Her throat felt raw.

They reclined their seats, threw the car blanket over them both, and then Michelle reached out for Charlie's hand.

269

"Goodnight, sweetheart," she said in barely a whisper. "I'm so glad we met. I felt the jolt of something when you went to pass me in the pub, and you put it down to the cheap carpet, but I knew it was you." Charlie replied with a grunt, her eyes seemingly impossible to keep open, and she drifted off to sleep with Michelle whispering sweet nothings in her ear.

CHAPTER THIRTY-SIX

CHARLIE HEARD HER mobile ringing, but she couldn't pry her eyes apart. Her head was cool and comfortable resting against the window. She tried to speak, but barely a hoarse, grinding whisper emerged from her lips. She was banged up so bad that she couldn't believe it. It had only been a few hours since she was talking and had her eyes at least open enough to drive. She knew she wasn't going to be able to make it today. *Holy crap,* she thought. *Uncle Lenny will lose it when he sees me!*

She heard Michelle answer the phone. "Hi, Uncle Lenny," she heard Michelle say. "No, I'm afraid she can't come to the phone at the moment. Can I get her to ring you back in a few minutes?" There was a brief pause, and she could feel Michelle's eyes boring into her. "Okay, no problem. I'll pass on the message." She felt Michelle reach back under the blanket and begin to stroke her arm. She moved her arm gingerly, and then began to move the rest of her body, very slowly and carefully. She turned to face Michelle. She heard her gasp. "Oh, my God, Charlie. What's he done to you?" Tears welled in Michelle's eyes and spilled over, forming little trails down her cheeks. Charlie reached over and wiped them away. She kissed her finger, reached over, and placed it on Michelle's lips.

Charlie tried to talk but couldn't. Only a stuttering hoarseness emerged from her lips. She motioned for Michelle to pass her the notepad and pen from the glove box.

"Ask Uncle Lenny what he wants, and why is he phoning so bloody early! Tell him I've lost my voice...nothing else."

Michelle phoned back and passed on the message, finishing by saying they would see them soon. 'He just wanted to know we were still okay to pick them up at the airport."

Charlie began writing again. *"Will you be okay to drive this car?"*

Michelle laughed. "We'll have to hope so, or we will be spending the rest of the cash on taxis. Come on now. Let's see if we can just manage a few more hours sleep without any company or disturbances."

***

MARTIN SAT IN the van, sleep overcoming him a few minutes after he'd roused. It had happened several times already, so along with the accompanying double vision he suspected he had a concussion. Hospital was out of the question. The ponce of a hotel manager was sure to have informed the police, so they would be looking for him now—definitely. He would hole up in a hotel for as long as it took to get fighting fit. Maybe see if he could ferret out a hit or two, just to keep his mind alert.

He still hadn't dealt with those two—not to his satisfaction, anyway.

***

IT TOOK NEARLY half an hour to swap seats and get Charlie in a comfortable position. Michelle then booked secure online parking at terminal one on Charlie's phone and programmed the SatNav for Nice airport. She looked across at Charlie, her face showing what looked like muted excitement.

"I've never driven a car as expensive as this before, or an automatic, so you will have to bear with me while I get the hang of it." She fiddled with the mirrors and various knobs, and if Charlie could have swallowed the huge lump rising into her throat, she would have. She was not a good passenger.

"Don't look so worried, pet," Michelle said in a cheery voice, "I have been told I'm an excellent driver." A statement to which Charlie tried to give a sweet smile. Charlie wanted to laugh at the statement, especially being called, 'pet' and noticing little bits of a Geordie accent beginning to emerge.

Before setting off, Michelle reached across and assessed the damage on Charlie's face. She had dampened down some tissues with what water they had left and made them into compresses for Charlie's eyes. The nick in her cheek was shallow and Michelle didn't think she needed stitches, but she would have been happier if Charlie had gone to the hospital. Now it would have to wait, but she wasn't happy at Charlie's refusal.

"Charlie, sweetheart. Why don't you let me take you to the hospital this afternoon and get you checked over? You might have some damage to your ribs or internal organs or something." She gently stroked her cheek and tried to look into her eyes. They had opened a little but not much, and now the bruising was beginning to take hold.

The reply was barely an audible squeak as Charlie replied, "Let me see how I feel later. For now, let's just get to the airport and pick up Uncle Larry and Gavin. It will be nice to see them again, although I have a feeling they will both have something to say, and it won't be anything good."

They arrived at Nice Cote d'Azur airport just after twelve, both thirsty and hungry. A short walk took them into the concourse and into Le Riviera restaurant. Charlie insisted on wearing her large dark sunglasses, which not only shielded her eyes from the sunlight, but also covered up the vast majority of the damage caused by Martin. Michelle, for the first time, dispensed with hers, although she was acquiring some odd looks.

"We need to get you something easy to eat and swallow." Michelle looked intently at the menu. "How about some gnocchi with four cheese sauce and lots of coffee to keep us going. What do you think?"

Charlie merely nodded in approval of Michelle's choice, but she was ready for some food as her stomach growled in protest at her abstinence. She wished now she had made more of an effort with her dinner last evening.

Michelle ordered and within a couple of minutes, there was a large pot of coffee in front of them. Michelle laughed. "I think they must have pinched this from catering. Everyone else just seems to have a cup." She took a tentative sip of the medium roast with cream and began to hum. "This is lovely. Charlie, do you need some help with yours?"

Charlie had the cup resting on her lips. She'd never realised how much you relied on your throat just to get the liquid in your mouth. "A funnel or a straw would be good. Otherwise, I'll manage," she squeaked in response.

Michelle smile. "Oh, sweetheart, if I could drink it for you, I would. Would you like me to ask for a straw?"

Charlie shook her head from side to side. "Don't you bloody dare!" she half squeaked, half spat. "I'll manage, thanks." Charlie had a feeling she would be doing a lot of managing in the next few days.

CHAPTER THIRTY-SEVEN

CHARLIE SAW HER Uncle Lenny and Gavin approaching the car with Michelle and her stomach did a flip. She knew they were not going to like what they saw but, unfortunately, there was no way for her to hide it. She was doing a remarkable job of impersonating a panda with her now almost round face and two black eyes. She could put on her sunglasses, but it would only delay the inevitable.

Her uncle looked nervously about him as he walked, but Charlie thought how well he fit in with his surroundings in his crisp white cotton shirt and cream linen suit. His tall frame and slightly greying hair made him look extremely distinguished. She thought Gavin, on the other hand, had a dress sense bypass. This was the man who normally wouldn't be seen dead in the street wearing anything that hadn't come from a designer store, and he was now walking across the car park in yellow knee length shorts and a Hawaiian shirt. Granted, the yellow was picked out in the multitude of colours provided by the shirt, but even so.

As they approached the car, Charlie tried to take a large gulp. She could see them talking in an animated fashion. As she tried to gulp, her mouth refused to produce any moisture. She purposefully swigged on the water bottle she'd bought. Her mouth kept drying in anticipation of the confrontation. Michelle passed Lenny the keys to his car and Gavin walked quickly to the back of the car. It looked as though he was going to be her companion, to wherever they were going.

"Jesus fucking Christ, Charlie! What did the moron do to you? Your face! Look at your face!" Tears welled in Gavin's eyes as he placed a protective arm around Charlie's shoulders and gently squeezed. "Sorry about the language you two, but what the hell?"

"Don't worry about me, Gavin, and I'm sure the lady has heard worse along her life's path," Uncle Lenny answered from the driving seat. Charlie had an idea he might take over the driving of his beloved car and was equally sure Michelle didn't mind a bit. "In fact, I couldn't have put it better myself. I'll leave my observations until later," he said as he turned briefly, smiling at Gavin and then a thunderous look crossed his face as he looked at Charlie.

Michelle chipped in. "Don't mind me, Gavin. I couldn't have put it better myself, either. He is going to get his comeuppance and the sooner, the better as far as I'm concerned. Martin has turned into some kind of maniac. I don't recognise the man I married. I am so sorry, Charlie." Michelle reached over the middle console and stroked Charlie's knee. "Are you sure you don't want to go to the hospital and get checked out?"

"It might have been a good idea for you to have insisted on it last night." Gavin was the most petulant grown up Charlie had ever known, complete with pout.

"I didn't want to go then, and I don't want to go now. I just want to lie down and go to sleep. I don't want any arguing from you two, either. I have a thumping headache as it is. Gavin, could you please take the top off the coffee cup. I always give myself a hernia trying to drink through the bloody hole. Thanks for getting them, by the way. Uncle Lenny, where are we going?" Charlie's voice was hoarse and weak, barely louder than a whisper, but she had no problem making her feelings known.

"I've borrowed Adrian Fineman's villa at Theoule for as long as we need it. He and Moira are going on a cruise to the Far East for a few months so this will be resolved by the time they get back, I'm sure of it."

"I bloody well hope so," said Gavin, in an odd tone of voice that gave the impression he wasn't convinced. "Where is Theoule, exactly?"

Uncle Lenny jumped straight in, wanting to show off his knowledge of the area. Charlie was a little puzzled. This wasn't like Uncle Lenny at all. He was always rather reticent in the talking department as far as strangers were concerned— under normal circumstances. *Perhaps they had bonded*, thought Charlie, given how much pressure they had both been under.

"It's just outside Cannes," said Uncle Lenny, "but it's quite easy to get to anywhere along the Cote d'Azur from there or even northern Italy. Perhaps we could make time to go on a few day trips while we are here. Especially as we shall have a police escort. No point being sitting ducks, is there?"

"So why are the police involved?" whispered Charlie, suspecting it had something to do with her uncle's insistence somewhere along the line.

"I put a word in the Chief Constable's ear. This was the best he could come up with at short notice. Once Winter had passed on the information about Martin Bailey's involvement with the emergency services computers and his ability to access any knowledge they held, he actually agreed with your assessment, Charlotte. Making things difficult for him was the best we could hope for. However, until Europol gets on board, we are very much on our own. He still hasn't had a reply to his request, as far as I know. The three people concerned were on the same flight as us, so they should be with us shortly." He shook his head in disappointment at the sorry situation.

"Too much to hope when the French are involved, I suppose," Gavin remarked as he continued to stare at Charlie's face.

She didn't want to talk, so she put her sunglasses on, her head back, and hoped she would be left alone for the rest of the journey to Theoule.

***

AS SOON AS Charlie saw the integral garage, she smiled. For a moment, she remembered her home—or at least how her home used to be. She was suddenly overcome with a feeling of such sadness that she threatened to break into a fit of sobbing.

Gavin broke the thought with a low whistle. "Wow. I'm impressed," he said as his eyes followed along the front of the three-car garage to the large patio seating area off to the right, ideally situated to catch the morning sun.

Breakfast on the patio came to Charlie's mind. She could taste the fresh croissants with salted President Butter on them and slathered with a healthy helping of Bonne Maman Raspberry Preserves. Her mouth began to water at the thought.

"I think I know someone with money," he said, looking straight at Charlie. His face was stern.

Michelle laughed. "I said the very same!" Gavin looked at Michelle, scowled briefly, and then looked away.

Charlie looked at her Uncle Lenny and tried to smile. He looked straight ahead not even bothering to pick up her glance through the internal mirror.

She kept her eyes away from Gavin's direction but realised she was going to have to explain her background sometime later. The Spanish Inquisition had a trick or two to learn from Gavin.

Charlie knew they were in for an eventful evening and the police hadn't joined in the mix yet.

After all the luggage had been transferred to the house, nosiness got the better of all of them. Even Lenny, who had visited previously, looked around the house as though it was his first time.

The house was elevated above the garages and storage areas, boasting a huge square metre footage. The master bedroom was elevated yet again with stairs leading to the middle of the room and having windows on all sides, which gave the appearance of a large lookout tower.

The other six bedrooms, all with en suites, were situated off a corridor that led from the back of a grand lounge, which had floor to ceiling windows on three sides. The terrace outside the lounge's patio doors led to the swimming pool and various lounging areas, affording views over the hills to the west.

It was a magnificent setting, carved out of the hillside. Three sides of the property had sea views, which its elevated position gave, looking out over the Golfe de la Napoule and the small fishing town of Theoule-Sur-Mer.

Gavin's eyes were wide, and he continually said, "O–M–G", as he wandered from room to room, taking in every item of furniture and admiring the interior design and furnishings. Michelle merely smiled in acceptance of her surroundings. Charlie and Lenny never broke stride.

"Will someone please make a decision about the bedrooms," Charlie said with a hint of annoyance in her voice. She was still having a hard time making herself heard over the clacking of the other three. "Please, I need to lie down." Michelle turned her head around and looked at her.

"Did you say something, sweetheart?" Michelle said, immediately getting the attention of Gavin and Lenny. Gavin raised his eyebrows high, pursed his lips as only he could, and gave the impression he had grasped the situation. Lenny looked more concerned, looking first at Michelle and then at Charlie.

"I think we should give the master bedroom a miss. It's out of the way, and we need to be as close as possible, especially at night. Who knows what this lunatic has in store for us." He held up his hand, palm up, in Michelle's direction. "I'm sorry, Michelle. I know he's your husband, but I don't think his behaviour can be described as anything but lunacy."

"I totally agree with you," said Michelle, her head dropping slightly.

Lenny looked slightly ashamed as he made his way towards the patio door. "Let's get a little air in here," he said as he turned the key in the door. With a flourish, he pushed them wide, and to the sound of an engine in the drive, announced, "The police have arrived."

Charlie squeaked but made sure she was heard. "Michelle and I are having the first bedroom on the left. You can please yourselves. I need to lie down." She decided she wasn't in any mood for the police. They would have to wait. She and Michelle picked up their bags and moved towards the bedroom. Gavin glared after them.

***

CHARLIE LAY DOWN on the bed and watched as Michelle decanted their clothes from the bags into the bedroom furniture. "Leave mine, Michelle. I'll do it later."

Michelle stopped mid-stride and looked at Charlie sideways. "What is wrong with you? I'm putting a few clothes away in a drawer. It's not rocket science, Charlie. Are you trying to be awkward because if you are, we are about to have our first argument." She continued with her task ignoring Charlie completely.

"I was only going to suggest you come and lie down, too," Charlie answered in her own defence.

Suddenly, they were both distracted when they heard a woman's voice in the corridor outside.

Michelle sat down on the bottom of the divan and tried to listen to what was being said. "Did I just hear a woman's voice?" Charlie nodded enthusiastically.

Michelle turned and smiled. "You," she said, pointing to Charlie, "need to get some rest, and I need to join you!" Michelle flung herself back on the bed and used Charlie's legs to crawl up to the top. Head to head on the pillow, Michelle turned and whispered in Charlie's ear. "I love you."

There was a slight pause as Charlie tried to moisten her mouth. "I love you back," she said. She had never been surer of anything.

***

THE WHOLE PARTY, minus Charlie and Michelle, after being allocated bedrooms, gathered poolside to have drinks. Gavin had made up a pitcher of Pink Floyd Cocktail and also brought out a selection of soft drinks he found in the enormous American refrigerator.

"The cocktail is Pink Floyd and there are soft drinks in the ice bucket. Help yourselves," he said holding up the pitcher and offering it around. The ice tinkled as it collided with the glass sides.

"What's in a Pink Floyd, may I ask? They may have been one of my favourite groups at one time, but obviously, my education was not complete." DCI Winter grinned as he waited for a reply. Lenny shrugged his shoulders.

"Vodka, peach schnapps, grapefruit juice and cranberry juice." Gavin swilled around the contents in an effort to cool the contents more quickly. "It might not look up to much, but it tastes—heavenly! Any takers?"

"I think I might force one down," said Winter. His eyes never left the murky pink liquid. "In for a penny...."

"Me, too," said Lenny, pulling a funny face, "although I might actually live to regret it." Gavin wasted no time and began to pour the liquid into three cocktails glasses.

Laura McCarthy and Jon Abraham both shook their heads and grabbed a diet cola from the bucket. Laura decanted hers into a highball glass while Jon drank straight from the can.

As the five of them sat around the table by the pool, each nursing their drinks, it was Lenny who spoke first. "Well, I think the time has come, Chief Inspector. Can you bring us up to date on what's been happening and how you're progressing? Martin Bailey nearly killed my niece last night. It was only Michelle's quick thinking that kept him from actually succeeding. I don't want to give him the opportunity to get so close again."

Winter swapped quickly into work mode and began to discuss details of what had been happening back in rainy Walden. The sun shone on the Cote d'Azur.

***

CHARLIE HOPED SHE hadn't died and gone to heaven. She could feel the coolness of the ice pack being moved around her face as she drifted on the edge of sleep. Wherever the ice pack went, so followed Michelle's lips, laying tender kisses there, hardly touching, but causing the sensation of warmth. "What an incredible feeling, Michelle. Thanks for doing it for me." Thankfully, Charlie found it okay to whisper and still be heard.

"You're welcome, sweetheart. Can I get you anything else?"

"You sound like cabin crew. 'Coffee? Tea? Or me?'" Charlie tried to laugh but couldn't. Michelle picked up one of the excessive number of spare cushions and hit Charlie's leg with it.

"Hey. You behave yourself." Charlie merely made a snuffling noise as she could feel the painkillers beginning to kick in, gently ebbing away some of the pain and relaxing her muscles.

"Will you be okay if Gavin and I nip out to the shops to get some food for dinner? We shall have the company of the delightful Laura to keep us safe. Lenny will be here if you need anything. Plus the other plods ready to hold your hand."

"I will be fine, and you two try not to kill each other. Don't let Gavin wind you up. He seems slightly pissed at you for some reason.

"Don't you worry about me. I'm a big girl and I can look after myself. Well, I can with Gavin, anyway. You rest up now, and I'll see you soon." Michelle kissed Charlie gently on the lips and then covered her with a coverlet. Charlie drifted off into a dreamless sleep.

CHAPTER THIRTY-EIGHT

SHOPPING DONE—ROAST chicken, salad and baguettes safely stored in the carrier bags along with the other shopping basics, Gavin, Michelle, and Laura then made their way back towards the car.

"Michelle, can I ask you something?" Gavin asked with a rather sharp edge to his voice. Laura immediately began scanning the other people around them looking for the face of Martin Bailey, not wanting to pry if this was going to be a personal conversation between the two of them.

"Yes, of course," answered Michelle in the most even voice she could muster. She had a feeling of nervousness she couldn't shake off.

"What's going on with you and Charlie?" Laura McCarthy's ears suddenly sprang to attention. She wasn't, however, averse to a bit of gossip.

"What do you mean? As in...?" Michelle knew exactly what Gavin was alluding to, but she didn't see why she should make it easy for him.

"As in, are you sleeping with her?" Gavin looked directly through the glass of Michelle's sunglasses and he saw Laura McCarthy begin to slow her pace in front of them.

"I would think you've worked out the answer already, Gavin. Yes, we are. Do you have a problem?"

"I do as a matter of fact." He began to slow to a snail's pace as his hand made its way to his hip. He looked like a coffee pot and Michelle wanted to giggle. "Charlie has been my friend a long time, and I don't want to see her get hurt. What on earth do you think you're doing? You're a straight woman, whose been married quite a few years from what I can make out, and in the space of a few days, you end up sleeping with my best friend." He began to raise his voice and he could see this angered Michelle. Laura McCarthy put a hand behind both their backs and guided them around the corner into a quieter side street.

The gathering gloom of early evening seemed to set the tone of Laura's voice. "Look, if you are going to have this conversation, why don't we sit down and have a coffee. There's a table over there—look." Laura pointed to a table on the opposite corner of the main street. All three picked up the bags and marched over.

Michelle caught the waiter's eyes and ordered three coffees.

Gavin wouldn't be dissuaded from his task, although his voice had been lowered. "What are you trying to do? Would the fact Charlie is loaded have made any difference to your decision, I wonder? You've put her in mortal danger and if you thought so much of her, I don't think you could have let it happen." At the mention of Charlie's wealth, Michelle's gaze shot up from the table to Gavin's face. He considered now he may have over-stepped the mark as he wiped the sweat from his brow.

The look on Michelle's face was thunderous. She looked directly into Gavin's face as she pushed her sunglasses on to her head.

"Listen to me very carefully, Gavin, because I'm not in the habit of repeating myself, especially when the issues don't really have anything to do with you." Michelle's voice was low, but slightly threatening in its tone. It made Gavin shiver. "When we met in the pub last Friday, I had been physically assaulted and raped by my husband. Charlie saw me in the toilets at work. She was very sweet and asked me if I was okay. It had all got too much for me and I'd had a crying episode." Michelle swallowed heavily at the recollection.

"I couldn't share what had happened with anyone. I couldn't bear the fact that if I went to the police, they would insist I went to the hospital and be examined. The thought of it made me physically sick." Laura reached to the side and placed her hand gently on Michelle's back.

"Michelle, you don't have to do this," she said, glaring at Gavin from beneath her sunglasses.

"No, Laura, he needs to know." Both women continued to stare at Gavin as he became more uncomfortable. "So after the police, Gavin, then what? He would be out there—and I would be on my own."

A tear formed in the corner of Michelle's eye and made its way down her cheek. "He was supposed to be going away for the weekend, and I thought I would get a chance to think out the situation. He changed his mind and followed us to the pub. He stood at the bar and glared at me the whole time I was there. I knew if I stayed until the end of the night, he would find some excuse to start trouble, so I left early." Michelle wiped away the errant tear with the back of her hand as the waiter approached and placed the coffees in front of them along with cream and sugar.

As he walked away, Michelle began to speak again. "He pulled me into an alley when I was walking along the street. Luckily, Charlie was going to her car and she saw what was happening. She stopped him and took me back to her house, but not before he'd done this to me." Michelle pointed to the faded bruises and the slight mark on her lip where the split had been.

Michelle reached, poured some cream into her coffee, and stirred aimlessly. "Something happened to Charlie and me when we tried to swap seats in the pub. As we passed each other, we touched and I felt such a surge of energy pass through my body like an electric shock. I could tell Charlie felt it as well." She smiled at the thought, but then her face became tinged with anger.

As the other two grabbed for their coffees, Michelle continued. "Since then, Gavin, I have tried at every turn to keep Charlie out of it, but she won't listen. I can't come up with any better plans than she has. Nothing which would ultimately keep us any safer. Along the way, I fell in love. I don't know how it happened in such a short time, it just did, and I hope Charlie feels the same way. She is so sweet and tender, and she cares for me a great deal, as I do her. To me, it doesn't matter what went on before, I don't care."

Laura McCarthy began to smile.

Michelle was just on the verge of ending her speech when another thought struck her. "As for Charlie's money, I didn't even find out until she needed to tell me. It's obvious you didn't know either, so how could I? I don't care if she is rich, flat broke, or owes a fortune—I love her. You can doubt it as much as you like, Gavin, but if you expect to keep Charlie as friend, then cut us a little slack. We're both new to the feelings of this love we have for one another, and we don't need you in the wings analysing it. I would like to be your friend too if you'll let me. But it's entirely up to you."

Michelle continued to gaze into Gavin's face to see if she could work out whether or not he believed her. Not because it made any difference, she meant what she'd said, but Charlie didn't need any added pressure right now. It was a long few seconds before Gavin replied.

"I suppose I can only believe you because, despite what Charlie looks like, and what your fucking husband did to her, she seems so easy and relaxed with you. You look as though you've been a couple for years. I can't deny what I see with my own eyes. I even understand the love-at-first-sight thing, but please, Michelle, don't do anything to hurt her."

"I would rather kill myself, Gavin, than hurt a single hair on her head. I have never felt more intensely about anyone, not even Martin." Gavin and Laura both noticed the look of sadness pass over Michelle's face.

Gavin nodded his face contrite. "I need the loo. Be right back."

***

As Gavin's back disappeared into the café, Michelle studied her companion. Laura McCarthy was tall and willowy, her frame topped off with a mop of unruly, short dark hair. Her face was angular, but at the same time had a soft appearance. Michelle had decided her nature was kind.

"Thank you for the support. I think Gavin was having a hard time grasping the situation. It's hard to describe what's happened with Charlie and me when I hardly understand it myself. I would never have thought a situation so horrible could lead to something so good." Michelle looked into the middle distance, turning over thoughts in her mind.

"It's not the first time it's happened. It's just a shame the bad had to happen though. George was just an innocent bystander." Laura McCarthy looked sad. "I understand this is none of your fault, Michelle, or Charlotte's even. At first, I was just annoyed you didn't trust us to look out for you, but now I'm convinced you were right to run. You certainly led us a merry dance." A wry smile crossed her face. "At least I got to visit the South of France."

"Every decision was made because we thought it necessary, not because we thought it would cause more trouble. Heck, even I wasn't convinced in the beginning, but Charlie made me see sense, thank goodness." Michelle smiled at the mention of Charlie's name.

"I'm glad it worked out for you both. At least you have each other. It doesn't always work out so well."

"It sounds as though you have personal experience. A statement from a broken heart?"

"Yes, unfortunately. It's a long story but explains why a Yorkshire girl now inhabits the Home Counties. Still, the move is a good one and I got a promotion, so everything has an upside if you look hard enough for one."

They ended the conversation as Gavin re-joined them. He smiled grandly at Michelle.

"I'm sorry I misjudged you." Gavin was genuine in his remorse.

"Accepted. Now come on, let's go see if we can get Charlie to eat some decent food. What do you say, Laura?"

"Sounds like a plan to me," said Laura as she hitched up the much too long cut-off leisure trousers.

Gavin smiled a genuine, heartfelt smile. "On the terrace I think, ladies. What say you?"

"I think it's a lovely idea, sir," answered Michelle and Laura nodded her agreement.

As Michelle left the money for the bill, she smiled at the thought of where it had come from. If only Gavin knew.

***

LENNY SORTED OUT some bottles of wine from the cellar and filled the fridge with white and the drinks cupboard with red. He placed a couple of bottles of white on the dining table and began to fill everyone's glass with the honey coloured liquid. He picked up his glass and raised it in salute. "A toast," he said, looking at everyone individually, "to the love of family and friends." They all clinked their glasses and repeated the toast, then sat in silence as the thought sank in.

Charlie had wanted to add survival to the toast. Survival. It really had come down to that. If anyone doubted it for a moment, then they only had to look at the faces of Charlie and Michelle. Martin had turned into a calculating, vicious psychopath, thanks to the use of the steroids and goodness knows what other illegal substances. Charlie, for one, was extremely worried Martin was closing in on them.

Charlie had been formally introduced to the police and the DCI had been kind enough to explain everything happening back in Walden. She had expected some kind of backlash from one or all of them, but hadn't found any trace of criticism. Winter was efficient, Abraham always looked shell-shocked, and McCarthy...was gay, she was convinced.

"So, DCI Winter, what do you think the best plan of action is?" Charlie whispered hoarsely as she broke her piece of baguette into even, small pieces.

"Please, call me Ian." A genuine smile broke out on his angular face as he lifted his wine glass to accommodate Lenny's approach with the bottle for a refill.

"I'm Jon, by the way, and this is Laura," said Jon Abraham, not wanting to be left out of the 'on first name terms' conversation. Charlie nodded in thanks.

Winter looked up from his wine after thinking about Charlie's question. "I think you should carry on as though you are on holiday and we will do our best to protect you. I had hoped to have heard from Europol so we could enlist their help, but we haven't heard a dicky bird yet. So we will carry on until we do. The Chief Constable is on their case. We will take shifts to make sure we have cover during the night, wakeful at all times." He turned to look at Laura and Jon, who both nodded.

"I think he will come here anyway. It's a lot harder to try to attack someone in the street. Too many unknowns." He took a mouthful of wine and narrowed his eyes. "Wonderful choice," he said and nodding in appreciation. "While we are in the house, we will keep a lookout for Martin Bailey's car and should you wish to go out anywhere, we'll take two cars. We'll follow wherever you go and then be close while you're on the street. Two will be with you, one in the house. We'll take it in turns."

As they began eating their meal, they all seemed to loosen up a little, each seeming to enjoy the camaraderie building between them. Gavin especially seemed to be enjoying the food and the company. "This spit roasted chicken is gorgeous," he said, wiping a little moisture from the side of his mouth with a sparkling white napkin. "It's so moist and full of flavour. I wonder how they get it like that," he asked, genuinely surprised.

Lenny jumped in with the answer. "They skewer the chicken on the spit, but inside is loaded with butter and herbs. As the spit goes around, the juices flow through the chicken and are absorbed. They also baste the chickens with any juice that comes out of them. They certainly do taste wonderful. Good choice." Lenny gave Gavin a slow smile, but there was something else in there, too. Did Charlie see a hint of wanting in those eyes? She was imagining things, surely. The thought came to her like a bolt from the blue, and she took a large gulp of her wine letting it dribble slowly down her throat, hoping it would clear her mind. It didn't. *Oh, my God! Uncle Lenny is gay!* Charlie couldn't understand why the thought had never crossed her mind before. Her mother's younger brother had always given the impression he was a lady's man, but Charlie could never remember seeing any evidence of it.

Any parties he attended, he had always been on his own. Quite happy to stand on the edge of the crowd sipping his drink, people watching. But never any girlfriend in sight. Charlie was still having trouble believing it, but there was definitely a look. She hadn't imagined it. She wondered why he had asked Gavin to stay in his home. It was so unlike him. She wondered if two and two actually did make four, in this case.

Charlie had thought their being together was just a reasonable solution to the situation they had found themselves in, but now realised there might be another possible motive. She then made a decision to keep her thoughts to herself. It was none of her business what her Uncle Lenny did or with whom he did it. He would tell her what she needed to know when he was comfortable doing so. She could live with his sense of timing.

Charlie finished off her meal long after everyone else, although the company was quite happy to sit at the table chatting, finishing off the wine, then coffee. When she had finished the whole of her meal, Michelle's face lit up with a bright smile. "Well done, sweetie. I didn't know if you would be able to manage it or not. How do the teeth feel now?" Jon Abraham turned and looked first at Charlie and then Michelle. As the disappointment crossed his face, Laura smiled.

"They are okay, actually. Better than I thought they would. In fact, I might not look human, but I feel a bit more like myself tonight. The general aches and pains have almost gone, but it could be the painkillers and the wine. My face is still a bit of a mess though."

"You look good to me." Michelle reached forward and placed her hand over Charlie's, and then asked, "What do you say we have an early night?"

"Could be the best idea I've heard in days." Charlie smiled inwardly. My, how she loved this woman.

Jon Abraham looked gutted.

They left the rest to load the dishwasher and they retired to the bedroom. Charlie looked out to the swimming pool. It looked inviting with its underwater lights casting a warm blue glow. Charlie saw Michelle walk towards her through the reflection in the glass and then felt her closeness as she moved into the back of her body and wrapped her arms around Charlie's waist. She locked her hands in front in a protective fashion. She rested her cheek in between Charlie's shoulder blades and let out a contented sigh.

"I love you, Charlie," she said in such a way Charlie had no trouble at all believing. "I told Gavin this afternoon I didn't care how it happened, I'm just glad it did."

Charlie breathed a sigh of relief in her contentedness. "I meant to ask you how the shopping expedition went. You managed not to kill each other—that much is obvious."

"I told you I'm no push over, and I'm not. Obviously, he's concerned about the speed in which we've come together, but I think he understands now. It's not like we had a choice, is it? Laura McCarthy did her best to be supportive, too. It was good to have an ally."

"No, I certainly didn't have any say in the matter. The minute I saw you crying in the ladies room, that was me—gone. If I'd had my way, I would have had Poppy Ryder checking you out and writing a dossier." Charlie let out a low chuckle. "I am nothing if not thorough."

Their conversation was interrupted as they heard the three police telling each other goodnight. Charlie snuggled in closer to Michelle.

"Would it have bothered you to find out I was married? Would it have stopped you taking things further?"

"No, probably not. I wouldn't have expected to succeed though." Charlie chuckled again. "What bothered me more than anything else was the fact we worked at the same place. It can be very awkward when a relationship goes belly-up, and you have to still work with the person concerned."

"You sound as though you are speaking from experience." Michelle reached and began to nuzzle Charlie's neck, occasionally dropping a soft kiss and a gentle lick.

"Once or twice, and it was never worth it. You, however, might have been a different story. I don't think it will be an issue anymore. Would you want to go back to working at Bamber and Brooks if you had the chance?"

"I wouldn't dare, Charlie. Given what Martin has done to poor old George, I couldn't face anyone. I would have to get a job somewhere else."

"What would you say if I asked you to give up working? To come and live with me so we could spend every waking moment together. You would never have to worry about anything ever again, and we could buy a large house with a granny flat so it would be possible for your parents to come live with us if they wanted to. How does this idea fit your ideas?" Charlie could feel the middle of her vest beginning to get damp from Michelle's tears.

"Charlie, I can hear what you're saying and I do appreciate it, but everything sounds so surreal at the moment. My life is so full of bizarre occurrences my head is perpetually trying to process. Please be patient with me, and I promise when this nightmare is finally over, then I can give some much-needed thought to what you are saying. I don't want you to doubt for one minute what I feel about you. I would never say I love you to anyone unless I meant it."

Charlie placed her hands over Michelle's and continued to stare out at the pool. She tried to absorb what Michelle had said and knew deep down she was right. It was not the time to make life-changing decisions.

Just then, Charlie's attention was caught by movement out in the pool. Gavin was in there, frolicking around like a ten-year-old splashing water and taking huge gulps and then spouting it out like a whale through its blowhole. He trod water and waved his hands in the air motioning for someone to come into the pool with him. Michelle was with her, the police had gone to bed, so there was only....

Oh, my God! Uncle Lenny, put some clothes on!

Charlie wanted to cover her eyes but didn't want to let go of Michelle or have to explain the situation. She turned around, keeping contact with Michelle, keeping her body between Michelle and the window. "What do you say we go to bed? I know I've had a nap, but I still feel as though I could sleep until Doomsday. What do you say?"

"I could never turn down an offer to go to bed with you, and I must admit, this sea air seems to be getting to me. I think a kiss might seal the deal though." Charlie didn't need to be asked twice and lowered her head, grateful the head-bursting sensation seemed to have dissipated. She rested her arms on Michelle's shoulders and leaned into the kiss. It wasn't passionate but warm and welcoming and considerate. Obviously, Michelle was still aware that Charlie was hurting.

"That will do nicely, ma'am. Bed it is."

Charlie turned the vertical blinds.

***

CHARLIE HEARD THE knock on the door and Gavin's cheery voice announcing, "Rise and shine, girls."

She did not feel like rising, she did not feel like shining, but those excuses would never deter Gavin. The next moment, the door flew open and in came a flouncing Gavin, tray in hand. "I thought you might like tea," he said in a lively voice. "Oh, my," he said as he began to titter.

As she began to order her thoughts, Charlie realised what Gavin was 'oh mying' about. She realised Michelle was draped across her, the bed clothes pushed to the bottom of the bed. Luckily, all the important areas were covered and only the back of Michelle was out there in glorious Technicolor.

"Don't be an arse, Gavin. Pull the bedclothes up." He stood there for a moment, surveying the situation, tilting his head from side to side and considering his options.

"Okay then, spoilsport. Let me get rid of this tray." He put the tray down on the bedside table and then grabbed the sheet from the bottom of the bed and flung it over the two of them in a large billow. "Don't say I never do anything for you," he said with a smile. "Enjoy your tea."

Charlie smiled as best as she could and replied, "Thanks, Gavin. You're a star," she said, hoarsely. Then, with a flourish, he was gone.

Tea, thought Charlie. *There is a God.*

CHAPTER THIRTY-NINE

AS THEY CAME to the end of a leisurely breakfast of croissants, which Gavin had gone to the bakery to fetch, and wonderfully strong coffee, Uncle Lenny spoke up. "Well, ladies and gentlemen, today you are in for a treat. I have made a unilateral decision and decided we are going out for the day. I am taking you for a visit to the Fragonard shop in Grasse, and we shall have a lovely drive through the hills and find some out of the way place for a long dinner. What do you say?"

Gavin jumped straight in. "Oh, yes. I'm up for a trip," he said with a broad grin.

"Girls?"

"Oooo, a perfume factory. I'd love to. I couldn't afford it the last time I was around these parts," Michelle said.

"Well, you have no need to worry this time. Today's on me," Uncle Lenny declared.

"Oh no, I didn't me—"

"Michelle, relax. There is no point arguing the toss, just say yes," rasped Charlie, as she gave her a toothy grin.

"Well, yes then, I'd love to, and thank you."

"Yes from me," said Charlie with a slight nod of the head.

"Good. Now, then, our brave protectors. Who's staying and who's going?"

Jon Abraham spoke directly to the DCI. "Sir, would you mind if I stayed here? I'm not really into perfume and the like, and although I did the night shift last night, I should be fine to stay awake until you get back." He looked hopeful.

"Well, okay, but it is against my better judgement. I would you rather be with an experienced officer at all times, but I suppose I have to let you be alone at some stage. You keep your eyes on the road outside and you don't let anyone through the door. If Martin Baily comes a knocking, you call me and the local gendarmes. The number is in your phone. No heroics!" He pointed to the back door of the property.

"Thank you, sir," he replied, although he did think he was being treated like a schoolboy.

"Right, all settled then," said Lenny with a smile. "I'll meet everyone down in the garage in half an hour."

An hour later, they were all in the car, sunglasses donned and on their way to Grasse, making their way through the hills above Cannes. Both Michelle and Charlie sat in the back, taking extended looks through the rear window, as the wonderful sight of the Mediterranean unfolded before their eyes—along with their tail of Winter and McCarthy. As they rose higher, they could see the subtle changes in the colour of the water as it faded from azure blue near the shore to a darker blue towards the horizon. Charlie could feel herself beginning to relax. She took Michelle's hand in her own, lifted it to her face, and kissed it gently. "A kiss for a lady," she said in a low voice. "And one I love very much."

"I love you too, pet. More than I would ever be able to tell you."

As they approached the outskirts of Grasse, Gavin suddenly became aware of the surroundings. "This seems a pretty little place with all its pink and pale orange buildings. It's really quaint. There is no doubt who it owes its gratitude to though, is it? Posters, placards and the sides of the buildings, all bearing the name Fragonard."

Lenny nodded in response. "Correct, Gavin. Perfume is big business in this town. It's known the world over, but let's face it—there are worse things to be associated with. I think I could be in the market for some new aftershave. What about you? My treat." He smiled a knowing smile but didn't say another word.

"Well, thank you, kind sir. Most gracious," Gavin beamed back at him

"What about you girls? Could I interest you in some perfume? It would be a shame to waste the trip."

"Well, Uncle Lenny, what's got into you? Treats? Am I missing something here?" Charlie threw out the bait, knowing it would probably be dismissed, and it was.

"It seems a shame to come to Grasse and not go home with a memento, and perfume is what it's all about." He turned his head and smiled at the two women in the back.

"Then it would be crass to say no. Thank you. That would be lovely," replied Charlie.

"Yes, it would. So thank you, Lenny," Michelle agreed.

The roundabout leading to the D104 to the top of Grasse looked beautiful in the late spring sunshine, the water glistening as it fell back into the pool beneath. Water features did so much to cheer a place up, and yet it was such a simple idea. The buildings on both sides consisted of low apartment blocks and shops hidden beneath delicate archways reflecting the typical Mediterranean look.

The sun glinted off the windows of the buildings above, and the predominance of pale pink and pale orange, along with the ivory and pale creams, gave the town a warm feeling. Gavin had been right about the posters as they neared the end of their journey. The Fragonard banner was indubitably evident.

At the next roundabout, they turned left onto the Boulevard Fragonard, and from then on, each twist and turn of the road afforded them with magnificent views over the Massif des Maures, the range of forested hills leading down to the Cote d'Azur. Charlie found the whole scene breathtaking. She was a little sad to think she had missed all this scenery on the visits she'd had with her father, and yet, as a teenager, Michelle had loved this part of the world, and never stopped doing so, from what Charlie could see. She desperately wanted Michelle to have new memories—good memories of the place she loved. Not ones that included being hounded by a husband who had, through his own devices, turned into some kind of a crackpot. Charlie could make that happen for her, and she would. Once this godforsaken mess was cleared up.

***

GAVIN WAS IN his element as they wandered through the factory and museum on the guided tour. He followed the lady, hanging on her every word, amazed at how many steps went into the making of a good perfume, and how complicated the process was. He stared at the perfume bottles and the stills, eyes bugging out at every new fact the lady shared with them. She explained about *Les Nez* and the way they blended and re-blended the essences until they reached their own unique perfection. The 'noses' were capable of holding the memory of over two thousand fragrances. Even Lenny was impressed with such a feat.

The tour ended with a visit to the shop, and each went in a different direction to see if they could find something to suit their individual tastes. As Charlie passed by the testers, she bumped into Michelle, who thought she had found the ideal perfume for herself. "Charlie, while you're here, just have a smell of this and see what you think. I've only just put it on so you might not get the full impact, but it will give you some idea.

It's called Fragonard. I know what you're going to say...original."

Charlie lifted Michelle's wrist to her nose, and before it even got anywhere near, Charlie was hit with the fragrant wall of delicate flowers, which immediately made her think of wild meadows, full of fragrant flowers.

"Mmmmm," was all Charlie could utter. The fragrance was so...Michelle. So feminine and desirable.

"Is that all you're going to say?" Michelle laughed. "Very helpful, Charlie."

"What would help? Would help if I said I wanted to rip all your clothes off and make mad passionate love to you? Would it help if I said I would like to lick it all off?" Charlie's eyes danced with devilment beneath their dark, heavy hoods, but she knew she had hit the spot. "I see that's helping."

"If it has such a rampant effect on you, I better have it." The smile was provocative and needy, and it wasn't missed by Charlie.

"I promise, if you wear it tonight, you're all mine."

"I'm all yours anyway."

"You're all mine...with bonuses." The provocative smile returned. Charlie's eyes rolled as Gavin approached.

"Michelle, sniff this, will you please?" he said as he stuck his chin out towards her.

"Why are you asking Michelle?" Charlie asked, pretending to be hurt. "You normally ask me."

"Well, why would I ask you when there is someone eminently more qualified than you are, dear." Michelle lifted her hand to stop the conversation before it got any more childish. She got hold of Gavin and pulled him closer.

"It smells very nice, Gavin, but you don't need quite as much as you're wearing at the moment, although it's too late now." Michelle wafted her hand in front of her nose.

"I'll wash some off in the toilets. Do you think it has pulling power?"

"Well, it would pull me, but I don't think I should say much at the moment," which was followed by a real belly laugh from Michelle. Charlie thought the comment was hilarious, and pointed at Gavin, laughing hysterically.

"You," he said, in his little-boy-hurt voice, "have no need to react like that. It wasn't that funny, Charlie. I don't know what a nice girl like Michelle sees in you." He flung back his head and stomped off holding his Suivez Moi close to his chest.

"What have you chosen, Charlie?"

"I have chosen this," holding a bottle of Ile d'Amour out in front of her. "You don't get a sniff. I want it to be a surprise."

"Oh, you just have to be different. What if I don't like it?"

"Then I will find a woman who does." An impish grin crossed Charlie's face making her look like a smiling panda. Michelle tapped her lightly on the arm. "I might let Laura have a smell to see if she likes it," said Charlie, sticking out her tongue.

"Hey, you. Behave yourself." Michelle smiled, knowing that Charlie didn't mean a word of it.

Lenny also kept his purchase a secret, gathering all their choices and putting them through for payment, along with Laura's, Winter's, and something for Abraham, too. Although they tried to insist they pay for their own, Lenny insisted they didn't.

***

IT WAS LATE afternoon and the shops were just beginning to reopen after lunch, so they decided to have a wander around the town, mainly in search of coffee and cake. They had missed lunch and were all ravenous. "I will never last until dinner time," said Gavin, whose stomach gave a loud growl, right on cue. "I need lots and lots of pastries."

"You can have all you want once we find a cafe. It's my treat for being awful to you," said Charlie, who smiled apologetically.

"You were very harsh, but I shall forgive you," he said, with a backwards flourish of the head.

"Are you two going to spend all afternoon preening each other's feathers, or can we find somewhere to sit down? My feet are killing me," Lenny protested, "so come on. We can re-park the cars further down the hill if we're lucky."

The cars were successfully re-parked, and a little cafe was found on the Boulevard Carnot after a little searching. Charlie found it amazing how little of the town was set up for the tourists. Everywhere else they had been on the Cote d'Azur was tourist driven. You couldn't go for more than a few shop fronts without passing a bar or cafe. Here, they had only seen this one cafe, with three tables in front and two seats per table. It was just an ordinary sandwich shop where they decided to take advantage of a little foot traffic. Admittedly, they hadn't looked on many of the streets, but this seemed to be the main one in and out of town.

"This coffee is delicious," said Lenny, savouring every mouthful. "The place may not look like much, but heck, the coffee..."

"I must agree with you there, Mr Stern. The coffee is delicious," Winter's said.

Lenny nodded in agreement and added, "Please, call me Lenny. Everybody does."

Ian raised his coffee cup and nodded his head in salute. "It will be a pleasure."

"This gateau is to die for, too. Mmmmm" Gavin hadn't stopped eating since they sat down. He'd already tried two different pieces of gateau and was seriously considering a third when Charlie gave him *the* look.

"If you can't eat your dinner, I will be seriously pissed at you," she said to him at the counter.

"All right, mother. Keep your hair on." For a grown man, he had moments of intense childishness, but Charlie loved him like a brother with all the responsibilities the position entailed.

Laura McCarthy laughed aloud at their antics.

The drive through the hills was quiet. Lenny was concentrating on the driving as the roads became narrower and the hairpin bends increased in frequency. He kept glancing nervously in his rear view mirror to make sure DCI Winter was still on his tail. Charlie could see Gavin holding onto the handle above the door, obviously alarmed when the severe drop into the chasms beneath became obvious.

The dream Charlie had regarding being chased by Martin came to mind, and along with it, a feeling of uneasiness she just couldn't shake. It worried her, as she had had these feelings before, and the outcome had never been good. Finally, as the road began to straighten out, the feeling eased a little.

Michelle had fallen asleep. She'd turned sideways as much as her seatbelt allowed and placed her arm across Charlie's midriff—her head on her shoulder. Her breathing was steady, obviously her mind uninterrupted by bad dreams. Charlie was glad. Michelle was living a nightmare so at least she had a little respite through sleep. Every now and again, the new perfume wafted up in Charlie's direction, driven by the slight warm breeze coming in through the window. It sent Charlie's mind into overdrive.

She had always been affected by scent. Today was no different. Her mind was replaying their time in the hotel in St Tropez where Michelle had had her first taste of Sapphic pleasures. Charlie squirmed uncomfortably. Her toes began to curl and she knew she needed to distract her train of thought before she ravished Michelle right here.

As if sensing her thoughts, Michelle mewed a little in her sleep, her hand sliding nonchalantly in a downward direction. She wondered, for a moment if Michelle was really asleep as she moved closer to Charlie and her head began to slip south until it rested on Charlie's right breast. As Michelle's hand began to move towards Charlie's crotch, so slowly it was almost undetectable, Charlie knew Michelle was awake.

She sat facing the front so Lenny could see her in his rear view mirror, only glancing away looking at the view occasionally, to keep things looking normal. *Surely to goodness, she's not going to do anything in the car!* Charlie was starting to panic. A thin bead of sweat began to form on her brow and top lip. She hoped a shift in body position might keep Michelle from going any further so she squirmed slightly from side to side.

Michelle obviously took this sign as encouragement, as her right hand began travelling even faster between Charlie's legs. Charlie could feel the pressure being applied through her linen slacks and her clitoris began to tingle at Michelle's touch. Michelle's head was also on the move, turning slightly so her lips were resting on Charlie's nipple, which was reacting to the sheer terror of the situation. She could feel it hardening against the thin material of her cotton vest, and the friction itself was causing further stimulation.

She felt Michelle's lips begin to tighten over the nipple and for a fleeting moment, Charlie envisioned her leaving the car with a wet patch on her vest. She shuddered at the thought of looking like a nursing mother whose nipple pads had failed to do their job. However, the thought was soon gone as Michelle began to apply further pressure to her crotch. She wanted to cry out but realised any sound would give the game away before it was finished, and she certainly didn't want to impede any progress. It had come too far now. Plus, she wanted to see just how brazen Michelle could be in her games.

The thoughts that followed only added fuel to the fire, which was burning low in Charlie's belly. Her clitoris was so swollen she could swear she could feel it pressing on her briefs. Michelle was tuned into her thoughts—it was obvious. As Charlie tried to push her hips forward without being noticed, Michelle began circling the linen material and with each sweep, further pressure was applied. Her teeth bit gently into Charlie's nipple and her fingers gave a deep, satisfying push. Charlie thought she was going to explode. The ripples of the orgasm made her shudder, but she merely put her hand to her mouth and coughed as though clearing her throat. Her head was swimming and her thighs throbbed from pushing down so hard.

Suddenly, Michelle changed position, as she would if she had been truly asleep. As she put her head back on the headrest, a slow smile began to cross her face. She opened her left eye as much as she could, winked, and then closed it slowly. Charlie sat there, trying to regulate her breathing. Michelle was going to pay for this...very soon.

CHAPTER FORTY

JON ABRAHAM SAT on the garden chair with the sunshade now ensconced firmly above his head. His mother would kill him the next time she saw him. He knew he was in the doghouse for letting himself get so sunburned. *Well, you have to get it while you can,* he thought with a titter. They saw so little of the sun in Walden it was a wonder they all didn't have ginger hair with the rust. He giggled to himself at the thought.

A white Audi took his attention as it roared up the road beside the house. The thrum of the engine distinctive as it faded into the hills. He had always wanted an Audi. Its look was his look he hoped—slick.

He laughed again at himself as he looked down at his swim shorts. Well, not at this very moment, but when he was dressed for work. He admired Paul Brett. His dress sense was spot-on. He tried to dress like him, but he just couldn't do it. He thought he should be grateful his parents still bought his clothes for him. Not many men of twenty-four could say the same. Well, not with a straight face anyway.

It was money in the bank for him. He didn't pay his parents money for his keep either. He'd tried, but they just flat out refused, so what's a man supposed to do? They said a young man should have money in his pocket to do the things all young men should do. Buy a car—well, it was under consideration; entertain young ladies—no luck there, yet; to go out with friends. He hadn't any of those to speak of either.

He didn't know why he was unpopular at work. He tried his damnedest to be efficient and to help people, but his timing always seemed to be off. His colleagues always thought he was trying to get one over on them and it just wasn't true. He was sure his promotion to detective had only come about because uniform was trying to get rid of him. He couldn't prove it and he didn't care—he was where he wanted to be. He couldn't see himself going far wrong with Paul Brett as his mentor. He was a hell of a detective.

An EDF van was the next vehicle passing the house on its way to someone with dodgy electrics. Suddenly, he felt at home, as he'd noticed more and more of these vans on English roads and had seen adverts for them on TV. He was surprised to find it was a French company. He wondered how many people had bothered to find out before they signed on the dotted line to switch from their usual supplier.

His thoughts were distracted by a French beret appearing above the top of the bushes lining the road. The man appeared round the corner of the drive. He was wearing blue overalls and carrying a large blue toolbox. He lifted the toolbox high in the air and shouted, "Bonjour, Monsieur."

Jon Abraham waved and replied, "Bonjour," which was the limit of his French.

The man was shouting something that sounded like instructions as he rounded towards the back of the house, to which he replied, "I'm sorry, I don't speak French." The only thing following…was a silence.

Jon slipped on his flip-flops and made his way to the back door. Gone were his boss's parting words of not opening the door for anyone. He needed to see what this bloody Frenchman was up to. He didn't want to be responsible for anything happening to the property in the absence of the others. He looked through the spy-hole but could only see the man's back and the top of his open toolbox. Hellfire! Why did things always happen to him!

He fumbled to open the door with the key that had been left in the locked door and slid off the two bolts from the top and the bottom. As he opened the door, he heard a swish and saw the man's hand move so quickly it was almost a blur. Using a speed defying his large size, the man sidestepped Abraham and grabbed him in a chokehold from behind. As he looked at his feet being dragged across the wooden floor towards the bathroom, it was only then Jon saw the knife sticking out of his guts. There was no blood. He couldn't feel his legs either.

It was only when he was thrown against the bathroom wall and he came to rest on the floor, propped against the same wall, he got to look into the eyes of Martin Bailey. Cruel and sneering, he leant forward towards his helpless victim and placed his hand on the large carving knife sticking out of Abraham's belly. As he wrenched out the knife, he slid it upwards, opening up the belly so Abraham's guts began to spill from his abdomen.

"I hope you don't mind, mate, but I'm going to need this for later."

As Jon Abraham tried to gather his innards and put them back where they should be, his last thought was... *My mum will kill me.*

CHAPTER FORTY-ONE

THE WINE LOOKED the colour of a ripened cornfield and tasted wonderful. Charlie took a large sip of the cold liquid and held it in her mouth a long time to savour the taste of the grape. She hoped it had a kick, too. She could do with being oblivious to everything for a short while. Her face ached. Her teeth ached. Her nose felt as though it was about to explode. She was sick of people looking at her as though she was Chi Chi the panda. Now the sun was down, she couldn't hide behind her sunglasses any longer. Also, the nagging feeling was back.

The restaurant was very chic—most of the dishes were served on flavoured foam, which looked quite pretty but didn't enhance the flavour of the food a jot. At the clatter of the last knife and fork being placed on the plates, Charlie spoke.

"I don't know about anyone else, but I'm bushed. Do you mind if we go back to the house and have coffee and dessert there?"

She looked to the other five for any sign of disagreement—none was forthcoming. Lenny settled the bill and within twenty minutes, they were pulling up to the garage at the house.

"Thank goodness," said Charlie. "Thanks for the wonderful day, Uncle Lenny. I'm just sorry I couldn't do the end of it justice. I'm beat," she said, as she dragged her aching body up the stairs. "I think I might have a quick float in the pool then go to bed."

"What a great idea, Charlie. I think I'll join you," said Michelle, sporting a wicked grin and little glint in her eye.

"Great idea," echoed Laura McCarthy. "I'll join you as well if you don't mind."

Michelle smiled. "Not at all, the more, the merrier."

***

WINTER DIDN'T SAY a word as he looked around the lounge and through the patio out towards the pool. "I wonder where, Jon is? I told him to keep an eye on the road." He looked troubled as he rubbed at the stubble on his chin. "He might be having a lie-down. He did do the night shift last night. He only had two or three hours of sleep after I got up. I'll get changed and join you by the pool."

"I'll go make the coffee then and break out the pastries I bought this morning. While the coffee is on, I'll get changed into my shorts then I can come in, as well," said Gavin, obviously still full of energy, no doubt fuelled by the immense amount of food consumed throughout the day.

"And I will go sit by the pool, put my feet up and read the papers. I have to remind myself this is not reality." Lenny laughed, although the body language reflected a certain level of anxiety. The situation was surreal and the day had been merely a diversion from reality.

The two women met up with Lenny outside their bedroom door. Both women wore bikinis, hoping the air would not cool too much. Lenny had opted for some pale blue shorts and matching Lacoste top. Charlie was seeing another side to her Uncle Lenny. For the first time in her life, she realised what an attractive man he was—how appealing he would be within the gay community. He waved a daily paper at them and smiled. "Time to catch up," he said, but there was just a hint of sadness in his eyes.

Charlie and Michelle followed Lenny towards the living room and nearly ran into the back of him at the door. They heard him mutter something under his breath and both looked at each other as though the other may have heard what he had said. His hand came behind him in a pushing motion—as if to push them away. Each one looked on either side of him. Michelle let out a cry. Charlie gasped. All three stood immobile as they looked at the scene in front of them.

There stood—Martin Bailey.

His right arm was draped around Gavin's right shoulder, his hand holding the carving knife conveniently placed at the side of Gavin's neck—right above his jugular. It looked as though he had Gavin's left arm pulled high up his back, not giving him any chance to strike out or cause any disruption to his task.

Martin smiled sweetly, as though he just sprung a birthday surprise. Gavin was in great pain—his face was contorted with fear. Several 'urghs' came from his lips. Gavin's eyes were wide and his bottom lip was quivering in fearful anticipation. He had a wet mark at the front of his shorts, which gave them a deeper colour patch. He had soiled himself.

Martin spoke first, in a calm, even voice making the whole scene quite bizarre. "Please, come and join us," he said with a smile. "We were wondering where you were. Ah, my lovely wife, looking as gorgeous as ever. The sun-kissed look suits you, Michelle."

The arrival of Ian Winter and Laura McCarthy threw Martin Bailey, as he dragged Gavin back towards the patio window. "More guests. My, my, aren't we popular? Who do we have here then?"

Michelle stepped forward, unsteady on her feet. Charlie wanted to grab her and give her some support, but she was frightened of escalating the situation, just in case Martin took it out on Gavin.

"Martin," she said with a slight tremor in her voice, "what do you think you are doing? Put the knife down and let Gavin go. He's never done anything to you. You don't even know him. If it's me you've come to get, then let's go. Just leave everyone else in peace." Charlie went to move, but Lenny put out his arm to restrain her.

"No, Charlie," he said softly. "No, buts. You will do as I ask this time. No questions asked." Charlie could tell by the timbre of her uncle's voice he was deadly serious. She looked at the back of Michelle's head and her tears began to fall. She felt helpless, and it wasn't a feeling she was comfortable with. Helpless. Helpless. Helpless—again!

At the door to the lounge stood Winter and McCarthy, obviously in police mode as they scanned the room. Winter spoke up in a firm, but non-threatening voice. "Martin, where's Jon? What have you done with him?"

Martin Bailey merely sneered in his derision in the face of perceived authority. "That's for me to know and you to find out."

He nodded towards the two standing in the doorway and said, "I think you should all sit down. Why don't you pour everyone a drink, darling?" Martin had complete control and he knew it. Lenny and Charlie crossed to one of the leather couches and sat. Winter took one chair, McCarthy the other. Both sides of the room covered.

Charlie glared at Martin. She wanted to break his neck. Michelle crossed the room and opened the drinks cabinet, took out the wine glasses and two bottles of red wine. She took the corkscrew from the drawer above the cupboard and proceeded to take out the corks. Her hands were shaking wildly. She filled the glasses a third full and began to pass them round, each person putting the glass down in front of them on the coffee table.

Charlie could see by the look in Michelle's eyes she had capitulated. The fight was gone. Charlie wanted to get hold of her and shake some sense—some fight into her, but the situation prevented it. She gave Martin a withering look.

"How's the knee, Martin? Any better?" she asked with a sneer.

Charlie saw the grip increase around Gavin's neck and saw how Martin's arm muscles bunched, beginning a choke hold on Gavin. Gavin's face began to turn red as he gasped for breath. Charlie wished she hadn't said anything, but couldn't help herself. She hoped Gavin would forgive her big, fat mouth. She knew she was skating on thin ice.

"Martin, put down the knife and have a drink," Michelle said, obviously trying to distract him. His face went puce.

"The time when you could tell me what to do has long gone. You sit over there and shut the fuck up before I cut this bastard's throat." The voice was low and compelling, with an edge filled with seething rage. He meant business. Michelle did exactly as she was told taking a place on the other couch, placing her at the side of Winter in the chair and away from Charlie and Lenny.

"Martin, just take me and leave the others in peace. What can you possibly gain from all this? You do know these are police, don't you?"

He nodded, slowly and deliberately. "Yes, I knew you were getting company. I just didn't think they would be invited to stay here though. How very thoughtful." The look in Martin's eyes was telling. *He's using something,* thought Charlie. He had the haunted, hunted look. He was definitely jacked up on something.

The distraction of Michelle speaking and the mention of the police seemed to be working on distracting him. His grip had loosened on Gavin's throat whose face was now nearly its normal colour. Lenny shifted slightly in his seat. "Can I just ask how you managed to track us down? I know mobiles aren't accurate, so it must be something else."

Lenny saw Winter's hand tighten on the arm of the chair as though he was ready to pounce.

"Clever man." Martin smiled. "Your car. Nearly all expensive cars have tracking devices, so I just found out everything about you. I saw her Audi parked outside your house."

He nodded towards Charlie and then looked back at Lenny. "I didn't see your car, but I saw you. I took a guess at swapping cars and then tracked it—all the way through France. Telling the police she was going to Germany was a good move on your part, but it didn't take a genius to find out it was a lie. She didn't turn left once."

Martin laughed in a maniacal way and everyone looked at everyone else as though wanting them to get his joke. Winter leaned forward and took a sip of his drink. Laura McCarthy looked at him with a questioning look in her eyes, but he continued to stare forward as if looking into an abyss.

"I knew it was only a matter of time before I found them. I only put on the performance at the hotel just to let them know I'd discovered where they were. I wanted them to live in fear. To keep looking over their shoulders. I wasn't prepared to find my wife batting for the other side though, although it actually doesn't surprise me so much. She certainly never showed me the amount of passion when we were in bed. Nice floor show, by the way, girls. I had fun myself, watching the moves."

He lowered Gavin's hand and grabbed at his own crotch to simulate what he had been doing while watching Michelle and Charlie making love. He quickly snatched up Gavin's arm again. Gavin cried out in pain.

Charlie moved her hands to either side of her body, ready to leap from the sofa, when she felt her uncle's hand on her forearm. Martin released Gavin's arm again as he reached for the drink from the side table. He threw back the lot and swallowed it in a large gulp. "Ah. Nice bit of plonk. Fill it up, Michelle." Michelle rose and retrieved the bottle from the coffee table, her hands wavering as she emptied the little that was left in the bottle, then opening the second bottle and filling the glass to the top.

Martin repeated the actions of the first glass. Down in one go.

"I fancy something a little stronger. What have you got? Never mind, I'll look myself." He picked Gavin up by the throat as he half dragged, half lifted him across to the drink cabinet, never taking his eyes off Winter and McCarthy, his head moving from side to side. He had, however, forgotten to secure Gavin's arm again, which hung limply at his side.

Charlie's mind was working in overdrive, trying to work out the various ways to get Gavin away from Martin. He still had the knife to his throat. They needed to slow down Martin's reactions so Gavin had a chance to break away. The alcohol just might do it. Once that was mixed in with whatever he already had in his system, they might just stand a chance.

Lenny must have been on the same wavelength as Charlie. "There's a nice drop of single malt there somewhere. I've been tempted to open it myself," he said, nodding toward the bottom cupboard of the cabinet.

"A man with taste. I couldn't have chosen better myself, Leonard." Martin picked up the bottle of Finlaggan and looked at the label. "I think this will do nicely." He took out a highball glass and set it on the drop leaf. He passed the bottle around in front of Gavin. "Open that," he demanded viciously.

Gavin took it with the hand that had been pinned to his side, but when he tried to grab the top, he couldn't do it.

"I'm sorry, I can't open it. I have no grip. I think I may have a broken arm." A single tear dropped onto Gavin's cheek.

"Get out of my way, you useless piece of shit. Fucking queers make me sick!" Martin took the bottle from his hand and pushed Gavin aside. He raised the knife and started waving it around haphazardly. A wild, uncontrolled look was showing in eyes as they were beginning to lose their focus and uncoordinated movements invaded his limbs. He was slipping. Slipping towards oblivion using the mode of his choosing.

"Don't any of you try to get to the door. The patio one is locked and I have the key. To get to the other one, you have to get past me and I wouldn't recommend you trying. Michelle, open the fucking bottle!" Martin's voice began to get louder and Charlie suspected the little wine he'd had was already beginning to take effect. Michelle did as she was asked, and Gavin scrambled to the seat at the other side of Lenny. She saw Lenny reach out his hand and squeeze Gavin's forearm in a reassuring and tender gesture.

Michelle passed Martin the open bottle of Finlaggan and he poured himself a highball glass—full. He took a large draught, savouring the flavour with a smack of the lips.

"Good stuff. Adrian has fine taste in single malt." The mention of Adrian's name made Lenny turn his head and look at Martin. "Oh, it was easy, Leonard. The French are manic about having everything recorded."

Martin took another large swig of whisky, eyes darting from one side of the room to the other while he did so. Charlie noticed Laura had moved forward in her chair, but Winter seemed distracted. Martin was drinking the single malt like other people drink water. Charlie was hoping the effect would come soon. She was waiting for his words to begin slurring, and then she would do something anything!

She looked at Laura, meeting her gaze. Laura shook her head so slowly it was almost imperceptible. The tension was palpable and everyone was now perched on the edge of their seats waiting to make a run for it. The silence was ear piercing.

The glass of single malt was nearly empty. Martin's hands were beginning to swing unrestrainedly from side to side. "I need a piss," he announced loudly, "now who do I take with me?" His eyes swung wildly from side to side surveying everyone in the room. "The common denominator is you," he said, waving the knife in front of him while pointing it at Charlie.

Charlie felt Lenny's body stiffen, his knuckles a deathly white as they tightened under the tension. Charlie put her hand on top of the one nearest to her and gave a gentle squeeze. She could feel her uncle's body quivering as he sat there in his helplessness. "I'll be okay," she whispered as she rose from her seat but wished she'd sounded more convincing.

"If everyone is not here when I get back or there is any sign of gendarmes, I will kill her. Do you all understand?" He looked at each of them with wide rolling eyes and waited for each them to nod. Each one of them did. He grabbed Charlie by the arm as she reached him and hustled her towards the bathroom. In a low voice, he then gave Charlie her warning. "If you don't do exactly what I say, I'll kill you anyway. Understand?" Charlie nodded her head in affirmation all the time wanting to commit murder herself, in the hope it would quell the feeling of hatred.

He pushed Charlie roughly through the door and locked it behind him, wanting to make it harder for Charlie to run from him.

She was transfixed with horror as she saw the body of Jonathan Abraham reared up against the wall of the bathroom. She tried to scream, but no sound would emanate from her mouth. She could feel the blood rushing from her face, her legs beginning to liquefy.

The bathroom floor was awash with blood and gore. Abraham's hands were inside his own body, lost in the morass.

Martin dragged her by the arm across the floor avoiding the carnage, and placed her with her back against the wall at the side of the toilet. "You stand and you watch. Get me?" Martin looked at her and waited for an answer. She nodded on autopilot—no idea what he'd said.

She couldn't take her stare away from Jon Abraham's face. She noticed his face was nearly as white as the tiles on the wall behind him. *How could it be?* Her eyes followed his body to the pooling of the blood as her mind equated the answer. She knew his exsanguination had been slow. The pooling was nice and neat. The poor boy had bled to death, seeing his lifeblood flow away from him. He knew he was going to die.

She tried to focus and get her thoughts back into hate mode.

He unzipped himself with a fumble, swaying back and forth in a wind that didn't exist. Inside Charlie's mind was deciphering his actions. She was hoping the single malt would kick in with a bang and he would just pass out—but no such luck. He fumbled to retrieve his penis from inside his underwear, and much to Charlie's surprise, he did actually manage it.

He began to urinate and Charlie tried desperately not to look, but she had to be aware of any change in his demeanour. Once he had finished, he didn't put his penis away but moved towards Charlie—staring, blinking as though he was trying to clear his vision. "I want you to get me ready for action. Do you understand?"

She took a big swallow, but when she didn't answer, he moved the tip of the knife against her throat, the other hand, he moved to the other side of her head. She felt the tip of the knife pierce the skin and blood begin to trickle down her neck following the curve of her body into her cleavage. She could feel it pooling, beginning to wet the band at the bottom of her bra. She winced and closed her eyes as the tip dug in, pain shooting towards her ear and down her neck. Her head was still throbbing mercilessly.

"Do it," he said, as he moved his face closer. She could smell the whisky on his clawing breath. She moved her head to one side to avoid it. He grabbed her hair on the back of her head and tilted it down so she could see what she was doing. All the time she could feel the knife. Her sword of Damocles. She was hoping he wouldn't slip or fumble and drive the knife deeper into her neck.

She grabbed his penis with a sharp tug and he answered by pushing the knife in a little more. She felt the blood begin to ooze a little faster, so began a slow rhythm in order to placate him, grasping firmly, pulling the foreskin backwards, then forwards, until she began to feel him beginning to harden. She glanced up at his face and saw he had his eyes closed.

Instantly, a plan flashed into her mind she prayed might work. She would get him to the point of readiness and then push him hard towards the back wall. The floor slick with Jon's blood, he was bound to slip. Hopefully, the whisky would help her. He was already wobbly and wavering on his feet, so there shouldn't be much left of his balance. She hoped it wouldn't take long.

Charlie began to feel sick. Sick with the degradation of it all. She felt dirty, used, and mentally abused, and she really needed for him to take the knife away from her neck. Suddenly, she saw beads of sweat appearing on his forehead. He leaned on the wall at the side of her with his other hand holding himself up in earnest. The beads began to merge together and run down his face. He took the knife away from her neck to wipe the sweat from his face.

The moment of chance had arrived—this was Charlie's out. She lifted both hands to his chest and pushed with all her might, gaining more leverage by bracing one leg against the wall. He lurched and then staggered, slipping on the blood-laden floor and half turning to try to regain his balance. He hit the floor with a resounding crash, the knife disappearing beneath him. He gave out a grunt as the air expelled from his lungs. A loud moan followed. Then nothing.

Charlie just stood there. In her head, she was out the door, racing down the road towards the village, but she just stood there—rooted to the spot. It was then she noticed a pool of blood getting larger and larger around Martin's body. Spreading. Spreading from him as though it was running away. *Perhaps it hates him too,* she thought. She followed its trail, watching in awe as it turned a little to one side and joined forces with Jon Abraham's now darker blood.

She should run to the phone and call the emergency services. Call out to Ian Winter. Call out to Laura McCarthy. That's what she should do—but it was never going to happen.

Charlie waited—and waited. Waited a little while longer, gathering her thoughts, and just watched. Watched as the blood continued to run until the pooling had drawn its last grotesque picture on the sparkling white tiles. For the second time in days, she walked towards Martin and knelt down to feel for the pulse in his neck, avoiding the now huge pool of deep red blood. His life's blood was at her feet, yet she felt nothing. It was worrying to her she felt an absence of any emotion—guilt, remorse, pity, sorrow—all missing. All she felt was relief, as though a great weight had been lifted from her shoulders. They were free. She and Michelle were finally free of Martin and his continuous incursions into their lives. The fear was gone—again, from her life.

As she felt Martin's neck, this time there was nothing. Not one pulse—Charlie was glad. Inside she was cheering. She pulled herself up as tall as she could, ran her hands through her hair, and unlocked the door. She saw the backs of the others as they scuttled back into the living room. She simply walked through the door and announced to the room, "He's dead—and so is Jon."

CHAPTER FORTY-TWO

THE WOOD FROM the fire gave a loud crackle and it roused Charlie from her state of dozing causing her to wake with a start. She could feel the moisture rising up through the dusk affected grass into the lounger cushion she had been laid on. She sat up, picked up the long stick from the grass, and poked at the dying embers, eliciting another set of loud crackles from the charred remains of the larger logs on top. She put on two more from the small pile near her feet.

"I think it might be time to swap over to the chairs. It's nearly time to start dinner anyway. Michelle, are you awake?" Charlie got to her feet and began to peel her jogging shorts away from her rump and her tank top away from her ribs. Her mind dipped into the past, remembering as her mother looked on as the policewoman began to peel off her clothing in the room at the police station, placing them in plastic bags. The smell urine and faeces clung to the inside of her nostrils. She could smell it now.

Michelle yawned. "Aaah ha," escaped her mouth as she stretched and arched her back. Charlie looked on, a stirring was beginning, and she could feel her folds beginning to moisten. It didn't take much. "Yes, I'm awake, just nodding off every now and then. Charlie, are you okay? You look a little pale, sweetie," she asked with concern, completely unaware of the effect she was having on Charlie.

"Yes, I'm fine. Just got up a little too quickly." Charlie lowered her eyes.

"What a load of rubbish. I might only have known you a few months, Charlie, but I know when you're not telling the complete truth. Will you please talk to me? I can tell when you're having a flashback. After what we've been through, I don't think anything will shock me ever again." Michelle walked over to Charlie and placed her hands around her waist. "Now then, what was it?"

"Nothing too serious, really. My backside and back were getting wet with the dampness and I remembered…"

"You remembered your clothes being taken off after they found you?"

Charlie was amazed Michelle could work something out so quickly. "Yes, that's right," she admitted.

Michelle just nodded in sympathy. "Would you like to talk about it, or is it one of those occasions where because it's been remembered, it will be enough for you to work it out?"

"The latter. I think we should…" Charlie's words were drowned out by raucous laughter as voices approached them.

Charlie turned and a smile adorned her face as Lenny, Gavin, and Poppy came into view. Each was grasping an open bottle of beer in their hand and Lenny lifted up two more as an offering to Charlie and Michelle.

"Thank you very much, kind sir," said Charlie to her Uncle Lenny, as she took the proffered beer and began to glug down its contents.

"Thank you, Lenny, much appreciated." Michelle took her bottle and lifted it in the air to clink her and Lenny's bottles together. "What brings you three down our way?"

"I just came to get blasted." Poppy smiled, first at Charlie and then Michelle. "Lenny asked me down for the weekend, so I accepted."

"I came to dance," said Gavin, a beer in his hand and obviously not his first. He put the bottle down on the grass. He sashayed forward, put his good hand on Michelle's waist, and pulled her away from Charlie and began to Salsa. "Durruh—duruh—duruh," he sang, as Michelle began to sway in rhythm with him.

Lenny answered the question. "It's Saturday night, sweetheart. The barbecue. Gavin and I are cooking." His smile was heart-warming. "Your parents have promised to behave."

Michelle struggled free from Gavin making her way straight to Charlie. "Don't think for one minute, madam, this gets you out of the camping because it doesn't. Just because the house is there and your room is there, don't think you are using it because you're not!" On the word *not*, Michelle nodded her head for emphasis.

"Honey, did I say anything?" Charlie pushed Gavin aside and took his place. "I said I would spend a week camping with you and I will. The week is up next Wednesday—not before." Charlie leaned forward and gave Michelle a brief kiss on the lips.

"How's your romance with the Welsh wizard coming along?" enquired Charlie taking a long pull on her beer, happy Poppy had now found someone to share her life with. The affair had almost been as quick as Michelle and Charlie's had been.

Poppy nodded, her face lighting up with a smile, confirming to Charlie she had indeed, found herself love. "Dafydd is fine, thank you. He's spending this weekend getting the cottage sorted out ready for my move. My kind of man."

"What about the new job? Are you excited?" Michelle absent-mindedly slipped her arm around Charlie's waist as the girls closed in a huddle. Gavin and Lenny seemed content to poke away at the fire as they conversed in low tones.

"It's only in a different place. Same job—inputting, but the pay's not bad, and I've been lucky to get it. It will keep the wolf from the door."

Charlie laughed. "But not out of your bed!" Poppy punched her playfully on her arm.

"You will come and see us before you jet off, won't you?" Poppy asked, showing seriousness on her face.

Charlie was touched at Poppy's open affection for her and Michelle. She leaned forward and took Poppy into a full-bodied embrace. "Just try and stop us!" said Charlie as she released her.

"I hope you and Dafydd will come and see us, too," said Michelle, replacing her arm around Charlie.

Poppy laughed out loud. "Now, let me see. Mold or Cavalaire. I wonder which one of us is getting the best deal? You don't have to ask me twice, and I suspect Dafydd will think the same. Has the sale of the villa gone through yet?" As if on cue, Poppy's mobile rang and as she looked at the display, she smiled.

Charlie nodded. "Final paperwork to be signed the week after next. You better answer your mobile," she said, pointing at Poppy's phone.

Poppy nodded. "Speak of the Devil and all that. He'll report me as a missing person if I don't answer him." She giggled and moved a little distance away to allow some privacy.

Gavin and Lenny approached them, picking their way carefully through the detritus that seemed to follow Michelle wherever she went. Clothes, towels, sun cream, and glasses surrounded the cushion where she had been earlier.

"Do you two ladies need some help clearing things away? They are going to get damp if you leave them on the ground much longer." Lenny seemed somewhat distracted as he drank his beer.

"No, we'll be fine. You go get the barbecue fired up, and we'll be with you shortly."

Gavin nodded to Lenny and said, "Come on, Gordon Ramsay—let's go cook up a storm. I will help as much as I can, using my good arm." Gavin went to collect Poppy, still talking on her phone, and the three of them made their way back to the home of Charlie's parents.

Charlie saw Michelle's eyes narrow at the mention of Gavin's injury. His corrective surgery on the damaged ligaments of his shoulder had gone well and the surgeon had predicted a full recovery. Still, Martin's murderous rampage continued to riddle her with guilt. As much as Charlie tried to reassure her it was not her fault, it continued to be a large stumbling block between them, but Charlie knew she would never give up trying to convince Michelle.

Charlie was surprised as she approached the smoking barbecue when she saw Ian Winter and Laura McCarthy laughing and joking with Lenny and Gavin. She smiled at both of them, genuinely glad to see them.

"Hello, you two. Glad to see you. How are you both?"

Ian Winter was the first to answer, although, for some reason, he looked like a fish out of water. "I'm fine, thank you," he answered, nodding in appreciation. "A lot better than last time we met." His eyes became downcast and sadness swept across his face.

Charlie was transported back to Jon Abraham's funeral and the look the on his grieving mother's face as they stood at the graveside, sobbing as they each threw in a red rose on top of the dark wood coffin. Ian Winter was not ashamed to do the same. Eaten away by his own guilt and the thought he had made bad choices the day Jon Abraham died in the South of France.

Charlie was in awe as Abraham's mother came to shake their hands and to thank them for attending.

"He died trying to catch an evil man. Thank you all for what you did," she said as she walked away, a lonely figure, walking towards the church, still mourning the loss of her precious son.

"I hate funerals," piped up Laura McCarthy. "Especially young people. He wasn't the most popular amongst us, but he was one of our own. I'm just glad his mum won't want for anything, but it won't bring her son back. They were obviously very close."

A tear escaped Michelle's eye and ran slowly down her cheek, not missed by Charlie, who placed a hand protectively around her waist. It wasn't missed by Laura, either.

"Michelle, I'm sorry. I keep forgetting Martin was your husband. In the end though, he was very dangerous..." Her eyes were downcast as her thoughts wandered.

Michelle tightened her grip on Charlie. "At the end, Laura, I have no idea who he was."

Lenny cleared his throat, emotion heavy in his voice. "The French police should have been there to help, and they weren't—that's all there was to it. Losing the request, for God's sake. Europol has a lot to answer for. Thank goodness, their forensics team seem to have more about them. They had no hesitation in substantiating what Charlie had told them. If Europol had passed through their information sooner, it might have been a different matter, too." Lenny picked up his bottle from the table and took a long draught. "I suppose no charges was a good outcome, but I feel it could have ended so differently."

They each seemed lost in their own worlds for several moments until Charlie finally broke the silence. "Uncle Lenny, I have something to tell you."

"Yes, sweetheart. What is it?"

"The steaks are burning!"

EPILOGUE

AS THEY STOOD on the beach watching the receding tide, Michelle and Charlie took the time for reflection. The tide had come and gone many times since their last visit. Michelle sighed contentedly as she swept her eyes across the bay, early autumn heat still lingering in the air making the first lights appear in Cavalaire sparkle.

"I have something for you," said Charlie, delving deep into her trouser pocket.

Michelle smiled. "What have I done to deserve a present? I can't think of anything special, just the same, mind blowing sex." A laugh left her mouth as Charlie bent down to kiss her.

Charlie passed her a flat, rectangular, leather topped box and Michelle stared at it.

"What is it?" she asked, excitedly, in the hope Charlie might tell her.

"Now, it's just as easy for you to open it and look as it is for me to tell you. In answer to your other question...just being you. You're a gift to me, Michelle. A gift from the universe or whatever else is controlling this mundane little world we live in. I love you."

"I love you too, honey, and you have no need to buy me gifts, but thank you." She flipped open and what she saw made her eyes pool with water. On a delicate gold chain sat a scroll of gold bearing an inscription. *To Michelle, my one and only love. It's time to make our footprints in the sand.'* Underneath, two sets of footprints walked together across the scroll.

The following kiss was strong and heavy with impending passion. As they strolled along the beach towards, Cavalaire holding each other closely, Charlie glanced back and saw her own and Michelle's footprints leaving a trail behind them. Strong and firm.

And that's the way life should be, thought Charlie.

The End

ACKNOWLEDGMENTS

I DIDN'T GET to this place by myself—published author. Yes, it's hard to believe when a forty-year dream becomes a reality. I'm just grateful it happened at all.

First, I must thank my publisher, Raven Press. Much gratitude goes to Trin Denise Robinson, who took a great leap of faith on an unknown. The same goes to Lyn Gardner for her timely input during the tricky times. And to Bronte Layne for the eye-catching and stunning cover and to Marg Farrell on the tremendous trailer.

Rogena Mitchell-Jones must be the best editor on the planet. She made a very difficult job—painless. For that, I will be eternally grateful.

I mustn't forget the nameless Submission Readers who do a first-class job as first contact.

I hope the book does them all proud!

Next are my family and friends. Denise Adams-Wright and Julie Gent, who nursed me through frustrations and disappointments with firmness and good humour. Lilian Doak, Barbara and Eric Bates, Stan and Kath Adams—thank you all for your tireless and loving support.

Thank you to my extended family, too numerous to mention by name.

I would also like to thank my friends Lorraine and Terry Groves, who provided my Welsh hideaway, always welcoming me into their home when a break was needed. The luxury of my lounger in the sunny garden gave me a tranquil and battery-charging retreat. Not forgetting either, Chumby Wumby, better known as the Merlinator, who provided hours of entertainment and big slobbering kisses.

Ruth Perkinson, friend and confidante, who has been there from the beginning encouraging me tirelessly. Ruth, I love you.

To Lucy and Kay Meurig Bowden, thank you for all the help with the technical stuff I didn't understand. You helped immeasurably.

My beta readers, Angie Cooper, Bobbie Carter, Julie Gent, Lorraine Groves, and Brenda Young were enormously helpful with their comments. Thank you, ladies.

Then to my Facebook family. Notably, Jeffrey Getzin, who took the time from his own writing to advise me on self-defence and for assisting with formatting issues.

Plus, all the other people, too many to name individually, who day in and day out inquired on how the manuscript was coming along.

Thank you all from the bottom of my heart.

And deep gratitude goes to you, the reader. I hope you all enjoy RUN.

ABOUT THE AUTHOR

Pat Adams-Wright was born in Halifax, a town of West Yorkshire, in the north of England. After qualifying as a Home Economics teacher in Liverpool, she moved back to her home town where after a variety of teaching jobs and a bad accident which claimed most of her mobility, she finally began working for Her Majesty's Inland Revenue.

Patricia has held a disabled status for many years, but running her own paranormal group help to while away the sleepless nights, but eventually had to retire, again due to mobility issues. Her ambitions had always included writing a book and at the age of fifty-eight, she began her first novel, Run.

She now lives quietly on the edge of the countryside with her partner of forty-two years, Denise, her sister, Julie, furbabies Tilly and Willow and cockatiel, Scotty-Pop...all of which are anxiously awaiting the release of Pat's first book!

***

If you liked Run, and if purchased via the Internet we hope you return to where you purchased it and leave a comment. If you would like to contact the author personally, please feel free to drop her a line at expat12300@gmail.com or by using the addresses on the following page.

CONTACT THE AUTHOR

TWITTER

@RPwriter

FACEBOOK

www.facebook.com/patricia.adamswright.5

EMAIL

expat12300@gmail.com

GOODREADS

www.goodreads.com/user/show/13604918-patricia

WEBSITE

www.pataw.net

42486228R00206

Made in the USA
Charleston, SC
30 May 2015